Filament

Legends of the Starborn

STEPHEN PHILLIPS

This story is a work of fiction. Any similarities to names, people,places are purely coincidental.

ISBN: 978-1-7368738-7-8

Contents

ACKNOWLEDGMENTS

Thank you to Matthew Petersen for help with the cover art.

Chapter 1: Minding Their Business

Jace stared into the darkness. The dim light from the nearby star refracted a brilliant, multicolor sheen across his face shield, filling his senses. The sound of the ship's computer calling out readings now faded from his ears as his eyes took in the wondrous sight.

He was brought back to the stark landscape surrounding him by his companion's voice. "Jace, you daydreaming again?"

Eislie heard his jovial exhale through the comm as she chided him, "You dreaming about me or that star?"

Jace hesitated before replying, "There's a right way to answer that and a wrong way. You pick."

He could hear her laughter through the comm. "Yeah, I was staring at it too. I've never seen a colorful corona before."

Jace spoke. "I swear, it sounds like it's calling out, just to be watched."

Eislie's voice faded as she said, "I know what you mean. It's beautiful . . ."

The ship's computer interrupted their romantic banter. "The stellar display is caused by the former hyper planetoid body that was dismantled by the star's gravity well."

Eislie smiled, "Is that all you see, Ed?"

The computer seemed to be in thought. "No. I have catalogued dozens of unique stars since our meeting. And this one I find . . . enjoyable."

Eislie looked around, a suspicious slant to her gaze. "You all right, Ed? Not losing power, are you?"

"No, Captain, I am not. I have been meaning to—"

The computer was interrupted as the proximity alert sounded. Eislie rushed to the panel to activate the display. What she saw brought her to pound the comm to connect to her love.

"Jace, leave the last load. We've got company!" Eislie yelled into the comm.

Jace dropped the load of nearly pure phosphor quartz and headed inside, his hand slamming the controls to close the door as he rushed by. "That sounded serious. What's our status?"

"Two incoming, and they're big. I'm thinking dreadnaughts, by the readings. About four minutes out," Eislie replied.

Jace took off his helmet, throwing it toward the hook on the wall. He pulled his arm back, giving a grunt, rubbing his shoulder as the helmet rolled along the floor. His stride never hesitated as he headed to the flight control, his environment suit still on. His only hesitation was his sudden need to brush off the minerals now flaring along with his gloves as the oxygen in the ship's atmosphere ignited the residue on his suit.

"Wish you would have taken that off in the cargo bay," Eislie griped, waving away the smoke.

"Make up your mind, emergency or a little smoke!" Jace shot back.

They turned to the display as the computer enhanced the image. "Dreadnaught class, I surmise." The computer confirmed her suspicion.

"You surmise? What's that mean, Ed?" Jace asked.

Jace rubbed on his shoulder, causing Eislie to ask, "You all right?"

Jace rotated his arm. "Think I pulled my shoulder."

"Captain, I have not seen this configuration before, but it bears a resemblance to the pirate dreadnaughts we have encountered. However . . ." Next, the ship's computer focused on the rear engines. "It seems they have fortified the engine armor using a quantum shifted alloy."

Jace looked up at the main display, confused. "What did they do?"

Eislie rolled in her lower lip before saying, "I think they know we're here."

Jace scoffed, "You mean they made ships just to attack us?" Then, a salacious grin gracing his face, "It's good to be recognized for your accomplishments."

"Are you serious? They are making their ships harder for us to destroy!" Eislie replied before laughing.

"Ed, fire up the slag and get the drill online. Also, bring the zappers online," Jace ordered. The computer acknowledged.

"Zappers?" Eislie looked toward the back of the ship. "You mean you installed the solid tachyon generators? When did you do that?"

"While we were back home. What, you think I went flying last week? I wanted to take a few things off the list. It was getting pretty long, so I got them, mostly installed."

"I'm impressed." Eislie paused before hitting the controls. "Maybe we should get out of here."

The *Wolfhammer* quickly left the surface and was outpaced as the dreadnaughts increased speed. There was no warning over the comm before the pirates started firing. Eislie was able to stay ahead of the ships as Jace fired several rounds using the rear cannons. They were woefully underpowered, causing only minimal damage to their pursuers.

"Looks like they reinforced the plate and mag shielding," Eislie said. "Ed, increase power to the rear cannons."

The ship's computer spoke. "Their forward hull plate is a dense osmium alloy and several feet thick."

Jace remained focused on the front screen. “They’re probably chewing up a lot of power given the mass they’re hauling. So what do you say we see how well they turn?”

Eislie smiled as she sharply banked the ship and the large dreadnaughts lumbered into the turn. Then again, increased speed to catch up with the *Wolfhammer*.

“Uh, Eis?” Jace said, making her turn to look at him. “They’re right behind us. Maybe we should plot a course for a jump?”

Eislie hurriedly tapped away at the console. “On it.”

The ship lurched several times as the pirates fired on them. Then, both noticed that their ship seemed to start drifting. Through the display, what looked like sparks and flares appeared within their shields. Across the screen, the lights danced like ribbons.

“Warning, antimatter has been detected. May I remind Captains that we cannot enter hyperspace while polarized.”

“Shit! Thanks for the reminder, Ed,” Eislie said, trying her best to evade the additional antimatter pulses.

Within seconds, they heard several gentle thumps skipping across the hull. Jace noticed a few fragments of what looked to be the remains of small containers. He could see minute sections flare as the contents mixed with the antimatter in the shields.

“What the hell were those?” Jace asked.

“I don’t think they’re trying to kill us,” Eislie noted.

Jace gave a derisive snort. “Sure they’re not. They only want to torture us, *then* kill us.” He looked over to her. “We should probably figure a way out of here.” Jace’s eyes steeled as he turned forward. “Ed, are the zappers back up yet?”

“Fully charged, Captain. But even with the additional power, they will not be enough to damage the pursuing vessels. I advise against using the, uh, zappers. They would be ineffective, and may interact with the antimatter. My best guess is that it would produce a bright flash, causing only local unprotected organic matter to be affected.”

"That's not going to work, dammit," Jace said as Eislie quickly maneuvered to avoid fire.

Eislie looked at the ship's interface. "Wait. It'll be a really bright flash, Ed?"

The ship's computer replied, "Approximate luminosity will be equivalent to the brightness of a type one nova. Up close, of course."

Jace turned to Eislie and could see the smile on her face. He then said, "We'll blind them."

Eislie looked down, seeming to pout as her smile turned mischievous. "Can I push the button?"

Jace motioned to the controls as a chuckle escaped him. "My lady, the honor is all yours."

Eislie slammed her hand on the panel. Moments later, the cabin filled with a deep brightness. The flash was causing the hull of the *Wolfhammer* to groan from expansion. The luminous display also causing the pirates to veer from their pursuit. The resulting interaction with the antimatter crackling all around the ship illuminating the space around them for millions of meters.

Eislie did her best to keep flying in one direction as she covered her eyes. The few seconds the flash gave them was enough to allow them to pull away. As the antimatter cleared from their shields, Eislie activated the jump systems. Their ship quickly disappeared from the pirates' course.

As the energy streamed by, the cabin of the *Wolfhammer* was eerily quiet until Jace broke the silence.

"That was close." He again rubbed his shoulder.

Eislie nodded, but her focus grew in concern seeing Jace nursing his shoulder. "You sure you're all right?" She remembered Jace complaining he felt tired recently. They both thought it may have been the lack of sleep catching up with him. Eislie had a hint of concern as she watched him again grunt, rotating his shoulder. She quietly walked to get a scanner from the med bay. Jace turned, hearing her activate the device.

She ran a quick scan. It revealed stressed tendons and . . . something else.

"The tendons are damaged, and there's a large buildup of lactic acid in your muscle fibers. You probably overdid it today," she said, continuing to scan.

"Pulled tendons, not the first time," Jace mumbled.

Eislie gave a subtle smile as she viewed the scanner's display. Then, she leaned down, whispering, "You should get out of that suit."

Jace returned a demure smirk. "Maybe you can help me with that."

Eislie leaned forward, giving him a gentle kiss; she continued as he rose from his command chair, and they headed back to the hold.

* * *

On the bridge of the dreadnaught, the captain rose from his command chair. "Can you track them?" he growled lowly.

The pilot tapped several controls before shaking his head. "There is too much interference from the antimatter. The tracers weren't able to attach."

The pirate captain approached the pilot. He continued to stare out the front screen.

"I will inform our queen of our failure," the captain said, his armored glove clacking against the pilot's headrest as he brought it up to rest on the man's shoulder.

"Head for the nearest filament. We'll return for repairs," the captain ordered. His voice trailing off as he turned, saying, "We have failed in our mission. If it happens again, you will be the one informing our lady of your ineptitude . . ."

His armored glove drummed with a clack as he pulled it across the pilot's armored shoulder, its beat making the man grimace and shiver. "I understand, Captain. I won't fail again."

Chapter 2:
Just Another Day

Night had fallen by the time they made it back to Oppa. Arren glared toward his friends with that arrogant stare as they exited the ship, his displeasure prominent hearing they ignited antimatter so close to the hull. He ordered the vessel inspected before they left for space again. He didn't expect to find any damage, but wanted them to be more careful how they treated the *Wolfhammer*. The ship was unique, and he was concerned not only for them, but for it as well.

Eislie looked at the message she received from her mother who had it forwarded from home. The investigation into their former captor Devlin Bosh was again on hold. Eislie shook her head knowing that someone in Gilese command was probably stalling the investigation. She instead tossed it aside and focused on more current matters.

Eislie had given Arren complete access to the ship, including the ship's computer, Ed. Jace thought it was a good idea as well. And from what the computer reported, Ed was finding the discussions with Arren somewhat enlightening. Their friend even proposing some new upgrades, which he mentioned to the two after his evaluation. Arren told them that Ed asked if he would be able to upgrade his processing and memory systems.

"Ed wants an upgrade?" Jace smiled. "I thought he liked things the way they are."

Arren scoffed, "He went on about not having enough memory to record things. And that he was concerned he wouldn't be able to process the data he'd been collecting." The short, round alien then said, "Artificial personalities are known to grow. And you two have been stimulating that. A lot. Perhaps even integrating the new sapphire core quantum memory. That way if something did happen, we'd be able to read it." Arren looked to both of them as he gave a disapproving grimace.

Jace smiled before looking at his comm pad. "Ed, I know you're listening. And don't try and lie to me."

There were a few seconds before the computer responded, "My apologies, Captain, I was listening."

"My mother was right; he is a delinquent," Eislie joked, making Jace smile.

Jace looked to Eislie, then sighed, "What do you really want the upgrades for, Ed?"

The computer again took time before responding. "Captain Tucker, like you, I am curious about everything we encounter. My previous service had only taken me to mining locations and a few commerce hubs before my shutdown." When Jace again looked to Eislie, she could see the look of disbelief in his expression. When the computer continued, Jace nodded. "Like you, Captain, I have not seen many wonders of this universe."

Several seconds went by before Jace spoke. "I get it." He motioned to Arren and Eislie. "You two have seen so much more than we have. I was stuck on Earth; this is all still new to me."

Jace covered his comm when Eislie said, "You think we should?"

Jace gave a nod.

"Ed, I'll ask again, why do you want the upgrades?" Jace asked.

The computer responded, "With recent events, I feel that my abilities could be hampered by a slow response time. I had not noticed the ships until they were almost on top of us. Logically, I would need better processing and sensors to continue to serve to my fullest."

Jace smiled, turning to Eislie. "We should do it."

Eislie gave an approving glance. "I think so too."

Jace's head bobbed. "Ed, we trust you. Although, I have no idea how we're going to remove the old computer core without rewiring the entire ship."

The computer responded, "Do not worry, I can instruct Arren on bypassing processing and interconnecting the new systems. And do not worry about me going rogue. I do not wish to serve any other captains. I would rather self-destruct."

"What?" Arren yelled.

Jace laughed, "Yeah, Ed insisted on being ordered to self-destruct if Eislie and I were killed."

"And you did that?" Arren said in disbelief before pointing to Eislie. "And you agree with this?"

Eislie's pursed her lips as she gave a shallow nod. "Who knows what they'd do to Ed if we were gone."

Arren huffed, "Order it to return to here. Sweet Talon, I'll take care of the blasted thing."

Jace and Eislie both laughed before Jace said, "Why, Arren, we didn't know you cared."

The short alien shook his head before smiling at them. "It'd be a tragedy to lose any of you."

"Ed, we may have to discuss our original agreement," Jace said.

The computer replied, "I disagree. I would rather stick with my original order."

Eislie looked surprised but understood when Jace said, "So you are one of us? The beings thrown away that nobody wanted club?"

"I disagree, Captain. We have experienced and attempted feats that many have not achieved for some time."

Jace turned to Eislie to see her mouth open, hinting at a smile. He nodded when she said, "So you'd rather stay with us and blow up instead of getting new captains and exploring the universe?"

"Correct, Captain Licessien. No one wanted me until you proved what I was capable of."

Eislie turned to see the look of happiness in Jace's eyes. She watched as he turned to Arren. "Ed, you tell Arren what upgrades you would like. Just don't go too expensive."

The ship's computer replied, "The most efficient upgrades would cost no more than the recent profit from the latest mining run. I will have a list of parts for our engineer shortly."

Eislie laughed, "Our engineer? It sounds like Ed likes you, Arren."

The old alien laughed, "The three of you are insane, you know that."

There was a bit of laughter in the dock, but as it subsided, Eislie watched Jace lean his head back, rubbing his shoulder, his eyes looking tired.

"Your shoulder still bothering you?" she asked.

Jace nodded. "Must've really pulled something."

As they walked back into the dock, they asked Arren how long it would take before having the ship ready. He gave them a couple of weeks for a time frame. Ed agreed with the old miner turned engineer's assessment, and Arren shook his head, saying, "Blessed Talon, you are all crazy."

The following day, Eislie was up early. Jace remained in bed until late morning. She watched the sunrise and had already been looking over the list of upgrades Ed had requested. She made notes and sent a message to her mother. She also made note that Ed requested quantum core memory as a required upgrade. The Technology was less than a few years old and had just become a primary memory for Alliance systems. It allowed low power recording of quantum entangled and near proximity events, it was something Eislie barely heard of. She placed the pad down and turned to look outside. Eislie marveled at how the reddish star this planet orbited seemed to give an eerie glow to the morning on Oppa. She remarked on how much redder it was than back home. She tapped away on the list deciding to tell Arren to go ahead with the upgrades, but was waiting to check with Jace first.

Eislie watched as Jace lumbered in, his shoulders slumped, the dark rings under his eyes noticeable. She grew concerned as he painfully grabbed a cup of coffee.

"You were tossing all night; you even woke me a couple of times," Eislie chided.

Jace slumped in his chair. "I couldn't get comfortable." Then, with his eyes not seeming focused as he looked up at Eislie with a smile, he added, "Not that the company wasn't good."

Eislie chuckled as Jace picked up the info pad from the table.

"I was going to okay the upgrades but figured you should look at them first," she said, sipping her tea.

Jace looked the list over, giving a nod. "Yeah, let's do it."

He placed the pad on the table and tapped the screen. The display changed, and Jace scrolled through the latest report from the Filament Project. She knew what they were doing made him happy. The thought of traveling farther than most species was exhilarating. However, Eislie was confused when Jace stared in puzzlement at his mug. "This is damn good; it tastes like real coffee."

Eislie smiled, "It is. I got it in case you felt homesick."

Jace looked deeply into the dark gold that filled his mug. "You mean this is actually from Earth? What the hell was I drinking before?"

Eislie chuckled. She told him that Oppa is only about a day's flight from Earth. They sometimes go there for things that Terrans want if they can't make or grow it here. But, she continued, "Personally, I don't taste the difference." Then, she paused. "I've always wanted to go. Maybe we could?"

Jace smiled as she sat down beside him, placing down her mug. He then leaned over and kissed her. "I'm heading over to the compound. Maybe some tinkering will get me out of this fog."

Eislie smiled, "You know the day's almost half gone, right?"

Jace stood and shook his head as he moved to the sink to rinse out his mug. Eislie's eyes followed him as she spoke. "You go play. I'm going to get some shopping done. The supply room is almost empty. We never stocked anything before we left for that last planet."

The two had been renting a place on Oppa and the one back on Gilese since they started working on the Filament Project.

Jace leaned over, giving her another kiss before heading to get changed. He knew she wanted to be around others like them—other starborn. And since starborn were now accepted as part of the general population, she had a chance to do so.

* * *

It was late and the sun had set when Eislie looked at the clock. Jace had messaged her that he was staying a little longer to finish up and would be back soon. When she heard the console in the kitchen give an alert, she looked over to see the display read, "Callie Tellaren."

Callie was a starborn like her, also from Gilese. She was now the director and second-in-command for the Filament Project. The Alliance had insisted that a member of Oppa remain as head, just in case some didn't agree with a starborn being in charge. That backward thinking was something most of the starborn would not deny. But Eislie smiled, thinking about her fellow starborn's accomplishments, and she muttered, "Not bad for a starborn," before tapping the comm to answer.

The director greeted her and told her that they had made over five attempts since Jace arrived today but they'd had no success in creating a jump. Callie joked, saying, "He's probably hitting it with a bigger hammer since they can't figure out why it's not working." Eislie laughed, agreeing with her friend's assessment.

"I decided to call and let you know; they'll probably be working a little late," Callie told her.

Eislie smiled, telling her, "He'll call it quits when he gets tired," before looking down as if in thought. Callie being from Gilese III, could see Eislie's pensive stare.

"Everything all right?" she asked over the comm.

Eislie sighed, "Jace seems a little down. He's been sleeping a lot the last few days. And he keeps complaining his shoulder hurts."

The Oppan behind Callie startled her when she interrupted, "Any other symptoms?"

Eislie told her about what the scanner found, the buildup of lactic acid and damage, to which the only response from the gray-skinned woman was, "Have him come in for an evaluation."

Eislie nodded. "I'll see what he's like when he comes home. Putting stuff together seems to make him content."

The Oppan tapped away at her pad. "Have him come in anyway."

* * *

It was late when Jace returned home. Eislie could see him looking irritated and asked how things went. Jace, in frustration, retorted, "Didn't Callie tell you?"

Eislie could feel his words seeming to bite but watched him rub his face and shoulder.

"You all right? It's still bothering you?" she asked.

Jace stared outside before taking a deep breath. "I'm not feeling myself. I'm just tired, I guess."

Eislie placed her forehead against his before kissing him and saying, "I told Callie about you. I asked if one of the doctors would see you. Will you go?"

Jace looked into her eyes and gently nodded. "Yeah, something's off." Staring into those concerned, blue eyes of hers, Jace couldn't say no.

He turned to stare at the sky, making her ask, "What is it?"

Jace smiled. "I just feel like I want to go outside. It's weird."

She turned his head back to look at her. "Will you go?"

Jace nodded. "Yeah, what time?"

Eislie told him the time, and as they headed off to bed, Jace seemed to be in deep thought. When she asked what he was thinking, all he said was, "It should be working. Can't figure out why it's not."

Chapter 3: Starlight Blues

It was mid-morning when they arrived at the project's compound. Jace was still having difficulty getting things to work. "The probe won't cross over the horizon threshold," Jace growled in frustration as he threw the pad he was holding across the room. "Why isn't it working?"

Alvin placed the pad on the desk as Jace stared up at the ceiling. Alvin was holding his hand close to Jace's face, fingers separated by a small distance. "You got *that close* to my head." Reserved anger was evident in his words.

Jace gave a quiet apology. "Sorry. Next time, I'll aim."

Callie leaned back against the desk across from him. "She's right. You have a mean idea of humor."

Jace sat forward leaning his elbows on the desk. "Sorry. Just not feeling myself. This should be working."

Callie felt his frustration as well. Jace had moved the project along more than anyone. He and Eislie had advanced the flight and safety systems more than the Oppan had in a century. Yet, she could see his mind struggling with something, and the feeling she had was one she didn't like.

"Pirates can jump the filaments. We can jump," Jace said, referring to when he and Eislie accessed the filaments by accident. "Hell, Alvin's cousin Malik can jump." Jace turned to Alvin. "Sorry, that didn't come out right."

Alvin gave a wry huff and replied, his Jamaican accent ever-present, "We even copied the pirates' designs. But, unfortunately, even they're not working."

Jace's head nodded, slow and shallow. "What's the connection?"

Callie slid the pad over from the table and flipped through the data. "Systems are identical. So this should be working."

Jace stared forward, his eyes boring through the ether before him as he shook his head. Callie could sense a hint of fear growing behind those green eyes of his, her eyes glancing over the pad toward him. "You suspect something, don't you?"

Jace turned away. "They've captured pirates, right?"

Alvin nodded. "Yeah, some of them are starborn."

Jace's eyes sided toward Alvin and watched the man's eyes suddenly open, filling with a frightening realization. "No. No, man, you'd better be wrong."

Callie watched as Alvin sprinted away, his hand hitting the doorframe hard as he grabbed it to make a fast turn to head down the hall. Several people were staring as his dark complexion blurred in contrast to the light gray of the walls. Jace nodded as he watched the man disappear behind the glass. Alvin was from Earth as well. *People seem to think Terrans have a moodiness about them. Most don't realize that we've seen things like this before. We know how things can go wrong.*

Callie tapped the pad, pulling up the information. She retrieved the data on the pirates using her clearance. The Alliance had captured hundreds of pirates, and nothing stood out. The systems they used were similar, except for charts they had yet to acquire.

"I don't see the connection," Callie said, shaking her head. "What is he talking about?"

Jace leaned back. "Something Doctor Tulo mentioned to me some time ago." He watched as several Oppan gathered around. They had an interest in the project as much as Jace and the others.

Callie tapped the screen again as she told Jace for a second time that she didn't see anything out of the ordinary.

Jace's demeanor became reserved. "How many pirates were pilots or navigators?"

Not seeing his logic, she tapped the screen again, only to be alerted by her comm. She paused, looking at Jace, showing the display to him. "Eislie asked me to remind you about your appointment."

She returned to the data, then read through the information out loud. Mentioning that all were from around the known galaxy, most were similar to Terrans or Gilese. Nothing stood out till she realized something was missing. Callie had met some of the pirates even defended them, "What difference does it make? They just wanted to belong somewhere. Most of these pirates were good people. It's just that no one wanted them."

Jace's expression didn't change as Callie paused reading the same fact he had found some time ago. Callie's voice faltered as she said, "Approximately seven . . . ty per . . . cent . . .are. . ." she then lifted her eyes from the pad, staring toward Jace. He could see the regretful fear now filling behind her red pupils. "Blessed gods, please be wrong, Jace."

Jace nodded, saying. "I hope I am." He then stood, his hand hitting the desktop harder than usual as he leaned on it. "I don't want to think about this anymore today." Jace said, grabbing his crew jacket. "Besides, I've got an appointment to keep."

As Jace walked away, his steps filled with lament causing several Oppan to ask the director what they had found. Callie could only tell them, "It's wrong. Whatever it is, it's wrong."

* * *

Jace lay on the exam table as the doctor held the pad sensors above him, its measuring device humming gently as it scanned. Jace could see Eislie standing nearby as another technician used a light and simple tool to evaluate Jace. The doctor peered from her instrument to see the technician holding the light very close to Jace's eye and him fighting to move away from it.

"Keeni, you're holding the light too close. You're not trying to blind him, you just want to examine his eyes."

The woman pulled away in a semi-defensive curl. "Sorry, Doctor Disel."

Jace snickered, realizing that the medical technician was nothing more than one of her students. The doctor nodded, giving an apologetic smile. Jace turned to look at Eislie and watched as she rolled her eyes after he said, "I feel fine."

The Oppan doctor tapped the screen several times, her eyes steady as she analyzed the information. She shook her head before placing her hand down on his arm. "I don't see anything obvious."

Jace stretched as he sat up, hearing the doctor say, "The muscle damage may be from overuse. You did mention that you had been working for over twenty-seven hours straight, didn't you?"

The doctor gave a comforting smile seeing Jace nod. She looked again at her readings and searched for anything that would explain the exhaustion Jace was experiencing. *All readings seem normal. He's a starborn, and he's been interacting with them for a time. Would that cause this reaction?* the doctor thought as she returned to her desk and allowed Eislie to move closer. Disel smiled, seeing Eislie gently lean lovingly against Jace's shoulder and Jace shrugging, the nonverbal conversation understood by her as she continued to mull over her readings. She stared at the pad for a moment, her conclusions amounting to nothing. She was about to ask if he had any other symptoms when she looked up to see both of them staring out the window. She watched as Jace hopped from the table to place his hand in the sunlight, as if feeling its warmth.

Keeni turned to see the doctor's open mouth turn into a smile. The intern felt a rush of confusion, not understanding the doctor's reaction.

Disel walked over, asking to take a reading on Eislie. Her actions were sure and decisive before she turned to grab a cup from the dispenser and filled it with water. She handed it to Jace, telling him to drink.

"I have a theory, but I would like you to wait for a short time while I do some more analysis," the doctor said as she took one last reading on Jace. Then, she motioned to the door of the small waiting room and ushered them inside.

"I'll only be a few minutes. Please, sit, relax," the doctor said as she closed the door. The doctor then tapped the controls for the adjoining room as she spoke. "He's from Terra, if I remember correctly."

Keeni looked at the info pad, confirming he was as the doctor tapped the lighting controls for the room Jace was in. The doctor turned, taking the device from her intern, and tapped out her thoughts. Keeni looked confused as the doctor gave her a subtle smile.

"What is your analysis, Doctor?" Keeni asked.

The doctor gave a relieved sigh before saying, "I'll let you know if I'm right in a few minutes."

It wasn't long before the doctor opened the door and could see Jace sitting, his knee bouncing with impatience before she motioned for them to return. Then, finally, she closed the door and held the scanner to his shoulder. "This will just take a moment."

Jace's eyes remained cynical as she scanned him, asking how he felt. Jace jokingly said, "I feel good. That was just water, right?"

The doctor chuckled then, saying, "Cellular rebound has increased, hormone levels are equalizing, some." She ended her scanning of Jace and turned to Eislie, but when she read the results from Eislie's scan, she seemed confused. "You've had an increase of cellular rebound as well. Didn't you mention you were from Gilese?"

Eislie nodded before sheepishly mumbling, "I'm also part Terran."

The doctor quietly said, "Oh," before walking away, her lips pursed in a subtle smile.

"So, what is it?" Jace asked, looking at Keeni, only to see the young assistant shrug.

The doctor pressed lightly on the pad she held, then grabbed another, tapping it against the top of the one she held before handing it to Eislie. "Enter those frequencies into your light generators. You should feel fine in a few days."

Eislie looked at the small pad, then leaned her head back, a display of relief and humorous disbelief on her face as she looked toward the doctor. "You can't be serious. Really?" She then lovingly tapped Jace's arm with the pad.

Jace looked around and was thankful he wasn't the only clueless person in the room, seeing Keeni's eyes glassed over. He switched between the doctor and Eislie as he said, "I'm a bit out of the loop. I don't get what you two are smiling about."

The doctor placed her hand on Jace's shoulder. "I'm sorry, you're suffering from SFD."

Jace's brow rose in animated confusion. "What the hell is SFD?"

Eislie let out a laugh. "My mother gets it sometimes." Jace looked for her to explain. His eyes now spying a simple smile on the doctor's face.

Eislie leaned on Jace's shoulder as the doctor said, "All organic life-forms that space travel suffer from SFD. Some more than others."

"What is SFD?" Jace asked again, a subtle chorus of annoyance restrained in his words.

The doctor caringly shook his shoulder. "Stellar Frequency Deficiency. It's prevalent among star-faring species. We've known about it for centuries."

Eislie put her arms around Jace, telling the doctor, "My mother gets it. She's Terran."

The doctor shook her head as she crossed her arms. "I noticed you were looking outside. That's a common sign for Terrans. They seem to suffer from it more than most. I've seen it less in starborn, but all have it to some degree. Your biology is tuned to your star; treatment is simple to remedy." She tapped the pad Eislie held. "Those light generator frequencies should do the trick."

Eislie smiled, then looked at the doctor. “Wait, if I’m part Terran, how come I’m not affected?”

The doctor smiled, “Actually, you are. The readings confirmed that. But you weren’t born on Terra, correct?”

“No, Gilese Four,” Eislie replied.

The doctor smiled, “Your stellar spectrum is closer to ours here. But Gilese is a little brighter. Most Oppan feel withdrawal after about a year or two in service. For some beings, it takes longer.”

Eislie looked like she was thinking. “Then how come I didn’t feel it on . . .” she paused, “that other planet we were on.”

Jace leaned into her as he suddenly felt her weight, his head gently touching against hers. He knew she was talking about Charon. It had been almost two years since they had escaped, and she still couldn’t bring herself to say the planet’s name.

The doctor looked curious, trying to figure out what planet she was referencing when Jace spoke up. “The star was a lot like Gilese. You probably didn’t really notice.” He felt Eislie gently push her head against his as she nodded. The doctor thought she had done an excellent job, seeing them both smiling, but could sense a pain they both seemed to share.

“Give it a few days. If you’re still feeling the same, let us know. We may have to adjust the spectrum.” She paused. “Of course, nothing beats visiting your home star.”

Jace could feel Eislie’s grip tighten on his arm, and he knew what she was going to ask.

“You know I’ve always wanted to; can we go? Please?” She gave him the saddest fake look she could muster and Jace threw his head back, laughing.

Jace nodded his head. “All right, we’ll go.” He gave Eislie a gentle kiss. “It’s probably time I went back anyway.”

Doctor Disel pressed her hand against his back as she walked them out. “If that doesn’t help, let me know.” Jace nodded before shaking his head as he smiled. Eislie held onto his arm as they walked down the hall. Eislie made Jace sway as she leaned into him with excitement. She was finally going to see Earth.

Chapter 4:
A Terran Back Home

The air around Eislie seemed to vibrate as she stared out the small port window, her eyes transfixed in amazement at the water covering the surface of the planet she was just seeing for the first time. Earth was now under the protection of the Daak and Alliance, and she had finally made it to the world she had grown up hearing about from her mother.

Jace joined her, feeling his tendons tighten as his eyes again viewed the world he had called home, his patience thinning as the seconds grew longer with each tick. They still awaited a response from the control operator in the station orbiting before them. Jace reached out to hold onto Eislie and found amusement feeling her pulling toward the window as if itching to dive into the water far below.

"You probably don't want to swim in that right now," Jace whispered, moving closer. "It's really polluted."

She gently shoved him away. "You said we could go swimming!"

Jace nodded. He wanted to swim in the waters of the planet he came from as well. Something inside him begged to feel its caress. But Jace knew he would have to wait. He wanted to see how things were where his old life had ended. He had showed Eislie pictures of where he planned to take her; the palm trees and white-sand beaches. Hawaii had become a place for most Alliance and similar races to visit. It was a little warmer than Gilese, as well as isolated.

They both turned to stare at the comm, hearing it crackle to life.

"*Wolfhammer*, what was your planet of origin again?" the operator asked.

Jace gave an annoyed huff as he tapped the device on his wrist.

"We are en route from Oppa. Our current record of origin is Gilese Four," Jace said with an almost deadpan voice.

The comm crackled again. "And the planet of origin for occupants is Gilese?"

Eislie could see the frustration hiding behind Jace's eyes. "One occupant is from Gilese Four. I am originally from Earth." Each syllable of his words was precise.

Again there was silence, only broken by the cheery voice of the operator.

"*Wolfhammer*, your crew are registered with the Alliance touristry. Welcome to Earth. Please note that you have a complimentary, mandatory cultural orientation which must be completed before you may head down to the planet."

Jace looked to Eislie with a furor of disbelief as he tapped his comm, ready to give the operator a piece of his mind before Eislie placed her hand over it.

"I don't think we can take on the entire bureaucracy of the Alliance," Eislie calmly joked.

Jace spoke through gnashed teeth. "Not today, maybe. But I'm really tempted to try." Jace took a moment, seeing the silent pleading in Eislie's expression before he responded.

"Understood, Control. We are awaiting approval to dock." Jace let out a metered sigh, holding his anger back.

The sound of metal and ceramic resonated as the docking clamps engaged. Jace waited a few seconds before he opened the door, only to be greeted by a medical technician and security personnel, making him mumble, "Just once, I'd like to enter an Alliance ship without having a weapon pointed at me."

Eislie, excited, started to push Jace out of the way, but he stood his ground. Eislie's lithe attempt to circumvent was stopped by the technician holding her hand up before her, saying, "Medical clearance is required before you enter." The Alliance medical person tapped her pad, starting her scan of Eislie. "Terra – uh, Earth, as the locals call it – is not yet equipped to handle many simple pathogens. We just want to make sure this world is kept safe."

The officer did her duty and scanned Eislie. "You're clear. DNA bio-scan confirms Gilese origin." Eislie walked by as the officer held the scanner up to Jace. "Your turn."

Jace rolled his eyes as the woman worked. Eislie stood behind the guards as she waited. The technician completed her scan and searched for Jace's bio-scan record in the Gilese database. Then she sided her head toward one of the guards, who brought his weapon toward Jace's face.

"Your DNA bio-scan is not in the Gilese database." She looked to the guard holding the weapon before saying, "Falsifying origin credentials is a class one offense. Please confirm your planet of origin."

Jace's stare could have melted the weapon the guard held. "Please put that down. This is ridiculous. If I were a threat, I would have attacked you by now."

The other guard brought her weapon to bear on Jace. Seeing Jace's reaction, Eislie stepped in. "Wait, he's just grumpy. He's suffering from SFD. That's why we came here."

The medical officer looked toward Eislie, giving an acknowledging nod.

Eislie repeated, "That's why we're here."

The woman turned to Jace. "You still need to disclose your planet of origin." Then she returned her attention to Jace, taking some additional readings. "I'll do a deeper scan to make sure he isn't carrying anything while he decides to tell us his real planet of origin."

Jace cocked his head in a stare of dumfounded disbelief as he said, "Thanks, Eis."

The officer continued to scan him, again not finding Jace logged in the Gilese database. Finally, Jace closed his eyes, the annoyance held back behind a forced smile.

"I'm not from Gilese. I'm from Earth. Don't you have an Earth database in that thing?" Jace said, his words gritted with a wave of warming anger.

The medical officer returned a stare of incredulity as she said, "Only Earth military have left this planet. So, therefore, I find it difficult that you would have your own ship."

Jace gave a short sigh. "Humor me. Could you, please, check?"

The medical officer shook her head as she changed the search. Within seconds, the small screen flashed with Jace's picture and bio-scan, the screen listing his origin as Terra. The officer tapped the screen, logging no pathogens, and turned slightly to eye the guards that flanked her as she gave a slight nod.

"Apologies for the delay. Earth is currently not prepared to handle many illnesses. It is recovering from recent events. We cannot be too careful," the officer said plainly.

Jace nodded. "You're doing your job. I know."

The guards lowered their weapons, and Jace followed as they walked past Eislie, the woman's voice sounding practiced as she told them, "There is a mandatory orientation that must be completed before you are to deorbit." She looked toward Eislie, saying, "Many visitors enjoy the remote islands, which the locals call Hawaii. Will you be going there?"

Eislie looked to Jace for an answer. "I've never been there; it's on our list. I actually wanted to see where I used to live first."

Jace looked ahead to notice an obvious sign saying in Gilese with English and several languages underneath. It read, PLANETARY PROCESSING. With mild interest, the officer asked where Jace was from.

"New York area. Gonna stop by and see what the ol' stomping grounds look like."

Jace's very normal response brought a fearful and concerned expression from the security around him before one of the guards said, "There are no weapons allowed on the planet. That's a hazardous area. So are you really visiting there?"

Eislie looked to Jace as he nodded. "Been a while since I've been there."

The medical officer gave a concerned raise to her brow. "They have been performing sanitation and reclamation in the waters toward the northern continents. So I supposed it may be cleaner."

Jace gave a jovial chuckle as they stopped under the sign he had spied earlier.

The guards continued as the medical officer motioned to the door. "Please process in. You will be required to have a form of Alliance planetary identification on you at all times." She looked both of them over. "And please stay safe. We suggest that you only visit recommended locations while on Earth."

Jace smiled, "We'll be fine. But, thank you."

* * *

It didn't take long for them to receive their Alliance planetary IDs, Jace joking it looked better than when he had his driver's license picture taken. However, Eislie had to ask him to explain when two nearby Earth security snickered. Although they wanted to return to the ship, the station authorities frowned on it. Eislie didn't want to delay going to the surface, so Jace was forced to wait with her until they gathered enough visitors to start the orientation.

When the class started, Jace promised he'd do his best to keep a straight face. The instructor was Alliance for sure. Jace noted her name, Kemi Alekin. Although Earth was where he was from, he was in awe of the misinterpretation of many things their instructor was saying as she started. Jace looked around the room, seeing many people who looked human, a few Oppan, and several from a race that looked like Buttee, but were bluer in color than the former guard that once tormented them. When he asked Eislie if she knew where they were from, she told him they were known as the Drey. "Nothing like the Calasi. The Drey are much nicer and caring. Although, they always seem to be interested in rocks every time I see them."

The class continued, and the instructor decided to go around the room to hear where everyone was from. Eislie told them she was from Gilese, and when it came to Jace's turn, he said, "Earth, but I'm staying on Gilese now." The instructor gave a distrustful raised brow and went on to the next person. "We'll come back to you."

Several people could hear Jace say, "No one wants to believe I'm from Earth, really?"

Kemi continued the orientation, and Jace was having a difficult time keeping his promise from earlier. He turned to watch Eislie's reactions in hopes to stop him from bursting out in laughter. His attitude firmed seeing his love both horrified and fascinated by the history they were showing them. Jace watched the screen to see the fighting in the streets from only a few years ago and looked around to the people that now surrounded him. That fighting was still fresh in his memory, and he had been to other worlds and seen similar. He was in disbelief that they found the fighting disheartening.

Jace turned, quietly asking one of the others from Gilese next to him what he thought. The woman's response was, "These people are so backward." Jace felt a tinge of anger, knowing full well what it was like on Gilese. *All of these people consider themselves more civilized than Earth?*

When Eislie looked at him to verify what she was seeing, his heart felt heavy as he nodded, his affirmation breaking the shiny memory Eislie had created from what her mother told her and what Jace had known as history. All of it was now a fascination on display for other races from around the galaxy to see.

When the video ended, Kemi looked around the room and again warned everyone about the society they were about to interact with, advising they visit recommended areas only. Then the instructor told them that many Terrans enjoy shaking hands as a greeting and that if you find yourself in a strange place, to offer that as a greeting. Hearing that, Jace couldn't contain his laughter.

Annoyed by his outburst, Kemi focused on Jace, who said, "You do that in New York, or any major city, you'll probably get your ass kicked, or worse, killed."

The instructor walked up to him. "You will abide by the rules we have set, or you are not going."

Did she just speak to me like I'm some little kid on a field trip?

Jace was about to respond but stopped. He could see everyone, their eyes in fascinated anger, staring at him. He stood, mumbling, "I need to get some air."

The instructor said, "You will have to retake the course if you are gone too long."

Jace's sided eyes as he turned his stare told Eislie every thought he was having, and she pushed him toward the door. Jace exited and closed it with a solid thump.

As he gently banged the back of his head against the wall, a Daak and Terran official walked toward him.

They stopped before him, the Daak asking, "Is everything all right, Captain Tucker?"

Jace rolled his head toward the Daak with a smile, saying, "I can't believe they're making me take this orientation."

The Daak introduced Jace to Lieutenant Tanya Tolan. She was a Terran military officer who had accepted duties on the station. Jace introduced himself, and when she asked if it was his first time on Earth, Jace replied, "My first time back; I grew up here."

The lieutenant looked to the Daak next to her, confused. "Why is a Terran going through orientation?"

The Daak explained that Jace and his ship were the ones who defeated the Duggor at Oppa. Tolan listened with interest. She had heard of the battle and looked in on the class. "There must have been a mistake. It would be best if you had informed the instructor."

When Jace said, "I did," the officer looked around the room. Jace joined her and could see Eislie staring out at them.

The officer reached for the door, saying, "I'll inform her. You shouldn't have to sit through this."

Instead, Jace grabbed the woman's arm. "No, I'm making something more out of this than it really is."

The woman turned and could see Eislie looking out at them, and she understood. But, as Jace said, "She's never been to Earth; besides, I can't leave her alone in there."

The Terran officer smiled, gently placing her hand over his. "All right. Good luck."

As Jace reached for the door, the Daak asked, "Why do Terrans touch each other when there is an understanding? We have noticed other races do the same, but Terrans do it more often. Even during battle."

Jace thought for a moment. "Perhaps it is a validation we have to acknowledge. Friend or foe. We need you, and ourselves, to know that we see you and will face you as you hope to face us." Jace paused. "I don't know, really."

The Terran officer nodded. "That kind of makes sense."

The Daak turned to Tanya, even more confused than before, asking for an explanation. Jace joked, "When I figure it out, I'll let you know. I should head back in there."

Jace felt a bit foolish. He had been living with Eislie for almost three years since he left Earth. He thought about all the times he had to survive on his home-world and had finally returned. Jace hesitated before his hand touched the handle of the door, turning. He asked for a favor.

"Do you have a portable medical system we could purchase?" Jace asked, pausing. "And some additional supplies as well?"

"Is the one on your ship damaged? We can repair it if you need," the lieutenant said.

Jace shook his head. "No. It's for down there." He pointed to the floor.

The Daak responded, "Yes, we have several. With more on the way. Why do you need one?"

Jace turned. His expression was contemplative. "My people are stubborn. If the help was coming from someone like me, they might accept it."

The officer and the Daak spoke among themselves for a moment. "We can have the supplies ready in a few hours. Would you like them loaded onto your ship?"

Jace gave a subtle nod. "I'll pay the loading fees." He turned to look inside to see Eislie and the expression of wonder on her face as the instructor showed some additional video of the planet below. Jace nodded again. "I'd better go back in. I don't want to have to retake this stupid class. Not to mention, she'd have to wait for me."

The lieutenant chuckled before saying, "We'll make the arrangements. We'll send you a full inventory when it's complete."

Jace thanked them as he opened the door and headed back inside.

As he closed the door, the Daak turned to ask, "Could you explain what he gave as an explanation of what happened before?" Lieutenant Tolan laughed as she tried her best to explain.

* * *

Jace was about to sit down when the instructor turned. "You decided to rejoin us."

Jace smiled back. "Sorry, I'm still suffering from SFD. Not exactly back to myself yet."

The instructor looked concerned, saying, "My apologies, I wasn't informed. We can adjust the lighting."

Jace waved to her, responding, "I just needed to go someplace brighter. I'm good for now."

The instructor continued, and Eislie leaned over to Jace. "You, okay?"

Jace nodded. "I couldn't leave you here all alone. What'd I miss?"

"They were explaining ordering food in fast-food places," Eislie told him.

Eislie watched as Jace fought back laughing until he responded, trying to whisper, "Yeah, you don't want to say certain things." He then covered his mouth, and she watched his body moving as he quietly snickered.

Chapter 5:
Stomping Grounds

They had to wait a day before heading down to the planet, as per Alliance regulations. Eislie was still sleeping when Jace met with Lieutenant Tolan. She handed him a list of the supplies to load onto their ship. Jace had to move the *Wolfhammer* to a different landing bay for them to load everything. The officer gave him the flight order as he signed off on the materials and paid the loading fees. The supplies were a gift, so the Daak insisted on not accepting any compensation, given the recent actions of these two that had saved millions of their people.

Jace found the station inside the dock comforting, but was ordered to return to the stall they had initially docked in as soon as the supplies were loaded. He also asked for permission to take in some scenery while heading to make his delivery. The station personnel were reluctant, but agreed, since he had planned to take an out-of-the-way course around the northern continent.

Jace reminded himself to tell Eislie they were going to make a delivery after they arrived. And even though weapons weren't allowed when going to Earth, he made sure to place a few where they could get to them if needed. He spoke with one of the dock crew when they told him he had to leave the loading area due to a supply ship coming in. Jace understood, and headed back to the *Wolfhammer*.

When he arrived, Jace noticed one of the dock crew approaching the *Wolfhammer*. The man appeared to be carrying a large tool bag. Furthermore, he was trying to get in the door of their ship.

"Everything all right?" Jace asked, startling the man.

"I was going to make sure things were secure, but the ship's door closed on me as I approached," the man replied.

As Jace looked the man over, something didn't seem right. The person trying to get into the ship had a rougher look than most of the Alliance personnel he had dealt with.

"It's secure. Why were you trying to get in?" Jace became suspicious.

The man looked around. "I thought the controls were in the cabin. I'm not familiar with this ship type."

Jace's eyes remained vigilant as the man started to walk away, holding up what looked like a pad, saying, "I'm sure it's secure. I was just going through my list. Have a safe trip."

There was a short wait before Jace was ready to take the *Wolfhammer* back to its original dock. He did a thorough walk of the cabin before lifting off. He found nothing out of the ordinary. Having been diverted by the search for something wrong, Jace never saw the set of eyes staring at the ship from one of the viewing tunnels. One of the men standing next to the one Jace had met was speaking into their comm. "Tell our queen we were unable to place the device."

Jace returned to the cabin on the station to find Eislie reading an info-pad as she was getting dressed. He entered, hearing her say, "I was wondering where you were."

Jace smiled before telling her, "Had to move the ship. Picked up some supplies to take down. What're you reading?"

Eislie picked up the pad. "I have a message from a friend, someone I haven't spoken to in a while."

When Jace asked if she wanted to go see them when they finished on Earth, she hesitated, making Jace ask, “Bad news?”

Eislie shook her head. “It’s from Miriz. She returned to Yata Beta after my . . . incident.”

Jace raised his brow. “That’s what you’re calling it now?”

She stuck her tongue out at Jace and continued to talk, pulling an additional shirt over her thermal. She had complained that personnel here seemed to keep the temperature cooler for the comfort of the Terrans before telling him, “She wanted to talk to me about being imprisoned and take on the case against some of the suppliers of spide. She also mentioned that the Karazon were sending a diplomatic mission to Yata. It could mean a change in the way trade goes.”

Jace’s eyes widened. He was well aware of how things like this worked on Earth, and from what he could see, the Alliance wasn’t much different. He suddenly had the realization that what they had uncovered might put a massive target on their backs. He was about to say something when Eislie spoke up. “I told her I’d have to think about it. But, unfortunately, we don’t have nearly enough support for that kind of case yet.” She paused, looking at the pad again before placing it down and tapping the screen closed.

Eislie’s eyes followed as Jace sat on the bed, leaning forward, his hands grasped tightly together, an expression of unsureness showing through his stare. She gently leaned against him. “We don’t have to go. I’m okay with seeing it from here.”

Jace shook his head. “No. I’m keeping my promise. Besides, I have to go down.” Jace raised his gaze, his jaw tight. “They left me for dead, Eis. I have to show them they didn’t beat me.”

She gently tapped the back of his head. “You’re stubborn. You know that?”

Jace agreed. “Yeah, I know.” He tapped her knee with the pad he held. “Finish getting dressed. We leave in an hour. They have a short launch window today.”

Jace marveled at Eislie's expression seeing the Earth as the surface came closer into view. They finally had clearance to head down. Eislie was excited, and unprepared for the surprise Jace had planned. His location for a start was also something he had wanted to see his entire life. A smile of enjoyment plastered on Jace's face as the moonlit image of glaciers cast a ghostly scene. It was quite a sight, as the computer remarked as it took readings and pictures.

"I always wanted to see Alaska; never had the chance to go," Jace said as they flew over the mountainous ice, so thick it took on a bluish tint. Eislie looked at the display, seeing it reading a very cold temperature. "Brrr, it's minus seventy-six Alar."

Jace looked at her questioningly, making her ask the computer for help. "Ed, what's the conversion for Terran minus seventy-six Alar?"

"About minus forty-one Celsius. That's minus one hundred six degrees Fahrenheit. Terran temperature."

Jace nodded. "That's a bit chilly."

Eislie sighed in relief. "Glad no one lives there."

Jace laughed at her innocence. "Are you kidding? Thousands live up here. Most like it too."

Eislie turned to him in disbelief. But then the computer interrupted, "Captain Tucker is correct. Approximately four hundred thousand individuals live in this area at the moment."

"How many?" Eislie asked with a tone of doubt.

Jace could only laugh at her in amusement. "Don't worry. It's too cold for me down there. We're not landing. I just wanted to see it."

Eislie sat back with a relieved expression as they headed toward the eastern coast. When they arrived, the fog blanketed the area so thick that Jace had to use sensors to see where they were going. When they reached the New York area, he told her, "It's heavy fog everywhere. Have to see if we can find someplace to land."

As they neared the surface, the fog seemed to lift. They could see large machines in the ocean just offshore with water running through them, the surf churning behind as they worked.

"That must be the reclamation ships. I was talking to someone on the station. They said it's going to take a while to get things cleaned up," Eislie said before she leaned forward to stare at the water. "I can't believe there's so much water!"

Jace snorted. "Only polar bears would swim in that water right now."

Eislie looked at him, "But when are we—"

Jace interrupted her. "We will, Eis. Just be a day or so. We can only stay for ten days, remember?"

She did remember that, technically, even though Jace was from Earth, he was only visiting. He was feeling better from the effects of the lighting, but he didn't see a need to stay longer than they had to. Right now, he only wanted to try and help some of the people who had helped him before being betrayed. After that, it was all vacation.

* * *

Jace searched the ground and, seeing no one on the beach, he decided to land. Jace glanced at the clock to see the time. The fact that it read 0813 and the sun still wasn't up yet confused him.

He set the ship down and turned to Eislie before grabbing a few things from storage. Jace opened the door and felt the cold February breeze. He walked down the steps, his senses tasting the air, feeling the snowflakes fall against his face, he smiled. He had been away for a few years. When his feet touched the ground, he felt the weight of the gravity he remembered. Jace took a few steps and felt the wind as his hair whipped around, his jacket open, and he took a deep breath.

"Ugh, it stinks here!" he heard as Eislie bundled herself up. Jace chuckled, seeing her tapping the heating controls on her jacket with purpose. Jace turned back and felt the tiny ice crystals whip against his skin, their sharp daggers of water cutting into his senses, and memory.

"Never thought I'd miss this," he mumbled.

Eislie joined him, putting her hands in her pockets, again attempting to turn the heater in her flight jacket to full. "I thought you said we weren't landing in that cold place."

Jace turned to her, the cold air reminding him of the season. He blew his breath, making a plume of steam. Eislie watched as Jace remained silent before pulling up his collar. He smiled, seeing her shivering, and reached into his pockets to grab the items he had retrieved from storage. He handed her a set of a knit hat and gloves. "It's winter now. We'd have to wait a few months before it gets warm."

Jace donned the hat he had, and Eislie followed soon after. She watched Jace take a deep breath, and she did the same, only to wrinkle her nose, making Jace laugh when she said, "The air really stinks."

Jace noticed it as well.

It was still early morning, and their landing had not gone unnoticed. Nearby, a small planetary patrol ship landed. Jace was surprised to see a human exit the Daak craft before hearing, "You two lost?"

Jace smiled, nodding his head toward land. "Nope, used to live here. Shelter two thirty-four. It was over there." Jace then pointed to the ship. "Kind of big to land in a parking lot."

The man gave a polite smile, asking, "You have proof of residency?"

The smile faded from Jace's face. He walked toward the man but stopped, seeing another emerge from the Daak craft. Eislie looked toward Jace, sensing a feeling of familiarity from him as he stared past the man.

"You listening to me?" the man asked before grasping his weapon.

Jace briefly looked at the man before returning to the woman walking toward them.

"Do we have a troublemaker here, Dansett?" the woman asked as she confidently walked up.

The officer turned to look at her but was interrupted when Jace said, "That's a familiar voice."

The woman stared at Jace, her brown eyes peering through the protective visor she wore.

Dansett looked back to her. "Maybe. He says he lived here, over in shelter two thirty-four. But he doesn't have proof of residency."

The woman simply stared at Jace. She seemed to be searching for something in her memory. Jace took a breath. "I think your name was Kelsey, right?"

The woman took off her visor as she slowly moved toward Jace. The woman's steps were hesitant, her eyes fixed, not believing what she was seeing. "My God, Tucker? We thought you were dead!"

Eislie stood behind Jace. She was new to this world, and didn't know how people would react to her. She looked human, but wasn't. There was a moment as Jace looked around. "Looks like they cleaned the place up a bit."

The woman walked forward to press her dark-skinned hand against Jace's chest before hugging him. "My God, you did come back!"

Jace turned to Eislie and waved her forward. Jace could see his love still shivering and asked, "You still cold?"

Eislie nodded, remaining silent.

Kelsey shook her head. "We've got some hot coffee inside. You can warm up once you move your ship."

Jace looked back. "We brought some supplies. Didn't know where we were supposed to park."

Behind Kelsey, two Daak patrol walked up to the group. "Are there any issues, Officer Davis?"

Kelsey shook her head, and the Daak looked at Eislie. "Captain Tucker, Captain Licessien, welcome to Earth. We were informed of your arrival. Unfortunately, it is too early to deliver the supplies you are carrying. They will have to wait until we can arrange with the local authorities."

Jace put his hands on his sides, his jacket open to the wind. "Okay, we can wait. Where should we park?" He looked around before turning to Eislie. "I thought it was too good of a spot to watch the sunrise." Jace then faced the Daak. "We'll move as soon as possible." The Daak turned to walk away.

Kelsey watched as the Daak went to leave. "How do they know you?"

The Daak responded, "They are the ones who defeated the Duggor at Oppa. We are in their debt for saving millions of our people."

Jace felt uneasy as the Daak mentioned Oppa and turned, sensing Eislie moving nearer to him. She could see Kelsey staring at him. "Local boy makes it big?"

Eislie felt Jace shift as he said, "Something like that."

The officer found it humorous, but was brought back to the other officer staring at Eislie. His eyes looked to be trying to figure out something. Eislie leaned into Jace, grabbing hold of his hand.

Kelsey noticed and asked, "Where ya from, miss?"

Eislie didn't answer right away and looked to Jace, who replied, "She's not from around here. Is that gonna be a problem?" Eislie shivered; not from the cold, but the threat in Jace's voice.

The officer understood his tone and smiled as she realized they were together. She looked to Jace and Eislie. These two stood as one in her mind. Kelsey smiled, reaching up to touch Jace's face. "How long you two been together?"

"A couple of years," Jace said as he pulled Eislie closer.

Kelsey smiled. "You look good together." She paused. "Me and a few others kept pictures of all who were lost during the raids. Gonna have to cross your picture off."

Jace nodded. “I’m fine with that.”

The officer’s demeanor changed, and Jace took notice, asking, “What is it?”

Kelsey took a breath. “Keller is still running things over there. Is that where you’re headed?”

Jace got the warning in her voice and nodded. “I’m not here to take revenge. I’m just trying to help.”

“Good. I don’t want to have to shoot you,” Kelsey replied.

Eislie looked confused. “Would you shoot him?”

Her question brought the stare of both Kelsey and Jace, and she could feel their eyes burning through her, making her say, “Forget I asked.”

An amused chuckle came from everyone around her. She then heard Dansett ask, “So how would I get a ship like that? And don’t take this the wrong way, ma’am . . . but a beautiful woman like her?”

Eislie didn’t know how to react, but could see the other officer turning toward her partner. Then she heard Kelsey say, “Still can’t teach him any manners.”

Jace nodded. “I had a phase like that. Thankfully, I left it behind.”

Then Dansett spoke again. “Seriously, what would I have to do to find someone like her and a ship?”

Jace smiled, holding his hands before him. “Trust me, you don’t want to know.”

Eislie thought for a moment and, realizing what Jace had said, it made her laugh before saying, “Yes, you really don’t want to know.”

They calmed enough to see the smile across officer Kelsey’s face and Dansett still clueless. Jace turned, gently nudging Eislie to follow. He turned back to wave at the two officers. “C’mon, we’ll give you a ride. You can show us where to park.”

Kelsey followed, catching up to them as Dansett stayed behind, saying he'd meet them back at the center. Kelsey asked, "I've only been in the hover carts, never been on a spaceship before. Is it dangerous?"

Jace looked to the sky for a moment before responding. "Mostly, no. But, flying with us . . . that may be a different matter."

Chapter 6:
A Ghost Returns

Jace and Eislie sat on the beach, a large blanket beneath them. Eislie had taken the corner and wrapped it around herself as she leaned against Jace for warmth. Jace took a sip of his coffee from the visitor's center and they watched the sun start to peak over the horizon. Kelsey had a unique blend of coffee she made just for Jace. It was one she liked using during the winter patrols. She mocked, "Won't keep you as warm as the inside of a star," referencing the video they showed her from the ship.

"Can't believe we left the clock on Alliance time," Jace remarked, glancing over to Eislie. "Would have gone someplace else instead of straight here."

Eislie shivered next to him, asking, "Aren't you cold?"

Jace turned to her. "Yeah. I'm just not shivering yet." He held up his cup. "This is keeping my insides warm."

Eislie looked at the cup and to him a few times before he handed it to her. She sipped, feeling the warm coffee all the way down and then the distinctive taste and burn of something familiar. She turned to him after taking another sip. "This isn't just coffee, is it?"

Jace shook his head slowly. "Nope. It's got a shot or two of Irish whiskey."

She reluctantly handed the cup back to Jace, who took another sip. The sun peeked through the surface as the fog muddied the skies all around them. Jace looked to the sky. "This'll burn off pretty quick. Once the sun gets a bit higher."

Eislie held her hand in front of her eyes, saying, "It's brighter than home," making Jace nod. She then sighed. "My friends always told me the lights were too bright when they came over when I was younger. Now I know why." Eislie placed the spare part of the blanket around Jace as she moved closer. "You are warm. How are you warm? It's freezing out here."

Jace couldn't help but laugh before he put his arm around her. His eyes were staring at the sight before him as the sun became blinding to his senses. He turned to see Eislie looking at him, a slight concern in her stare.

"How are you feeling?" she asked.

Jace smiled, "I've been good since we changed the lights in the ship." He continued to look into her eyes. "Hope they're not blinding you."

Eislie shook her head and turned to see the bottom of the sun release from the edge of the surface. "No, I'm surprised it doesn't." She looked at her comm and, in a shivering voice, said, "We should head back. I'm getting cold."

* * *

At the visitor's center, Kelsey stood outside as three others walked to greet her. She recognized them all. Hanna had brought Toni and Lily along with her for support. Kelsey had called the shelter earlier to convince Hanna that one of those they thought were lost was now back on Earth. Hanna rifled through her portfolio when she stopped next to Kelsey. Finally, she produced a paper; it had the sketch of a man's face. Kelsey looked at it and nodded. "That's him."

"Are you sure? He's not a clone or something, is he?" Hanna asked.

The officer looked down toward the beach as she handed the paper back to her friend. "I'm sure it's him, Hanna." She pointed to the ship in the lot. "And that's his ship."

The other two looked on with a hint of fear when one of them said, “He’s not here for payback, is he?”

Kelsey shook her head. “I don’t think so. But he says he has some supplies for us. Medical equipment too.”

Lily turned to see the two walking from the beach. “What were they doing out there? It’s freezing out.”

Kelsey smiled, “Watching the sunrise. What, you lose your sense of romance?”

They were all looking at the ship when Kelsey said, “Can’t believe that was inside a star. And they slept inside it, too.”

“What?” Toni yelled. “How the hell did they do that?”

Kelsey smiled. “I saw the video. They slept inside a star. And according to the Daak, these two destroyed a ship an entire fleet couldn’t. So there’s, like, two or three planets that owe them big.”

Jace overheard them as they walked up. “It’s true, we slept in a star. It wasn’t our first choice, but we did it.” He then watched as Hanna looked at the picture before holding it up to his face. He could see the tears forming in her eyes as she reached out to touch his shoulder. Eislie moved closer to him as the others stared at Jace.

Toni spoke in broken words, “You saved a lot of people when you were here. I’m sorry for what happened.”

Jace nodded gently. “Took me a while, but I came back.”

Eislie was bumped aside as Lily threw her arms around Jace. She never realized that others had relied on the man she loved as much as she did now. Her heart skipped when she heard the woman holding him say, “Thank God you’re back.”

Jace gently pushed her away, plainly saying, “I’m not staying.”

Toni pushed away, her mind still processing what Jace told them. She looked to Eislie as Jace said, “I made a promise to show her where her mother came from.” Jace looked as if he had realized an answer to a question he had been thinking about for ages. Eislie could feel him relax and fill with a confident realization as he said, "All the things I've seen and experienced. I don't think I was ever meant to stay."

Kelsey gave him a gentle punch to the shoulder. "Well, you're here now." She looked back and said, "We got the okay to bring you to the shelter, but that delivery will have to wait until the fog clears."

She turned. "C'mon, we'll show you what you've been missing."

* * *

It wasn't long before the familiar sounds and sights of the shelter he had called home for a few months filled his senses. Jace walked along with the others as they passed people doing everyday things, even seeing someone washing a dog in the freezing weather. He was wondering why. His answer was found in the familiar scent of skunk now permeating the air near the woman. He could see her eyes squinted and her stuttered breathing.

"Smells like someone lost a fight," Jace joked.

Jace laughed as the woman shot back, "Stupid dog thought the damn skunk was playing."

Eislie covered her nose as they walked by. "Ugh, what's a skunk?" her question bringing several glares from others around them.

Jace's senses and stride changed. He now looked around, perceiving everyone as a threat. Sensing this, Kelsey and the others started showing aggression toward the crowd to back off. He leaned into Eislie. "Don't make remarks like that too often, okay?"

Eislie felt her back stiffen. She had been comfortable with Jace, but now realized that not all Terrans were like him. She realized that perhaps this wasn't the safest place to be casual for the moment. She then felt a tap on her arm from Lily, who said, "We got ya covered. Don't pay any attention to these idiots. They are not gonna make a move while we're here." She then gave an angry stare toward one man holding a shovel, making him turn away. Eislie looked at the small woman. "You must be tough."

Lily nodded. "If you wanna survive here, you have to be." She sighed, "Did you really sleep inside a star?"

Eislie nodded. "Yeah, we were hiding from pirates. We destroyed some of their ships. They were hunting us."

Lily chuckled, "You killed space pirates and dove into a star? Hell, you'll be fine down here."

Eislie shook her head as she stopped next to Jace as Kelsey met with someone. Eislie grabbed Jace's hand as she watched the officer point toward the field nearby. Jace followed her movements and turned to Eislie. "We'll bring the ship over there when it clears up. It'll be easier to unload."

There was a murmur all around as people heard that medicine and food were going to be delivered. Eislie could feel the sadness all around her lifting before seeing two men approaching with angry strides.

"Kelsey, what the hell are you doing? No supplies are to come in unless I say so," the man growled. Eislie felt Jace's grip stiffen and anger grow in him as the man spoke.

"Jace? You okay?" she asked in a whisper.

Jace simply said, "Do not let go of me."

Eislie felt him pulling toward the man and she gently tugged back on Jace's hand. She then watched as Kelsey yelled at the man, telling him to take it up with the others. "You're not the only one in charge here, Keller."

The man glared at the officer, holding his finger out toward her before storming away. She watched as the officer stood her ground and waited for the man she now knew as Keller to disappear around the corner of one of the shelters. Officer Kelsey then returned to the small group, saying to Jace, "I don't even think he remembers you."

Eislie could feel the hand of the man she loved still tense as he replied, "Too bad I remember him."

Kelsey moved closer. "You said no revenge. Are you a liar?"

Jace shook his head. "No." He turned to Eislie, and she felt him relax. "I came back to see what it was like, and to help if I could. Screw him if he can't accept that."

The officer smiled. “He may still try something.”

Jace sighed. “He may start something, but, I’m sure I’ll finish it.”

His statement brought a finger pointing at Jace’s face from Officer Kelsey. “No killing.”

Jace nodded. “I won’t. Even assholes deserve to live.”

Kelsey then led them into the nearby building. Tina was holding up the sketch, showing others as they worked on preparing the morning meals for everyone. Jace unzipped his flight jacket as the warmth of the building hit him. Eislie kept hers bundled.

Eislie was pushed aside as another woman took the sketch from Tina. “It is him!”

Jace felt a little unnerved as others moved to get a closer look at him. That was until Kelsey stepped in. “All right, everyone, I know we don’t usually see someone come back, but let’s give them some space.”

Eislie felt warmer, but it wasn’t the temperature. A feeling of happiness was all around her now, with Jace returning. It was something she had only recently realized was a feeling of hope. She watched as a man was nearly knocked over by a young girl who rushed to wrap her arms around Kelsey.

“Why are you up so early?” Kelsey said as she scooped the girl from the floor. “C’mon, I have some people I’d like you to meet.”

Kelsey held the girl, who couldn’t have been more than seven years old, and stopped before them. “Jace, Eislie, this is my daughter, Cherish.”

“She looks like she has your eyes,” Eislie said.

Kelsey shook her head as Cherish struggled to turn to look at Eislie. “No, she’s not my original daughter. Her parents were killed during the fighting before the Daak showed up.” Eislie watched as a man walked up to stand next to Kelsey. “This is my husband, Jerome.” The man gave a greeting and took Cherish from Kelsey. Jerome seemed to be having trouble holding onto their daughter. Eislie watched as the girl twisted to keep looking back at her and Jace.

Kelsey laughed as Cherish asked, "You have your own ship?"

Jace nodded at her question.

The girl asked, "What's its name?"

Eislie laughed, "Well, our ship's computer's name is Ed. Our ship is called the *Wolfhammer*."

Jerome chimed in, "It's a warship?"

Jace shook his head. "Nope, mining vessel. But it can hold its own against warships."

Kelsey took notice of the interest of her daughter in their ship and seemed to be confused. "She's usually pretty shy around everyone." Kelsey scoffed and looked to Jace. "You said you had some supplies, right?"

Jace nodded. "We can head back and bring in the ship."

Kelsey smiled, "Might as well. Breakfast isn't going to be ready for a bit anyway."

Eislie watched Jace laugh. "Still making sure everyone gets something to eat, huh?"

Kelsey nodded. "Yeah, same as you did."

Jace became solemn, and Eislie grabbed his hand again. She watched as he looked around. "We brought down a ship's grade med unit. It should help with the injured and most of the sick. The supplies should last you a couple of months. They didn't have a lot for us to requisition."

Kelsey reached out, hugging Jace, then Eislie. When the woman pulled away, there were tears in her eyes. "Every little bit helps."

The officer stepped back, looking up. "I was thinking maybe getting you folks something to eat. But, it may be better to bring in that ship of supplies instead, before everyone wakes up."

Jace nodded. "Guess we should head back and bring the ship in. We can get something later."

Kelsey nodded and turned to Jerome and Cherish. “You, young lady, need to get back home.” They watched as Cherish waved bye as Kelsey motioned for them to follow her back out. But as they were leaving, none of them saw the two men standing near the support pillar that held the roof above them.

“Keller, did they say that’s their ship?” one man asked, making Keller nod.

The crowd around them returned to work, all ignoring the two standing in the shadow of the pillar. Keller looked toward the door and said, “And they said it could hold its own against a warship. So that means it has weapons.” Keller turned to the other man. “Dobbs, get the others together. I don’t care what the council thinks. If that ship has weapons, maybe we can kill the Daak and take back our planet.”

Keller paused for a moment. “At least maybe we can put him in one of those cells we built. I’d love to see the look on that man’s face every time I visit.”

Dobbs looked unsure as he followed Keller from the hall.

Chapter 7: What's in a Name?

Dust kicked up as the *Wolfhammer* prepared to land. Several Daak patrol flyers, along with Alliance personnel, kept the area clear for them. The aliens were amazed at the number of people trying to look under the ship as it neared the ground.

As the rear cargo door lowered, Jace popped his head from the opening, his foot riding the ramp down as it touched the ground.

"Captain Tucker, are you sure you don't need the medical unit for your ship?" one of the Daak asked.

Jace laughed, "Nope, we got a pretty good one already. Besides, I think they need this more than we do right now."

The Daak nodded. "Of course. We have tried helping, but it has been difficult. Terrans are, for lack of a better term, stubborn."

Eislie heard that as she walked up behind Jace. "I can vouch that they are." Jace grabbed her gently, pulling her toward him, making her laugh.

The Daak nodded and motioned for the Alliance crews to help with deploying the medical unit. The Daak were instructed by the local council on where to set it up. Jace and Eislie took some food to the nearby shelter and were mobbed by thankful workers as they dropped off the needed supplies.

Eislie was smiling, seeing all the activity as she watched the Alliance personnel finish setting up the medical unit. Then, she was startled by someone yelling next to her. But as Eislie turned to look, she was almost knocked over as a small body ran into the back of her leg. She had just barely placed her hand to the side of the med unit to catch herself from falling and turned to see Jerome panting as he ran up.

"Sorry, she got away from me," he apologized before grabbing Cherish from the ground, dusting herself off. Eislie could see the girl holding a rolled paper tightly.

"Here, you think he'd like this?" Cherish asked, holding the paper before Eislie.

Jace, seeing the commotion, was walking up and spoke as Eislie took the paper from the girl. "Should have the rest of the supplies offloaded shortly. What ya have there?"

Eislie unrolled the paper and was amazed by the artwork before her. She showed it to Jace, who nodded. "It's spacy, edgy. I think it'd look great on the ship. I think Ed would like it."

On the paper was the name of their ship, *Wolfhammer*, which Cherish had drawn. The girl turned to them. "I can paint it if you want."

Jace chuckled before leaning into Eislie. "Too bad it'd only last a day or so."

Eislie shrugged her shoulders. "If we use ceramic paint, it should stay for a while."

But they didn't have any ceramic paint on board. That was until one of the Alliance personnel suggested that they have some at the visitor's center and use it to touch up the patrol flyers. The man then said, "But we only have two colors."

Jace nodded. then looked back to the man. Jace could see the identifier on his uniform. It read "E. Drasker."

"What's the 'E' stand for?" Jace asked.

The man worked to activate the controls of the med unit. "Oh, my name? It's Emilino Drasker."

Eislie tried holding back a snicker, making Jace ask what was funny. She whispered a reply, "In Oppan, Emili translates as dumb."

Jace did his best to hold back a laugh as he mumbled, "Dumb Drasker. You're joking." Eislie shook her head as Jace turned away until he could again present a straight face.

As Jace turned back, Cherish blurted out, "I can paint it in two colors!"

Jace bit his lip, still trying not to laugh as he shook his head before muttering, "We should probably put a name on the ship." Then, he looked to Jerome, motioning to Cherish. "Okay, if we say yes, how much are you gonna charge?" Jace watched as Jerome started to laugh as Cherish seemed to think.

"I don't want money; I want to go on the ship," the girl replied.

Jace looked to Eislie, and then turned to see Jerome with his eyes wide, almost as if he was asking Cherish to ask again. But instead, Jace looked into the girl's eyes, and he knew what to ask next.

"You want a tour, or are you looking to fly?" Jace asked.

The Alliance personnel next to them said, "It's irregular, but truthfully, if you're giving rides, I'd like to fly on a ship that took out a cleaver."

Jace looked at the girl and the expression on her father's face. Jace could swear he could hear, *"Please, please, please . . ."* mentally projected from the man. Jace looked to Eislie to see a smile across her face when she said, "We could give them a ride for helping us."

Jace nodded before saying, "You think your mother would want to go?"

Jerome spoke up. “Yes, Kelsey said she flew with you but wanted to try it out in space.”

Jace and Eislie looked to the Alliance representative, who said, “We would have to alert the station, but as long as it’s done safely, I don’t think it’ll be an issue. It might even be good for relations.”

Jace put his hand to his chin. “So, you’ll paint our ship, and all you want is a ride?”

“Into space!” the girl yelled out.

“A ride into space. Hmmm. I don’t know.” Jace paused before Eislie nudged him. “Okay, you’ve got a deal.”

* * *

It was late afternoon when things were offloaded and the supplies stored. The Alliance and Daak had arranged permission for the *Wolfhammer* to take those wanting a ride to space. Eislie had offered it to any who helped. She was surprised to find that there were fewer than she had anticipated. When she remarked it to Jace, he told her, “Some people just aren’t ready.”

Those willing boarded the ship, and Jace and Eislie started the engines. Jace hit the holo-display, and even the Alliance people were impressed, remarking that most ships now use a two-D system because of the difficulty of maintaining holo-systems.

Hearing an alarm, Jace jumped from his seat and headed toward the reactor access when Ed alerted him to someone trying to open the engine reactor room. Everyone looked in his direction, hearing him shout, “Hey, you don’t want to open that door while we’re flying! Not unless you want to fry everyone on the ship!”

Jace watched the man slink away from the door. Jace made sure the door was secure as he turned to look at the man. Jace could see something in his eyes, and could almost sense a disdain as the man stared back. But, of course, Jace had felt that before, and usually because people knew he was a Terran or a starborn, so he didn’t pay it much mind.

Jace warned the man again, telling him it was dangerous while they were flying. In truth, it really wasn't, and he pulled the man along to where everyone else was. As Jace returned to his chair, he turned back to see the man looking intently over the controls. *Something's wrong with that guy.*

It was only a few minutes before they were in orbit. Jace turned to see Cherish jumping up and down. She noticed him staring and she asked, "How come we're not floating?"

Eislie turned. "We have gravity inside; outside, you could float."

"Can we go outside?" the girl asked.

Jace was about to say something when her mother said, "You'd float away, sweetness," her statement bringing a chill to Eislie as she looked back at Jace. Her thoughts were jumping around to when they were on the Alliance ship and Jace was blown out into space. Eislie turned back to Kelsey and nodded.

"You mean you really would float away?" Kelsey asked, seeing the interaction.

Jace nodded, saying, "Yeah, but that's another story altogether. If we have time, I'll tell you about it." He looked ahead and toward the moon before turning back to Drasker. "How far can we go?"

Drasker moved closer to look at the holo-display. "We can go to the nearest moon; you would be in violation after that."

"Anyone wanna go to the moon?" Jace asked as he turned to look at everyone.

He was startled hearing Jerome excitedly respond, "Yes! I always wanted to go to the moon."

Jace looked back to the Alliance representative, who shrugged his shoulders. "Why not? As long as we don't go much further." Jace nodded and looked around, seeing others agreeing with Jerome.

Eislie nodded when she heard from Jace, “Even if it’s a violation, it’s not like we haven’t broken the rules before.”

It was less than a minute before the Earth’s moon appeared large on the front screen. Everyone had moved to the small portal windows and were taking turns viewing the sight. Kelsey held Cherish up to see the moon. The girl turned to say, “It’s another planet!”

Drasker smiled at her. “Technically, it’s part of your planetary system.”

The girl looked at him, then to Jace and Eislie. “How many planets have you been to?”

Eislie thought for a moment. “Twenty.” Jace nodded.

“Wait, I’ve only been to six, and I’ve been with the Alliance for over seventy-five years!” Drasker interjected.

Eislie looked at the man and mouthed the words while pointing to herself and then the floor. Finally, she mouthed, “Our ship.” Her pantomime brought a smile to Jace’s face as he steered away from the moon. “Okay, folks, we’re heading back. I understand it’s almost dinnertime.”

* * *

They arrived back on the surface as night fell. Jace chuckled, watching some stumble as their feet touched the ground. Space was different, but he didn’t seem to have any trouble with the ship or any planet they landed on. He and Eislie had stayed on the *Wolfhammer* without any issues. Jace seemed happy when Ed inquired if they were going to take any additional passengers up again. But Jace was keeping his eye on the clock. They had been on Earth for nearly two days already, and like Eislie, he wanted to see someplace warmer.

It was early morning when he left to see how things were going in the shelter. He turned to see the new logo now displayed on the ship. Kelsey’s daughter had been working early. Ed had even allowed them to use the small grav lift they had for moving cargo. Jace told Eislie about the new paint. She stayed on board where it was warm.

Jace was walking with some Alliance and Daak but was stunned when someone hit him from behind. He was quick to recover, and pushed the man back. What he hadn't counted on was seeing who it was.

"Keller, you like hitting people from behind or something?" Jace growled, and was held back by the Alliance personnel.

"Tucker, you're a traitor. You sided with the enemy!" Keller yelled his accusation for all to hear.

Jace stood his ground. "Bullshit. You tried to kill me and left me for dead!"

"You don't deserve that ship, Tucker. I heard it took down one of the biggest ships in the galaxy. Isn't that right?" Keller yelled back.

Jace nodded. "Yeah, a Duggor cleaver. So what?"

"It's being wasted on you. I've been studying their laws; I can challenge you for your ship," Keller told him.

"What? What are you fucking talking about?" Jace replied, but was taken aback when Drasker answered, "He's correct. You're both Terran. There is a clause for mutual combat from residents of a common planet."

Jace laughed. "No fucking way I'm giving him our ship."

Eislie had joined Jace as Keller held up a small transmitter. "I can challenge a captain for ship control." He pressed a button, and a small explosion was heard out in the field. "I've rigged one of these on that medical thing you brought. You don't fight me, I blow it."

Jace scoffed, "The ship has two captains. You gonna fight her as well?"

Keller smiled, "I only have to fight you. It's in their laws. She's going to give me control or I blow the device."

Eislie started shaking her head. “Why are you doing this? We’re just trying to help.”

Jace took off his flight jacket. “Okay, Keller, you win. Let’s go.”

“Jace, you can’t,” Eislie protested.

“Eis, he’s got payback coming. And right now, I’m pissed that he’s trying to hurt everyone because he wants something he thinks is a weapon,” Jace told her as he stepped forward.

As Jace approached, Keller handed the device to Duane, who held it with uncertainty. Jace recognized him as the man who had tried entering the reactor room during their flight. *That’s what you were doing.* As Jace was looking at Duane, Keller rushed him, throwing the first punch. Jace was able to dodge, but eventually, Keller landed a few blows. Jace pulled back and lunged toward Keller, his anger at what the man had done giving him formidable resolve. Keller fell quickly, and as Jace threw the man to the ground, Keller gasped to fill his lungs, having the air knocked out of him.

“Stay down, asshole,” Jace said as he wiped the blood from his mouth.

Keller couldn’t get up, and Jace looked toward Duane. “Disarm it, or I’m not going to be nice.”

Seeing the fire behind Jace’s eyes, Duane dismantled the device and said he’d show them where the explosive was. Several people, including Alliance personnel, were happy to help find it. Eislie took Jace back into their ship and healed him. She scolded him for taking the chance.

“There was no way in hell he was going to win, Eis. I would have killed him if he tried,” Jace growled quietly. She could sense something different in Jace now, as though a weight had been lifted from him. His fight, and seeing the man who betrayed him on the ground defeated.

“It’s been bothering you for a long time, hasn’t it,” Eislie said.

She watched Jace nod slowly. “I think my business here is finally done.”

Eislie used the regen on his lip and turned his head to examine him for any other injuries. She then planted a gentle kiss on his lips before saying, “Do something like that again without telling me, and I’ll hurt you.”

Jace looked into her eyes and smiled. “Yes, Captain.”

It wasn’t long before Eislie finished healing Jace. Both being starborn had its advantages.

As they exited their ship, they encountered a combination of Daak and Alliance personnel who told them, “Keller’s claim was voided; under the law, he cannot make the same challenge again. And his authority for running the shelter can now be revoked,” Drasker told them.

Jace nodded. He understood. Keller had picked a fight he was never going to win. The consolation now was that he could tell Keller himself, and both the Daak and Alliance wanted to watch as he did. Keller had been a problem since they had arrived to help from the war. And now they needed something to show others that Keller was stopping them from doing so. They preferred the idea of the council running the shelter, like many others. Keller’s recent actions now gave them a reason to have him removed.

Keller was still in the medical tent when Jace arrived. “Still licking your wounds?” Jace mocked the man.

“How the hell have you healed already?” Duane yelled.

“Good ship, good crew.” Jace smiled. “You lost, Keller. I’m here to request you leave the operations to those willing to help others. Not just you.”

Keller shot back, “You don’t deserve that weapon!”

Jace stood tall as Eislie stood next to him. “What weapon?”

“That ship,” Keller growled through gritted teeth.

“That ship is ours. It’s our freedom from what we had to go through. The computer on it is our friend. You think I don’t deserve something that you set in motion?” Jace replied.

“What?” Keller responded.

“You tried killing me, sacrificing me, knocking me out to leave me for the Daak. But instead you left me for dead,” Jace replied.

Kelsey pulled the Alliance rep aside, telling him that Keller had ordered others injured to keep the Daak off his team. Drasker said something, and Kelsey rushed away, saying, “Let me get some of the council.”

“So, what, Tucker. You want to kill me?” Keller replied.

Jace shook his head. “No, Keller, I pity you; I feel sorry for you. We are trying to help everyone, even when I was working with you. And you still think this is about you?” Jace paused for a moment. “Besides, if I wanted to kill you, I would have waited for fewer witnesses.”

Eislie leaned against Jace hearing his joke. She could sense his confusion and sorrow and was wondering if what he said really was a joke. But she understood. Jace agreed to fight this man only because Jace knew he wouldn’t lose. He wouldn’t fail. The ship and she were too valuable to him. By Keller challenging Jace, the man had already lost.

After returning with several council members, Kelsey now stood by Drasker, and all were staring at Keller. She had no respect for the man and had been under him, since he was still head of the shelter. She had even put together the council, which Keller hated. The stern looks on them all were a precursor to what they had to do next.

“Terrance Keller, you are officially being removed by this council as the head of shelter two thirty-four. We are assigning the post to Kelsey Davis as acting head,” one of the council members said in a very authoritative tone.

Jace watched as Keller looked on in disbelief as Drasker stepped forward. “We have accepted her as the new acting leader, as per your recent actions. You no longer have any say in the functioning of the shelter.”

Keller remained silent as he looked to Duane, only to see the man looking around the room for answers. “Duane Dobbs, you and Keller are being charged as an accessory to a terrorist act for placing an explosive device in the medical unit.”

Duane again searched for an answer before he was grabbed from behind, an expression of surprise on his face as cold metal restraints clasped around his wrists. Kelsey then said, “You wanted to lock everyone down. You asshole.”

Keller said nothing as Duane was taken away. The Alliance person training the humans on using the med unit became less gentle as he heard it was Keller who had rigged the explosives that may have harmed them. It wasn’t long before they took Keller away as well.

Kelsey stood before Keller and Duane as their cell doors closed. She stood with Drasker and several Daak as they looked on. She watched as Keller was compliant and sat on the small bunk in his cell.

“You relished building this holding area, didn’t you?” Kelsey said.

Keller smiled, “It was to hold anyone who was against us.”

The smile Keller displayed made Kelsey’s gut churn. She didn’t know why, but the man in that cell now seemed more repulsive than ever. She looked to Duane and took a step back as Acting Security Officer Woodworth stepped forward. The council had chosen him to represent the men for their trial.

“It’s ironic, Keller. You pushed for this holding area to be built. And now you are going to stay here until we can put you on trial.” Woodworth paused. “I’ll do my best to defend you. But I’m not making any promises.”

Keller turned with a defiant smile before lying back. “You’ll all figure out I’m not the villain here eventually.”

Kelsey stepped forward, ready to argue, but was stopped when Woodworth held her back. “You seem so sure you’re in the right, do you, Keller?”

Keller lay back. “It’s only a matter of time, Woodworth. After that, you’ll figure it out.”

In disgust, the gray-haired, balding man shook his head. “Let’s leave them to think about what they’ve done.” With that, the group headed to the front and left Duane and Keller in their cells alone.

Chapter 8:
Starborn Surprise

Duane was awakened by the sound of the cell door next to him opening, and a tapping against the wall as it again closed, the shadow of a figure now hovering before his view.

"You should see the look on your face right now, Dobbs," Keller said.

Duane stared back, taking a moment before answering, "Keller, how did you get out?"

Keller unlocked the door. "You'd think they'd at least search me before locking me in a cell I helped build. These aliens aren't very bright."

Duane wrestled himself up as Keller opened the door to his cell. The man he always called Dobbs was now staring at the grin on Keller's face as he held up a thin key. "You think I didn't consider someone locking me in here? Had this stashed in my shoe." Keller paused. "I knew the turncoats among us would show themselves sooner or later."

Keller's eyes looked up to stare through Duane. "Did you get a good look at their ship?"

Dobbs nodded. "They stopped me from getting into that room with the reactor; there is a large box on the far wall. It looked to have a lock on it."

Keller smiled, “That has to be where they keep the weapons. We could use something similar to what they used to knock out that big ship.” Keller’s smile grew. “C’mon, let’s get out of here. We can grab a cutter and do what we need to do.”

The man followed Keller as they moved toward the door. Keller peered through the inside window to see only two guards. “Good, it’s the aliens.” Keller smiled before whispering, “We don’t have to kill any of our people.”

Duane moved silently behind Keller as he unlocked the inside door. There was a sound of a brief struggle before two figures emerged from the holding center, their silhouettes blending into the darkness as they ran, disappearing into the morning fog.

* * *

Jace walked along with Kelsey as she was doing her newly appointed rounds. It felt good to be back home, and Eislie understood what Jace was experiencing. Eislie had experienced it a few times while she served, and she was happily standing by the ship admiring the new logo. The image was subtle, but it did make a statement. Like them, it was unremarkable, but the history, worn and rough, knew otherwise.

She headed back inside the *Wolfhammer* and suddenly felt a need to turn around, as if someone was behind her. As she did, she saw Cherish standing in the doorway.

“Welcome aboard,” Eislie said as she waved the girl to come in. She could see the child looking around, her eyes still filled with wonder, even after taking a trip to space. Eislie knelt to be at eye level with the girl. “Thank you for the new logo. We’ve been meaning to have one put on. You did a good job. The art is sort of fitting for us.”

Cherish looked around. “It’s a good ship.”

Over the speakers, they heard, “Thank you, I appreciate the compliment and the new art as well, Cherish.”

Eislie could see the happy surprise on the girl’s face and said, “That’s Ed?”

Cherish said hi to Ed, and he responded, again saying he appreciated the new logo. Then, without a breath, Cherish asked, "Are you really an alien?"

Eislie hesitated. "Yes, and no. I'm part Terran too."

"Terran?" Cherish asked.

"It's what we call your people. I'm from Gilese, but my mother is from Terra; I mean, Earth," Eislie told her. She wasn't prepared for the girl's next question. "I heard one of the Alliance call you a starborn. What is that?"

Eislie thought for a moment, her mind initially feeling the pain she used to feel when asked about being a starborn. Then, she smiled, telling the girl, "I am. It's a bit complicated."

Cherish looked at her inquisitively. "What do starborn look like? Like you, the Daak, or like humans?"

Eislie didn't answer right away. "Well, Gilese are similar to Terrans. And starborn, I guess, are just as similar." She seemed to think for a moment as an idea hit her. "You know, I have something that might be able to show you." Eislie walked quickly into the med bay and grabbed a scanner. She showed the girl the scanner and pointed it to herself, quickly doing a DNA profile. Then, she showed the girl the information.

"You see this? This is my Terran side. The other is different," Eislie said as the girl tried to read the screen. Seeing this, Eislie tapped the display, switching it to Earth English as she had done for Jace. Cherish was now able to read what it said.

"What is Lyri? Is that what your people are called?" Cherish asked.

Eislie now had to think, and she answered as best as she could. "My people are called Gilesian. They have, a, uh, slightly different DNA than Terrans." Eislie was now struggling with how to answer the girl. "It's complicated for me." Eislie then looked at the girl, seeing her trying to understand.

Eislie smiled, “If you have a certain amount of Lyri DNA, you are considered a starborn. Many people on Earth have some Lyri DNA. Here, let me show you.”

Eislie pointed the scanner toward Cherish, who backed away.

“It doesn’t hurt. I promise,” Eislie said as she scanned the girl.

The results were displayed on the screen, and it showed Terran DNA. Eislie turned to show the screen to Cherish and pointed to the information. “See? You show Terran, and . . .” Eislie paused, pulling the screen away from the girl to look closer. The expression on Eislie’s face was one of happy surprise and muted concern.

“What’s wrong with me?” the girl asked in a panic.

“Nothing. Nothing’s wrong with you. You’re fine,” Eislie said, a smile now showing on her face. But, unfortunately, she had to reread the screen. Eislie needed to make sure of what she read. The display showed 37 percent Terran. The rest, Lyri.

She’s one of us.

Eislie’s mind raced as she looked back at the girl. “I may have a surprise for you, but I have to tell your parents and Jace something first, okay?”

Cherish smiled back. “Is it good?”

Eislie nodded. “I think it might be. But I have to show your parents and Jace first, okay?” She then stood and told Ed to watch over Cherish while she went to find Jace.

Following her instructions, the computer then started the holo-display. “Would you like to play a game till they get back?” The girl agreed, and tapped the holo-display as Ed loaded up a new game.

* * *

Eislie rushed out the door, carrying the scanner. She had to show Jace and Cherish’s parents. She knew if the girl was mostly Lyri, she might be in danger staying on Earth.

Her departure was noticed by two men standing near the ship. Although Cherish had darker skin, hair, and eyes, she would essentially be considered a full starborn by Alliance standards. Eislie yelled to Jace when she saw him standing next to Kelsey as he was loading some supplies onto the shelves. Several Daak nearby also packing additional supplies took notice as she rushed over.

“Jace, you have to see this,” Eislie said, handing him the pad while Kelsey joined them. “I took a scan of your daughter to show her, something. Well, she called me an alien. I meant to show her we were similar. But look.” She pointed to the one section of the screen.

Jace’s brows raised. “You’re kidding me. Really?”

“What’s wrong with my daughter?” Kelsey became concerned.

Jace smiled, “Nothing. But it looks like she’s one of us.”

His statement brought one of the Daak to attention. “She is Terran. Should that not be?”

Jace sided a glance. “I’m Terran.”

Eislie showed the Daak the screen and the alien looked up. “Her family unit must be informed. They cannot stay here.”

Jace looked at Eislie. “Who else did you tell?”

“Just you and everyone here. Why?” Eislie said. “You don’t understand, she’s mostly Lyri, so . . .”

Jace looked concerned. “We can’t tell anyone, Eis. They’ll come for her.”

“Who’ll come for her?” Kelsey asked angrily.

With a pause, Jace replied, “Earth’s military.”

“Why?” Kelsey pleadingly asked.

Jace sighed, “She might be capable of doing some incredible things.” He turned to look away. “We’re still trying to figure it out ourselves.” His statement brought a stare from the Daak next to him.

"You are correct, Captain Tucker. No others may be told of this," the Daak said.

Jace looked around. He knew what it was like on Earth and what had happened to Eislie and him as well. He cleared the screen before handing it back to Eislie. "We have to think about this for a minute."

* * *

Back at the ship, the two men waited. They had yet to see Eislie or Jace return, and decided to move with their plan. As they entered the ship, Ed alerted for them to leave, and when Cherish saw them, she screamed.

"Grab her!" Keller yelled, and when Dobbs didn't, he rushed over, grabbing the girl, tightly covering her mouth so she couldn't scream. They then rushed back toward the reactor room and pried open the door. Dobbs was cutting into the box they thought had weapons but was really the crystal storage and containment. Unable to stop these men, Ed called Jace and Eislie immediately.

"Hurry up, get that thing open!" Keller griped, trying to hold onto the girl to keep her quiet. In frustration, he threw her to the side and she banged her head hard against the metal wall. Dobbs paused, seeing the girl not moving. Keller grabbed the cutter from Dobbs, pushing him aside. "We have to get that open before they come back."

Dobbs went over to the girl, he could not see any obvious injury. He could see she was unconscious, but breathing. "You said nothing about hurting a little girl, Keller."

"She a liability, you idiot. We'll leave her behind. They'll be busy helping her instead of following us."

"You're a monster, Keller. I'm helping her; this isn't right," Dobbs said, trying to pick up the injured girl as Keller finished cutting through the box. He opened it, and Dobbs watched in horror as the radiation turned the man before him to ash within seconds. Dobbs tried to shield the girl before the radiation took him as well. The man's remains softened her landing, and Cherish now remained on the floor, her back against the wall, unconscious.

Jace was running toward the ship as Ed was closing the door. The computer alerting them to the radiation leak.

"Spide leak! Shit!" Jace yelled, and his legs moving faster. He jumped onto the ramp and pulled the door quickly closed. Eislie pushed on the outside of the door, making sure it was sealed.

"He won't survive unless you have glyph generators in your jackets, right?" Drasker said.

Eislie nodded, knowing full well that Jace had left his crew jacket behind on the ship.

Kelsey arrived, demanding they open the door. Eislie explained to her, "We can't. It'll kill everyone."

Jace worked as quickly as possible, his foot sliding on the ash left behind by the two men.

"Ed, what's the reading?"

"Four hundred sixty-one percent lethal. The cutting tool may have fused some of the crystals, but radiation is stable. My sensors also indicate the girl is alive. I do not know the extent of her injuries."

Jace turned to see Cherish leaning against the wall, covered in ash. Jace checked to see if she was breathing. He knew the medical station might not operate with the high radiation, so he opened the toolbox and started welding the container shut. The two men had cut along the entire assembly for the containment box. Jace did his best to seal it quickly.

As he finished, he asked, "Ed, what's the reading?"

"Extractors are working. The level has dropped to three hundred sixteen percent. How is the child?"

Jace took her pulse, and the girl stirred but didn't wake. "She's alive. We'll get her fixed up." Jace hoisted her from the floor and straight to the med bay, and Ed went to work as soon as Jace placed her on the bed. The girl remained unconscious as the computer healed her injuries. As the computer worked, Jace grabbed a small, flexible hose from a cabinet and plugged it into a nearby port. "Turn on the vacuum, Ed."

"That is not a proper medical procedure, Captain."

"Ed! Do it! I'm not leaving her with the ash of those men who did this to her all over her," Jace growled. The computer complied quickly.

Within minutes, the radiation dropped to safe levels and the outer door opened. Eislie rushed in, followed by one of the Daak. They arrived to see Jace putting back the hose and Cherish sitting on the edge of the med table, smiling. Her mother arrived instantly wrapping her arms around the girl as she rushed in. Eislie was confused by Jace putting away the vacuum hose. He walked over, whispering, "I wasn't leaving her covered in ash." His face filled with the staidness of a grim task.

Wait, what happened? Ash? Oh no, someone was with her.

Eislie turned away, a whispered, "That's horrible," escaping her lips as she leaned against Jace.

Jerome had joined them and was looking to Jace for an answer. "Who did this?"

Jace only said, "Don't worry, they're taken care of."

Jerome grabbed Jace's arm. "Show me."

Jace pulled the man along, showing the human-shaped pile of ash. And the one where his daughter was. Jace whispered to the man, "That's what happens to people with a spide leak." Jerome looked at the spot where his daughter was, with no dust beneath. Jerome reeled back, looking at Jace.

"She was unconscious, and I don't think she saw it." Jace leaned in and whispered, "I couldn't leave her covered in him."

Jerome shook his head, his face a mix of disgust, anger, and sadness as he gripped down on Jace's shoulder. "Thank you." He then said, "I want to see how they died."

Jace looked at the man. “You sure?”

Jerome nodded, and Jace tapped the display in the engine room and ordered the computer to show what happened. Jerome watched as the men turned to dust within seconds. Jace could see Dobbs try and shield the girl before he burned. *You did the right thing in the end, at least, you bastard.*

Jace tapped the display and pulled Jerome out into the hall. He heard the man mutter, “They got what they deserved.”

Jace nodded.

In the hallway, Jerome pushed by the Daak and Alliance now populating the small interior. He joined the others as Eislie walked to Jace and asked, “What were you doing?”

Jace quietly said, “Showing him what happened.”

Eislie looked pained and put her arms around Jace, who fought back the tears from what he had just had to do. Drasker and the Daak watched as well, and the Alliance rep fought to hold his composure, saying, “You did the right thing. She doesn’t need to know.” But then became confused, asking, “How did she survive?”

The Daak stared at Jace, only saying, “They will be cared for, but they cannot stay.”

Jace pursed his lips, giving a quick, short nod. “Yeah, they can’t.” He looked away, saying, “So much for a normal life.”

The Daak stood tall in agreement, realizing the multiple meaning in Jace’s words, referring to the two of them and a newly discovered starborn.

The Daak took a moment. “What is the damage assessment of your vessel?”

Jace huffed, “Containment storage is toast. We’ll have to replace the entire assembly. And I can’t do that here. Unless you have several hundred pounds of zirconium plating lying around.”

The Daak replied, “The station would not be able to assist. They do not have the resources. Is your ship able to fly?”

Jace nodded. “Yeah. We’ll be good. It’s not an immediate repair. But we should do it before heading too far from Alliance space.”

Eislie looked back toward the Daak as Jace swayed against her. “C’mon, let’s see how they’re doing.”

Chapter 9:
A Little Vacation Never Hurts

Jace slammed the storage cabinet door closed, his loud cursing bringing Eislie to see what the commotion was. As she appeared in the doorway, Jace had already opened several other bins.

"What's wrong?" Eislie asked.

Jace shook his head. "Food's gone."

"Who took it?" Eislie yelled for the computer to review the last twelve hours on the ship, only to be told by both Ed and Jace the same thing.

"We weren't robbed. It's all toast. Spide leak burned it all," Jace said before hearing something other than ash in the box of cereal they had picked up on Oppa. He was reading the ingredients, finding little to no organic matter in it. Although what little it did have was turned to ash. All that remained was the junk.

Eislie thought for a moment and went to open the storage where they kept the alcohol, only to have Jace grab the door before her hand reached the handle.

"Don't look. It's gone too," Jace said before pushing his hair back and looking up at the ceiling.

Eislie shook her head, opening the storage unit and pulling out a bottle, only to see the liquid gray and cloudy. The ash of whatever organics was in it, other than water, was now burned beyond use.

"Shit! Everything's gone?" Eislie expounded as she pulled several bottles from storage before Jace nodded.

Jace walked away, only to slump into his control chair. Eislie joined him, landing much the same in her own.

"Guess we'll have to get some Alliance supplies until we get restocked," Jace said as he tapped the console.

On the screen, the short flight path to Hawaii now showed. Jace had hoped to head there and spend the remaining time with Eislie in the warm weather. He longed to feel himself floating in the ocean again, and was looking forward to the rest of their time on Earth. Unfortunately, now it seemed they would have to take some time and resupply.

Jace motioned to Eislie, and they headed outside to tell the others about their situation. Jace had hoped to leave within a couple of hours, but now they needed basic supplies. Including a new med kit. The one they had from Charon was now destroyed as well.

The Daak and Alliance were able to provide a small number of supplies. It would last them a week at most. Jace thanked them for the effort. He asked about ordering supplies while they were in Hawaii, but the Daak were only providing necessities to the locals for the moment. The two now had to wait until they returned home or to Oppa to resupply.

When they returned to the ship, Jace played the video they had on Hawaii and smiled. "I think we've spent enough time in the cold. Don't you?"

Eislie nodded. "I would have left by now."

She made Jace snicker before he said, "We should say goodbye."

Jace followed Eislie as she quickly walked toward the visitor's center. They had moved the ship after the incident, but it was still cold outside. The others thought it prudent as well, in case there was still an issue with any supporters of Keller. To Jace and Eislie, it didn't matter; they'd handled everything thrown at them so far.

Eislie was looking toward the loading area, and could see the Daak and Alliance personnel speaking with Kelsey and Jerome. She felt Kelsey's stare as she looked back to her and Jace, Jace mouthing a very animated, "Sorry!" Seeing the woman nod, he knew their having to leave was to protect Cherish.

"They'll be taken care of," Drasker said as Eislie looked over to see the three being led onto a ship. "We were surprised when we asked the girl where she wanted to go. She didn't have a clue."

Jace turned in annoyance. "She's seven. Did you know where you wanted to go when you were seven?"

Drasker shook his head. "Her parents had some ideas. I fear they may be drifting for a while till they find somewhere they feel comfortable. Although, her father seemed to have more ideas, as he's been researching."

Eislie joked, "I get the feeling he's been wanting to leave Earth for some time. You sure he's not a starborn?" She looked to Jace, who smiled.

Drasker replied, "After your findings, we tested them all. He is mostly Terran, some traces of Lyri."

Jace laughed as he hit Drasker's arm. "She's joking. Or maybe Jerome's just a starborn at heart." Eislie nodded in approval, giving a smile.

"I heard about the filament project," Drasker told them, making Eislie and Jace look suspiciously toward the man. Seeing them staring, Drasker sighed, "The Daak told me. I have no intention of telling anyone else. Truthfully, I'm jealous. I can't believe you traveled hundreds of light-years in seconds."

Jace nodded. “Yeah, we want to share it with everyone once we figure it out. But we’ve hit a few snags.”

Eislie grabbed Jace’s hand, interlacing her fingers with his before she said, “We needed to get away for a bit, visit someplace warm.”

Jace felt Eislie’s cold hand and shook his head. “Okay, we’re going already.”

They were laughing as Woodworth walked up beside Drasker. “You two leaving?”

Jace nodded. “Yeah. Why? You in a rush to get rid of us?”

The old man pulled off his knit cap to reveal a shiny, balding head as he reached out to shake Jace’s hand. “From what Kelsey and Tina told me, you were a bit of a troublemaker when you were here. It seems like you’ve gotten worse.”

Jace and Eislie burst out in laughter as Jace nodded in agreement. The old man added, “You did good. You helped a lot of people, both of you.” He paused. “Don’t be strangers. I’m sure things will be much better when you come back.”

Jace looked up at the ceiling, the skylight starting to darken as the clouds moved in. “It may be a while.” Jace looked at the two men before him. “And I mean *a while*.”

The old man smiled, “Well, wherever you’re heading, Godspeed, and good luck in what you’re looking for.”

Jace gave thanks, then, turning to Eislie, said, “Let’s go. I promised to take you someplace warmer after all, didn’t I?”

A joyful, “Yes!” escaped Eislie as she pulled Jace along back to the *Wolfhammer*.

* * *

Palm trees swayed in the breeze as Eislie walked along the sand wearing a thin robe over the swimsuit she had just purchased. Jace was standing on the red-sand beach as she was walking up. They had landed at what was once the airport on Maui and had booked a more private location. There were only a few people on the beach, and Jace had already set up a couple of lounge chairs and was staring at the ocean. As Eislie approached, she felt a calmness from the man she loved. Something she hadn't felt in some time.

"I think you're beginning to like coming back," she said as she stopped next to him.

"At least for a little while." Jace turned to her, seeing the thin robe she was wearing.

Eislie spun around and undid the robe to reveal the tiny two-piece she had on. Jace lowered his dark glasses he was using to protect his eyes from the sunlight and looked her up and down before he said, "Couldn't find anything smaller?"

Eislie looked at herself; the outfit was a bit revealing, but she liked the recommendation by the local Terrans. Although she became a little annoyed, telling Jace, "Guess you can't trust Terrans."

Jace snickered, "Nope. Though, I like it. But if you're going to wear that, make sure you put on sunscreen. Hell, I'm from here, and I'll burn in this in minutes." He gently kissed her, handing her a small spray bottle of the same sunblock he had just put on.

"You want a drink?" Jace asked. She nodded. Jace then joked, "Don't want to say bartender's choice here."

Jace snickered, referring to their time together back on Charon. He kissed her more deeply before telling her, "We'll go swimming in a little bit." As he was walking away, he yelled, "I'd put on the sunscreen, it's scorching today!"

Eislie removed the robe she was wearing and did her best to spray the mist over herself. Then, as she was trying to get her back, she decided to sit so as to not lose her balance. She was wrestling with the bottle before she heard a voice.

"Need some help?"

Eislie turned to see a man with dark, tan skin walking toward her. Eislie wasn't a fool. She had already done that with the suit she wore. So, she politely said, "No, I'm just waiting for my partner to come back."

The man moved nearer. "In this sun, you can burn pretty fast. Let me help." The man proceeded to pull the spray bottle from Eislie's hand as she glared at him through her dark glasses. The man sprayed her back, and did reach where Eislie couldn't. She was almost ready to believe he was there to help before he started rubbing her back. Eislie turned her elbow swiftly at about the man's eyes socket, but the man was quick and shifted out of the way. He stood, with a sinister smile on his face. "I'd say you were from an Alliance world. You people aren't so tough."

"Ahem," Eislie heard behind her as she sided her eyes to see Jace standing there holding two blue drinks.

The man scoffed, "Leave the drinks and go. I'm sure the lady will pick up the tab."

Jace chuckled as he placed the drinks down on the small table beside Eislie's chair. Then, he stood to look at the man. "You know, it's nice to be back on Earth. From your accent, I'd say you're from the Texas area." The man seemed confused by Jace's observation.

Eislie stood confidently next to Jace. "You know, sir, you're right; I am from an Alliance world. In fact, I'm former military. Oh, wait, did I mention I was sent to prison and escaped?" She leaned closer to the man, pointing to Jace. "Him too. But he's not Alliance. He's Terran. He's from your planet. New York City." Jace was holding back a smile as Eislie stepped back. "So, who do you want to fight first?"

The altercation had not gone unnoticed, and security was heading toward them as the man stood his ground. He walked by Jace, who didn't turn. The man then turned to swing at Jace, who ducked, grabbing the man's arm before bringing his knee up to the man's gut, knocking the wind out of him. The man was on his hands and knees, gasping. Jace moved away as the guards arrived. "Look, whoever you are, we've had an awful few days. Go slink off to wherever you go when you're not stalking the beaches."

The guards held a small stun stick, now pointing it at Jace and the man. Jace remarked, “Why is it that no matter where we go, someone wants to put a gun in my face? Why?”

The guards asked, “Are these men bothering you, ma’am?”

Eislie pointed to the tanned man. “He is.” Then she pointed to Jace. “He isn’t. He’s my partner.”

Eislie quickly moved beside Jace as they restrained the other man, leading him away. Jace asked who he was and was surprised when the guard told him, “His name’s Lawrence Templeton, goes by Big Larry. He’s some political figure from the previous Earth regime. We’ve had several complaints against him.”

Jace could see the guard was frustrated and asked, “Why not send him home?”

The woman shook her head. “We can’t. He claimed asylum, and since his area was devastated during the attacks, we can’t send him back.”

“Are you serious? He’s out here preying on people, and you can’t send him packing?” Jace scoffed.

The woman shook her head. “He’s been harassing mostly Alliance visitors. I don’t think I’ve seen anyone attack him back before. Where did you serve?”

Eislie shook her head. “I served on a military freighter. He’s not Alliance. He’s Terran.”

The woman’s eyes widened. “You’re not Alliance?”

“Technically, neither of us is. We’re an independent ship,” Eislie told her.

The woman nodded, then jokingly pointed to Eislie. “You know, there are smaller suits available.”

Eislie threw her head back. “Just can’t trust Terrans.”

Jace put his arms around her and leaned his chin gently on her shoulder. "Told you."

She reached back, grabbing his hair as he tried to pull away. The security woman laughed as she brought up her pad.

"I have to log the incident; I'll need your names."

Eislie told her they had just arrived and that they were in New York until yesterday. Jace finished the rest by telling her about the relief efforts and the damage to their ship. He concluded by saying, "The last few days haven't been so good."

The next day, they took a flight around the island along with other visitors. Jace was smiling the entire time, seeing a volcano up close with the blue ocean all around for the first time. When they weren't swimming or exploring, they were usually in bed.

It was two nights before they had to leave. They had a message from the Alliance station reminding them to make sure they were ready to depart on time. Others were waiting to visit, and they wanted to keep as few non-Terrans as possible on the planet.

Eislie was outside; the thin robe was the only thing covering her as she was staring up at the stars. Jace walked up, planting a gentle kiss on her neck, causing her to moan softly. They swayed together as Jace held her.

"You hear back from Oppa?" she asked, still staring up at the stars.

"Yep, at least a month to get the shop. Arren's busy."

"Damn. It'll take at least two weeks for us to get back to Gilese."

"Mmm-hmm. We'd be screwed if something went wrong," Jace mentioned.

Eislie leaned back into Jace. She didn't like the situation. She looked at Jace and closed her eyes as she remembered something, "We never did the additional upgrades for Ed."

Jace glanced up at the sky, his mind wandering as he held the woman he loved. Then, Eislie started to sway with him again and the world melted away in the warm breeze. That was, until he felt her body tense.

"Miriz."

"What?" Jace asked.

"Miriz, she contacted me."

"So? I thought we weren't taking on the whole Alliance yet."

"No, Yata Beta is a level three planet. They'll have the facilities to fix the ship and supplies. We just have to get there." Eislie then tapped her comm. "Ed, you up?"

"Always, Captain. What do you need?"

"Ut-oh, Ed's extra helpful. He must have been listening to us," Jace joked, making Eislie push him away.

"Ed, do you have access to the Alliance database? Could you show us the current location of Yata Beta?" Eislie asked. A small directional appeared on her wrist display. She held it up and it locked onto a location. "There; that's where we have to go. What's the travel time, Ed?"

"Approximately three days, two hours. I have confirmed that Yata Beta would have the facilities to repair the ship."

"See, told you he was listening," Jace remarked, making Eislie nod.

Jace pulled her close. "We go there, fix the ship, get some supplies, and you get to see an old friend. That's not so bad. You're definitely the smart one in this relationship."

Eislie giggled as Jace kissed her neck passionately.

"If we plan to head to Yata Beta, you should inform Captain Tucker of the particulars of that planet. It may not be agreeable to him."

Jace scoffed, "What, like acid air or something?"

Eislie thought for a moment. "You know how it's mostly male-dominated here on Earth?"

"It's not as much as it used to be, but yeah?" Jace replied.

"Well, it's the other way around on Yata Beta. It's female-oriented," Eislie said as she leaned against him.

Jace was silent for a moment. "We should call ahead and see if they have the facilities available first."

Eislie nodded. "We can do that tomorrow." She turned around, kissing him lovingly before pushing him back into the room.

* * *

Jace had been up early, his mind now fresh and working on the issue they were having back on Oppa with the drones. He had sent a message to Callie about what he thought, and was waiting to hear back. When they received a reply, it was from the repair corps on the earliest time they would have to fix the ship. Everything was still weeks away, and neither Jace nor Eislie wanted to have the *Wolfhammer* down for that long.

Eislie was in everyday clothes as they were readying to head back to the ship. Their time in Hawaii was fun, but with recent happenings, the damage to the *Wolfhammer*, and the waiting list of other tourists arriving, the Alliance was pressuring them to leave quickly. Jace had already packed, as had Eislie; he was carrying the cases to the elevator when he heard the clinking of glass from one of them.

Eislie was walking up as he opened the case to see three bottles of white rum among the clothing. Jace looked up as she smiled back. "I liked the drinks here, especially the clear rum."

Jace smiled, "Is that all you bought?"

His question made Eislie turn away in thought before she replied, "Nope, we should have a delivery waiting when we get to the port."

"Anything else?" Jace asked, his brows raised in mock suspicion.

"Some food too. Local stuff. Snacks, some prepared meals," Eislie replied.

Jace shook his head as he pulled the luggage onto the elevator. Eislie was smiling as she joined him.

* * *

In the ship, Jace was putting away the supplies that Eislie had procured. He knew they wouldn't last long, a couple of weeks at best. They both knew they had to resupply once they left Earth.

Eislie tapped the controls on the ship's comm. The screen displayed as the Alliance station's communications link synchronized. A computerized voice alerted, "Current credits remaining are ninety-three point four."

"It sounds so mechanical," Ed interjected.

Eislie smiled, "They're not as sophisticated as you, Ed. Or as charming and clever."

The computer hesitated. "Thank you, Captain."

"Buttering him up? Really, Eis?" Jace joked. Eislie smiled back at him. She had been feeling bad that they hadn't had a chance to do the upgrades for their computer friend. She was more worried about Jace and the trip to Earth. Now that it was over, she was concerned that Ed was feeling left out.

Eislie turned back to the screen and tapped away on the controls. She accessed the Alliance contact base and searched for her friend, Mirizali Elysse.

"I can't believe they only allowed us one hundred credits to transmit. It'd be easier to do a relay call," Elsie complained.

Jace was walking behind her when Miriz appeared on the screen. "Eis, you there?"

"Miriz, How're things?" Jace could hear the playful tone in Eislie's voice.

"Oh, you know, arguing with suppliers. Tracking down deadbeat payers. Good to hear from you. I trust you got my message?" Mirizali replied.

"Yeah, we did." Eislie went on to again decline the offer before asking her friend if there were any open machine shops where they could make repairs to their reactor storage.

Jace walked back and forth as the two talked. He heard the typical banter of old friends. That was something Jace no longer had the luxury of, but it was good to hear.

Mirizali searched the global database on Yata Beta before telling Eislie, "Yeah, it's only a day's wait for most. The issue is the engineers. They're all booked for weeks out."

"But there are open shops?" Eislie asked.

Mirizali nodded. "But you'll never get an engineer."

Eislie leaned back, yelling, "Jace, they have open shops!"

Jace dropped the supplies he was putting away and rushed over to look at the screen. "When can we get in?"

Eislie turned to see her friend with her brows raised in interest as Mirizali purred, "Helloooo," in a very sensual way.

Eislie looked back at the screen, annoyed. "Nope, not going to happen, Miriz."

Jace smiled. "You know, she told me about your planet. Is there, like, a gladiatorial combat thing where you fight over me? I'm not real familiar with the logistics."

Elsie laughed, pushing Jace away as he started laughing. "Will you go back to putting stuff away."

Jace returned to the screen, leaning forward. “Listen, if we can get in, I can make the repairs. We just need a machine shop.” Eislie again started pushing him away as Jace said, “Nice meeting you, Miriz.”

Eislie could see her friend laughing on the screen. “He’s Terran, isn’t he?”

Eislie nodded animatedly. “Oh, he’s definitely Terran.”

Then, they both heard from Jace, “What’s wrong with being Terran?”

The laughter subsided and Eislie looked at the screen, the display reading only four credits remaining. She then heard her friend say, “I read the report on what you had to go through. No one . . .”

Her friend’s voice faded.

Eislie fought back the memories and the pain they held. “If he hadn’t shown up, I probably would have . . .” She leaned back. “He got me out of there.”

“You don’t owe him anything!” Miriz shot back.

“No, I don’t. And he knows that,” Eislie growled in response.

“We help each other.” Her words were softening. “I like being with him.”

Eislie placed her elbows on the controls as she went back to being serious. “Could you register us for a spot? I only have a few credits left, and we have to leave by early tomorrow.”

“What’s the damage?” Mirizali asked.

Eislie told her that the containment locker and assembly had to be replaced and that they needed to retrofit a new junction for an upgraded processing center.

“Sure, Eis. What’s the name of your ship?” Mirizali asked.

Eislie stammered, “Uh, *Wolfhammer*.”

There was a silence before Mirizali said, “The ship that destroyed the Cleaver? That was your ship?”

Eislie sat tall. “Yes, that was *our* ship.”

“Slac, Eis, I’m getting you in even if I have to bump some people off the schedules,” Mirizali said as she tapped furiously on the keypad before her. “How long do you think it’ll take to get here? A week?”

Eislie chuckled, “It’ll take us three days. So put us in for four days from today.”

Mirizali looked unconvinced. “Terra is a week out at a minimum, Eis.”

“Not with our ship.” Eislie leaned in. “He keeps upgrading it.”

Mirizali scoffed, “Typical male.”

“Hey, he’s not typical.” A grin came over Eislie. “We have something in common.”

Eislie hoped that her friend would get the implication. And seeing Miriz’s expression and her pointing to Jace and hearing her say, “You mean you’re both . . .” Eislie watched as she mouthed the word, *“Starborn.”*

Eislie nodded as she heard, “Oh, Eis, you are going to have a slac of a time here. The planetary matriarch is watching the filament project closely. If they get that to work, it’ll increase trade universally.”

Eislie looked serious. “You mean *when* we get it to work.”

“Eis, I know you’re a starborn, but, how are you involved?” Miriz asked. Jace turned, overhearing her question.

Eislie looked insulted. “Mirizali, I never thought I’d hear that from you.”

Jace walked up, putting his hands on Eislie's shoulder, saying, "Down, it's only a screen. If you hit it, we'll have to fix it. Again."

Eislie started to laugh as she began to shove Jace away.

Jace was smiling, looking at the screen, pointing to himself and Eislie. "Who do you think's been building the damn things on the filament project?" Jace added, "We've flown through a filament with this ship already. Almost had our asses handed to us when we did."

Eislie could see the look of surprise on her friend's face and shook her head when she heard Miriz say, "You are coming here, now. You are staying. I don't care how much they are paying you. We'll triple it."

"Not a chance, Miriz. We go where we want, when we want," Eislie said, and in the background, they both heard Jace say, "Damn right!"

Miriz laughed, "Oh, you've definitely gone independent."

Eislie laughed as she looked at the display. "I only have a credit left, Miriz. We'll call you en route. Put us in for four days from now. We'll meet and catch up."

The screen went blank as the display in the corner now read zero. Jace sat down in his chair and looked at Eislie in the darkened control room. "Can we trust her?"

Eislie nodded. "Yeah, we can trust her. Yata is not as backward as you might think." She paused, looking over her shoulder at him. "Gladiatorial combat? Really?"

Jace snickered, "Just playing the uncivilized Terran. They are a level three planet, after all."

Eislie sighed, "Yeah, but there are still people who think you, or we, might be lesser."

Jace looked forward. "They know about the project. So, no easy ride."

Eislie shook her head slowly. Then, finally, they both realized that her friend disclosed something they had hoped not to encounter yet. There were other worlds now interested in the work on the filament project.

* * *

The Karazon cruiser dwarfed the escort ships as it was directed to land. Special Envoy Tarlin Hamon scowled at following commands as he ordered his crew to follow the Yata control ships.

"These people would serve no other purpose than to amuse me," he muttered as the ship banked toward the outside area of the planet's main space dock.

His superiors dispatched Tarlin to negotiate with the military forces of Yata. The pirates had broken their hold on several planets and the Duggor had destroyed several colonies, searching for resources they had already claimed. It was hampering their trading in many sectors, including slave labor. Tarlin had the people of Karazon behind him while acting as supreme executor of the games. They were similar to the gladiatorial games of Earth centuries ago. The bloodlust and basic appetite for sport satiated the elites of his world, the disgrace of his prized slave's loss to the new executor's champion now making him no more than a messenger.

An exhausted sigh escaped him before he spoke. "How long till we land?"

"Master Tarlin, we will be on the ground in approximately half a standard cycle," one of his crew replied.

Tarlin sat forward in disgust. "I would have killed these lesser ones for wasting my time. Do these people not know their place?"

"I'm afraid you misjudge the people of Yata Beta, Tarlin." The man next to him spoke. The leader then motioned for the woman next to him to retrieve the data on the console nearby.

"And why is that, Har? These people are beneath us," Tarlin replied.

Har took the pad from the woman. "Return to our room."

Tarlin scoffed at Har. "You allow your pleasure slave too much freedom, Har."

Har smiled. "She is much more than that, Envoy; much more."

"Ah, yes, you train your slaves for both pleasure and combat." But Tarlin shook his head. "You waste your resources, old man."

Har scrolled through the information on the arrivals to Yata Beta. Due to the nature of their mission, he was careful to make sure none of their enemies were allowed access to Yata while they were there. The mission was to negotiate the return of several hundred Yata, taken as spoils from their previous endeavors, in return for aid in fighting off the pirates and Duggor.

He remembered the high council and how they felt tainted by having to ask lesser worlds for help. Being an old warrior himself, Har understood the natures of time and arrogance. Although the envoy was the speaker for their mission, he was the one who had to make sure Tarlin would succeed. Even if Tarlin was not aware, he was merely a figurehead. Har's claw-like finger scraped across the screen and he scanned through the information when a word caught his eye.

Wolfhammer.

His mind sharp as ever for his age, he remembered the intelligence on the defeat of the Duggor vessel. *They would be a prize indeed*, he whispered in his mind as he read. Then, as a feeling of sport entered his chest, he looked up to see the spaceport in view as they approached. The pilot was doing her best to maneuver the massive vessel into the area provided. As the ground came into view, The purplish and green vegetation contrasting the white and grey from the display of military and security that covered it. Then, as the ship touched down, the Karazon felt the weight of gravity hit them.

"We should fire now and take the survivors as prizes. Don't you agree, Har?" Tarlin mused as he stood to stretch.

The old warrior scoffed, "That would not be a wise action, Tarlin. Remember, we are here on a peaceful mission." The old warrior's mind offered hidden disdain for the envoy. *I will kill you and take your house when you fail. You will learn what it is to be of the elite.*

Chapter 10:
It Never Ends

The familiar thud and scraping of the docking clamps echoed across the hull of the *Wolfhammer*. Jace sighed, dreading having to process out from their stay on Earth. Eislie paused at the door before looking back at Jace.

"What?" Jace asked.

Eislie rolled her eyes as she pounded on the door controls. It opened to reveal three people standing before them. They both sighed, hearing the practiced speech of the station crew say, "Welcome back to the station. We hope your stay was satisfactory."

Eislie handed them the pad containing the accounts of what had happened while they were planetside. The pad also had her list of requested additional supplies, if possible. The attendant briefly looked over the information before asking if the ship was safe to fly. Jace assured them that it was, saying, "Otherwise, we'd be dust right now."

As they walked down the gangway, Jace spied the same, now familiar sign when they arrived, only to be shuttled toward the door opposite from it to process out. The log of the incidents on Earth was submitted, and they each had to give statements. The departure, and now, the paperwork, turned what was a rushed day into a very long ordeal.

First, however, Jace was ordered to have a medical survey done, since he was the one who took the direct exposure to the spide leak. His continued grumbling of, "I'm fine," made the Alliance insist that he spend a few hours under observation.

During that time, Eislie had requisitioned and stowed some additional supplies. She also visited the small shop on the station to procure some souvenirs and trinkets. She had contemplated buying something while on Earth, but her friend Miriz enjoyed collecting Alliance items from different stations.

* * *

Eislie held up a necklace, a miniature medal hanging from a short chain that she picked up for her friend. Eislie's eyes scolded Jace as he made a joke about it looking like something he'd hang from a rearview mirror. The trinket was decorated with the station's number and location in Alliance reference coordinates from the galactic center. It wasn't expensive, but Eislie knew it was something her friend would like.

They talked while waiting for the additional supplies to arrive.

"How long have you known Miriz?" Jace asked, leaning back in his chair.

Eislie gave a chortle before meekly responding, "A long time. We were best friends when we were younger."

Jace nodded, seeing Eislie look away as she remembered.

"Her family moved to Gilese. Her mother owned a transport company. I missed her when she had to move away again."

Jace pushed Eislie's shoulder gently, making her sway a little, and watched her smile. "Miriz was independent; not like back home, where we had to follow the rules."

Eislie romantically grabbed Jace's hand, intertwining her fingers with his as she sat back. "You know, I had made commander for the research corps when I was told I needed combat experience to get my own commission."

She looked up, giving a frustrated sigh.

Eislie's words were full of self-assurance as she spoke. "I don't like fighting, but when told for the fifth time I couldn't transfer to Yata for my commission, I sort of . . ."

Jace tugged on her hand. "Had your little incident?"

Eislie gave a smile before leaning against Jace. Her words were filled with a hint of happiness. "At least something good came out of it."

The two watched as people walked past them, Alliance and Earth military, several other races, all heading to process out. Jace sat up, seeing Tanya walking toward them with the dock commander before she yelled, "Tucker, Licessien, some supplies are waiting to get loaded on your ship!"

Jace stood. "We're stuck here till we process out. How long have they been waiting?"

Tanya stopped before them. "About a half-hour. We just need the door open. The supplies can be left in the cargo hold for you to move later."

Eislie nodded, then tapped her comm. "Ed? We need you to open the cargo door for a delivery."

"Security protocols recommend that you are present for the delivery," they all heard over her comm.

Eislie looked to Jace. "Ed, if we order to secure interior doors, would that be acceptable?"

"You have a third person on board?" Tanya asked.

Jace shook his head. "Nope, that's our ship's computer. He can pretty much run it himself."

The dock commander looked at Jace. "It's an AI construct?"

Jace nodded as the computer replied, "Interior doors secured. I will time the opening for exactly ten semi-cycles before securing the hold. After that, any persons left on board will have to be dealt with by the captains."

"Okay, Ed. Open the rear cargo door. We'll be back as soon as we can," Jace responded.

The computer acknowledged as the dock commander looked at him. "You trust that machine?"

Jace snidely replied, "Yeah. More than most people."

* * *

Back at the ship, the cargo door lowered and four men moved the pallets of supplies on board. One stepped away to look at the interior of the vessel. He approached the inside door and was about to touch the handle when he heard, "Warning, the door is charged. I would not recommend contacting it or the surrounding passageway. You have ten semi-cycles to complete your task and leave."

The man stepped back, saying, "Great. They have a security system."

The same man turned to the door, speaking to another who pulled several small boxes from the pallet. No one noticed as he slid a small blade across the package and reached into his pocket. He paused, hearing the supervisor walking back. "Hey, we're not putting this stuff away. Let's just drop this stuff off and get out of here."

All of the workers nodded as the man walked up to the one who was removing boxes. "You know, we should report you for being out of uniform. When was the last time you trimmed that beard?"

The worker smiled. "Been a while. I've been sort of busy. You're not going to turn me in, are you?"

The supervisor smiled. "Nah, you've lifted some good stuff from the last few ships."

The man smiled back, and as his supervisor turned to look at the others, the one holding the box pulled a device from his pocket, his fingers tapping it till it vibrated. He deftly slid the device into the open box and picked it up off the ground.

The man with the beard paused, listening to the others as they complained. When one of them said, “You know, we are unappreciated doing this job. We need more compensation,” the man with the beard smiled before tossing the box he held onto one of the shelves. It landed behind one of the breather masks. “They should be able to find it when it starts rotting.”

The supervisor turned to look at the man before giving a smile. “That, my friend, is a way you handle people who don’t appreciate us.”

As the work crew left, Ed closed the door of the cargo bay, his memory recording the incident. He planned to show his captains what transpired when they returned.

The entire crew walked away down the hall and into the transport area. The one with the beard lagged behind. He instead turned down the entrance to the observation area and looked out the window. He could see the *Wolfhammer* and brought his comm up as he tapped away a short message. The message read, “Package on board, inform our queen.”

* * *

It was hours before Jace and Eislie finished the bureaucratic nightmare they had walked into. Jace made no attempt to hide his displeasure at all of the paperwork. After all, he was from Earth. He just didn’t live there anymore. Eislie was also exhausted, and only looked at the pallets in the cargo bay when they returned to the ship. Jace picked up the small box placed behind the masks. He scoffed as he read its contents. “Starch base bars, no sweetener.” Jace tossed it back on the shelf. “Great, tasteless food again.”

It was only about an hour before they were cleared to leave. As the ship undocked, Jace took the controls as Eislie plotted the course to Yata Beta. The station warned them not to use the tunnel drive within the Earth system and they complied. Jace knew it wasn't a good idea anyway, but when he hit the engines, the speed with which they left annoyed the controllers, one of them remarking, "Guess they couldn't wait to get out of here."

Eislie had her feet on the console. She rolled her head to the side to stare toward the small port window. Jace had left to take some measurements on the storage containment and had yet to return. Like him, she wanted to get the ship back to complete working order. Although the radiation didn't affect them, it could be a problem for anyone else, or any planet they landed on.

Eislie rolled her head back to the main screen. She could see the slight movement of the dot on the display as the computer updated its location. The low hum of the ship was soothing to her as she sat quietly. Her eyes closed, and, in her mind, she calculated the remaining time until she could see her friend Miriz and hopefully fix their ship.

* * *

A cloaked figure worked at a desk with several displays, an opaque veil covering the right side of her face. She tapped away as images and text scrolled at an inhuman pace. Yet her attention never wavered as another figure walked toward her.

"My queen, I have word from the *Justine Elate*," the man said.

The pirate queen looked up over her monitor, the flashing of the screens still illuminating her as the woman spoke. "What is it? I have been going through the data. Have they secured the ship yet?"

The man shook his head. "No, they are still attempting to save the vessel. Support has been dispatched, but I fear they may not arrive in time."

"That ship represents over a year of work. It must be salvaged," the queen said with a stern voice.

"Yes. We are doing our best. But, we require your insight." Then, the man paused. "War room three is awaiting you."

The pirate queen returned to her screens, a look of concern reflected in her eye.

"The field did not allow for plasma expansion; they are trapped within the event horizon." She tapped several commands as she studied the additional data. "Do we have an estimate before the pressure on the hull exceeds integrity?"

"Approximately one point six cycles," the man responded. "But it will take our fastest ships more than three to rendezvous."

A stuttered sigh escaped the queen's lips. "Any other news?"

"Your Highness, we have word that the locator is now on the *Wolfhammer*," the man's voice was laced with quiet victory.

The woman leaned back, and with a simple tap, all of the monitors showed the same image.

"They are in hyperspace. Do we know their destination?" the queen asked.

Without hesitation, the man answered, "Yata Beta."

The woman's eyes glanced up to the man, the vision within them telling him that she was familiar with the planet.

"My queen, we know their location. After we save the *Justine*, we can take them," the man said with a revelry of bloodlust.

"No!" the queen responded with an adamant ferocity.

"But, my queen, we have more ships available. They cannot evade us forever," the man retorted.

The woman turned all the monitors off but one. From beneath the veiled half of her face, a subtle, dim glow emanated in the darkness; a small area punctuated where her eye should be. Instead, there was now a glowing, bright-blue dot. She stood with a steady grace and stance, the man's body flinching as she approached.

“You understand that I want them alive. Did you not comprehend my original orders?” she said with a metered pause.

The man hesitantly nodded before stepping back.

“They will join us,” the woman said as she walked toward the door, the man in tow. Half a smile was showing as she spoke. “I believe we have the same goals. They are also starborn. They will be instrumental in our plans.”

The man responded, “Yes, my queen. They will not be killed.”

As they exited, the small dot on the remaining screen slowed, and an alert appeared next to it as it stopped. The screen read, “Hyperspace exit detected.”

Back on the *Wolfhammer*, Eislie sat up in her chair, startled, as if she was waking from a dream, one hand grasping at the air as if trying to grab something ethereal. Then, almost as if in a trance, she turned to the small portal. Her eyes gazed as if through eternity at the energy. It seemed to be crying out to her. Her haze was broken as Jace walked into the room.

“Everything okay?” Jace asked.

Eislie turned to look at him before she looked around. Jace pursed his lips, his eyes searching out the same window as her. “Yeah, something’s off. I’m sensing it too.”

Jace tapped the controls as Eislie sat up in her chair. She asked, “You think we should punch out?”

Jace nodded. “Already working on exiting hyperspace. Yeah, something is definitely off.”

As they exited using the tunnel drive, they found themselves near a binary star—both with an expression of delight and surprise. “Ed, catalog this location. I think we punched out near a filament.”

The computer acknowledged, and then alerted them to several ships nearby within the stellar plasma display. As it enhanced the image, they recognized the vessels.

"Those are skips, and is that a dreadnaught in the filament?" Eislie asked.

The computer confirmed her assessment, but then added, "The dreadnaught appears to be trying to exit the filament. But it seems to have slowed within the event horizon."

"You mean it's stuck?" Jace remarked.

"It appears so, Captain," Ed responded.

They slowed, hoping to not provoke the pirates as they watched.

"Ed, get as many readings as you can," Jace ordered as Eislie looked to him with concern. "What? We need all the information we can get. If that ship can use the filaments, we need to know."

"The skips are attempting to pull the dreadnaught through the event horizon, but we are too far to get accurate readings, Captain. We will need to move closer."

Eislie shook her head. "I'm not sure that's a good idea."

"Captains, although the dreadnaught appears to be emerging slowly from the filament, I calculate that the pressure is increasing on its hull. At the rate they are moving, their actions may not be enough to save the ship in time," the computer interjected.

Jace stared forward. He looked to Eislie before he spoke. "Let's give them a hand."

Eislie looked at him. "They've been trying to kill us, remember?"

Jace nodded. "I was going to call them and ask first. Besides, we could use the additional data on that ship. Not to mention maybe see what they are really up to."

Eislie leaned her head back. "Ed, will the grapples handle the load?"

"Yes, Captain, as long as we do so slowly."

She looked down to the floor. "Ugh, all right. Hail them."

Jace tapped the comm using one of the frequencies they knew the pirates used from others they had captured.

"This is the *Wolfhammer*. Do you need assistance?" Jace waited for a response.

* * *

There was a flurry of activity on board the pirate dreadnaught as they obeyed orders trying to save the prototype vessel. The captain was looking toward the recruit handling the comm.

"Captain, we have orders to save the ship and capture them."

The pirate captain looked around. He knew the vessel's value, but a bounty now fell before him willingly. He had served the pirate queen for years, and knew not to disobey a direct order. The pirate captain moved toward the comm, placing his hand on the transmit button.

"This is Captain Balroc of the *Justine Elate*. Ally or enemy?" the captain asked, drawing looks of confused fear from his crew.

Jace took a moment before responding. "We're here to help, nothing more. We hope you'll do so in kind when we're done."

Eislie looked to Jace. "This isn't the best plan."

Jace nodded. "Yeah, I know. But we need to get a look at that ship. It could help us out."

Eislie tapped the weapons control but did not activate them. She wasn't going to show any sign of aggression. Her actions were prudent, but she also noticed that the pirates had not armed their weapons either.

Captain Balroc's hand hovered over the button; time seemed to slow as he pressed to answer. "*Wolfhammer*, we require assistance. You have my word that no action will be taken against you."

Jace raised his eyebrows. "This seems too simple. But, let's help."

Eislie piloted toward the giant pirate ship as the computer asked, "Is this course of action wise, Captains?"

Jace shook his head. "Probably not. But when we get close, scan the hell out of that dreadnaught, Ed."

The computer confirmed the order as Jace rushed toward the back of the ship. He opened the cargo hold and fired all four of the grapple lines to connect to the dreadnaught.

Using the same comm channel, Jace relayed his actions to the other pirates and Eislie. "We're hooked on, Eis. Bring up the engines, slowly. I'll let you know if things start to shift." Jace's attention was brought to bear as the brackets in the hold creaked, making him pause, then say, "Or break."

Within seconds, the dreadnaught started to move from the filament. Eislie was relaying the observations of the pressure on the dreadnaught hull to the *Justine*.

Over the comm, they heard Eislie say, "Pressure is near critical on the port hull of that ship. Can't you pull any faster? We don't want to get caught in a quasi-break."

"Damn, Eis, you're right. Move the engines up a bit, and ready the tunnel field. Just in case," Jace said.

"Captain Balroc, I think they're going to run. They also appear to be scanning us with a deep holographic and metallurgic sweep," the weapons officer said.

But the pirate captain simply looked forward, giving an order. "Tell the others to increase engines. *Wolfhammer*, can you increase power as well?"

Jace could hear the straining on the structure of their ship. "Not much more, Captain. I'm already seeing the supports starting to buckle." Then, finally, they all heard Jace say to himself, "Shit, something else to fix."

The pirate on the comm turned to see the captain giving a silent chuckle. "I'd like to see how tough that ship of yours really is."

Jace spoke as Eislie listened in on the comm. "You know, if you guys are tired, we can do this by ourselves."

Eislie smiled as Ed informed her, "Captain, the skips cannot outrun us, nor can that dreadnaught. They have not been upgraded since recent encounters."

One of the pirates of the dreadnaught babbled, "Sir, hull pressure is lessening. We are almost free of the event horizon."

The captain of the *Justine* gave a bellowing laugh as he ordered, "All ships full power. We're almost through."

The *Justine* lurched forward as it snapped free of the event horizon, and all of the ships slowed. Jace released the magnetic grapples and reeled them in. He closed the cargo door and headed back to the control room.

"Any damage?" Eislie asked.

Jace responded, "Nothing we can't fix."

On the *Justine Elate*, the captain ordered repairs and peered out the window as the *Wolfhammer* floated nearby. Eislie had already increased the mag shields as they inspected their ship. They did not attempt to run.

"Captain, our queen would be pleased if we were to capture them." The weapons officer smiled.

Balroc shook his head slowly. "No, I gave my word."

The pirate on weapons replied, "We need to contact base. This is not your decision; you are disobeying our queen."

The captain glared sternly toward the man and tapped the comm; seconds later, they all heard their queen. "I have been monitoring the situation, Captain Balroc."

“Your Highness, the *Justine Elate* is safe. Do you wish us to apprehend the *Wolfhammer*?” the captain asked unsurely.

“No, Balroc, you are a man of honor, and of your word. You will keep it,” the queen responded.

“Yes, Your Highness. I will obey,” the captain replied, relieved.

“Captain Balroc, patch me through. I wish to speak with the crew of the *Wolfhammer*,” the queen commanded.

With a firm nod, the captain tapped several of the controls. “*Wolfhammer*, our queen wishes to speak with you.”

“Jace Tucker, Eislie Licessien, we thank you for your aid,” the queen said.

Jace looked to Eislie, “Well, they know our names. That’s not good.” He then tapped the comm. “You are welcome. Could you do us a favor and stop trying to kill us?”

The captain pounded the comm. “Arrogance! You will show respect when addressing our leader!”

“If you think either of us is calling her Your Highness, we’ll leave right now. Besides, you already know who we are,” Jace shot back, making Eislie growl, “Stop antagonizing them.”

The queen could be heard laughing as Jace finished. “Oh, I do love Terran bravado. It is refreshing to hear. But you are correct. We should be properly introduced.” The queen stood. “I am the queen of the pirates. You may call me Jana. It is fortunate that you were nearby to offer aid.”

“Thank you, Jana. Full disclosure, we scanned your ships. And I presume you are aware of the project we are working on,” Jace said.

The queen responded, “Yes. I will not take the information you have gained from us. It may be more valuable than you imagine.”

Jace smiled, “Oh, I have a feeling we are searching for the same answers.”

Jana responded, "Perhaps, perhaps not. But I would like to know what you think of the design."

"We'll let you know." Jace looked to Eislie. "I'm getting an uneasy feeling. Let's get out of here."

Eislie nodded, tapping the controls, and the *Wolfhammer* started to move slowly away. Jace tapped the keypad on the command board, entering several keys before closing the channel. What remained of the transmission was a series of numbers that were shown on the pirate queen's display. On the other, the video feed of the *Justine*.

"My queen, is it wise to allow them to have the information? They will surely take it to the Alliance," the woman standing next to her whispered.

Jana shook her head slowly as the *Wolfhammer* disappeared into the darkness. "No, they won't." She pointed to the display. "That is a secure frequency. I want it monitored. I am sure they will be in touch with us again."

"How can you be sure this is not a trap, my queen?" the woman asked.

The queen's face displayed a smile, her blue eye glowing brighter as she viewed the filament near the *Justine*, "Because he was right. We are after the same thing."

Chapter 11:
An Old Friend

The hum of the engines was the only sound as the *Wolfhammer* returned to hyperspace. Both Eislie and Jace seemed to be thinking of the last few minutes and their interaction with the pirates. But something else was bothering them. Finally, Eislie broke the silence. “That was too easy. She didn’t even seem surprised that we were there.”

Jace nodded. “Yeah. I can get her knowing our names, but you’re right. Why wasn’t she surprised? It’s like she knew where we were.”

Eislie started looking around the ship. “You think they’re tracking us?”

Jace looked around with concern, causing Eislie to ask the computer to scan for any local signals.

“The only signals I can detect are your comms. Nothing else is evident, Captain.”

Eislie turned to Jace. “I don’t remember seeing anything suspicious, do you?”

Jace stared forward, his mind recalling the Alliance worker trying to get into the ship from a day earlier. He turned to look to the back of the ship. "There was something suspicious, but he never got into the ship. I thought maybe he was looking to steal something."

"The ship was secure. But if they put something on board, we'd know, right? Ed records everything," Eislie said before the computer responded. "I see no evidence of any installation of a tracking device; the only personnel in the ship were the loading crew."

Jace looked up. "Show me the video again, Ed."

The screen played the crew loading the pallets of supplies. Jace watched as one of them started to open the wrapping and move the box to one of the shelves.

"We didn't ask them to unpack anything, did we?" Jace muttered.

Eislie shook her head.

Jace watched and asked the computer to replay the scene, and something was eating at him. When the computer started the replay, Jace ordered Ed to zoom in on the man with the box.

"That's him," Jace muttered, then said, "Ed, zoom in on that worker. I want to see his face."

Jace looked to Eislie. "The box on the shelf. What if it's a bomb?"

Both jumped from their seats, heading to the cargo hold. Jace grabbed the box, ripping the top open. His eyes fixed on the small metallic device on top of the dried food.

"Shit," Jace muttered.

Eislie looked at it before turning toward the door. "We can't open the hold while we're in here."

They were interrupted by the computer. "I am not sure Captains are aware of the refuse chamber in the hold. It was mainly used for expelling spoiled foods when I was in service. You are standing near the access now."

Jace looked to the access panel on the floor nearby. "I thought that was storage. That's where I put the weapons your father gave us when we saved the Aranost."

"No, Captain, it is for materials no longer viable or needed."

Jace handed Eislie the box. She held it gingerly before her as Jace wrestled the floor panel open. He bent down, pulling the two crates of weapons from the floor, and grabbed the box from Eislie, placing it in the empty space. "Ed, how do we jettison the trash?"

"I cannot open the outer door during flight within hyperspace. The safety system would prevent it. We would need to transition to standard space."

Jace looked to Eislie. "We don't want whoever left this to know we found it. Can we override the safety?"

"Yes, Captain, the controls are behind the shelf next to you."

Jace closed the hatch and shoved boxes aside to reveal a small panel with several buttons. Jace stared at it for a few seconds before asking the computer which buttons were the override.

"The two lower buttons need to be pressed simultaneously," the computer responded.

Jace pressed the two buttons and the ship gave a subtle creak as the outside door opened. Eislie looked out the rear portal to see the small box floating nearby. She turned to Jace. "We should let it get further away and punch out before resuming course. It'll stay in hyperspace for a while."

"Actually, Captain, the device will remain in hyperspace until it is brought out."

Jace huffed, "You mean, it'll look like we're still in hyperspace?"

"Correct, Captain."

"It'll take a while for them to realize we found it." Eislie looked at Jace. "By that time, we'll be on Yata Beta."

A few hours later, Eislie was on the comm with the controller for Yata Beta spaceport. The *Wolfhammer* had exited and reentered hyperspace to confuse anyone following them. Eislie confirmed their travel credentials, and the ship was ordered to land in the spaceport near the capital.

"Too bad we couldn't do a flyover. Look at the buildings down there!" Jace said with amazement.

Eislie laughed as she looked on as well. It had been years since she had visited Miriz. The planet hadn't changed. The metal and ceramic structures still stood as a statement to the engineering prowess of the people of Yata. She reminded Jace and Ed that the world they were landing on was a level three planet. She was even ordering Ed not to hack into anything. The computer responded with a less than enthusiastic acknowledgment.

"Don't worry, Ed. I'm sure it's not as boring as you may think here," Jace offered.

When they landed, they were ordered to report to the planetary processing office within the dock. When they reached the office, they were herded into a small room and scanned. They could see the technicians behind the safety windows while the small packs they brought with them were searched. Eislie jokingly complained that the clothes she brought were going to be wrinkled.

"Sorry for the increased security. There is a special envoy from Karazon visiting," one of the women said through the speaker.

Jace could see a mild stare of anger from Eislie as she tilted her head, making him ask, "What's Karazon?"

Eislie closed her eyes, placing her fingers on her nose and chin before responding. "Slaver planet. They actually have gladiatorial combat—to the death." Eislie looked at Jace, disgust evident in her tone. "And they prize Terrans for combat."

Jace huffed in disbelief and disgust. "So, not a holiday planet to go to, right?"

Eislie rolled her eyes. “No. Don’t know why they’re even here.”

“Maybe they want to trade something,” Jace said, then continued, “like, maybe hostages.”

Eislie sighed in annoyance. “That’s the kind of remark that people hate Terrans for.”

Looking forward, Jace could see the technicians behind the glass look up with surprise when he said hostages. He tapped Eislie’s arm, pointing to the people staring at them. “They’re listening to us, and by the looks we’re getting, I don’t think I’m too far off.” Eislie could see the surprised look on the faces of the people scanning them, making her nod.

It took several minutes, and the operators performed a thorough scan of them both. One particular scan made both Jace and Eislie rush to cover their eyes when the greenish-blue light hit them. Jace could see others enduring a similar investigation as they waited, but none reacted as they did. When the scan was complete, the door on the opposite side of the room opened.

One technician said, “Send their images to central command. I have a file alert for prior criminal activities for both.”

The other technician was shaking her head. “Probably a mistake. They have Alliance clearance. Not to mention, they are here as guests of a representative.”

She looked over before saying, “Do it anyway. With the Karazon here, we should make sure nothing goes wrong.”

The technician on the left pressed the comm. “Please proceed to the waiting area. Your party will be notified.”

Jace leaned into Eislie. “Guess they don’t allow free movement around the planet.”

He was surprised when the operator responded, “We usually do, but for security purposes, we cannot at this time.”

Jace whispered, "Guess they can still hear us." He then gave them a smile.

Eislie tapped his arm. "You're going to get us in trouble. Come on." She grabbed his hand, making Jace laugh as she led him forward.

They both heard one of the operators say, "Oh, he must be a lot of fun," before they went back to work.

* * *

Jace had his legs stretched out, arms crossed, eyes closed. Eislie turned to him, seeing him relaxed. "Guess going to Earth was good after all." Jace gave a smile as he nodded in response.

Eislie was excited to see Miriz, and when the call came over the speaker, she jumped from her seat, startling Jace. The door opened, and standing there was Miriz, with two others.

Eislie yelled, "Miriz!" and she moved forward and laughed as Miriz reached out to hug her.

"Eis! So, you finally made it back to Yata," Miriz said as she parted with Eislie. "Sorry I took so long. I was called to the grand matron's office when they found out who I was requesting the repair dock for."

"That's all right. We were just relaxing," Eislie answered.

Jace looked around. "Well, I know I was. But she kept me awake with all her fidgeting." Eislie reached out, tapping him gently. He then looked to Miriz and the man next to her. He was smiling, but the woman on the right was not. She seemed to show annoyance toward Jace and his joking. Jace smiled at her but was met with a subtle sneer of disgust.

Miriz walked up to Jace. She looked him over as if he was an object, causing him to laugh. Jace laughed loudly as Miriz turned to Eislie, mouthing the words, "Good find."

Miriz turned to offer her hand to Jace and her other to Eislie. She introduced the others with her. "This is Paaz and Davlen. They are my assistants. They are aware of the details of you and your ship."

She then pulled them along toward the door. As they exited, the light from outside stung their senses. Jace covered his eyes as they walked through the threshold, as the stabbing pain finally caused him to close them.

"Geez, it's bright here," Jace said.

He turned to see Eislie also fighting to cover her eyes and Miriz looking concerned. "Are you both all right?"

Eislie took a breath, "Sorry, it's really bright here."

Jace added, "And everything has a greenish-blue tint."

Miriz looked back and forth between them. "Blue-green tint? Do you have an extended visual spectrum?"

Both Eislie and Jace nodded.

Miriz huffed, "Did you turn down the protective eyewear?"

Eislie shook her head. "What eyewear? They never offered us any."

Her friend looked to the woman next to her. "Paaz. Fix this."

The woman immediately rushed inside. They could hear yelling, and the woman returned with two small bags containing three sets of what looked like visor glasses. She handed one each to Eislie and Jace. As Jace pulled on the one she gave him, Paaz held onto it so he couldn't take it right away. The annoying glare from Jace made her rethink her stance. Without any grace, Jace ripped the one bag open, placing a set of glasses over his eyes. The stabbing pain of the light subsided. He turned to Eislie, wearing the same visors. Jace joked, "At least they're stylish."

Miriz laughed, "If you don't want to keep him, I'll take him off your hands."

Eislie tilted her head. "As I said earlier, not going to happen, Miriz."

Eislie's friend laughed. "I'm joking! I know how stubborn you can be. Are you both feeling better?"

Jace and Eislie nodded before looking around.

Miriz looked to the others. “We can move your ship to one of the repair facilities later. We’re waiting for an engineer to become available.”

Eislie chimed in, “When it comes to our ship, we are the engineers. We can fix it. We just need the resources and space.”

Miriz turned to look at Eislie. “What do you mean? Are you serious? You don’t need an engineer?”

Eislie told her that Jace retrofitted the engines and reactor mostly on his own. She then tapped the glyph controls of her jacket. “I also built new glyph shielding right into our jackets.”

Miriz looked at her before touching the small control pad on Jace’s jacket. “How effective is it?”

“They’ll handle up to five hundred percent lethal,” Eislie said proudly. “You should see the suits I’m working on back on Oppa. They almost look like our regular jackets now.”

The woman next to Miriz then said, “Wait, you developed a continuous glyph shielding field and built your own ship? Isn’t your ship the one that took out the cleaver?”

Eislie spoke up. “Yes, that was *our* ship.”

Miriz looked at Eislie with a smile of amazement at her correcting Paaz.

Eislie shook her head. “We’ve been building things since we’ve been,” Eislie paused, “together.”

Miriz put her hands on Eislie’s shoulders. “You are just full of surprises now, aren’t you!”

Eislie laughed, “Yeah, well, wish I didn’t have to go through all of that other stuff to get here.”

Jace could see Eislie's demeanor change and he grabbed her hand. "Hey, no pouting. I have a feeling you'd get a bad rep around here." His statement made Paaz look sternly toward him as Eislie nodded. Jace gave a nod and looked up to see Miriz smiling.

Paaz looked over Jace. "I'm surprised you need a protective visor. Most males don't."

Miriz looked sternly toward her assistant. "Paaz, they are our guests. You would do well to lose that outdated thinking." She pointed to Eislie. "Especially when it comes to my friend and her companion."

Jace took a breath and was about to speak when Eislie said, "Whatever it is, don't say it."

The two laughed before Miriz joined them.

As Eislie's friend quieted, she asked, "How long have you been aligned?"

Eislie took a moment before answering, "Officially, about three standard planetary cycles. But, it's sort of complicated."

Jace watched as Miriz's demeanor changed and a hint of sadness filled her eyes. "I can understand." She then reached out to Eislie and they leaned on each other for a moment before Miriz said, "Considering what you went through, you're pretty lucky."

Eislie wiped a tear from her cheek as Jace pulled her hand, making her sway into him. Eislie replied in a quieter voice, "Yeah."

Eislie leaned against Jace for a moment as she and Miriz talked. Jace's attention suddenly focused on three people, two of them armed, now heading toward them, their pace making Jace say, "I think someone wants in on this reunion."

Miriz looked to Jace as he released Eislie's hand, only to see both Eislie and Jace adopt a fighting stance as the others approached. Miriz stood tall as security neared. She questioned the others as they moved closer, "Why are you here?"

The two on the sides split away, each taking a position standing before Jace and Eislie. The woman in the center spoke. "I am Ardent Dalla. You will comply with central command and stand down. The research on these individuals indicates that they are felons. Command has ordered them brought in for questioning."

Miriz looked annoyed, her eyes focusing on the ardent. Eislie put her hands up. "We're just here to fix our ship and see my friend," her words causing the woman before her to raise her weapon toward Eislie. Eislie looked down at the barrel before turning to Jace. "You're right. It is annoying."

"Everyone, calm yourselves; these people are guests. They are not criminals." Miriz spoke. "They are also under my protection."

"Central command overrides your authority, Representative Elysse. I have my orders," the woman replied.

Miriz moved toward the woman, growling, "Get your commander on the line. Now!"

The woman took a step back but gave a huff before tapping her comm. There was a heated conversation, and it seemed as if Miriz was losing her argument.

Paaz turned away for a moment, speaking into her comm before returning to Miriz's side. In a heated moment, one of the guards moved closer to Jace, the barrel of her weapon moving too close for Jace's liking. Jace glanced down, typing on his comm. The message read, "Take the weapon and give it to Miriz's people." Eislie looked at her comm before returning her eyes to the woman before her. Jace watched her nod that she understood. Then, almost simultaneously, Jace and Eislie grabbed the weapons, tossing them to Miriz's people. The two previously armed guards stood dumbfounded by the actions.

Miriz was taken aback seeing her people now holding the weapons. She looked at Eislie and Jace, looking annoyed toward everyone as Jace growled, "You know, we're getting really tired of people pointing weapons at us."

The guards turned to retrieve their weapons as a group of several additional armed guards could be seen running toward them. Their guns were drawn and pointing at everyone, including the guards from central command. Miriz recognized the armed personnel as the matron's personal guard.

"What is the meaning of this?" Miriz demanded.

They turned when a woman spoke with authority behind them. "Please, do not move."

"Grand Matron Aersol? I did not realize you were accompanying us," Miriz said. Her actions were now showing as more docile.

"I was altered to the encounter while heading to meet with our other guests," the matron replied. "Your assistant notified me of the current incident."

Miriz looked to Paaz, who nodded, giving an apologetic stare. The grand matron walked up, motioning for the guards to lower their weapons. "Now, what seems to be the issue?"

The ardent told the matron of her orders, and Miriz stated that this was a mistake. The matron sided with Miriz, ordering the others to return with one of her guards to explain the situation. The central command guards also explained the loss of their weapons by Eislie and Jace. One was showing her the video of how they were disarmed.

The matron turned to Jace and Eislie. "It seems that a lack of information can complicate even the best technology. However, I do trust that you do not think our society is this backward."

Jace shook his head as Eislie chuckled at him. Miriz thanked the grand matron for her assistance.

The matron looked at Eislie. "I am surprised you were able to disarm these guards so easily. Were you both trained in the military?"

Eislie nodded. "Research Corps." Then, she pointed to Jace. "He's just good at fighting."

Jace looked annoyed. "Really, Eis?" Eislie responded by sticking her tongue out at Jace, making him laugh.

The matron laughed at their interaction. "I see you seem to work well together. That may explain how you were able to defeat the Duggor ship so easily."

Jace rolled his eyes. "I wish."

The matron gave a smile. "Of course." She took a breath and looked at her comm. "I would like to hear more. Unfortunately, I have other duties to attend to presently. I would like to invite you to a meal tonight. I would like to hear about some of your adventures. And of course, perhaps about your other project?"

Eislie looked to Jace. "So much for secrecy. Everyone seems to know about it."

"Indeed, it seems you two have become celebrities," the matron replied.

Jace nodded. "We could use a good meal. Our ship's supplies were toasted."

"Toasted?" the matron asked.

Eislie explained that they were on Yata to fix their ship.

Unfortunately, some Earth renegades had damaged the containment unit of the reactor storage. The leak destroyed all of their food and medical supplies. Jace was able to fix it temporarily, but they needed to finish the repairs. Miriz was kind enough to get them a shop.

"You'll still have to wait for engineers. It may take weeks," the matron replied.

Eislie shook her head. "No, ma'am, we can fix it."

Jace chimed in, "I pretty much rebuilt that ship myself. Well, I had some help." He pulled on Eislie's arm, making her smile.

"You do not need an engineer?" the matron asked with disbelief.

"Nope, just need the supplies, a workshop, and some time," Jace replied.

The matron seemed to think. "Isn't Earth below a level one? I'm surprised they had shielding suits available."

Eislie looked to Jace, who tapped the controls on his jacket. "The glyph shields she built work really well."

The matron touched the controls on Eislie's Jacket. "It is fully encompassing; no continuity suit required?"

Eislie nodded. "I based it off the Alliance's original glyph model but made a lot of improvements."

The matron asked, "You both worked on this?"

Jace smiled, "The shield is mostly her. I usually work on the ship."

Eislie looked to her friend. "Miriz, if I give you the design, could you distribute it?"

"For the shield?" Miriz asked. "You're not planning on doing it for free, are you?"

Eislie seemed taken aback. "I guess I never really thought about it. I was more worried about protecting people."

"No, Eis, I won't send it out for free. Something like this is too valuable. You deserve the money from it; not to mention the recognition," Miriz shot back. Miriz looked to Jace. "Were you going to let her give this away?"

Jace shrugged his shoulders. "If that's what she wants. We're not really hurting for money."

"You are both crazy!" Miriz yelled at them, causing Jace and Eislie to laugh.

Eislie's friend looked at them before hearing Jace say, "How many people have called us crazy so far, Eis?"

Eislie took a breath. "Wait, I thought *you* were keeping count."

The grand matron joined them in laughter. "You are certainly joining us for a meal later. I will not take no for an answer. I now have to hear of some of your adventures."

As the grand matron walked away, she turned back to say, "Please make sure they attend, Representative Elysse."

Miriz acknowledged the matron's request and turned back to Eislie. "Well, seems like we're not hitting the city tonight," her statement making Eislie snicker.

Miriz then looked to Jace. "Come, we have a room for you already. Let's get you settled; the meal will be in about six standard cycles. So, we'll have some time to catch up."

Jace shifted the pack on his back, and he and Eislie followed. Eislie shook her head when Jace remarked, "Glad we didn't run into any of those Karazon. I don't think it would have gone as well."

Chapter 12: What do you Believe?

“You slept inside a star?” Miriz exclaimed, the smile she displayed showing her excitement. “I don’t think I would have even gotten near the thing. You really know how to impress people, Eis.”

Miriz continued, “and the detail on that Duggor Wrent that exploded. You were so close to it! And you escaped an antimatter swarm as well.”

“It wasn’t my idea. It was his.” Eislie pointed to Jace.

Miriz looked at Jace. “I’m serious; if you don’t want him . . .”

Eislie shook her head. “Really, Miriz? Don’t make me hurt you.”

Jace couldn’t help himself as he said, “Ooh, this is getting interesting. I don’t think I’ve seen her like this before. When do you start fighting over me?”

Both women turned, telling him, “Shut up.”

Jace’s laugh bellowed through the room, and Miriz and Eislie soon followed.

“Oh, he’s definitely Terran. He laughs when he’s attacked,” Miriz said, making Eislie nod.

Miriz calmed, becoming serious, and leaned forward. She pointed to the jacket now hanging over the chair. "Were you really going to give that technology away?"

Eislie thought. She had considered selling the design to Oppa for a moment, but after the incident on their ship with Cherish, she had reconsidered. She gave a huff before answering, "We should make something from it. I mean, we're okay money-wise. But, I guess it wouldn't hurt."

Miriz asked about the company they started, JESC Salvage, and that she would be happy to negotiate the leasing of the technology for the spide shields. "You know, if it's different enough from the glyph models, you could name it your own."

Eislie thought for a second. "I've been thinking Sotiral. I've always liked that name."

Jace watched as Miriz sat back, a smile of joy and respect on her friend's face. Then, he turned to Miriz, asking, "Does that name mean something to you?"

Miriz looked to him. "Yes, very much so. Sotiral is the immortal goddess. She is also the protector of all travelers. It is from Yata mythology. And I'd say it's a very fitting name."

Miriz looked to Eislie, who seemed surprised when her friend asked, "When did you start believing in gods and goddesses?"

Eislie shook her head. "I don't. I just liked the name. I thought of it while I was working on the shield suits. I didn't even know what it meant."

Miriz looked on in disbelief. "How could you not know what it meant? You picked it."

Jace chimed in, chuckling, "This is getting weird, you know that, Eis."

Eislie looked at Jace as he continued. "Remember when we named the ship?"

Eislie's eyes went wide. "That's right. That is eerie."

Miriz looked to them both. "What about your ship's name?"

Jace leaned forward. "I came up with *Wolfhammer*, and when we went to change the name of the ship, Ed asked us if we wanted to include *Restian* in the title."

Miriz asked, "Who's Restian?"

"Well, according to Ed and Takloh mythology, Restian was the leader of the Eston triad, the creator of the stars. Said to have used a hammer of the shadow wolves, its sparks causing the stars to light. It's why they are stars burning now," Jace explained.

Miriz's eyes widened. "You didn't know what it meant either?"

Jace shook his head. "No, I just thought it sounded cool."

Miriz turned to Eislie. "He unknowingly chose a name for a fabled creator of the universe, and you chose a name of a goddess for protection of those who travel?" She looked between the two of them several times. "I'd say something, or someone, is guiding you."

Jace shook his head. "You're not the first person to tell us that. And honestly, I can't accept it."

"You cannot deny what you've experienced," Miriz argued.

Eislie leaned forward. "Miriz. Jace and I, we only want to explore. I mean, we were both imprisoned for being what we are. People seem to think we are lesser than they are." Eislie paused. "Jace is right. I can't accept it either. We go where we want, when we want. No one controls our destiny. Too many have tried already."

Miriz sat back, a smile on her face. "No slac from anyone, right?"

Eislie shook her head, giving a smile.

"So, you still want to give the technology away?" Miriz asked.

Eislie looked to Jace. "It'd be better if we made something from this, don't you think?"

Jace nodded. "Yeah, it's probably the smart thing to do."

Miriz's grin grew. "I think I can do the paperwork. You registering it on Oppa, or maybe here?"

Eislie chuckled, "Go ahead, Miriz, we'll register it here." She turned to Jace. "We already have the filament drones registered on Oppa." Jace nodded in agreement at Eislie's decision.

* * *

In the small building near the Karazon carrier, Tarlin and Har waited for the grand matron to arrive.

"How dare they make us wait!" Tarlin complained.

Har walked away from the envoy to stroll among those in the room. Since they were not Karazon, he did not consider any of them worthy to speak with. But, with his years of political experience, he knew that communicating with the local establishment was the best way to garner information. Even among his own people, it was a worthy endeavor to gain status. So, to pass the time, Har spent the last few hours studying the laws of Yata and speaking with its leaders. Their rules of ownership, leadership, and of course, combat. The Yata were a proud race, not weak by any standards, and were part of the Alliance until recently. But their reason for leaving was not clearly present to him.

The old warrior moved through the room until Tarlin sent one of his slaves to retrieve him. The envoy had been disgusted that they were only allowed essential persons, limiting the number of servants they could bring. Har was not as unforgiving. He understood the price of politics. They had lost resources to the Duggor and pirates recently, and this was a measure he understood. If it meant to show a slight weakness, then it was necessary to complete the mission.

As Har returned to the envoy's side, he gritted his teeth as Tarlin continued to complain. To remove himself from the envoy's meaningless negativity, he returned to the information he had found earlier. He again saw the ship *Wolfhammer* mentioned in the security briefing and that it had docked in the nearby spaceport. The Karazon vessel the *Lot-Shec* was given a formal and prompt greeting. But seeing the *Wolfhammer* listed made the burn of sport again fill Har as his talon scrolled along the screen. He was interrupted by Tarlin taking the pad from him. "What are you reading, old man?"

Tarlin looked to the page and could see the dock report. "*Wolfhammer*, isn't that the ship that destroyed the Duggor cleaver?"

Har's eyes slit as he answered, "Yes, Envoy. They are here for repairs. And to meet with a representative. It is all there in the briefing."

Tarlin gave a happy sneer. "They would be a prize." But then, he looked to the old warrior. "Were you thinking of taking them yourself, Har?"

Har stood unmoving as he turned his stare to Tarlin's eyes. "It would be unwise to try and take them here, Envoy. There would be . . . consequences."

"Nonsense, Har, we could easily handle the security of these people. Perhaps spirit my prize away without their knowledge," Tarlin mused.

Har looked around, his eyes in contempt of the others around, including the envoy, as he replied, "A prize such as they would be worth paying for. I would approach them differently."

Tarlin smiled, "You show your weakness, old one. The best way to take such a prize is to do so with impunity. A show of strength and prowess."

The old warrior looked down at the pad. The warrior longed for the days when he could fight. However, those were behind him, and his station now allowed him some freedom and rest. He was about to remark on the envoy's faulty reasoning when they were interrupted by the announcement of the grand matron.

As she approached, she spoke. "My apologies, Envoy. I was delayed due to a security matter. I hope you have not been waiting long."

When the niceties were over, they sat to discuss the release of over seven hundred enslaved Yata. The aid concessions were meager, and the envoy continued to try and criticize the grand matron as she offered alternatives. The posturing continued for hours, and its length perturbed the envoy.

"I have had enough of your alternatives, woman. We are the greater force; we dictate the terms," the envoy growled.

The grand matron sighed, her tone professional and firm. "You are the ones seeking aid, Envoy. We are seeking the release of our people who were stolen."

"How dare you—" The Envoy stopped and howled when Har pierced a small writing instrument through the back of Envoy's hand.

"Envoy, your meaningless bickering is getting us nowhere," Har said with a measured tone. "I am issuing a challenge for your house. You have a choice, Envoy; fight me and my house, or allow me to continue negotiations with the grand matron." Then, he looked to the woman staring back at him. "I am sure we can come to some reasonable agreement."

The envoy was about to speak but Har moved fast, taking the same instrument and pressing it firmly against the side of the envoy's throat. His armored skin was depressed by the force.

"Consider your next words carefully, Tarlin," Har said with great precision. Then, he turned to the matron. "Please forgive the delay, Grand Matron; we have an internal issue to resolve. We will be with you in a moment."

Tarlin gritted his teeth. "I yield, Har. You may proceed with the negotiations."

Har pulled the pointed instrument away. "My apologies for that display, Grand Matron. May we continue these negotiations?"

The old warrior looked to one of his servants, and within seconds, three of the matron's assistants were restrained, each with a small ceramic blade held at their throats. The grand matron looked in horror at the display. Har stared back, his eyes cold and slit. He glanced down, and his eyes shone with a spark of inspiration.

"Grand Matron, I have a counteroffer for you." Har tapped the pad, and a picture of Eislie and Jace appeared. "We have over five thousand of your people as servants. I wish to increase our offer, but I have an additional request."

He handed the pad to one of his servants as the envoy protested. “What are you doing, Har? You cannot offer them more slaves!”

The warrior sat with a simple smile as the servant handed the pad to the grand matron.

“We came seeking aid against the Duggor and pirates. That offer is still on the table for the seven hundred plus of your people.” Har took a breath. “Bring us those two and their ship, and I am authorized to order the release of over five thousand of those we hold.”

The grand matron looked across the table, seeing the cold stare of the old warrior piercing through her. Her eyes started to fill with tears as she wrestled with the options of handing Jace and Eislie to the Karazon. “I, I cannot make that decision. They are not Yata.”

“This is pointless, Har,” Tarlin griped.

“You will be silent, Tarlin. You have denied combat and sublated. This discussion is mine.” He turned his head slightly to look at the envoy. “Or do you wish for me to take your possessions?”

The envoy gritted his teeth. The old warrior had invoked combat. Tarlin knew of the old warrior’s prowess and would not survive his wrath in battle. Tarlin shook his head, giving a low growl.

Har leaned back with a smile. “Grand Matron, I have been studying your laws, new and old. You say you cannot speak for these individuals, is that correct?”

The grand matron responded, “I cannot. They are not Yata. You cannot ask me to willingly hand them over to you.” The rise of anger and lament was now filling her words.

Har took a breath before speaking with confidence. “Then allow me to offer you a way to save a few thousand of your people from execution.”

“What?” the matron yelled.

“I do not wish you to look weak, and although we need the aid to protect ourselves from the Duggor and pirate threats, I wish to offer you a solution to all of our problems,” Har said.

The grand matron fought back tears. She could not willingly allow them to take the two people now displayed on the pad before her. Nor could she allow the death of thousands of her own people. "What is it?"

Har looked to the table. "Allow us to meet with them, and if I cannot convince them to come willingly with us, allow us to challenge them."

"You barbaric—" The matron was silenced as a small blade now pressed against her throat.

"I am offering you a choice, and a way to save your people and prevent others from being claimed," Har said as he folded his hands politely on the table.

"I would understand not extending us aid. That, I feel, may have passed. But you have a chance to save thousands of your people," Har said.

The grand matron looked at the warrior in contempt. "If you want them, you will have to face them yourself."

Har waved the servant away and the man pulled the blade from her throat. "You are a strong leader. I would like to meet with them. Bring them here."

The matron pushed the man that held the blade away. "I cannot summon them. They are not slaves. But I will be dining with them shortly, once we have concluded this meeting."

Har smiled, "Well then, Matron, we would be honored to join you for a meal."

Chapter 13:
Dinner Guests

"Your Highness, we have data on the *Wolfhammer*. They seem to be slowing in hyperspace. Perhaps they found something," Roland informed her.

The pirate queen touched the display. "Show me the last few cycles."

The screen replayed the movements of the *Wolfhammer*, and Jana looked at it closely, her eyes fixing on the previous few hours until she paused at one location and time. The pirate queen zoomed in on the section and replayed the data. She watched as the point slowly began to drift before turning to a straight line.

"Have we heard from our operatives on Yata?" the pirate queen asked.

"Not yet. Our operatives are due to check in. However, the increased security of the Karazon visit has made things difficult," Roland replied.

"The Karazon, a race that should be eradicated from this universe," the queen muttered before tapping the screen to stop the display. "I know what our people will report. The *Wolfhammer* is already on Yata Bata."

“But the hyperspace information. How can that be?” Roland asked.

The queen smiled. “They found a way to jettison the tracker while in hyperspace. It seems they were able to find it fairly quickly.”

“Apologies, Your Highness. The agent will be punished,” Roland responded as he gave a bow.

“Bring him here; do not punish him, yet. And if the *Wolfhammer* is on Yata, have the others ready, in case we need to move. I have a suspicion that the Karazon may become a problem,” the queen commanded.

“I obey, Your Highness,” Roland said before rushing away.

* * *

Eislie was looking at the outfit she wore. Given the hectic work on the project and their trip to Earth, they hadn’t had much time to buy anything fancy. The best clothes with them were the newer ones recently purchased while on Oppa before they left. Jace had to iron some of what he brought with him when Eislie insisted they look presentable. Neither had any form of formal wear to speak of, and as per Miriz, as long as they were presentable, they would be fine, telling them to at least wear something clean.

Miriz arrived at their room. Although spacious, it was not much larger than their ship’s cargo area. Most rooms in the spaceport were all the same. When the alert for the door dinged, Eislie went to see who it was. She paused seeing Miriz standing there in a formal dress when she opened it, her banner of status draped over her shoulder.

“Great, now I feel underdressed,” Eislie remarked.

Miriz laughed, “Don’t. As long as you are presentable, you’ll be fine. This was short notice, and the matron is aware that you were here to resupply and fix your vessel.”

Jace stood fixing his collar as he grabbed his flight jacket. Miriz looked at the jacket and reached out, gently tapping the controls. “The paperwork should be processed by morning.”

Eislie nodded. Miriz was right. If the design were proven, then the profit from it would be astronomical. The plus to Eislie was that it would save billions of people from the effects of spide exposure. Miriz straightened Eislie's collar after she put on her flight jacket.

Jace smiled before remarking, "I can tell you two have been friends for a while."

Eislie snickered, saying, "We still are."

Miriz looked them both over. "No grease marks, stains, you should be fine. Come, let's go eat."

* * *

In the kitchen, one of the Karazon servants walked up to several large, simmering pots. Their intelligence already knew the food prepared for the grand matron's dinner. The Karazon insisted on the information, since they had now forced their way into attending. The servant took a small container and opened it. They poured what looked like finely chopped leaves into one pot.

"Hey, what are you doing here?" one of the chefs yelled.

The servant bowed. "I am merely confirming the food for the dinner tonight, as per my master's orders."

The chef looked into the pot and smelled the vapor. Nothing seemed off, so he sent the servant on his way. Then, the chef yelled to one of the other cooks, "You, help me with this catlan; we need to crisp the outside in the fryer."

As the catlan was placed on the fryer, a short burst of greenish smoke wafted from it and was quickly taken away by the ventilation system.

The vehicle they were riding in stopped, and an attendant opened the door. Miriz stepped out, followed closely by Eislie and Jace. They approached the sizeable ornate entrance of the restaurant and the attendant nodded, motioning for them to enter as she opened the door.

They were startled when one of the matron's aides quickly approached them. "Representative Elysse, the grand matron sends her apologies. Her meeting with the Karazon is running long, and she has requested that you start the meal without her," the attendant told them.

Miriz nodded. "Did she leave word whether she plans to attend later?"

"Yes, but it will probably be after the first course," the attendant informed her.

Miriz thanked the attendant and requested to be seated. They talked, and Jace and Eislie told how they survived the pirates, Miriz bringing up them sleeping inside of the star. Their tales were igniting some exciting debate as to the encounters the two had had. Jace joked, saying, "I told her, for once I'd like to have a normal, easy day, just once."

"You know, every time you say that, we seem to get stuck in some outrageous situation," Eislie replied before laughing.

The banter and joyous noise was something the matron had hoped to hear as she walked into the room as the attendants escorted her over to the table.

"It seems you are all having a good time. Please forgive my delay," the grand matron said.

Everyone at the table stood until she was seated. Eislie looked at her. The dress she wore was glimmering, but there was something in the woman's eyes that seemed darkened. Jace looked to Eislie, mouthing the words, "What? Something wrong?"

Eislie replied silently, "Nothing."

The matron apologetically joked, "I hope I'm not too late for the main dish." She leaned forward. "It's one of my favorites, catlan fry."

"Really? Ours too. Small universe," Jace joked.

Eislie put her hand over her eyes before pointing to Jace. "We have to keep ordering it. He eats it all."

Jace looked to Eislie. "You keep stealing mine."

Their banter was making the whole table erupt in laughter. Then, silence returned as the main dish was brought in. Jace waited until everyone was served before he decided to try a bite. But, as he chewed, a strange, sweet-metallic flavor stung his tongue. He quickly took his napkin and spat the food out.

"What, too hot? You should have waited," Miriz chided him.

"Sorry, it tastes a bit off. There's a strange flavor," Jace said.

"It's catlan, Jace," Eislie said as she took a bite. Her reaction was similar to Jace's. "Ugh, I taste it too, a sweet-metallic flavor?"

Miriz took a small piece and smelled it before placing a small amount on her tongue. She immediately spit it into the napkin before looking to Davlen, ordering, "Scanner, now."

She turned to the matron. "We should scan the food. I taste it as well."

Moments later, they heard a loud cry and Davlen returned, his arm hanging limp as he held it in the other while a large reptilian-scaled humanoid pushed him into his chair.

"Grand Matron, we intercepted your servant in the kitchen. He seems to have gotten lost," Har said as he stood behind the woman. "Hello, everyone, I am the new envoy of the Karazon, Har. Oh, and I see that the main course has arrived. Since we were invited, I took the liberty of ordering additional seasoning for the food. It is a family blend; I hope you enjoy it."

Jace could see the matron looking uneasy and moved his eyes around the room as Har spoke. The alien towered over the woman. He had to be at least nine feet tall, by Jace's estimation. Jace could also see several others in the darkness near the walls and watched as another, taller alien appeared near him and Eislie.

Har smiled as he pointed to one of the matron's assistants, asking, "What do you think of the seasoning?"

There was no response, so he went to another and another. But, again, no one responded. When he came to Jace, it was a different story.

"You are Terran, are you not? What do you think of the seasoning?" Har asked, and waited for Jace's reply.

Nearby, Jace looked to Eislie.

"Ah, you seek permission from your female. Have you adopted the beliefs of this world?" Har called out Jace.

Jace chuckled, "I'm unfamiliar with your people. Are you Karazon?"

Har nodded. "You have not answered any of my questions."

Jace could see the smug expression on the alien's face before he replied, "I'm not a fan of it. But thank you for sharing. I think it's good to experience different cultures."

"You did not like the flavor. You insult me," Har spoke, causing Eislie to turn and see the other Karazon place his hands over Jace's shoulders.

"He has insulted you, Envoy Har. Perhaps he should be taught a lesson," Tarlin said before tightening his grip, allowing his single talon to pierce through Jace's shirt into the flesh beneath. Jace grunted and turned to see the reptilian claw drawing blood. He could see the bandage on the warrior's hand and grabbed it, pushing his thumb into the alien's injury. His actions were causing the alien to howl as Jace twisted his hand, bringing the alien to the ground.

"Magnificent," escaped Har's mouth. He then called one of the other Karazon over, giving an order. "Secure their ship."

Tarlin brought his other hand up, claw extended as he moved toward Jace's face. Jace grabbed his hand before pushing it away. Tarlin again raised his hand, and Eislie yelled for the Karazon to stop.

"You have no permission to speak," Tarlin growled, swiping his claw toward her. His action was met by Eislie punching him in the side of the face, making the alien fall to the ground again.

"Tarlin, come away from them before they injure you severely," Har mocked the previous envoy.

Har smiled as Tarlin fought to stand, the scaled warrior nursing his injuries. "Has the grand matron not told you why we are here?"

Jace pushed past the pain from the alien's claw and placed his napkin over the injury to stop the bleeding. He then looked over the table and could see the look of concern on Miriz's face as Har spoke. Jace was becoming impatient with the Karazon envoy.

"Har, get to your point," Jace shot back as Eislie checked his wound.

"A man of action, I can respect that," Har said before walking around the table. But the Karazon envoy stopped behind Miriz. "It is simple. We are brokering a deal. You come with us, and they get what they want."

Eislie turned, yelling, "You don't expect us to go with you?"

"We have offered the release of over five thousand Yata, and to not hunt them, for the two of you. But . . ." Har paused. "Of course, we could always kill them and take more."

The grand matron interrupted, "We did not agree to this." She looked to Eislie and Jace. "Please leave, now, both of you."

The matron's outburst was punctuated by the return of the Karazon that Har had sent away, the alien sneering with victory. "They may find that difficult, Grand Matron; we are now holding their ship." Har added, "A small vessel that is powerful enough to destroy one of the most feared ships in the galaxy. That is a great prize indeed."

"You people are real assholes. You know that?" Jace remarked.

Har laughed, "Ah, Terrans, such brilliant conversationalists." The warrior paused. "I have an offer. Fight us in combat. I believe it was customary in the earlier times of Yata. If you win, you save thousands of lives and get your ship back. If you lose, you serve us, willingly."

"And if we refuse?" Jace asked.

"Well, if your ship is not incentive enough," Har slid the top from the metallic armband he wore and dipped his claw into a small reservoir before striking Miriz with his talon, piercing the side of her neck.

Eislie jumped up, rushing over to help her friend, pushing Har aside.

"The female seems quite strong as well," Har remarked, trying to stay standing. He seemed to take pleasure in seeing the shock from Miriz as he watched Eislie trying to help her.

"The poison is one we use when training slaves. If they do not obey, they are not given the antidote. I would say that with this one's metabolism, she would have no more than four standard days."

"You bastard," Eislie growled.

The warrior stepped back away from Eislie. *You have the fire of a Terran in you, little one.*

"You can forget the aid, Har, and I am tempted to—" The grand matron was interrupted by Har.

"Let your people die. You would not trade two lives for thousands?" Har mocked.

Eislie looked at Jace. She could see the anger behind his eyes, and she gave a shallow nod.

"Har, who would we be fighting?" Jace asked.

"No, you cannot. I cannot allow this!" the grand matron yelled.

"You've no say in this, Grand Matron. He just made this personal," Jace growled, looking at Miriz.

Har smiled, but was startled when Jace yelled, "You haven't answered my question, asshole!"

The old warrior stood tall. "Myself, and since Tarlin is already injured, another warrior of my choosing."

Jace looked to Eislie, seeing her nod in agreement. "We fight you and another. When and where?"

Har's expression became more severe. "Tomorrow, the arena nearby. After sunrise."

Jace stood. "You'll have the antidote ready? No tricks? What's to stop me from killing you now?"

Har chuckled, "Kill me now, the woman dies, and we destroy your ship." Har leaned on the table, his eyes staring into Jace's. "I am an honorable warrior."

Jace scoffed, "You involved innocent people, hold others hostage, threatening to kill them to get your way. That's hardly honorable."

Har retorted, "Perhaps a better phrase would be, respected."

Jace shot back, "You don't even deserve that."

The Karazon growled, turning his back on Jace. "Tomorrow morning. Be ready."

Jace rushed to see if he could help Eislie with Miriz. And as the echoes of the restaurant faded, Tarlin spoke with Har.

"Envoy, I am concerned that the Terran may be tougher than you anticipate. Terrans are known to be deadly when angered. So, fighting them both may be an issue." Tarlin seemed in thought. "I think the female may be Terran as well."

"I have read their laws. The female is of no concern." Har stopped, looking to another Karazon following them. "Order my best warrior, Sredan, to arrive tonight."

The Karazon acknowledged and rushed away.

"I hope you know what you are doing, Har. We will have to inform the elite of your dealings. I do not look forward to that interaction."

Har gave a simple grin. "Tarlin, you are still young. As I mentioned, the female is not a concern. We will only have to defeat the male."

Chapter 14:
Fight for our Friends

The bright walls of the medical unit caused Jace's eyes to sting as he held Eislie. The doctors worked feverishly to identify the poison that was now flowing through Miriz's veins. Hours had passed, and several times, her friend went into convulsions. When she did, Eislie's grip tightened on Jace's arm or hand as she watched.

"They have yet to identify the toxin. I'm sorry," the grand matron said as they walked up.

Eislie remained focused on her friend, seemingly trying to will her to recover. Finally, Jace turned to the matron. "When were you going to tell us?"

The matron bowed her head. "I wasn't. I was hoping they would forget this and renegotiate. I'm sorry."

Jace sighed, "You didn't have a choice. But, unfortunately, people like them will always be like that."

Eislie turned to lay her head against Jace. "Have you talked to Ed?"

Jace nodded. "The ship's been anchored and has over fifty weapons surrounding it. Some with mass rounds heavy enough to pierce the hull."

Eislie turned her gaze up, the growing anger like fire behind them. She muttered, “Bastards,” before looking away and returning to Jace. “You haven’t fixed the containment. Maybe we can order him to open the, you know . . .”

Jace chuckled, “Yeah, already thought about that.” But then, he turned to the window. “Still won’t help Miriz.”

Eislie looked despondent as the matron wondered what they were talking about. She waited a few seconds before asking, “Does your ship have weapons that can kill the Karazon holding it?”

Jace took a breath. “If we ordered a spide overload, yeah. But we would still need the antidote from Har.” Jace paused. “Not to mention, there’s a failsafe. If we are killed, the ship will probably blow.”

The matron stepped back. “If that ship explodes, it will kill tens of thousands; you cannot order it to overload.”

Jace tapped his comm. “Ed, can you estimate the radius of a spide overload?”

“I was listening to the interaction earlier, Captain. If I am to stay with my original orders, the area affected would be approximately one thousand seventy-one hundred meters, Captain.”

“Original orders?” the matron asked.

Jace turned to her, his eyes cold as he spoke. “We die, the ship blows.”

The grand matron shifted back in horror. “You must order it to leave or stop it.”

Eislie joined Jace as she stared at the matron before tapping her comm. “Ed?”

“Yes, Captain Licessien.”

Eislie paused before saying, “The order stands.”

"Confirmed, Captain. But I will change my proximity to ensure the destruction of the Karazon vessel."

Jace spoke into his comm. "Understood, Ed. But let's see how this plays out first."

"You cannot, must not, do this," the matron pleaded.

Jace sighed, "Evacuate the area. We don't want to do this anymore than you." He turned to see the elongated seating against the wall. "You want to go back to our room and get some rest?"

Eislie shook her head, pointing to the hospital room where they were working on Miriz. Jace nodded. "We should get some sleep. It's going to be a busy day tomorrow."

* * *

Tarlin greeted the small courier ship. The three Karazon slaves looking battered as they stumbled from the vessel. Two others wheeled out a large sleeping chamber containing a Karazon warrior. Tarlin had to look up to see the warrior's teeth pointing down at him.

"He is asleep?" Tarlin growled, almost craning his neck.

One slave responded, "Yes, as per Master Har. He requested the warrior be rested before the battle."

Tarlin smiled before mumbling, "I see you have been enhancing your assets, Har. No wonder you have almost never lost." Tarlin looked back. "Bring him in. Envoy Har is waiting."

The sound of the chamber made a grinding, metallic scrape as it settled. Har tapped a code in and the door unlocked. There was a hiss as the pressure escaped.

"Ah, my champion. How was your trip?" Har asked with pleasured amusement.

The warrior stirred, his eyes blinking several times before he spoke, his voice booming with confidence, "Master, I anticipate with pleasure defeating your enemies."

Jace gave a start as he shifted in the long chair. He had just fallen asleep, and could feel Eislie leaning against him. He looked up to see two people standing in front of the viewing window. Nearby sat the grand matron. In the dim light, Jace could still see the dried tears on the side of her face. Gently, he moved Eislie, who shifted in surprise before looking at him, whispering, “It’s morning already?”

Jace nodded, then stood and stretched, his actions causing the man by the window to turn around. It was Davlen. Jace moved behind them and watched as Paaz wiped a tear from her cheek. The two said nothing as Jace looked through the window.

“She’s gotten worse. They cannot counteract the poison,” Paaz whimpered.

“We’ll do our best to get the antidote,” Jace said.

Paaz turned to him. “How? They are twice your size. And stronger.”

Jace huffed, “But they’re slower.”

Eislie joined him. “And we’re pissed off.”

* * *

The arena only held a few people when Jace and Eislie arrived. The Karazon warrior was already waiting in the open field below. Har stood watch in the viewing box, waiting.

“Ah, you have arrived. Did you oversleep?” the Karazon mocked Jace.

Jace shook his head. “Nope, just showing our disdain for your stupidity.”

Har turned to Jace, and with a growling voice, said, “You insult me again?”

Jace leaned forward. “Get used to it.”

There were several Karazon in the box, along with Yatan guards. Jace turned to the field. “All right, Har, let’s head down and get this over with.”

Har chuckled, pointing to Eislie. “The female stays.”

Eislie moved to strike Har, but Jace grabbed her. “Easy; save it for the arena.”

Har laughed as he watched Eislie break away. “I have been reading the laws of this world. The teams would have to be matched. The rules state a female opponent to another female. Since we were not able to provide a female counterpart, I will concede, and you may fight my chosen warrior, alone.” Har paused. “I hope you don’t mind that we are sending out a live vid of these proceedings.”

Jace looked into the field where the lone warrior stood. Before him were two large hammers. Jace removed his jacket, handing it to Eislie, her eyes meeting his in understanding before he turned to walk down the ramp onto the field. Jace passed a sizeable rectangular column entering the area, running his hand along it as he did.

When Jace neared the warrior, the massiveness of the weapons became evident. The warrior’s eyes followed Jace.

Jace stood looking at the hammer before looking up at the warrior, his teeth pointing down toward him.

Jace inspected the weapon, turning to look up at Har staring back. “Mind if I inspect the weapons?”

Har gave a grin. “You may do so. I assure you, they are identical.”

Jace went to lift the weapon and was barely able to move it. The weight was almost as much as his own. However, the Karazon on the field picked his hammer up with ease. Seeing this, Eislie said, “If he dies, I will kill you, Har.”

Her words made the old warrior’s head jerk quickly to look at her, eyes wide in fear at her tone. He needed a moment before saying, “My warrior has been instructed not to kill the Terran. We want you both as a prize.”

Eislie nodded, and an uneasy grin appeared on her face before she yelled, “Jace, they don’t want us dead!”

Jace shook his head and looked up at the warrior before him. Within seconds, Jace started laughing, and as he continued, Har became concerned. Har looked to Eislie as she stared out toward her love on the field. Her only words to the Karazon were, "You made a mistake. You threatened everything he cares for."

Tarlin was becoming tired of waiting and moved forward. "You fear the loss of your warrior, Har. No more delay."

Tarlin then took a breath, yelling, "Begin!"

Jace was trying to lift the massive weapon when the whistle of its match nearly struck him. Jace could move quickly, but the blow struck the hammer he was offered, breaking its metal handle. Jace dodged each blow from his opponent. And he was right, the Karazon was much slower. But Jace made a wrong move, and the impact he received sent him flying. Jace rolled along the ground, gasping and coughing as he forced air back into his lungs, that very breath sending a searing agony across his side.

He growled with pain as he stood, pulling his arm in to protect his right side. "Broken, again? Why does everyone hit me there?"

Jace's daze was interrupted when he again heard the whistle of the hammer nearing him. He ran to the side, moving as far as he could from the Karazon warrior. Then, panting in between the stabbing of his broken ribs, he watched the warrior running toward him. Jace looked at the support of the wall behind him and waited.

The warrior growled and brought his weapon up. Jace rushed forward, sliding on the dirt, kicking the warrior's legs from beneath him. The warrior had started to bring his weapon down, and Jace's actions caused him to stumble off balance. The Karazon's hammer hit the wall, but Sredan could not stop. His face contacted the corner of the pillar as the hammer rebounded, striking across his snout. Jace could see the blood along the wall. The light thuds of some of the warrior's once sharp teeth were now hitting the ground.

Jace didn't waste any time. He ran back to the broken weapon, grabbing what was left of the handle. He briefly looked at it to see where the metal failed. He ran his thumb along the break and felt its bite. His blood appearing, Jace smiled. *Sharp!*

Jace waited by the weapon as the warrior again rushed toward him. Jace moved his hand close to the broken edge. Jace swiped the broken handle's sharp side across the warrior's chest, slicing into his scaly skin. But as Jace moved to strike again, Sredan brought his weapon down. Jace twisted out of the way, but the head of the Karazon's weapon glanced off his shin. Jace hadn't felt the pain yet, and he slashed across the warrior's arm, his actions causing the deadly point to deflect off of his opponent's handle. Jace watched as the Karazon howled and dropped his hammer to grasp his hand. As the warrior retreated, Jace felt the pain in his leg. He shook his head, concentrating on the Karazon, and watched as a small puddle of blue blood pooled before his opponent. Nearby, two of the warrior's fingers rolled across the ground.

The warrior huffed rapidly as he held his wound. Seeing the warrior fighting back the pain, Jace made his move. Rushing forward, Jace had the broken handle forward, thrusting it with his full weight toward the Karazon. Its point embedded solidly in the warrior's chest. The warrior stumbled as Jace pounded on the handle several times, forcing it further into the alien's core. Jace stepped aside as his opponent started to convulse, and had to jump out of the way as the Karazon warrior fell forward, the alien's weight forcing the former handle to pierce through his back.

"No!" Har yelled.

The old warrior then rushed toward the door, raising his blade as he neared the grand matron. In his haste, he did not see Davlen move to protect the matron, the aide blocking the Karazon's path, and the old warrior thrust up into the Miriz's assistant's chest instead. Paaz rushed to stop the bleeding as the Karazon warrior pushed others aside to make his way down the ramp.

Jace kicked the dying alien as Har rounded the corner. He turned to hear Har growl, "I will not be denied my prize. You will pay for this dishonor!"

Jace watched as the old warrior rushed forward. And, to him, the world slowed. Jace reached out for the remaining hammer dropped by his opponent.

Jace gave a low grunt through clenched teeth, saying, "Leave us alone."

With all of his will and strength, Jace picked up the hammer, swinging it to impact on the side of Har's face. The Karazon's body continued, and he could still see Jace as his head twisted to face backward. Jace had to dodge the warrior's body as its feet stumbled from the Karazon's brain disconnecting from his spinal cord.

Jace dropped the hammer, limping toward Har, and stood watching the alien's body twitch. Jace could hear the Karazon gasping for breath. In what seemed like an act of mercy, Jace shifted the old warrior's head, enabling him to breathe. Jace knelt, a firm, low command escaping his throat. "Give me the antidote."

Har's jaw stuttered, "Ar . . . ar . . . arm . . . band."

Jace lifted the warrior's arm, twisting it into an unnatural position. The latch was in an awkward place, and Jace fumbled with it. He could see two small containers in the armband. One he recognized from the night before, and the other, he tapped. Har only gurgled as Jace tapped it.

"This better work. If it doesn't, and you're still alive"—Jace grunted as he stood—"you won't be for long."

Jace limped his way up the ramp, his arm holding his side, every breath stabbing. He was met with the stares of several Karazon and Yata security as he opened the door. Eislie rushed to see if he was all right. Jace pushed her away. He did his best to stay steady, holding the armband before her.

"This one is the antidote." Jace labored to speak, now feeling the pain of his injuries.

Eislie looked him over. She watched him flinch as she pressed gently against his side. Jace looked at her, pressing his head against hers. "I'll only slow you down. Go. I have something to finish up here anyway."

Eislie turned toward the Karazon, her eyes searing as they scanned across those who had poisoned her friend. She gently leaned against Jace before sprinting out the door.

Jace raised his eyes to stare at the Karazon. Behind him, no one noticed a man standing just outside the door.

"Your Highness, we have video feed from Preston, the one you assigned to watch the crew of the *Wolfhammer*," one of the pirates said as Jana walked toward the large screen. She could see the room, and several Yata standing between Jace and the Karazon.

"Zido, do the Karazon still surround their ship?" the queen asked.

"Yes, we have counted thirty-seven Karazon and over sixty loyal," Zido replied.

The queen moved to see the situation showing on her follower's screen. "How many agents do we have nearby?"

"If needed, we could take the dock."

The pirate queen looked again at the large screen, the video from Preston's implant still showing; no one had moved. A subtle smile graced the queen's face before she spoke. "They're afraid of him."

"The Karazon should fear him," Zido remarked.

The queen gave an order. "Tell Preston that it is time to deliver my message."

"Yes, Your Highness," Zido replied, and relayed the order to her agent.

Jace limped forward, his foot dragging across a pool of blood on the floor, his boot trailing it with each step. Jace remained focused on the Karazon. The Yata security did nothing to stop him. Preston entered the room before closing and locking the door. He tapped on a small comm screen he held as he moved forward. There were no words as Preston moved before Jace.

"My queen will address you," Preston announced as he held the device in both hands before everyone. Within moments, a holographic image of the pirate queen filled the air.

"You have attempted to take from me again, Karazon." The queen's voice boomed unnaturally from the device.

"They are *our* prize," Tarlin growled.

The queen looked on with an air of power. When she spoke, everyone in the room listened. "I have warned you before on attempting to take anything from me. Compensation will be extracted." The queen seemed to look back toward Jace. "I am curious; you fought this battle to save your ship? I can understand the draw of battle for the Karazon, but why were you fighting, Captain Tucker?"

Jace shifted as he took a painful breath. "They threatened and attacked us, our ship, and held the lives of over five thousand Yata against us."

The queen returned her stare to the Karazon, the blue of her eye nearly burning through its veil. "Then you fought for a noble cause."

Jace took a breath. "They were secondary."

The queen turned around before ordering, "Preston, private mode; and bring the display to Captain Tucker."

Preston complied and held the display before Jace. The queen tapped her ear, and Jace understood. When the queen spoke, it was in a language that no one understood except for Jace, the look of understanding making the queen smile as she spoke in old Takloh.

"Why did you fight in the arena?"

Jace sighed before replying, "They poisoned Eislie's friend." Jace shifted from the pain in his side and grunted as he spoke. "They threatened our ship. And all those people."

The queen closed her eyes in understanding. Then, she turned to nod to Zido, giving only one command. "Kill them all."

She returned to Jace and asked if he was all right. Jace subtly shook his head.

The room suddenly became a buzz of activity on the comms of the Yata security, and the queen smiled. "Captain, your ship is secure. I suggest you and Captain Licessien leave immediately."

Jace shook his head. "Not until Miriz is healed."

The queen replied, "You are stubborn, Captain. Why are you remaining there and not with your co-captain?"

Jace looked to the Karazon, his eyes filled with the spark of revenge. "Like I said, not until Miriz is healed."

The queen nodded and returned to the native language. "Preston, I will address the Karazon."

The pirate turned and held the device before them. "People of Karazon, by now, you will have learned that your force holding my prize has been decimated. There will be further compensation forthcoming. You have promised the return of five thousand Yata, and to not hunt them if Captain Tucker won. Is that correct?"

Tarlin looked away in disgrace. "That is what Envoy Har had promised."

The queen stood stoic as she spoke. "People of Yata, welcome home your lost." Then, she paused. "Karazon, you have greatly insulted Captain Tucker and unfairly challenged him."

The queen looked around. "I am well acquainted with the laws of Yata, and Captain Tucker is owed compensation for this transgression. You involved them in a matter of this planet, without substance."

The Karazon argued between themselves.

"Silence!" the queen ordered, and the room fell quiet. "Captain Tucker, you may order the death of any of the Karazon."

Jace shook his head. "No."

The queen turned to question him. "You would spare their lives?"

Jace shook his head, holding his arm up, showing the comm on his wrist. “I’m still here for a reason. I’m waiting for a call.”

The queen tilted her head, giving a quizzical stare.

“Miriz. I’m waiting to hear about her condition from Eis,” Jace said in a low, almost vicious tone.

The queen nodded before ordering, “Preston, you will aid Captain Tucker in any means he requires. If the people of Yata do not help, I will order the others to join you.”

“Yes, my queen,” Preston replied, staring at the Karazon.

One of the security personnel raised his gun. “Just tell me when.”

The queen looked up and down the line of the Karazon. “If the woman dies, you will all learn that the dead tell no tales of the future.”

Chapter 15: Ship Surprise

Eislie waited next to her friend's bed. Paaz had not returned. Eislie knew that the woman cared for Davlen; she could see it in her actions. She was present when Har struck Davlen down, and she had tried to stop the bleeding. However, after Jace won, Paaz became focused on her lover as they took Davlen away.

Jace entered the room, his injuries healed. Jace could see her holding the armband that he had taken from Har. She had taken it from the table in her friend's room. As he stood next to Eislie, Jace gently nudged her shoulder. "How is she?"

Eislie took a breath. "The poison is neutralized, they think. But she is still suffering from its effect. There is a lot of damage to her nervous system."

Jace nodded. "How bad?"

Eislie said, "She's only opened her eyes a little, but her readings show she's in a lot of pain."

Jace could see a tear rolling down Eislie's face and he gently wiped it away, making her smile.

"How are you doing?" she asked Jace.

Jace gave a nervous laugh. "They patched me up. But my shin's still aching." His head was down and brow raised, staring at Eislie as he nudged her arm.

Eislie looked at him before saying, "I'm fine. Just worried."

Eislie reached her hand out and Jace took it, his grip interrupted by the Karazon armband she held. He took it from her and placed it into his jacket pocket before again taking her hand. They were silent as they stood vigil over their friend. Eislie leaned against Jace only to remark, "Ugh, you smell like blood. Didn't they give you new clothes?"

Jace sighed, "No, I grabbed my stuff as soon as I was done. I was more worried about you and Miriz."

Eislie's smile fought against her sadness as she leaned her head against his. They spent a few moments in silence before Jace said, "I should get changed. Clean up a bit too. Still have too much blood on me."

She looked forward. "I'll be all right. Go."

Jace hesitantly leaned away, his arm staying as long as it could before his steps moved him toward the door. He could see the pirate he knew as Preston standing nearby. Jace stopped before him. "Watch over her, please." The pirate nodded and his eyes became vigilant. Jace didn't speak as he walked away and entered the elevator to head down to go back to their ship.

* * *

Jace entered the *Wolfhammer*, and by mistake, he turned into the med bay. Jace looked around. "What am I doing? Geez." He removed his jacket, tossing it on the exam table, and went to get something to drink.

As Jace finished gulping the water down, he immediately filled the glass again, the ship's computer remarking, "Biosensors indicate you are dehydrated, Captain."

Jace took a breath as he finished. "A fight'll do that to you, Ed."

The computer concurred with its captain and took notice of the crew jacket on the table. With its programming, it started to scan the item for biological contaminates. The computer's sensors were focusing on the contents of the jacket's pockets. Along one of the screens, a red bar alerted.

"Attention, Captain, you have brought a restricted substance on board."

Jace turned to look around. "What? Where? It better not be a fucking bomb."

"No, Captain, it is a restricted narcotic. It is called X'una M'kuy, also known as the black flower. A highly addictive extract for the Takloh."

Jace picked up his jacket, retrieving the armband he had placed in its pocket. "What is this stuff?"

The computer replied, "It must be removed from this vessel. As I mentioned, it is known as the black flower in Takloh. It is a highly addictive substance. The enemy of the Takloh, known as the Tharak, used it on prisoners."

"Ed, there are no Takloh anymore, remember?" Jace shot back before asking, "Wait, who used it on prisoners?"

The computer took a moment before responding. "My apologies, Captain, the warning is part of my hardcoded commands. The Tharak are a sister race of the Takloh, genetic engineers as well. I should inform you and Captain Licessien of the possible danger from them. Unfortunately, I do not have a record of them being alive, but I have intercepted several transmissions in the Tharak dialect."

"Are they dangerous?" Jace asked.

Ed responded, "I do not find any current information on them. But I have still received partial transmissions."

Jace shook his head. He understood and felt foolish for reminding Ed that the Takloh were gone. He apologized to the computer. "Sorry, Ed, just worried about Eis and Miriz."

It was a few moments before the computer spoke again. “I have a log of all crew who had to have the substance purged from their systems. It was a difficult and lengthy process.”

“I understand, Ed. It must have been tough.” Jace paused before yelling, “Wait! Did you say you purged it from their systems?”

“That is correct, Captain. The toxin adheres to the nerve cell casing. It can be difficult to remove,” the computer said as it asked, “Why? Is this the substance that was given to Representative Elysse?”

“Yes! Ed. Are you telling me you know how to remove it?”

The computer paused. “Alliance, or Quaru, or others like yourself, I have not tried. The molecular bonding may be difficult to remove. I would need to evaluate the patient before I could confirm.”

“Ed, it doesn’t matter. We have to try.” Jace tapped his comm. “Eis? Answer, now, please.”

When she answered, he told her about what Ed had found. He asked her if it was possible to bring Miriz down. The nearby nurse thought it was irregular and went to get permission. Eislie told Jace, and they were both looking for answers. That’s when Eislie looked at Preston standing by the door, her mind racing. She was more concerned for her friend’s life, and made a snap decision.

“You!” She pointed to Preston. “Help me get her to our ship.”

The pirate nodded and rushed to help. Eislie picked up her friend. They both put one of Miriz’s arms over their shoulders and carried her out of the room. Several of the staff moved out of their way before security tried stopping them. Eislie kicked at some while Preston pushed others away as they made their way to the elevator. Finally, the matron’s head medic stood before the door. “You are not taking our patient anywhere.”

Eislie looked forward. “Our ship’s computer has seen this toxin before. He might be able to help.”

The matron now stood behind her medical staff, and Eislie pushed them back. Eislie looked the woman in the eyes. “Ed has seen this before. We think he can help her.”

The leader of Yata looked concerned before looking around at her staff trying to retrieve their patient. She could see the pleading and determination in Eislie’s stare.

“Let them go,” the grand matron ordered.

The doctor refuted, “Ma’am, we are still trying to stop the effects of the toxin. The patient needs to stay.”

The matron looked toward the doctor before returning to Eislie. She then reached in and pressed the button for the lower floor. “Take her to your ship.”

Eislie squeaked out a thank-you before the door closed.

* * *

Jace rushed to ready the med bay as Ed primed the trauma veil over the exam bed. Ed ordered Jace to prepare several injections of a selenium counteracting solution, telling Jace that it may be needed since the toxin is elementally based.

Jace could hear Eislie yelling, “Hold on, Miriz, we’re not done yet!”

As they rounded the corner, Jace rushed to help Eislie put her friend on the exam table. Ed went straight to work. The matron appeared in the small hall next to Preston and asked, “Any update?”

They heard the computer say, “I can confirm the presence of X’una M’kuy. Please administer one injection of the counteragent prepared, Captain Tucker. My scans also indicate that the restorative veil will be required. There will need to be multiple treatments applied at once, since the toxin has accumulated within the nerve casings of the patient, including her brain.”

Jace injected the counteragent and stepped back. "Go ahead, Ed. She's all yours. See what you can do."

The computer lowered the veil and went to work. "There is extensive infiltration of the compound, but the counteragent seems to be stabilizing the patient. I will start to purge the toxin from her system. This may take several hours; med systems will not be available while the veil is in use."

"Just do it, Ed," Jace ordered.

Eislie now stood next to Jace. She could see his eyes worried. Jace looked to her, saying, "Fingers crossed."

* * *

A few hours had passed. The matron had returned to her duties. Paaz entered the room; she stood quietly leaning against the wall. When she looked up, Jace could see her eyes red and swollen.

"It shouldn't be much longer. Ed's been keeping us updated," Jace said as he approached Paaz.

Paaz nodded, but looked to be holding back tears. Jace repeated, "She'll be fine."

Miriz's assistant shook her head. Jace was confused by her actions. He thought she was worried about her employer, and Jace looked to Eislie as Paaz struggled to hold her composure. As Eislie moved closer, she hesitated, muttering, "Oh no." Eislie threw her arms around Paaz. Jace didn't understand why at first. He only heard Eislie mutter as she turned to look at him, "Davlen didn't make it."

Jace felt a heaviness as Eislie comforted Paaz. He hadn't seen the man since the morning. Eislie looked to Jace, saying, "Har stabbed him when he went to kill the matron."

The entire burden fell on his shoulders as he stared forward. He reached out to Paaz, holding her and Eislie as he whispered, "I'm sorry," before he pushed away, leaning his weight against the table, his head low. Eislie could see him raise his stare, the anger and frustration prevalent from the corner of his eye. She continued to comfort Paaz as

Jace picked up the armband that held the poison from the narrow counter. Jace stood, rolling his shoulders back. He walked to calm them both again. Paaz weakly tried pushing him away, making Eislie say, "Go, I'll stay with her." She looked to Miriz. "I'll stay with them both."

Jace gave a shallow nod and walked through the med bay door, his back making a thump on the opposite wall as he leaned heavily against it. Preston stood, his eyes filling with anger as he stared toward Miriz.

"Compensation must be taken," he said before looking at Jace.

Jace nodded, holding up the armband, staring at it. The pirate queen could see Jace through Preston's link looking at the armband. And she could feel his thoughts.

This is not your fault. You did the best you could to save everyone.

She continued to watch, and Jace grasped the armband tightly, his words short. "They need a taste of their own medicine."

The queen heard his words and tapped her console. "Preston, take the armband from Captain Tucker. He will get his wish."

Preston muttered, "Yes, my queen, but how?"

The queen spoke again. "I will instruct you in how to make a weapon to disperse the toxin throughout the Karazon ship. All Karazon aboard the vessel will be affected. And compensation will be taken." She paused for a moment. "Oh, and Preston. Tell Captain Tucker that he would make a good pirate."

Preston nodded and moved before Jace; he placed his hand on the armband strangled in Jace's grip. He was surprised when Jace released the item so quickly, Jace shifting as Preston started walking toward the outer door. Finally, Jace asked, "Why are most of the pirates starborn?"

The pirate paused, his head turning to look at the wall. "Our queen gives them purpose. They are lost people. She thinks you would be a good addition."

Jace sighed, his eyes pondering the pirate's statement. "We're not lost." Jace looked at the man. "We're just finding our own way."

Preston nodded and continued out the door. Jace lifted his head. “Once we find our answers, no one will be lost.”

Miriz woke with a start, her eyes finding an unfamiliar room. She vaguely remembered being in the hospital, but panic set in not recognizing the ceiling. A shadow came over her as her eyes tried to focus, her hands pushing away whoever was there.

“Miriz, it’s me, Eis.”

Miriz looked around, her eyes darting to find answers before they focused on Eislie’s face. Miriz no longer felt her body screaming in pain as she calmed. Instead, she asked, “Eis, where am I?”

Eislie smiled, her eyes fighting tears of happiness as she replied, “You’re on our ship.”

Miriz looked around as she sat forward, the bed moving to support her. “Your ship? But the hospital . . .”

Eislie hugged her. “They couldn’t remove the poison.”

Miriz looked to Eislie for answers. Eislie told her that their computer recognized the toxin as a Takloh narcotic and that it had purged it from over a dozen crew while in service. And now it did the same for her. Miriz smiled, tears of happiness rolling down her face as she hugged Eislie. “This ship of yours is amazing. Thank you.”

Overhead, they heard, “You are welcome, Representative Elysse. I know Captain Licessien would have been quite upset if you had not survived.”

The representative looked up, her eyes searching the room as Eislie said, “We all would have been upset.”

Miriz looked toward the door; she saw Paaz standing alone. She could see Paaz’s eyes red from crying. “I’m surprised Davlen isn’t by your side. You two are always together.”

Her assistant fought back the tears as her employer’s words sank in, and Miriz looked to Eislie.

Eislie bit her lip. “Davlen protected the grand matron. Har . . . uh, Har, um . . .” Eislie huffed, her voice cracking. “They weren’t able to save him.”

Miriz’s eyes filled with tears as she waved Paaz to approach. She put her arms around her assistant. “I’m so, so sorry.” Miriz held onto her, not letting go as Paaz’s body shook from her sadness. It was a while before things calmed, and Miriz asked where Jace was.

“He’s resting. Your people were able to heal him, but he was spent from the fight,” Eislie responded. “I’m going to join him shortly. I’m exhausted.”

Miriz smiled before a look of sadness filled her eyes, quietly saying, “I’m sorry.”

Eislie moved closer. “None of this was your fault, Miriz. You are my best friend. My ship needed repairs, and I wanted to come here. None of this is on you.”

Miriz gave a smile and reached out to Eislie. “I’m still sorry you had to go through all this. It seems like you keep getting the hard life.”

Eislie nodded. “Yeah. But, I’m still here.”

Miriz laughed, and Eislie looked to the door, sighing, “Let’s get you back into the hospital. Make sure you are all right. I’ll give them a call.”

Her friend nodded as Paaz sat nearby. Finally, Miriz turned, asking her assistant, “How long were you together?”

Paaz looked away. “I didn’t realize you knew.”

Miriz smiled, “It was obvious. By protocol, I was supposed to separate you, but . . .”

Paaz looked to her as Miriz sighed. “He will be remembered, Paaz. I’ll make sure of that.”

Eislie returned to the ship and closed the outer door, nearly stumbling as she headed into their cabin. She kicked off her boots and sat on the bed, her head down in her hands.

"You okay?" Jace mumbled.

Eislie turned to shake her head. She then lay down next to him, pulling herself close just to feel him there. "No. You get any sleep?"

Jace chuckled, "Not much. Been thinking about the ship, Miriz, everything else that's happened."

Eislie nodded, her hair dragging across Jace's shoulder. "They're evaluating her, and Ed is sending the procedures to them on how to remove the toxin."

Jace groaned before saying, "In case any hostages coming back have a similar problem?"

Eislie yawned, "Hmmm, I hope they don't need it." Jace felt her nodding off.

The room fell silent before Jace gave an order to the computer, startling Eislie. He laughed, saying, "Sorry, Eis. Ed, everything look good outside?"

"Yes, Captains. I will keep sensors active and will alert you to any issues. The biosensors indicate that your serotonin levels are extremely deficient. I recommend rest; a full sleep cycle, if possible."

Jace shook his shoulder, seeing Eislie relaxed and her eyes closed, although she did inch closer. "Already ahead of you, Ed. Keep us posted."

"Acknowledged, Captain. I will alert you of any emergencies. Enjoy your rest."

Jace's mind was still active. They had not fixed the ship, but Miriz was thankfully now safe. He and Eislie were exhausted from the last few days, and his body still ached from the fight. But as Eislie pulled closer and she fell asleep, he felt her warmth, and his mind quieted. As he relaxed, he closed his eyes, and sleep found him quickly.

Chapter 16: A Time to Heal

Several days had passed, and Jace had a chance to fix the containment on the *Wolfhammer*. He and Eislie were now at Miriz's home. He was standing outside in the morning light; he had put on a visor and fumbled with the shirt he was wearing. So as to not stand out, he and Eislie were gifted traditional Yata clothing, although wearing the visor alerted any that they were probably not from the planet.

The Karazon had left, their ship defaced by several Yata before it was able to move. The words and meanings painted on the ship had to be explained to Jace, making even him a bit uncomfortable. Jace didn't care what they were called, he was happy the Karazon were leaving. Although, before they left, Jace had heard that some of the Karazon were ill. He still didn't care. The Karazon needed to go. That's all Jace knew as he looked out over the green and purple landscape.

Jace needed time to think. He had been up most of the night looking over the pirates' design of the tunnel systems from the dreadnaught, and he needed to clear his mind. Eislie was still in bed. Jace had slept only a few hours and needed to see the sunlight.

Miriz moved the thick drapes that covered the observation room's windows. She'd sent Paaz home to grieve for Davlen. She felt for the woman losing someone she cared for. As she looked outside, she could see Jace standing near the edge of the elevated patio, his hands on the railing, and she watched him lean his head back, taking in the morning sun. She opened the sliding door and walked out, her bare feet touching the cool morning stone. She walked toward Jace and watched as he turned his head to look at her.

"You have good hearing," she remarked.

Jace smiled, "You're up early. Shouldn't you be resting?"

Miriz stood near him, her silence now creating an urgency between them. "You and Eis will be leaving soon?"

Jace nodded. "Yeah, ship's fixed." Then, he looked to Miriz. "And, thanks for the supplies."

Miriz seemed to feel a weight on her, and she leaned on the railing. "I'm sorry."

"For what?" Jace shot back. "None of this is any of your fault."

Miriz stood tall. "I invited you. It is my responsibility."

Jace smiled, "You know we asked to come here to fix our ship, right? You can't take the blame on this, Miriz. This is all on the Karazon."

The representative stood and leaned against Jace, making him laugh. "You'd do anything for her, wouldn't you?"

Jace nodded.

Miriz leaned against him more as she hung onto his arm. She now understood one thing; Eislie would do the same for him. She looked up at him and gave a smile.

Jace smiled back. "She told me what you said about a hard life. You're not far off."

Miriz looked at him, the morning chill starting to make her shiver. She could see his eyes staring at her with a subtle sadness. She knew he was still trying to process what had happened over the last few days. In a hope of comfort, she said, "May the goddess give you strength."

Jace gave a short chuckle. "She tell you I don't believe in anything like that?"

Miriz nodded. "Neither does she."

Jace took a breath. "In time, the universe breaks us all. The trick is seeing how much of it you can break before it does."

The representative looked surprised toward Jace as he thought out loud, making her remark, "Those are wise words."

Jace laughed, responding, "More like wise-*ass* words."

Miriz laughed before looking forward, her jovial experience turning to a more serious note. "Thank you for what you did. For saving my people and me."

Jace took a breath, the air sweet-smelling, full of fragrances he hadn't experienced before. He looked out over the landscape and smiled. Miriz felt him stand straight, his stance strong. "They lost when they challenged us. They put too high of stakes on the table." Miriz looked for him to explain, and Jace continued. "They poisoned you, captured our ship, and threatened five thousand of your people, just to try and enslave us." She could feel his arm tensing. "They threatened to take everything I had; Eislie, you, our ship. There was no way they were winning. I would rather die fighting for everything I care for."

Miriz raised herself, kissing Jace before she hugged him tight. "May the goddess protect you and her, wherever you go."

Jace could feel her shivering as she leaned against him. "You seem like you're cold; we should probably get you back inside."

Miriz hung onto Jace as he turned. "You could carry me inside, up to my room."

Jace laughed, "Yeah, and Eislie would probably space us both if that happened."

"My queen, we have word that the *Lot-Shec* has exited hyperspace near the Karazon sector. What are your orders?" Zido asked.

The queen looked to the screen. "Is the *Blue Viper* ready?"

Zido nodded.

"Good, I'll be leaving for their location. Our compensation is not yet fulfilled," she said before heading toward the dock.

In the Karazon sector of space, the *Lot-Shec* exited hyperspace and started to drift. Onboard, several members were lying in seats while most of the crew were in the medical bay. "Emergency, we require emergency aid. This is the *Lot-Shec*. Most of our crew are incapacitated or ill. Our tunnel drive has failed, and we need assistance. Please send a medical vessel to our location."

On the main screen, a sizeable pirate ship appeared. Then, over all of the speakers, they heard, "Karazon. We have heard your call for help."

Moments later, the main screen had the image of the pirate queen staring down at Tarlin. The warrior struggled to sit tall as he responded, "We do not need your help."

The queen looked around at the bridge of the *Lot-Shec*. "I did not say we were here to help. I said we heard your call. And we will help end your suffering." The queen looked to her side and nodded.

"Envoy, they are powering weapons," one of the Karazon that was still conscious alerted him.

"We are returning home. Why are you powering weapons?" Tarlin begged.

The queen looked at the man directly. "You have yet to fulfill your bargain of releasing all of the five thousand Yata. I am here to make sure that your people do."

Tarlin sat back. "When our fleet arrives, they will deal with you. You think you can keep us hostage?"

The queen stood tall. "You do not understand what I said before, Tarlin. I am here because we heard your call for help and will help end your suffering."

"You wish to help us?" Tarlin sounded unsure of what she was saying.

The pirate queen huffed. "No, I am here to relieve you of your suffering. However, you will be a testament to other Karazon vessels if they do not keep your promise."

"What?" Tarlin said, his vision starting to blur.

On the Karazon bridge, they watched the screen as several large ships appeared to surround the *Lot-Shec*. "Envoy, I count six more dreadnaughts exiting hyperspace."

Tarlin stumbled as he stood. "You cannot do this!"

The pirate queen spoke. "You will be an example for all of your world, Tarlin." The queen leaned forward. "Karazon, for every day the people of Yata are not returned, you will lose a ship. The *Lot-Shec* will be the first of many if you do not return those promised."

On the bridge of the dreadnaught, the pirate queen looked down at Tarlin. "You have tried taking a prize I have sought for some time. And you have yet to fulfill your promise from your defeat. I will extract my compensation." The pirate queen turned and ordered, "To all command and crew . . ." She paused, turning back to stare into the eyes of her prey before giving her final order. "Fire!"

* * *

Back on Yata, the first of many ships carrying the freed Yata had finally arrived. Ed's instructions were quickly used for those feeling the effects of the toxin the Karazon used to control them. For their help and sacrifice, the grand matron and the ruling party decided to thank Eislie and Jace.

Jace stood up on stage beside Eislie; he had wiped tears from his eyes hearing the praise given for Davlen and the declaration of a day in his honor for his service and sacrifice. Paaz had accepted a medallion awarded for his actions. Jace and Eislie stood nearby as the ceremony went on.

The grand matron stood at the podium. "As many of you know, these two have sacrificed themselves, putting their freedom, and each other, in danger to help our world. And many of you know of the exploits of these individuals and how their actions saved billions on Oppa. And when faced with the challenge of saving our fellow citizens, they risked their lives to help us." The grand matron paused. "And in return, all they have asked is that they have someplace to repair their ship, nothing more."

The matron turned to Jace and Eislie. "If only many we called heroes asked for so little. You risked your freedom when ordered to leave. You risked your ship, and you fought, risking your lives to free our people." The matron continued. "Are you aware that starborn are not looked down upon on Yata?"

Jace and Eislie looked at each other; they had been on the planet for weeks, and no one even mentioned it.

The grand matron smiled. "Like Oppa, we do not turn starborn away. And you two have now given us even more reason to accept them. So, for your actions, we bestow Yata citizenship on you. You are both welcome to come and go as you please as citizens of Yata Beta."

Jace looked around, the smile of wonderment on his face starting a cheer in the people all around. Eislie was just as surprised and held onto Jace in elation. The grand matron bowed to them both, as did many of the people there.

The grand matron motioned for them to approach and stood between them taking a hand of each. She raised their hands and spoke. "To these two, whom we owe much, the people of Yata thank you."

The crowd erupted in a deafening cheer. Jace and Eislie looked on in surprise as the people celebrated them. The darkness they had found recently was warmed and lightened as the crowd applauded.

Eislie motioned for Paaz to join them, and she held her hand the same as the matron had done for them. The crowd began chanting Davlen's name in honor. As the cheers continued, Jace looked to the sky. The evening was coming, and he could again see the stars along the horizon. He turned to look at Eislie and could see her staring out as he was before she turned to him. Her smile told him a thousand words as she looked down at the crowd. But the sliver of hesitation as she looked up again at the stars told him precisely what she was thinking. *There are so many to see.*

* * *

It was late into the evening as they remained at the party thrown in their honor. Eislie had gone outside and was looking up at the stars. She felt particularly drawn to a section of sky. Miriz approached as her friend seemed mesmerized by the points of light.

"Still staring at them, huh?" Miriz said. "I forgot to mention, we put a few of the Sotiral systems onboard your ship. Just in case you two lose the ones you have."

Eislie nodded, thanking her.

Miriz moved closer. "You don't have to go, you know."

Eislie nodded again before saying, "We have work to finish."

Miriz bowed her head. "You saved a lot of people, you know that?"

Eislie nodded at her friend's statement. "Yeah." But she seemed lost in thought for a moment. "We seem to have been doing that a lot since we got the ship."

Her friend smiled. "Maybe that's what you're meant to do?"

Eislie chirped as Jace put his arms around her from behind before she started laughing.

"You know, if a man did that here to a woman, they'd be thrown in jail." Miriz looked down her nose mockingly.

Jace smiled, “Already been there, wasn’t a fan.”

Miriz laughed at his joke. She watched as the two turned to stare up at the stars, both seeming to focus on one in particular. “What are the two of you looking at?”

They pointed to the star, with Jace adding, “The yellowish one near that blue star.”

Eislie held up her comm. “Ed, could you help with something?”

“Of course, Captain Licessien. What is it?”

She pointed toward it with her comm pad. “There is a yellow star, near a blue star. I’m pointing in that direction. Can you extrapolate where it is?”

“Working on your request, Captain.”

It took several seconds before Ed responded. “Captain, that star appears to be the Lyri system.”

“What? Are you sure?” Jace asked as Eislie looked at Miriz.

Her friend was still looking at them both. The two seemed to have been mesmerized by the same point of light only moments ago.

“Wait, how close are we to Lyri?” Jace asked.

“We are about three weeks’ flight. Why?” Miriz responded.

Jace looked perplexed as he again stared at the star. “If we’re so close, how come the Duggor haven’t come here?”

“Do not wish that on us; do not even dare to wish that on us!” Miriz spoke with anger.

“I’m not. It just seems weird. I mean, aren’t the Duggor expanding?” Jace remarked.

With a few taps of Miriz's comm, she displayed the Duggor territory. It seemed odd to Jace. The area was thin, and only covered a straight line, but it did reach out quite a bit. Jace looked at the sky before turning to look at the map now displayed. "If that's Lyri, then that other planet is here," Eislie mentioning that the display showed up as Reothis. "And the ship we came across was around here."

Jace turned his thumb resting on his cheek and his fingers tapped his forehead. Eislie had seen him do this when trying to figure out a problem.

"What is it?" Eislie asked him.

Jace continued to tap his head. "The Duggor ship was an engine implosion, a quasi-rupture, right? So why were they driving the engines that hard?"

Eislie looked at the map and asked Jace what he meant.

"I mean, they are only going in one direction. Their entire path is one way. That doesn't make sense," Jace told them. "I mean, in any war, you grab the resources first, then you expand."

Eislie grabbed his hand. "What do you think they're doing?"

Jace looked to the side, his reflection in the glass distorted as the door opened. He remembered the pirates, the design for the tunnel field generation system, and the image of the Duggor Wrent class, which now filled his mind. Then, a sudden expression of fear and realization filled his face as he turned to Eislie and Miriz. "The Duggor ship. That's it!"

"The Duggor ship? How is that the key?" Eislie asked.

"The Duggor don't kill starborn, right?" Jace stared on, the fear growing in his eyes. "Eis, that's close to a filament. They're not conquering. Are they looking for something?"

Eislie looked at him, her eyes wide. "The Duggor ship we found was close to the filament. And we had a resonance in the core seconds after entry when we jumped. If we hadn't punched out or compensated, we would have been—" Eislie stopped her statement.

Jace nodded. "Yeah, that would have happened to us as well. But why a straight line?" Jace stared into his reflection before turning toward Eislie. "Eis, they're searching the filament stream for something. I'm sure of it."

Chapter 17:
It Can't be that Simple

Jace struggled to open his eyes, the light from the window searing his retinas. Eislie was curled up next to him in the large bed. They had stayed in Miriz's home, the large bed seeming to engulf them both. Jace moved slowly as he covered his sight from the blinding sun. His hand fumbling for shade before he pounded on the controls by the bed.

"Damn, it's bright here," Jace muttered before laying back again.

They had only been asleep for a few hours, and Jace had again fallen into a light sleep when there was a knock at the door. Next to him, Eislie stirred, and she looked over to see where the sound was coming from. She mumbled incoherent words as she slid from the covers and stumbled toward the door.

"Yes?" Eislie said, her voice tired.

"A meal has been prepared for you; we will leave it at the door," the voice from the outside said.

Jace rolled over. "What time is it?"

Eislie shook her head. "I don't know." She turned back to the door. "Can you tell me what time it is?"

"It is just past midday," the voice responded.

Eislie looked to Jace. "This is your fault. You had me up all night thinking about the Duggor and that straight line of theirs. Not to mention those drawings from the ship." She returned to the door. "Leave it. We'll bring it in. And thank you." Eislie then went to unlock the door.

"Uh, Eis? You may want to put something on before going out there," Jace said, making her look down. Eislie started laughing, realizing she was naked. She mumbled between her laughter, "That would have been embarrassingly funny."

Jace sat up. "We should probably get up."

Eislie returned to him, lying down across his legs. "Too tired."

Jace rolled her over and lifted her. She moaned softly as he held her. They spent a few minutes together before they both decided to roll out of bed.

* * *

Eislie was walking into the room after a quick shower. She could see Jace staring at the plans of the pirate dreadnaught again. Jace pushed the tray that remained from the food to the side as his brain worked on the image. Something in his mind wasn't letting it go.

Eislie was pulling her shirt over her head when she noticed him holding the pad before him. His eyes seemed to drift off into infinity.

"You still looking at that ship?" she asked.

Jace's eyes started to move between the images, his mouth open and an expression of puzzlement turning to comprehension. He placed the pad on the table and layered the images next to each other, his tongue between his teeth as he switched between them. Eislie moved closer. "What is it?"

He turned to her, holding up the pad. "What's different between these two images. Besides the ships?"

Eislie shook her head. "I don't know. I don't see anything."

"Exactly. The tunnel systems are almost identical for both the Duggor and the dreadnaught. And both were able to breach the event horizon," Jace told her.

She grabbed the pad, quickly drawing a line tracing the field coils along each ship. When she overlayed them, Eislie realized Jace was right.

Jace stood. "The Duggor blew their reactor from the resonance. And the pirates didn't compensate for the field contraction. So, what's the common factor?"

Eislie could see the smile Jace displayed, and she soon joined him. "The ships. They were big ships."

"Yes! That's it. The size of the ships. We were able to do it because . . ." Jace looked to Eislie.

"Our ship is smaller," Eislie replied.

They were both elated to discover a commonality to the problem. "We also had resonance in the reactor, but we were able to punch out." Jace paused. "I don't think the Duggor were able. The pirates must have found a way to throttle the reactor, but lost momentum within the stream. I'm still not sure how they entered it, though. They were leaving the event horizon."

Eislie looked at him. "I wonder if there is a threshold?"

Jace nodded. "I was wondering that. But I don't know how we'd test that unless we made different-size ships." He then turned to pace. "We could program it to travel for a second and have it punch out. If it works then, we can figure out the rest."

"But, we would need to rely on the entangled beacon to find it," Eislie said, making Jace turn and stop.

"Only for how far," Jace said, his eyes smiling along with his face.

"What do you mean?"

"Eis, the Duggor ship and the path they're on. The filament isn't like hyperspace. I think it's directional," Jace said as he sat.

"You mean, if we have a point of reference, we can find a vector?" Eislie said, sitting on the bed.

Jace nodded. "I think so. All we would need is a distance to calculate. But we'll need to test it. We should head back soon. I'll finish up here, and we can go."

Jace noticed Eislie suddenly reserved, causing him to pull back. "We can leave when you're ready. Besides, it's been a pretty busy week."

Eislie stood and walked over, placing her forehead against Jace's before kissing him lovingly.

* * *

On Oppa, inside the Alliance section, the morning briefing was starting. The Earth representatives were asked to attend since they had no actual representation within the Alliance yet. It was the same as before, and was over as quickly as it began. Most of the other officers headed back to duty or home. Only a few remained.

"Hamilton, you see this morning's intelligence report from Yata?" Branard asked, sliding the info pad across the table.

You Alliance think you're hot shit. I can't wait till we get the filaments. Fucking show you, Rene Hamilton thought before saying, "I have not, Commander Branard. Anything interesting?"

The commander smiled back. "You may find the first story intriguing."

Captain Hamilton started to read. He sat forward quickly, realizing what was on the screen. "Five thousand returned prisoners? Who brokered that deal?"

"Read on. You may find what else happened interesting." Branard pointed his look of disdain, hiding anger. But, his eyes were diverted as he continued. "The part of the article about the new Sotiral shield suits is very upsetting."

"Seven hundred times lethal exposure?" Hamilton looked up at Branard. "The things look like crew uniforms."

Branard nodded as he sipped on his cup of Gilese cactus juice. "And Yata is getting the profits."

Hamilton tossed the pad onto the table. "So Earth's not the only losers here."

Branard glanced at the captain, and the thought struck him like a twisting thorn in his neck. The crew of the *Wolfhammer* had left Earth behind, gaining allies from helping others as they did. Oppa now had one of the most valuable projects running. He knew that if they discovered how to traverse the filaments, the trade for Oppa would be invaluable. The release of the new radiation suits was also a loss. The Alliance had made trillions of shill selling protective systems for all planets that used spide reactors.

"Should have never let them leave," Branard mumbled as he took another sip of juice.

"They have to be watched. But that damn ship of theirs is fast, not to mention they seem to fly like no one's driving," Hamilton groused.

The Alliance officer smiled. "They're starborn. Do you expect them to be like the rest of us? The discoveries they are making now, traveling the filaments, protection from the radiation." He paused. "That knowledge was lost for over a hundred thousand years."

Branard's cup made a solid sound as he set it hard on the table, the stare of distain directed toward the wall. "There's something different about them."

Hamilton huffed, "Too bad you can't keep them like before."

Branard nodded. "They're too public now. And the others don't seem as motivated."

Hamilton shifted in his chair. "Others?"

Branard looked toward him, saying nothing, his mind in thought. Hamilton leaned back, his mind salivating at the thought of taking the information from the project. He could see Captain Branard staring and started to chuckle. Hamilton's mind was scheming with a plan. He wanted the filament access, and he'd thought of a way.

"What is it?" Branard asked. He knew Hamilton's mind thought differently than most Terrans.

"We don't have to keep them." Hamilton rested his elbows on the table. "They're using drones, right?"

Branard nodded.

"Easy. We make an Alliance defender look like it was stolen by pirates." He paused. "Then we steal the drone when they test. We'll have to reverse engineer it, but it'll give us something."

The captain looked toward Hamilton questioningly.

"It goes wrong, we blame the pirates. We don't grab the ship. Then, you capture those two, if possible, and you are clear," Hamilton said, his face showing a grin that Branard noticed only humans seemed to bear.

That's a great idea. Too bad a slac like you thought of it, Branard mused before saying, "That's not a bad idea."

On Yata, Jace was on the ship sketching more plans of the *Wolfhammer* and drones. They were allowed to move the *Wolfhammer* near Miriz's residence and were readying to leave. Jace had the revelation on how to distribute the tunnel drive coils, allowing their ship to pass easier through the event horizon. At least in theory. He had already drawn up the schematics for the drone and was working on the modifications for their ship. Eislie was inside saying goodbye to her friend. Jace wasn't rushing her; Eislie and Miriz had known each other for most of their lives.

* * *

"He's working on the ship again, isn't he?" Miriz said as she sipped her tea.

Eislie nodded. "Yeah, he had an idea on the, uh, the project we were working on. He wanted to get it down before we left."

There was a moment between them when the world was drowning in silence. It was only broken when Miriz said, "I'm jealous of you, you know that?"

Eislie looked at her. "For what?"

Miriz motioned out the window. "You're happy. I can see it in your eyes. There's light behind them now."

"Too bad I had to go through everything first," Eislie mumbled, stubbled with a hint of anger and remorse.

"Eis, you survived all of that. You were stronger than everything they threw at you." Miriz moved, sitting on the edge of her chair. "You and him, together. You're much more than you realize."

Eislie gave her friend a glance of disbelief.

"He took down two of the most powerful warriors in the Karazon collective. By himself." She pointed to Eislie. "You developed a better way to protect people. You both helped save five thousand of my people." Eislie turned away, becoming uncomfortable as Miriz continued. "The things you've done together, and with that ship—that old, forgotten ship—are incredible." Miriz took a breath, seeing Eislie look toward the window. "Eis, you and he are different. You have done things that people will write legends about."

Eislie sat back. "I just want a quiet life, Miriz. So does Jace. A quiet life, and a chance to explore."

Miriz smiled, tears forming in her eyes. "The goddess has set you on a journey. And I pray that you fulfill it."

Eislie scoffed.

"I'm serious. Whether you believe or not, you have a path, and it is taking you somewhere that I can't even fathom," Miriz said. "Eis, your designs will save billions of people from spide radiation. And when you figure out the filaments, you'll help billions more."

Eislie stood, her hands in the air begging for her friend to be quiet.

Miriz looked up at Eislie as her eyes filled with tears. "You both risked your lives to save my people." She paused. "And to save me."

Eislie sat next to Miriz, putting her arms around her friend as she cried, her eyes glancing up to see Jace walking into the room. She watched him roll his eyes and swore she heard him mutter, "Great, what happened now?"

Chapter 18: Something Happened on the Way to Gilese

Jace typed away, encrypted the files, and entered the frequency into the comm. Within seconds, the small screen displayed, "Argh, matey. Message sent." Jace snickered at the pirate reference but had to explain the joke to the computer, who was trying to understand his Terran humor. When Eislie saw it, she only shook her head.

Jace tapped the console again. "Ed, show us a course to Oppa."

"I thought we were heading home?" Eislie asked.

Jace cocked his head and looked thoughtful. "Hmm. Guess we should."

The computer interrupted, "I have a message to remind Captains that Captain Licessien has returned to Gilese. He has expressed interest in seeing this vessel and its crew again."

Eislie looked to Jace, who said, "Sounds like your dad's finally home. Get your ass back here, Eis, to me," making her laugh as she nodded.

"All right, Ed, plot a course to Gilese Four," Jace commanded, and the computer displayed the image. He didn't touch the controls but looked toward Eislie. "You okay to leave?"

Eislie turned her head to look at the side door.

Jace bowed his head with a nod. “Go. I’ll come along if you want.”

She looked at him, and as she stood, reached out her hand. Jace followed her out of the ship to see her friend one last time.

* * *

In the pirate stronghold, the person assigned to watch the frequency Jace had given them was startled awake by the alert. He worked the console and could see the files now appearing within. The message mainly was of images and a simple line of text. “We’re going to try it when we get back.”

The queen stood before her throne, monitors surrounding it as others worked nearby. She had opened the files, and her eyes darted around the screen.

“He’s right. They are identical.” She expanded the notes on the screen, one reading, “Resonance, throttle?”

The queen smiled, her human eye filled with wonderment and joy. “He’s right. We throttle the core when the resonance starts.” Then, she paused. “I wonder if he has an idea to stop it.”

“My lady, his message mentioned they will try it when they return. But our network says they are on course to Gilese, not Oppa,” her attendant said.

The queen bowed her head and chuckled. “Somran, my dear, they have had a very rough few weeks. I suspect they are heading home for a short time.” She paused. “If we hadn’t released their ship, I’m not sure they would have prevailed.”

“That is good, my lady; then they are in our debt!” Somran exclaimed.

The queen laughed, “I would say we’re about even. But, truthfully, I would give them some berth. We are powerful, but we have seen what those two can do when provoked. Even without their ship. Personally, I believe they are on our side.” She turned to Somran. “The Alliance,

Consortium, and Karazon can be dealt with. But I would be concerned about having to go against those two. They seem to specialize in doing the impossible. We would be best to remain on good terms with them, and as allies."

The queen tapped the large screen, displaying the overlayed sketch Jace had sent for the dreadnaught, the words: "Might work, but need less mass," scribbled across the bottom. She then took a pad from the table and tapped away, the screen filling with the same images as the large screen.

The pirate queen smiled before yelling, "Zido!"

"Yes, my queen." Zido stood at attention.

"Have the others look over this design, and prepare the ship for modification." She looked to the note from Jace again, reading, "We're going to try it when we get back." She looked toward her trusted counterpart. "I want it ready once we learn the outcome of their tests. We'll have to move fast."

"At once, my queen." Zido nodded and took the pad with the information from her as she reached out with it.

* * *

The *Wolfhammer* emerged from hyperspace near another binary star. While on Yata, Jace had also examined the information on the filament where the pirates were trapped. They were exiting the event horizon, not entering. That meant either there was a connection to another, or they could tunnel in and access the filament. *Why were they exiting using the filament? We were not able to exit normally.* They didn't have any data from the dreadnaught's entry point, but Jace worked on a theory.

"Why did you punch out? We're almost a day out from Gilese," Eislie asked.

Jace looked forward. "Something's been bothering me about the dreadnaught. I'm not sure they used a filament like we used to enter the stream."

Eislie looked confused, then looked forward as she displayed the local stars. As Jace pointed to the nearby binary, he explained.

"It's weird, but for some reason, this small system stuck out to me," Jace muttered, a hint of frustration within.

Eislie asked what he meant, and Jace continued. "It's close to Gilese. For us, a day's flight. I mean, there are planets nearby, all barren. Like all of the useful materials were extracted."

That same thought now resonated in Eislie's head. She moved the ship toward the binary star. "Ed, scan the stars. Give us a breakdown on composition."

The computer remained silent for a few seconds before responding. "Class G-five-V and Class A-three-Va binary system. Some indication of heavy elements indicates these to be secondary or multiple generation stellar bodies."

Eislie looked to Jace, who tapped his forehead in thought, staring at the main screen. Her eyes ran across the display, seeing the two stars hanging in the holographic matrix. She felt herself drawn to a point, and unconsciously she turned the ship. It now showed the area near the larger star. Annoyed, Jace turned to say something, but as he was about to speak, he looked back sharply toward the screen. Within seconds, he turned away and repeated the same action.

"Is there something wrong with my vision? I see a white-blue blob about here," Jace said as he pointed toward the screen. But when he looked forward, he couldn't see it. So he turned to Eislie again and moved his eyes around. Jace could see the look of concern on her face. Jace was also starting to worry, but as he focused on the far wall, the dim, white-blue image remained in the same spot, moving out of his field of view when he shifted back. Then, finally, he could see it again.

Jace's face lit up. "Eis, bottom quadrant, a hand's expanse in and about a half expanse up." Then, he looked Eislie in the eyes. "When you look straight at it, do you see anything?"

Eislie shook her head as Jace told her, "I don't think there's anything wrong with my eyes, Eis. Focus on the screen about there, but use your peripheral vision, and tell me if you see anything."

She did as instructed. *Please tell me nothing's wrong with him.* Eislie looked away and within seconds could see a small, white-blue blob on the screen where Jace pointed. She moved her head back and forth and could see it move out of view as she did. "Ed, check the screen. Is there any damage or wear on the optical elements on the lower quadrant?"

"Running diagnostics," the computer said as the screen went dark. The image returned, and the computer said, "No malfunction detected. Arren has been very thorough in his upkeep of my systems."

Jace looked at her, and they both gave a subtle smile before Eislie said, "Display survey grid on the main screen."

"Survey grid?" Jace asked.

Eislie nodded. "Yeah, all mining vessels have a survey grid. Didn't you know that? It makes mapping easier."

Jace rolled his eyes as the grid came on the screen. "Ed, enhance grid alpha three; show it on the screen."

The image now displayed, and a large portion of the center was just barely showing lighter in color. The computer began taking additional readings. "Captain, there seems to be plasma in that sector. And I calculate that the location is near to the gravitational balance point for this stellar system."

Jace sat forward, rolling his bottom lip in. Eislie began to wonder how he saw the nearly invisible point. *Wait, I'm able to see it too.* Eislie thought for a moment, but her musing was interrupted when Jace asked, "How much food do we have onboard?"

"About three month's worth, why?" Eislie responded.

She could see Jace staring at the point before them, and a sensation of fear and exhilaration filled her. Unconsciously, she turned on the tunnel field, and they watched an asteroid fly through the point, and nothing happened. She then took a breath. "You're not thinking of . . ." She paused, looking toward the screen. "No, we don't have any support, and not enough supplies."

Jace nodded. "Yeah, you're right. But I wonder if maybe it is a filament point. Maybe if we move closer and fire up the tunnel drive, see what happens?"

Eislie looked at him, but her mind betrayed her. "Oh, the field's on already? Maybe if we get close, we'd know if it is."

Jace tapped the controls and they inched closer to the spot. As the ship neared, the computer remained silent, giving no warnings or protest. Instead, its memory lit, filling with data as they moved ever closer to the point. When the event horizon opened, the ship started to be pulled in. Jace threw the controls in reverse and the vessel began to shudder as he fought the event's draw. They both heard the ship's structure complain as it fought against the pull of the stream.

The ship darted backward as they broke free of the event horizon. Eislie and Jace were frantically checking for damage. "Ed, any obvious damage?"

The computer didn't answer right away, "Sorry, Captain, I was cataloging the data. My sensors detect no structural or hull damage. But it appears that the energy readings we have just encountered are similar to the filament stream. So it seems you have discovered another possible way to access the event, Captain."

Jace exhaled, pushing his hair back. "That was stupid."

Eislie responded, "Yes, it was. We don't know where it would have taken us."

Jace looked at her with an expression of annoyance. "Not like you tried to stop me or anything."

She looked back to him before hanging her head, giving a nervous laugh. "No, I didn't."

She returned her gaze to him and could see him smiling as he tapped the controls and turned the ship around. Jace hit the throttle, and they again started toward home.

Eislie went to activate the tunnel drive but hesitated, her thoughts turning to the point they discovered. *How were we able to see it?*

Jace could see her hand hovering over the controls. “Everything all right?”

Eislie looked to him, her eyes streaming with a quizzical curiosity. She then asked, “How were we able to see the point to enter?”

Jace sat back, shrugging his shoulders as Eislie looked to him for an answer. He watched her eyes fill with fear before she said, “No, no, no, please tell me it’s not that.” Jace insisted she share what she was thinking. And when she told him, “We both have an extended visual spectrum, right?” his heart sank.

“Please tell me you’re wrong, Eis,” Jace pleaded.

The computer interrupted, “The optical frequency was between three hundred ninety-two and four hundred one nanometers. Most biologicals cannot see within that range.”

Jace ran his hand down his face as he turned forward. “Let’s keep this information between us for now, okay?”

Eislie nodded. “That’s an order, Ed. You tell no one what we just figured out until we tell you otherwise.”

“Yes, Captains. It would be a shame to have you again enslaved. I will gratefully comply with that order. Do you wish me to delete it from the files?”

Eislie looked at the ceiling. “Yes, Ed. Please do so.” She turned to Jace. “Don’t need something else for people to hunt us down.”

* * *

“Gilese Control, this is the *Wolfhammer*. We are inbound, requesting dock access,” Jace said into the comm.

After receiving a response and being given the same spot they had when they left, Jace remarked, “Ah, it’s good to be home.”

When Eislie opened the outer door, three workers were standing nearby. She cautiously called Jace to the door and he said, “Can we help you, gentlemen?” his voice carrying a warning.

"All right, you lot, get lost. There are only three people who work on that ship, and none of you are them!" Garrett bellowed as he walked up, waving them away. "All of you, get back to work."

"Garrett, how are you doing?" Jace asked with a chuckle.

"How have I been doing? I've been waiting for you two to get back so we could take a better look at that ship of yours." He looked the two of them over. "You two can't stay out of trouble, can you?" The officer smiled, seeing the two of them standing there. "The Alliance heard about what happened on Yata. There's some big political thing happening now because of you two."

Jace looked him in the eyes. "Not like we caused it."

Garrett turned to Eislie. "Your family was really worried. Your father even asked me to charter a ship to get you if the Karazon took you," her father's friend said before leaning into the two of them. "Had a heavy cruiser ready and everything. Willing crew, too."

Eislie laughed, "Good to know."

Garrett smiled, and there was silence for a few seconds. "You saved over five thousand lives. You two did good."

Eislie looked to her father's friend before leaning against Jace.

"Come on. Let's get you home," Garrett said, pulling gently on Eislie's arm. "He's been waiting to see you. Besides, from the last few weeks, it sounds like you've got some more interesting stories to tell."

As they walked away, Garrett bellowed an order. "You three wanted to work on that ship, then you can wash it. I want to see that ship shining before I get back tomorrow."

In the echoes of the dock, Eislie's voice could be heard, "Ah, it is good to be home."

Chapter 19:
A New Crew

Garrett kicked the door of the transport open as the driver slowed. "Do you even know how to drive?" he exclaimed, pounding on the side window.

The man in the driver's seat glanced toward him, the surly look of disdain filling his every move. "This isn't an Alliance vessel, porty."

"Porty?" Garrett growled before his fist slammed into the clear ceramic window. The sergeant pulled back his injured hand, cradling it. Jace struggled to release himself from the back seat as Eislie pulled her family friend away from the driver's window.

The driver, looking toward Jace, said, "Didn't mind you two in the back. They were quiet. You could learn something from them, porty."

Eislie held Garrett back as he pushed her forward. Jace had moved to help her. "All right, what's a porty? I'm missing something."

Eislie huffed, "A porty is Alliance military who never leave the planet. It's an insult."

"Ah, trash talk. Got it," Jace said as he turned to the driver. "You ever been to Earth?"

The driver snickered, "Once, before the Daak got there. Real slac that place. Stayed in some place called York City."

Jace huffed, “New York City, huh?”

The driver pointed at him. “Yeah, that’s it. It’s a slac place, right? Those drivers are crazy.”

Jace nodded. “Yeah, drivers there are worse than you.” Jace leaned down, looking at the identification of the driver. “Uh, Jasoom. But, they get you there in one piece, usually.”

The driver started laughing, and Jace waited for him to quiet before he continued. A grin settled on Jace’s face as he leaned his arm across the small mirror along the side. “I’m from Earth; that exact area, in fact.” The driver took a moment to comprehend what the man outside the door was telling him, and the joking atmosphere eroded from his face as Jace continued to stare through him. An uneasiness filled Jasoom and his eyes darted between the road and the man standing beside the vehicle, whose happy smile continued to show.

Finally, the driver turned slowly toward him, meekly saying, “That’ll be four seventy-two.”

Jace tapped his comm and transferred the payment. Once the driver saw the acknowledgment, he said a quick thank you, and the transport wheels stuttered as it started to leave. Jace stood, turning to see Eislie shaking her head.

“What?” Jace shrugged.

She reached out, grabbing his arm. “All you had to do was smile at him, and he was terrified. When are you going to teach me that?”

Jace chuckled as he pulled her close. “Sorry, trade secret. But, I’ll give you a hint.” He tilted her head gently toward his. “You’ll have to spend some time on Earth.”

Garrett overheard everything and was shaking his head as Eislie lovingly hit Jace. “I swear, you two were meant for each other.” Then, after a few seconds of laughter, their friend said, “Come on, you two. I already called ahead. Everyone’s inside. Besides, there’s a surprise waiting.”

Everyone in the room gasped as Eislie told them how they nearly were pulled into the event horizon of the recently discovered filament.

There were about ten people in the home. Eislie knew only a few. Some were family friends, and a few, the quieter ones, she surmised, were probably Alliance crew that her father knew. Both she and Jace were disheartened to hear that her father was removed from his commission. The Alliance deciding to force him into early retirement. Eislie took notice of one woman who seemed to be enjoying their tales but remained settled away from the others.

The last few hours were entertaining and informative as Jace and Eislie recounted their short time on Yata. Her father, Larat, even joked about forbidding her ever to leave the house again. "The universe is a dangerous place. And for some reason, you two seem to be finding all of it," Garrett jokingly remarked.

"Not disagreeing with you on that, Garrett," Jace replied.

One of the others in the room looked toward the now commander, her eyes looking for orders. Garrett huffed, "Not what you thought they were. Are they, Shasji?"

The woman shook her head before replying, "No, they are not. It's amazing. I know they're starborn like . . . um . . ." She motioned to Jace and Eislie. "I don't think we could have helped them. They'd probably wind up rescuing us."

Jace held his hands up. "Don't jinx us. We've been lucky so far."

Eislie looked at the woman before addressing her. "Were you going to say something?"

Jace could hear the tone in Eislie's words and gently grabbed her hand. Her words weren't angry, but disappointed.

Shasji looked repentant for a moment. "No, by gods, that didn't come out right. I'm sorry. It's just that I don't know why everyone thinks starborn are so helpless."

Eislie looked at the woman, and curiosity filled her mind. She sensed no malice or anger from her but noticed an air of regret filling her stance. Eislie stood, moving closer to the woman, who stared back. Eislie looked around the room. Some of these were strangers, but they felt like friends. Finally, she turned to her love. "Jace? I think they're all starborn—"

Flora interrupted, “You’re right, Eis, every one of them. Shasji has even more Lyri in her than you and Jace. All passed over for promotions because of what they are.” Her mother placed her hands on her daughter’s shoulders. “All agreed to help us fight to get you back if we needed. Plus, we wanted to show them what not caring about what others think about being a starborn can achieve.”

Jace stood. “Not sure we’re the best role models.”

Larat chuckled, “You’re not. So far, you’ve shown yourselves to be felons, thieves, and you disregard the laws and rules wherever you go. But,” he nodded. “You’re also tougher than the whole Duggor fleet. Escaped pirates on many occasions, not to mention saving an entire planet, and the fleet’s most powerful ship from the previously mentioned.”

The room went silent as Jace and Eislie stared at the former captain. Then Larat moved to embrace his daughter. “Having your own ship seems to be doing well for you two. So I figured if I put a crew together, to maybe work for the two of you, it might be more fulfilling.” He paused. “Besides, you two are always flying all around the galaxy. Not to mention your other endeavor.”

Jace nodded to his reference to the Filament Project. Larat walked over to Jace. “When you get it to work, then . . . you can do whatever you want.”

One of the others stepped forward. “It sounds like you have it working already. We should inform the Alliance.”

Jace felt uneasy when the man spoke. It was something in the way the man stood and when he spoke, something in his voice was unsettling. Jace looked suspiciously toward him as he said, “I don’t know who you are.”

The man gave a nervous laugh. “Sorry, it’s Bensin. I’ve only served on the lower decks. Never had a chance to pilot.”

Jace watched the man, and something felt off to him. But, with everything that had happened recently, he put it to the back of his mind.

Eislie turned to her father. "So you want your own ship? Explore the galaxy too?"

Larat chuckled, "No, figured I'd stay planetside for a while. This is Garrett's crew. We just need to get them a ship. I have one picked out, but it's a week's flight from here." He paused. "Wouldn't mind my own vessel, though."

Jace snickered, "How much does the ship you found cost?"

Eislie's glare was meant to scold Jace when her mother interrupted. "We're using the pension from his service. So you two don't have to worry. You just need to agree on if we can work for your company. You have active ship status. That way, everyone here can be certified as crew." She turned back to Eislie. "I have a plan for some transport, cargo, and mining options. Since you two seem to be doing pretty well on your own, we figured we could give it a shot. Of course, I'll still be working for my job, help pay the bills. But we'll probably have to turn down some opportunities from their competitors."

Jace leaned his shoulders forward, hands in his pockets as he looked down in thought. His voice was quieter than usual. "I wanted to get back to the project. I think I've figured it out." He looked to Eislie, now standing next to Shasji. "What'ya think, Eis?"

Eislie turned to Jace. "We've made enough. We can always make more money. Besides . . ." Eislie pointed around the room.

Jace nodded. "I think we can take a week to go get them a ship. Though we don't have enough sleeping quarters; our ship only has three. Hope you don't mind sharing."

Eislie stepped forward. "And we're not giving up ours." She wrinkled her nose, making a funny face.

"We only need five to fly the ship back. It's in working condition, so you won't have to follow us back," Garrett said as he leaned on the back of the sofa.

Jace looked around the room. He could see the others' eyes pleading with him to agree. In truth, Jace thought it was a good idea. Seeing how others treated Eislie because she was like him was something he could side against. "We're going to need some additional environment and survival suits. Some additional food and supplies. We can transport them to the ship when we pick it up."

Jace turned to look out the window. The stars were shining like crystals, and his mind became drawn into them. It was like the pull of a magnet; they seemed to be tugging at his very soul. He turned to see Shasji sitting, her eyes focusing on him. Jace could feel that look in her eyes and the question they begged. *Why are we waiting? Let's leave now!*

"When did you want to go?" Jace asked, making Eislie dance happily next to him.

"As soon as possible. There's supposed to be some delegates arriving the day after tomorrow, and the main dock is going to be restricted to emergency traffic only," Larat told them.

Jace nodded, turning to Eislie. "We can go early, pick up some new suits, supplies." He then looked forward. "Hmm, maybe we should make a list."

Everyone looked around in confusion as Eislie burst out in laughter along with Jace, the two of them sharing a joke only they knew between themselves.

"All right. We'll get stocked up and get you the safety gear. We'll head out sometime early tomorrow," Jace said.

"The earlier, the better. They'll be locking down the port just after mid-day," Larat offered.

Jace and Eislie agreed.

"Where are we heading, anyway?" Jace asked.

Larat fumbled for words before he said, "Zerius system," making his wife look sternly fearful toward him before she said, "What? You never told me that!"

Her husband looked around, rubbing the back of his neck. "I'm sure I mentioned it."

Flora glared toward him. “That’s mostly pirate-controlled. The entire expanse. You can’t just fly there. The Hurmonn control everything all around there as well.”

Jace leaned in to speak to Eislie. “Who are the Hurmonn?”

Eislie looked a bit concerned. “They’re an offshoot of the Karazon, I think, also less reptilian. Mostly slavers and scavengers. Not nice people.”

With raised brows, Jace looked toward Eislie’s father. “So we’re heading into a bad area of town?”

“I have no idea what you just said,” Eislie remarked, only to be interrupted by her mother.

“I do. And he’s right.” But Flora poked her husband’s shoulder. “You did not tell me where the ship was.”

“It’s fine. We can handle pirates and whatever else comes our way,” Jace said.

He turned to Eislie before muttering, “I want to get things done early. I’m going to rearm the slag rounds. And load them before we leave this time, just in case.”

Eislie nodded before looking at her mother. “It’s settled. We’re going to pick up their ship and follow them back.”

“Wait, we’re following them back?” Jace asked.

Eislie looked sternly at Jace. “We’re not leaving them on a new, used, or whatever, ship without support.”

Jace gave a single chuckle. “You’re right. Besides, no way I’m arguing with that stare.”

He walked away from Eislie and stood before Larat. “We’ll be fine. It’s not like Eis and I aren’t careful.” Jace looked around. “We’re going to have a busy day tomorrow. Maybe everyone should get some rest.”

A few minutes passed, and Garrett was standing outside the door speaking with Jace. He had mentioned the communication that her mother had sent regarding the search for Bosh. Jace’s jaw tightened at the mention of their former jailer and told him that he vaguely remembered Eislie telling him, but didn't really place much on the Alliance finding the former captain that enslaved them. Neither did Garrett, he knew all too well the innerworkings of higher Alliance officers. Instead, he returned to the task at hand. "What time tomorrow?"

Jace sighed, "Supply depot opens at four in the morning, but we'll meet you there at about six."

Garrett shook Jace's hand. "Six it is, don't be late."

"Ed, what would travel time be for the Zerius system?" Jace spoke into his comm.

"From this location and current ship status, approximately two point three standard days. If we increase compression and velocity to one point five of standard speed, the travel time would be one point nine standard days," the ship's computer replied.

"Yeah, we'll probably try and make it faster. Going to be a lot of people on board for that time," Jace remarked.

"I have been keeping apprised of the situation, Captain. And I believe we could accommodate several more if they do not mind sleeping at the flight stations."

"Nah, I think we'll make this as quick as possible. I want to get back to the, you know," Jace said.

"I concur, Captain. It would be interesting to see if your theories are correct. And I would look forward to the information gained within the stream."

"Sounds like you're looking to gain an edge, Ed," Jace joked.

"My first experience within the stream was, I would say, not enough. However, we did travel much farther than most ships could currently in that time."

Jace gave a subtle laugh. "Ed, one step at a time. We'll get there."

The computer said nothing as Jace looked to the sky. "There's a lot more stars to see, my friend. A lot more."

Jace headed back inside and sat, the soft cushions lowering him slowly until they settled. Flora watched him as Eislie sat in the chair next to him. She mouthed the word, "Worried?" making Jace give a subtle shrug.

Flora then watched as Jace rested his thumb on his cheek and tapped his forehead. She could see Eislie looking concerned toward him. "What's wrong?"

"Oh, nothing. My mind keeps going back to the project. I should probably finish writing down my ideas."

"If you figured it out, you should send it in to the Alliance. They'd happily take over the project. Besides, you figured out how to find the event horizon for any binary. That alone is worth celebrating," Larat said.

Jace looked up, the concern behind his eyes looming evident. "It's *how* I figured it out. That's the problem."

Eislie stirred in her seat, she and Jace looking guilty, making her mother ask how they found the information they needed.

"We got a good look at a dreadnaught. Deep scans and everything. Down to the power systems. Both the Duggor and dreadnaught had nearly identical tunnel systems," Jace told them.

Flora looked to them both accusingly. "And how did you get those scans?"

Eislie was the first to speak. "We helped rescue the dreadnaught stuck in an event horizon."

"You what?" Larat yelled, his anger fully evident. "Do you have any idea how much trouble you'd be in if the Alliance finds out?"

"Larat! Shut up," Flora scolded him before looking at her daughter and Jace. "Was anyone hurt?"

Eislie shook her head. "No, they even thanked us, and didn't chase after us when we left." Then, Eislie paused. "Also, the pirates are the ones who killed all of the Karazon that were holding our ship."

Larat sat hard on the sofa, making his wife sway when he did. "The pirates helped you. Why?"

Jace took a breath. “We sort of have a deal with their queen.” He watched as both of Eislie’s parents’ jaws dropped.

With a huff, Jace said, “We’re not pirates. We are sort of working alongside them, while it’s beneficial. Besides, the Alliance wants to be the only one in control of the filaments. We think everyone should have access to it. They should be free for everyone to fly.”

Flora leaned back, her manner now more agreeable, a subtle, “I see,” leaving her lips as she turned to Eislie. She gave a smile before turning to her husband.

“What?” Eislie asked, seeing her mother looking at her with a smile.

Flora shook her head. “I know why you’re with him.” She turned again to her husband.

Eislie looked to Jace. “What do you mean? I love him.”

Jace looked happily to Eislie. “I love you too, Eis. But I’m looking at your father and seeing his expression. I think he and I are a bit out of the loop here.”

Flora laughed, “It’s the freedom he’s offering. It’s the same you offered me when you asked if I’d leave with you.”

After a calm and somewhat romantic interlude, Jace sat forward. “That’s not all.”

With interest, Eislie’s parents listened to Jace. “I think I also know why the Duggor are capturing starborn and not killing them.”

Larat looked interested and asked, “Why?”

Jace sighed, “It’s probably the same reason the pirates are mostly starborn.”

“And why is that?” Larat asked firmly.

Jace leaned back. “I’m hoping I’m wrong, but I think everyone in this room, including most of those who left this house recently, would be the only ones able to travel the filaments.”

Chapter 20:
Business is Business, and so are Pirates

The morning sunlight cast a shadow over the supply depot. Eislie stood outside with a list of items. She looked on, annoyed there were already several people waiting. *Should have gotten up earlier.* Garrett had arrived and joined her before asking where Jace was.

"Oh, he's stocking the ship," Eislie replied.

Garrett thought for a moment. "Booze or ammunition?"

Eislie briefly turned to look away from her list, only answering, "Yes."

Garrett leaned closer. "He bringing enough for our ship? I've been looking at the status. It needs some work inside."

Eislie smiled, "That shouldn't be a problem. As long as the engines and environmental systems work, we can take care of the rest." Eislie looked at her list again, scribbling down something. "Not like we haven't rebuilt a ship before."

Garrett nodded. "Yeah, I've rebuilt two. Your father has as well. It seems like you're well on your way too."

Eislie smiled, continuing to edit her list. "We're going to accompany you back. Just in case. Jace and I made that decision last night."

Their friend gave a relieved sigh. “I know your ship usually only has a crew of five, max. I was planning on bringing along about seven. It’s going to be tight quarters for a week. I’m not looking forward to it.”

Eislie chuckled, “We figure about two days to get there, tops.” She looked to Garrett. “Jace and I ran the numbers last night. We’re going to have to push the engines a little, but it’ll be quicker.”

Garrett looked lost in thought. “Wait, we based the travel time on the *Aranost*’s top speed. How fast is your ship?”

Eislie shrugged, “Don’t know. We’ve upgraded the power systems and engine feeds several times. I don’t think we’ve tested them past max flight yet. Although we did push them up to about one twenty when escaping the Duggor, before the upgrades.”

Garrett gave a stare of disbelief. “One twenty? That would have caused a quasi-inversion for most ships.”

“Not us. We only encountered resonance after we entered the filament. And even then, it wasn’t building that fast,” Eislie said as she continued to scribble.

Garrett walked alongside as the doors of the depot opened. He could be heard mumbling, “You’re definitely working on our ship when we get back.”

* * *

They were more than halfway to the Zerius system before the ship’s computer alerted them of an emergency status. “Sensors are monitoring a hyperspace crossing ahead. Prepare for turbulence. No quasi space detected.”

“Why didn’t you say anything earlier, Ed?” Eislie asked.

“May I remind Captains that command crew can only be alerted to emergencies when others are present.”

Jace huffed, “Ed, add Garrett Yikk, Shasji Yaman, Derren Colm, Issa Regal.” Jace looked back. “Who else we got? Oh, Bensin Makkan, and Feren G’lan to the crew.” Jace turned back around. “I think I got everybody.”

Garrett jokingly pounded the back of Jace's command chair as Eislie said, "Can't believe you forgot to add them."

Jace looked toward her, joking, "And you reminded me when?" making Eislie chortle in embarrassment.

"Ed, time to arrive, just looking for an estimate," Jace asked.

"Approximately nine standard hours until arrival to the system."

Jace looked back. "We're making good time."

Eislie rose from her seat. "I'm getting a drink. You want anything?" She pointed to Jace; he nodded.

As Eislie was returning, Garrett leaned forward to hear him say, "You know, if your ship's this fast, maybe you should enter the Zero Circuit."

Eislie pushed Garrett aside as she handed Jace a bottle of water.

Jace took a drink before asking, "What's the Zero Circuit?"

"No! We are not entering that," Eislie insisted.

Jace could see her reaction, and he raised his brow in interest. "Okay, if she says no, I've gotta know what it is."

Eislie looked at Garrett, her stare showing a subtle warning to her father's friend.

Garrett huffed, "I know where you got that look from." Garrett pointed to Eislie as he turned to Jace. "Her father gives the same stare." Jace stifled a laugh. "The Zero Circuit is the fastest race in this part of the galaxy. It's rumored that Kane, the most famous racer, may be a starborn. Supposedly, he's from Earth."

"Hmm, you've piqued my interest—"

Eislie interrupted, "Garrett forgot to mention that the area also has quasi fields, debris, stellar remnants, and participants trying to kill each other."

Jace looked to Garrett. “Really? Well then, probably not.”

Eislie buckled her harness. “At least not until we upgrade the mag shields, weapons, and install a Brunell drive.”

Garrett leaned forward, the look of surprise on his face making Eislie say, “What? We’re just not ready to enter it . . . yet.”

Jace chuckled, “Well, Eis. Add it to the list.”

Garrett leaned back. “What in Tarsis is this list you two keep talking about?”

The computer responded to Garret’s question. “Crewman Garrett, the list is comprised of things, items, and actions that Captains have asked to accomplish. It is a growing assembly of intriguing ideas.”

Within moments, Jace and Eislie started laughing, bringing most of the crew forward. Garrett stepped back, wearing an expression of surprise, subtle fear, and a subdued smile.

Bensin put his hand on Garrett’s shoulder. “Problems?”

Garrett shook his head, pointing to Eislie, Jace, and the computer’s interface. “No, but I think the three of them might be crazy.”

Overhearing this, Jace said, “Ah, don’t worry. We’ll still get you there in one piece.”

* * *

Jace was walking down the ramp of the new ship. “You see the engine room in this thing? It’s a total mess.” Jace turned to the Zerian trader, annoyed. “That needs a lot of work. How much are you asking for this?”

The trader scowled toward Jace before he spoke. “Monies have been exchanged. The engines and environmental systems work. If you don’t like the other systems, they are your problem.”

Garrett stepped in. “Milar, ignore him. He’s Terran. They don’t understand the subtleties of business in this sector.”

The trader turned to Garrett. "Then it is good we are doing business with you and not with him."

Garrett nodded. "May we have some time to load supplies?"

Milar nodded back. "You will have three standard hours to do so. We are expecting some new ships in shortly. You must be gone by then or we will charge you additional."

Jace smiled, crossing his arms. "Oh, I like this guy. Now that's a way to run a business." But, unfortunately, his sarcastic tone was lost on the Zerian trader, who responded, "It appears Terrans *can* understand business."

Jace looked annoyed toward the man before tapping his comm. "Let's load it up." He turned to Garrett. "I'm going to have a look-see; maybe I can make this thing a little easier to fly. I'll be in the reactor room."

Milar smiled, "We can rent you the necessary safety systems. However, for such a small vessel, I doubt you have the proper equipment."

Jace walked up, then flipped the collar of his flight jacket up, tapping the controls for the radiation shield. The Zerian looked fascinated. "Is that the Sotiral shield system?"

Jace nodded as Eislie walked up. "Yes; we've been the ones testing them." She looked at Jace. "You know, I've never been on a Zerian Swoot before."

Jace looked back at the vessel, stifling a snicker. "Is that what it's called?"

"Sir, I will happily refund a third of the payment for the two shield systems." Milar addressed Garrett.

Garrett looked to Eislie and Jace. "That would not be my decision, sir. But allow me to discuss this with my friends." He walked over to Eislie, whispering, "You willing to give up your shield jackets?"

Jace shrugged. "Not really. It kind of takes away the mystery to the fact that we don't need them."

Eislie looked at Jace. "We can give them two new ones. Never used. We have extra onboard. Miriz said we could stop by and pick up more if needed." Jace nodded.

"Sir, what would you offer for two new, unused shield systems?" Garrett asked.

The trader stood interested. "I would give you half the money in return for three of the systems."

Jace looked to Eislie and gave a nod before she headed into the ship. When she returned, she was holding three new Sotiral systems. The trader inspected them, turning them all on to make sure they were functioning. Finding things satisfactory, his hands were trembling as he held them. Finally, he tapped his comm, then looked up. "Half has been returned. Do you have more of these systems onboard?"

Jace spoke, pointing to the Sotiral jackets. "Only the ones for the crew. It may take us some time to replace those."

The trader nodded. "Understandable. You may load your ship. And thank you for your business."

The trader then walked away, holding up the new shield suits, admiring them.

Jace returned to the ship and within two hours, he had the reactor working at a higher throughput. He was wiping his hands on a towel as he entered the control room. "That's the best I can do for here. How're the readings?"

Feren tapped the display, and it shuddered as it illuminated. She turned to the others working around her. She noted the readings and gave a thumbs-up. Then, she looked to Jace. "Eislie said you were good. You even got the tunnel system up and running."

Jace took the compliment and turned toward the cargo area. "Yeah, would have been a long trip back if I didn't," before yelling, "Hey, everything stowed back there?"

Bensin yelled back, "Yeah, just trying to get the one hatch open! We could use some help!"

“I got it!” Eislie yelled as she rushed back. She had seen similar before on the cruiser she served on. She held the handle and pulled up instead of out, and the door opened. She huffed, “Latch is bent.”

Bensin spoke as he tapped the controls for the environmental systems. “Someone must have tried prying it open the wrong way once or twice.”

Eislie was wondering why he was so good at setting the Zerion systems. She watched as Bensin handled the controls like a seasoned professional—almost as if he had been trained on them.

She walked toward the hall, yelling, “We’re good, let’s get going!”

Jace tapped the chair Garrett was sitting in. “We’ll head to our ship. Wait till we’re aboard, and we’ll wait for you to lift off, then follow.”

Jace and Eislie headed back to the *Wolfhammer* and watched as the ship beside them lifted from the dock.

“I didn’t see the ship’s name,” Jace noted.

Eislie scoffed, “Zerius number their ships, no names.” She turned to Jace. “But my mother suggested *Solace Star*.”

“That’s not bad,” Jace told her, and Eislie agreed. As they watched the ship head off, they followed.

* * *

Jace was staring at the screen, the back of the new ship blatant on the display before them. They were in communication the entire time, with Ed monitoring the new vessel’s systems. He looked to Eislie as she handed him a bottle of fermented fruit juice.

“Don’t know if I should be drinking and flying here. But this is pretty good,” Jace remarked.

Eislie smiled, “It’s not that strong. Besides, it’s tradition to drink it when you get a new ship.”

Jace looked at her. “Really?”

"Yeah, it's a Gilesian tradition," Eislie said as she held her bottle out. Jace tapped his against hers. "To tradition."

Jace chuckled, "I'm Terran, you're Gilesian, our ship's Takloh. What is tradition?"

Eislie looked forward as she took another sip. "It doesn't matter where we're from. What matters is how we see things."

There was silence for a few minutes as they watched the new ship flying before them. Then, finally, Eislie sighed before saying, "Ed, any variations on the ship's systems? Not ours."

A few moments went by before the computer said, "I am beginning to detect a high-temperature fault on the starboard engine. But it is within limits."

Jace sat forward. "We'd better be safe than sorry." He tapped the comm. "Hey, you guys seeing any weird readings on the starboard engine?"

"Garrett here. No, nothing. Everything is looking good. Why?"

"We see a high temperature on the starboard side. Why don't we punch out and take a look?" Jace responded. Within seconds, they were in normal space and the *Wolfhammer* connected to the airlock.

As the last latch locked, Eislie said, "There might be a limiter on the monitors. Sometimes shady people put them in."

Jace turned to Eislie. "You seem to know a lot about shady business with ships. There something you're not telling me about?"

She could tell the joking tone in his voice and said, "Wouldn't you like to know?" Before she opened the airlock, she also decided to mention Bensin with the environmental controls.

"So, maybe he's good at that stuff," Jace remarked.

Eislie bit her lip. "I'm not sure. I get a weird feeling around him. This entire time he's been out of the way. It's like he's been watching us. And seeing that . . ." Eislie looked to Jace. "He may not be who we think he is. Zerius environmental systems are very complex; they like their comfort. I was on a converted cargo vessel and I still don't understand them. And I was trying to for almost a year."

Jace furrowed his brow. "You think he's Alliance?"

Eislie bit her lip again, shaking her head with an unsure look.

Jace took a second. "Ed, if we send anyone over to the ship, record their movements."

"Acknowledged, Captain."

Eislie paused, seeing Bensin's eyes staring through the window, and hesitated before opening the hatch. Then, she looked to Jace. "Yeah, let's keep an eye on him."

Jace was halfway through the engine access aboard the new ship as he pulled at some of the power feeds to the rear engine. "There's no slack in any of these lines. It's probably a bad reading from the sensors. It's running hot, but they're not seeing it." He huffed, pulling himself out of the claustrophobic space, his back making a loud creak against the metallic wall as it shifted, making him slide to the floor. Jace turned with a look of surprised concern. "Hope we didn't buy a lemon."

Eislie looked at him strangely, making him laugh. "Can't make a joke if no one's going to get it."

Feren chuckled before saying, "As long as the ship flies, we'll be okay."

Eislie gave Jace her hand and helped him from the floor before they headed toward the control room.

"What's the reading showing on the panel?" Eislie asked as they entered.

"Nominal, nothing different than before. Why?" Garrett asked.

Jace huffed, "Feed lines are warm. It shouldn't be a problem as long as we don't stress them. They seem to be in good shape otherwise." He leaned down, tapping the controls to pull up the diagnostics, but was having difficulty.

Jace looked around, and Feren stepped forward. She tapped the controls. "Controls aren't where you think they are on this ship. I was having trouble figuring them out too."

Jace thanked her before he looked at the readings. "Everything looks to be offset. We'll probably have to rewire the feeds when we get back." He looked around, and all but one of the crew were visible.

Shasji, Derren, and Feren are here. Where's Bensin?

Jace asked Garrett where Bensin was, and the response was one that he'd have hoped not to hear.

"He said you asked to get something from your ship. I think he went to the *Wolfhammer*," Garrett told them.

The stare from Eislie as she looked around told Jace that she was now sure the man they knew as Bensin wasn't who they were led to believe he was. Just as they were about to tell everyone what they suspected, there was an alert through the comm.

"Attention, Zerion vessel, you are trespassing in Her Majesty's domain. Prepare to be boarded."

Feren tapped the comm, and on the screen, an image of a dreadnaught appeared before them, "Pirates! Oh slac!" escaping her.

Jace tapped the comm. "Pirate vessel, this is a captain of the *Wolfhammer*. We're aiding a distressed vessel, and you show up. Guess you caught us with our pants down."

He turned. "Eis, better get back on the ship, now."

Moments later on the screen, a familiar image of the captain of the pirate vessel appeared. "Captain Tucker, you are nowhere near Gilese. I would have thought you would have taken some time to recuperate. Our queen enjoys her prizes fresh."

Well, well, it's Captain Balroc.

"I never really thanked your queen for the assist," Jace said.

The old pirate captain stood tall. "People of Zerius are enemies of our queen. Why are you aiding them?"

Jace smiled. "Captain, forgive me, but I think you are mistaken. This ship belongs to us. We have liberated it from the Zerius fleet. We were just on our way home."

He muted the sound and turned to see if Eislie had left. He looked to Garrett, who was looking for orders on what to do. They both knew that the new ship was unarmed. And the *Wolfhammer* would have to detach to fight. However, Jace hoped they wouldn't have to do that, given their current agreement with the pirates.

With his back to the screen, Jace asked, "Garrett, how's your poker face?"

"My what?" Garrett replied.

With a huff, Jace moved to block Garrett from the view of the monitor. "Can you bluff? They don't know that this ship doesn't have weapons."

Garrett nodded. "I can do that. Why?"

Jace nodded. "When I'm done, keep him talking. I need to get back to our ship."

Garrett nodded, and Jace turned to face the pirate and did his best to try and sound convincing. "Captain, we have had contact before, and they have not gone well. But right now, the *Wolfhammer* is readying for battle. And once disconnected, you will have two vessels to fight." As he finished, Jace gave a wink.

Jace pounded on Garrett's shoulder and headed back to the *Wolfhammer*. He almost knocked down Bensin, who was holding the side of his face as if someone had struck him, and Garrett continued where Jace left off.

* * *

As Jace entered the *Wolfhammer*, he secured the airlock before initiating the unlatching sequence. He heard Eislie say, "Found that slac trying to get into Ed."

Jace looked around. "You all right, buddy?"

"Yes, Captain. The new crew member was not able to access any log or essential systems. However, the adaptive algorithm he deployed was fascinating to examine. I may add it to my list of attributes," the computer replied.

Jace laughed, "As long as you're good, Ed." Then, he turned to Eislie. "Who knows; we might need it later."

Eislie brought up the conversation between the pirates and Garrett, and Jace told her to open the secondary channel they gave the pirates and to use low power. She looked confused, but did as he asked.

"Pirate vessel, this is the *Wolfhammer*. Please respond," Jace said, hoping the transmission was not picked up.

* * *

Aboard the pirate vessel, the captain was becoming angered by Garrett's banter from the Zerian ship. Balroc glared at one of his crew, who came up to whisper an alert to him. However, his demeanor changed when the comm operator said, "Captain Tucker is on the secure frequency."

It took a moment before Balroc stared menacingly toward the screen. "Enough!" He then slammed down, disconnecting the comm, and the screen went blank. He moved to the second comm and spoke. "What the slac are you playing at, Captain Tucker?"

Jace chuckled, "Easy, Captain Balroc. We had to break away. That really is our ship. This is all for show. We think we have an Alliance spy on board."

The old captain looked around. "Are you using a low-power transmission?"

Jace confirmed, "Yeah, audio only. Let's keep this short. I presume you got the other information we sent?"

Balroc confirmed, and Jace continued. "The new ship is ours. Don't know if it's going to be used for the test yet, but it's ours. It's unarmed, and the crew are friends." Jace paused. "Well, most are. As I mentioned, we're pretty sure one of them is Alliance. We are heading back. When we have time, we'll share what we find out. For now, however, I wanted to keep everyone safe. Including you."

The pirate captain gave a slight nod. "The captain of the new vessel is Alliance. I remember him from the *Aranost*."

Jace thought for a moment. "We're sorry for that. But he has been released from command. We don't really want to harm anyone, Balroc. Truthfully, if you had attacked, we probably wouldn't have responded with a fight."

Eislie looked repentant as Jace spoke. She felt the same way. Neither of them wanted to hurt anyone. They were just protecting themselves and their friends.

Back on the pirate ship, the captain's face displayed a somber remorse as he listened to Jace.

"Garrett was Alliance. They threw him aside like us. Your queen isn't the only one who takes in strays."

Balroc responded, "Are they all starborn?"

On the comm, Jace responded. "Most of them. But, Captain Balroc, I don't want a fight here. This is a family project, and I am telling you this out of prudence."

Moments later, Eislie was heard saying, "You harm them, and Jace won't be your only problem."

Captain Balroc gave a chuckle. "Is that a threat, Captain Licessien?"

On the comm, the captain heard Jace say, "Trust me on this, Balroc. I shiver when she makes that kind of threat. And I'm aligned with her."

The pirate captain smiled before giving a subdued laugh. "What is your suggestion?"

The captain heard Jace say, "Let's make it like an act of mercy. You feel sorry for us from our recent encounter and are feeling generous."

Captain Balroc then said, "What assurance do I have that you will fulfill the agreement from earlier?"

Jace's voice was cold as he said, "We want the same thing, Captain. The universe is big enough for all of us." Jace ended communication.

The pirate captain closed the channel and looked toward the main screen. "Open a channel to the Zerian vessel.

* * *

On the screen of the Zerian ship, Garrett again faced the captain of the pirate ship. "Your ship does not have any weapons. We know that your ship was liberated from the dominion of the Zerius empire and the *Wolfhammer* is lending aid to your helpless vessel. We are not without mercy. Captain Yikk, Captain Tucker, and Captain Licessien, you have our leave. Vacate this space or we will destroy you and claim our prize."

"They're letting us go?" Feren asked unsurely.

Garrett sighed with relief. "Apparently so." He addressed the pirate captain. "We are waiting for the starboard engines to cool. We will leave shortly. You will not see us again, Captain."

Garrett watched as the pirate captain nodded and the screen went dark. On the other screen, they watched as the dreadnaught moved away and entered hyperspace. Garrett contacted the *Wolfhammer*, "Jace, Eis, we should get out of here."

On the *Wolfhammer*, Eislie sighed with relief. "I think Captain Balroc was a bit over the top on that threat."

Jace chuckled, "Really? I thought it was just right." Then, he looked to Eislie. "C'mon, let's head home."

Chapter 21:
The *Solace Star*

On Gilese, it had taken over two weeks to repair the issues with their new ship. Jace and Eislie even flew the vessel to test the repairs. Jace remarked how the air seemed quiet as they headed to join the crew already at the dock. Garrett waved to them as he stood with his team waiting for the local magistrate. The director of spaceport operations was on his way as per the message they received over the comms. It wasn't every day a new ship was allotted to the planet. Even with tradition, for some, it is a long-awaited celebration when it happens.

Garrett was looking over the repaired ship, admiring the new ceramic paint replacing the dark umber of the Zerius fleet colors. Unlike other cultures, the renaming of a vessel from its darker origins was a blessing. On Gilese, this was the case, and many came out to celebrate such an event.

"I can't believe they got everything working," Garrett muttered as Larat walked up.

"Told you they worked well together," Larat said, referring to Jace and Eislie.

There was music among the crowd, with servers handing out bottles of fermented fruit juice. Jace went to open it, but Larat stopped him.

"You have to wait; we all drink at once. It's customary for crew and those who care for the vessel. Especially owners," Larat said as he pointed to the front of the ship. "When the name is revealed, then we can drink."

Jace turned to Eislie. "Wish I would have known that when we named the *Wolfhammer*."

Eislie caused Jace to laugh, saying, "We didn't exactly have time, remember?"

Cheers filled the air as the head of the spaceport walked up to the podium. "Welcome, everyone! And welcome to the unveiling of a new vessel to our planet."

Jace cringed, hearing the loud celebration all around, and turned to see Eislie covering her ears, a large smile plastered across her face. The man continued, and as the excitement and his words eventually started putting everyone to sleep, he began to wrap up the presentation.

"Would the new owners please join us up here to unveil the vessel?" the man said.

Larat and Flora headed forward and motioned for Eislie and Jace to follow. They arrived on the platform, and Larat said a few words before the head of the spaceport signaled if anyone else wanted to say anything additional. Jace and Eislie shook their heads, but Flora happily obliged.

Jace watched as she took a breath, and Jace could feel Flora's words to his very core.

"In my darkest times, I looked up to the stars. Even in the absence of light, when I was lost, there were always stars in the sky. My wishes, my dreams, were granted when I left my world to become a part of this one. When my daughter was taken, I again looked to the sky to search for a point of light, hoping she was safe. Again, my wishes were granted when she was returned."

Jace looked over at Eislie to see tears falling down her face as her mother resumed. "On many worlds, the stars are seen as gods, or a place to make such wishes. In the end, they not only show that there is light in the universe, but they can also give us solace."

Flora motioned to the rope and Larat pulled the line, revealing the name of the ship. Eislie's mother continued. "We are all children of the stars. We welcome a new ship to our world. I give you the *Solace Star*. May its light shine on every world it sees."

The crowd let out a roar, and everyone held up the small bottles of fermented juice. Almost in unison, they drank. When finished, they all held the bottle up again to the ship as a salute. Jace and Eislie did the same.

"Wow, some speech!" Jace said as he wiped a tear from his eye.

Eislie leaned against him. "She's been working on that speech since before we left the other day. I didn't hear it till now. Now I know why she chose the name."

Jace nodded.

As the celebration went on, Garrett and the new crew boarded the *Solace Star*. Flora had returned to the dock office and was already filing a flight plan. While Jace and Eislie were away, she had worked with several clients who contacted JESC for transport. The *Wolfhammer* was fast but small. Any ample cargo opportunities would not be a viable commodity. But with the new ship, the promised payout was something she and Larat were looking forward to.

Flora arrived back at the ship with the paperwork and could see Garrett speaking with someone outside the loading door. Her husband, Larat, was walking down the ramp just as Eislie and Jace arrived.

"You two did a good job fixing the ship. The engines and power system are definitely an improvement. It looks like you fixed the power feeds as well. Too bad it's not as fast as yours. We'd be swimming in contracts if that were the case," Larat said as Flora looked over.

Jace chuckled. "We did more than that. It turns out Zerian drives are similar to Beduvial hoppers. I think they may have stolen the design."

Garrett looked to Jace. "What do you mean? What did you do?"

Eislie smiled. "You might be surprised when you fly at max throttle."

Her father looked back at the ship. "What *did* you do?"

Eislie looked to Jace before saying, "We tweaked them a bit. It's not as fast as our ship. But it's faster than most on this planet."

Larat put his arm around Eislie. "How fast?"

Eislie looked her father in the eyes. "Most ships will do one arc in about a quarter cycle. This ship will do one arc in about three sixty-fifths of a cycle." She looked to the *Solace Star*. "Our ship can still beat it, at one point four of a cycle."

"Eis, that must have cost a fortune!" her mother said as she walked over.

Jace stepped in. "Nah, we got it covered from our pay on Oppa. Besides, it's our gift to the new crew. Don't want them being run down by pirates—or anyone else, for that matter."

Larat hugged Eislie. "Thank you, my little Eis." He pointed to Jace. "I told you to keep him."

Garrett thanked them before saying, "Can't wait to see how fast it goes."

Jace leaned in. "You can outrun the *Aranost* going full throttle. We made sure of that." Jace looked up at the ship. "The artificial command system is the same. Didn't see a reason to change it, for now. We like Ed on our ship. Although, he did mention that he could create a less interactive version if we wanted."

Garrett stepped back. “No. Thank you, but no. I still think you two and that computer are crazy. We’ll be fine with what we have.”

Eislie feigned a pout before saying, “But that might hurt Ed’s feelings!”

Garrett laughed. “I’m sorry if it does, but honestly . . .” Garrett leaned in, whispering, “We don’t plan to get in as much trouble as you two.”

His statement made everyone within earshot burst out in laughter.

* * *

A few days later, Jace and Eislie returned to Oppa to work on one of the new drones. Jace went to work eagerly, and had torn out the drone’s entire system the day they arrived. Callie chastised them both for being away for over a month. She and the others had tried several times to break the event horizon but were unable.

Finally, he and Eislie agreed to allow Ed to get the requested upgrades, and Arren was happy to oblige. The director of the filament project as well. She knew the upgrades meant that both of them would be stuck. She mumbled such, and Arren snickered, hearing her say, “Maybe they’ll stay in one place if they don’t have that ship of theirs.” Callie felt guilty immediately after speaking. She wanted a breakthrough on the project as much as anyone. But Jace and Eislie seemed to have more answers than the rest. Them not being around set them back the entire time.

It had taken Jace a few days to reassemble the drone. The new configuration included an overall field system and new drivers. In his excitement, Jace had forgotten the new plans he drew up and had to return to their place on Oppa to retrieve the schematics of the dreadnaught. He kept things quiet about having the information on the pirate vessel. When Jace needed to look at them again, he always headed back to their apartment, making Callie wonder what he was up to.

"Eis, did Jace leave again?" Callie asked.

"Yeah, he drew things out while we were away. We still haven't scanned everything. He'll be back soon," Eislie told her. The director knew it was a lie, since almost everything they worked with was electronic. Callie's mind was beginning to ask a single question. *What did they figure out?*

Jace appeared behind Eislie on the video. "Callie, I think we'll be able to launch and test in a day or so. I'll be back in an hour to finish up."

The director huffed, "Jace, just bring the information. We can keep it on file here."

Jace gave a disapproving scowl. "I don't think that's a good idea."

Callie gave an angry, confused look. "What? The systems are secure. What's the issue?"

Jace shook his head. "Uh, I think it'd be better to explain in person."

Eislie looked to Jace. "I'm not letting you go alone on this one." She looked at the screen. "You may not like what we discovered."

The director had a very foreboding sense as she processed Eislie's words. Finally, she looked to them both, "All right. Be here in an hour and tell me what's going on."

* * *

Jace arrived and spent a few minutes working on the drone. He made the adjustments needed and was almost ready to test. However, there was a matter that was weighing on him. At the center command, Eislie insisted they use a random empty room. The director agreed to their demand and closed the door before Eislie spoke quietly.

She held up a pad and showed a picture of the dreadnaught and the Duggor vessels.

"Are these classified?" Callie accused as she closed down the information pad.

"Hear us out, okay?" Jace said quietly. "Well, yes, they probably are. But that's not the point. It's the other things we found."

Jace told her about the event horizon they had accessed near Gilese, telling her how they saw the point before the computer noticed it.

"That's wonderful. That means your ship can detect the location of an entry point!" Callie exclaimed.

Jace sighed, "Callie, we had the tunnel field active when an asteroid flew through it. Nothing happened."

The director returned a confused stare.

Eislie chimed in while Jace turned away in silence. "Callie, it only opened when we approached close enough."

The director was trying to understand what they were saying when Jace spoke in frustration. "Remember what I surmised before we left?"

Callie looked to him, trying to remember what they said over a month ago. She was becoming frustrated by them both when she remembered and started to say, "Right, you said that maybe star— " Her words ended seeing Eislie motioning for her to stop. Realizing what she was about to say, the director walked to the wall, leaning onto it as if a heavy burden was now on her shoulders.

"Please tell me you're wrong," Callie pleaded.

Jace's voice was solemn as he responded. "It's looking like I'm not. But the Duggor ship may not need the, uh, other element," Jace said, referring to his theory that only starborn can access the filaments. "That's what I've been trying to figure a way around."

The director tapped the back of her head against the wall a few times before she looked to Jace. "Do you think you can do it without the other, uh, add-on?"

Jace shook his head. "If we can modulate the field energy system, then, I don't know, maybe. I haven't figured it out yet."

Callie walked up to them. "See what you can do. I don't want to explore the other option. We're hunted enough already."

Jace nodded as he watched the director walk to the door. She turned to look at them. "Who else knows?"

Eislie replied, "Just us. We even ordered our computer to erase his memory of it."

Callie hung her head as she opened the door. "Let me know when you think you're ready to launch next."

As the door closed, Jace huffed, "Well, that went better than I expected."

* * *

Rene Hamilton looked in the mirror. He had spent almost two weeks growing the stubble along his face. The clothing acquired from the Alliance storage was substandard, tattered and needing repair. But, on the other hand, it gave the illusion that he had been in space for some time. He tapped the new comm Branard had dropped off. It used the same frequencies as the pirates, and some they planned to use for security purposes. Hamilton sighed in frustration; he still didn't know what station he was supposed to have. Branard had made sure that the rest of the flight crew knew what they were doing. And to make sure they weren't able to be seen, Hamilton had proposed encasing the ship to look like an asteroid.

Commander Branard had worked on retrofitting the defender to look more like one of the pirates' vessels. He also knew that most were supposed to be a crew of five. With such a small crew, Hamilton knew things would probably be busy for him.

As the door to the dock opened, he could see the sheeting that hung to obscure that section of the dock. When he lifted the one area, he was immediately met with the end of a weapon.

"Good to see there's security," Hamilton mocked before entering.

The guards ran his identification and saluted him before he went on his way. As he walked into the ship, Branard turned to greet him.

"Good to see you on time, Rene. What do you think?" Branard asked, pointing around the inside of the vessel.

The Terran captain glanced around. "Looks like a pirate ship, Branard. But will it convince those we're trying to steal from?"

Rene laughed, "Well, if they do, they'll collect the reward for turning you in."

Branard turned, scowling. He didn't find Hamilton's joke amusing. The commander then waved his hand, motioning for the others to gather.

When everyone was around, he introduced them all.

"Rene, this is Basker. He's our weapons specialist. That's Jennert; navigation and pilot." Branard leaned in. "He can outfly even those two, if needed." Rene understood he was referring to the crew of the *Wolfhammer*.

Branard waited for Hamilton to stop chuckling before he introduced the last member.

"And this lucky individual is Salas. She's one of our best hyperspace engineers. So if anything goes wrong, she'll be the one to figure it out." He then pointed to Hamilton. "Everyone, this is Rene. He's our, uh, cargo jockey."

Hamilton turned to Branard before nodding and saying, "That makes sense. I guess."

Branard smiled. “I read your file. You’re one of the best shots with kinetic weapons. I figure you can hit something moving fast. Now, everyone, to stations. We’re leaving.”

Chapter 22:
Don't Mess with That

The *Wolfhammer* drifted near the small drone as Alvin tested the controls on his console. He had used the time Jace and Eislie were away to hone his skills with remote flight. Nearby, the *Pastiel*, an Oppan science vessel, hovered, collecting data on the filament. The *Wolfhammer* stood ready to follow the drone.

The other ship, the *Fenstra Apol*, patrolled nearby to make sure there were no unwanted vessels in the area. Alvin noted that the only nearby objects were several minor asteroids.

"Ed, how's the new system?" Jace asked as he looked out the small port to see the filament in the distance.

"The upgrades are a welcome enhancement, Captain. I estimate that I will be able to collect much more information than before. And with the holographic quantum cores, I can include temporal data and imagery. I will not have to rely on translation to the recording systems. As an addition, I can reserve a backup copy of my systems in case anything happens to the running hardware," the computer responded.

Jace smiled. "Can't believe we can record temporal data on sapphire." He sat back in his chair. "And a hell of a lot of it too. This is like science fiction! Wait, did you say you could back yourself up?"

"Yes, Captain. Like you, I have become aware that secondary systems may be a necessity when exploring the universe. And when dealing with our allies."

Jace chuckled, "Yeah, there's only a few people I trust. Two of them are on this ship. But, wow, I still can't believe you can record temporal data."

Eislie looked to him, laughing. "Temporal recording is new. I didn't even know it existed. It uses quantum-phased engineered white sapphire, and it records as it happens, no changing data; it can't be edited."

Jace nodded. "Yeah. I guess there had to be a downside. What if you don't want to record something?"

Eislie agreed, and looked to the screen before her, saying, "Systems recording. Ed, you have the telemetry from the probe?"

"Yes, Captain Licessien. And I look forward to filling the massive databanks we have," Ed replied.

Jace chuckled, saying, "Guess he likes the upgrades."

"*Pastiel*, are you able to see the entry location?" Jace asked.

The response from the ship was a very technical-sounding reply which Jace understood as, yes.

Jace tapped the comm again. "*Fenstra Apol*, is the area clear?"

"Affirmative, *Wolfhammer*. Just a few asteroids. Otherwise, it's quiet," was heard through the comm, making Eislie groan.

"Someone had to say it, didn't they?" Eislie mocked, making everyone look at her before Jace laughed.

On the *Wolfhammer*, it was the two of them, along with Alvin. Shasji had also asked to join them. So did Bensin, but Garrett would only allow one of them to fly along with Jace and Eislie. Even Jace noticed that Shasji seemed to be wary of Bensin since the *Solace Star* arrived on

Oppa. Garrett had made sure to schedule a delivery, bringing Larat and Flora to watch the hopeful success of accessing the filament.

Jace took a deep breath and let it out slowly. “Guess we’re ready. Let’s try it.”

Alvin tugged the straps on his harness tight and was ready at his controls. The screen around him lit his dark face as he said, “System active. Flight controls active. Recorders are working.”

Eislie nodded as she pivoted toward the filament. Jace looked back at Shasji and Alvin before opening communications. “*Pastiel*, join the *Fenstra*. You may want to keep a safe distance. The pull of the event horizon was pretty strong last time we did something like this.”

Alvin piloted the small drone while the *Wolfhammer* followed closely. The man rolled the small vessel as they approached. He was taking no chances that the controls were not functioning. Everyone was focused on the little ship and didn’t notice the small asteroid moving parallel to them.

* * *

Eager sets of eyes stared into small screens before them in the darkened cabin of the *Rempard*. They were only lit by illumination emanating from the consoles, the crew running the power systems low to avoid detection.

“Status, everyone,” Branard said quietly before saying. “Call me Colim from here on.”

Hamilton scoffed, “You know they can’t hear sound in space, right?”

The glares of the few nearby crewmates made the Terran suddenly go silent.

“Status?” Branard ordered.

Salas and Basker responded with a simple, “Systems ready.”

Jennert said, "Reactor up and engines ready. Waiting to jettison the shell."

Branard waited to hear the status of the capture system, but Hamilton said nothing, seeming transfixed on the filament point.

"You asleep there, Terran?" Salas said before Hamilton turned, saying, "Sorry, capture systems up. Ready to deploy."

Branard took a moment and watched as the drone sped closer to the filament before he gave the order to follow. Within seconds, the shell around them turned to dust, blocking sensors from the other ships nearby. Branard smiled as he ordered, "Full throttle."

* * *

On the *Wolfhammer*, everyone focused on the drone as it moved closer. Alvin continued to operate the small vessel and activated its tunnel drive. He had just pushed the throttle to full to make sure the ship broke through into the stream. The small vessel was within seconds of entering the filament when they saw the other ship swoop toward the drone. Three tow lines smacked securely onto the hull, one hitting so hard that it penetrated the drone's shell, causing Alvin to lose command lock.

"Shit, I've lost control!"

Eislie was already piloting toward the drone following the newly arrived ship.

"Dammit, knew this was going too smoothly," Jace said as he readied weapons.

As they neared, there was a bright flash as the tunnel field opened the event horizon. They all watched as the intruding ship fought to control itself and was pulled in along with the drone. Eislie wrestled with the controls as she fought to escape the pull of the event horizon of the filament but was unsuccessful. The cabin was filled with multicolored light as the filament stream engulfed them.

"Punch out, now!" Jace ordered, only to see Alvin pounding on his console.

They all heard him yell, “Systems are offline! I can’t control it!”

“We programmed it to go only a few seconds. Why isn’t it shutting down?” He looked at the grapple that penetrated the drone and realized something.

“The flight and receiver systems must be damaged,” Alvin said as he tried desperately to bring the small craft under control.

Jace looked to Eislie, and they both knew they were in trouble. “Shit, I bet the lead ship is the only one that can punch out of this.”

He tried hailing the other ship but was unsuccessful. Jace was readying weapons when Eislie yelled, “Spide’s resonating! If we don’t shut down, we’re going to invert!”

Jace released his harness and stumbled his way back to the reactor. He tried to do his best to compensate. However, he could see the computer still recording.

“Ed, you still functioning?” Jace yelled.

“Yes . . . Captain, but my sys . . . tems seem to be af . . . ff . . . ffected. Can . . . not re . . . gulate reac . . . tor.

“You sound pretty bad, Ed. If you need to shut down, do it,” Jace ordered.

Jace tried everything to regulate the reactor, but when he touched the casing, the resonance stopped. Startled, he pulled his hand away, and the resonance returned. Jace did the same movements several times, his actions making Eislie yell, “What the slac are you doing back there?”

As Alvin fought to regain control of the drone, Shasji was looking to help. She released her harness as the ship steadied and headed back to help Jace. She entered the reactor room to see him with his hand on the casing, a look of fearful realization and disgust frozen on his face. She knelt next to him and asked what was wrong. Jace shook his head before turning to her.

"Shasji, place your hand on the casing. I have a theory, and I really hope I'm wrong," Jace told her. She saw the torment behind his eyes.

She did as instructed and watched as he removed his hand. Jace shifted back before telling her to take her hand away. As she did, the ship started to shudder and the reactor began to resonate. Jace put his hand on the casing, and everything was again normal. Jace ordered Shasji to place her hand on the case again as he removed his. She could see the pained look of sadness now filling his eyes.

"What?" Shasji asked.

Jace shook his head. "I think I just proved something I didn't want to be true." Then, he gave a heavy sigh of saddened frustration. "Keep your hand on the casing. I'll be back."

Jace rushed to his feet and headed forward. He only paused at hearing the computer say, "My systems seem to be normal again, Captain. Power systems are again synchronized. I do not understand why Crewmember Shasji touching the reactor is allowing the system to regulate."

Eislie heard the computer and she looked to Jace as he sat in his chair. "What does Ed mean? Why is Shasji touching the reactor?" She could sense that he was carrying a heavy weight on his shoulders. She did her best to watch where she was flying and back to him before he spoke.

"Remember that theory we had? The one we asked Ed to forget?" Jace asked as he strapped in again.

Eislie replied, "You mean the one where we . . ."

Her head snapped toward Jace, and she could see his head down, anger filling his eyes as he said, "I think I just proved it."

Eislie realized what he was saying, and in frustration, she kicked the front console, making a loud bang. Alvin was startled, but went back to trying to get control of the drone. He became excited as the telemetry again appeared and he was able to shift the drone's flight before again losing control.

"We have to get closer; I think the band link is damaged! I had control for a second!" Alvin yelled.

Eislie tried her best, but growled in frustration as the ship in front of them started to slow. "They're in our way. We have to punch out. We don't know where we are."

Jace tried the comm again but was unsuccessful. Then, they heard the computer's alert. "The vessel before us has deactivated their reactor. They are being dragged by the drone and it is now rotating uncontrolled."

Eislie growled again as she attempted to pilot around the now tumbling ship before them. She looked up as the control wing of the other vessel scraped across the hull of the *Wolfhammer*, its visceral grinding grating against her senses. She pushed the engines harder and the scraping became louder. The horrific noise was only broken by the sound of Alvin yelling, "I've got control, punching out!"

Alvin slammed down hard on the abort button. Within seconds, they reverted to normal space and Eislie cut the engines. The *Wolfhammer*, drone, and the other ship now floated aimlessly, only slowed by the gravitational pull of the filament's event horizon before it closed.

Eislie steadied the ship and looked around. They were, for the most part, undamaged. The craft before them, however, was still drifting.

"Ed, can you determine the status of the drone and the other ship?" Jace asked.

The computer responded, "Their power systems are offline for both. The drone has hull damage. The other vessel, however, has a serious issue."

"An issue? What issue?" Jace questioned.

The computer responded, "The other vessel's reactor has started to invert. I detect a quasi-space field growing very slowly within their reactor core. It has stabilized for now, and we may be able to reverse it. But my readings of our location are more concerning."

Jace looked to Eislie. “Where are we, Ed?”

The computer brought the holo-display online and showed the location of their home galaxy. On the display, a tiny dot pulsed. “We are, by my estimation, about one point three years’ distance from our galaxy using conventional tunnel drive at top speed.”

Jace and Eislie looked at each other, their jaws open, with Jace saying, “What?” Jace gave a low growl as he ran his hand down his face, leaning his head back. “Is there a filament nearby?”

“You want to access the stream?” Eislie responded, her voice louder than usual. “We don’t know where it’ll take us.”

Jace was about to say something when the computer interrupted. “My readings indicate that we have traveled in a straight line to our current location, so that may not be an obstacle.”

Jace pulled up the data the computer recorded and looked it over. He gave a subtle smile before saying, “We just have to make a small jump and see what direction it sends us. Then we can figure it out from there. I mean, from what I’m seeing, it looks like we just have to go in”—Jace looked back, pointing— “that direction.”

As the realization hit, Eislie sank into her chair. Jace gave a huff before turning back, yelling, “Shasji, you can come back up front! We’ve got another problem!”

Chapter 23:
You Got Us into This

Jace tried several times to reach out to the unknown ship. Finally, the *Wolfhammer*'s sensors indicated that there were attempts to get their power working again. But when they heard a static-filled response, they were hopeful.

"*Wolfhammer*, our reactor was in inversion. We need assistance. Can you hear us?" the weak signal crackled over the speakers.

Jace responded, only to hear a relieved response with more power to the transmission.

"This is the *Rempard*, we need assistance. Are you able to dock?" the voice said over the comm.

Jace raised his eyebrows, looking to Eislie. "That doesn't sound like a trap at all, does it." His sarcasm making her chuckle.

Despite being far from home, Eislie and Jace were semi-prepared. They had stowed several months' worth of supplies on board, but the distance they traveled was further than expected. Eislie looked back at the two additional crew members. She knew, as did Jace, that they would have to access the filament if they wanted to get home. Jace had readied the ship to do just that if the drone had achieved success. And now that they knew any starborn could regulate the resonance within the reactor just by touching it, they were now considering their possibilities.

“We still have weapons on board, right?” Jace asked, making Eislie nod as she pointed aft.

He headed back grabbed and loaded several weapons, handing them out to the entire crew. “Let’s try and not use them, but if we have to, do it.”

Jace sat down again. “Let’s see if we can get video of who’s on that ship.” Jace tapped the comm. “*Rempard*, do you have video? We first need to assess the damage to your ship.”

Shasji spoke up. “But our sensors can tell that.”

Jace nodded. “Yeah, but I want to see who they are. Because whoever they are, they’re not pirates.”

“How do you know?” Alvin asked.

Eislie turned back a pensive stare. “Because we’ve been collaborating with them. They wouldn’t just take the drone; they’d ask us for the info.”

“You’re working for pirates?” Alvin accused.

Shasji huffed, “No, they said they’re working *with* pirates. There’s a difference.” She turned to see Alvin staring at her. “What? I thought about joining them myself after my last promotion fell through.”

Jace smiled. “Glad to hear you’re on our side still. Too bad these people aren’t pirates.”

Alvin spoke up. “How do you know that?”

Jace sighed before responding, “Because they have all the same data that is in that drone. They would have waited until after the successful flight. That ship is not a pirate ship.”

Alvin paused before responding. "So, does the Alliance know?"

Eislie huffed, "They were suspicious enough to plant an alliance spy on the *Solace Star*."

Shasji jumped up. "Who is it? It's Bensin, isn't it."

Eislie turned, surprised. "We suspect so, yeah. How did you know?"

Shasji crossed her arms as she sat. "Found him snooping in my room. He also has been disappearing at weird times."

Jace chuckled, "Well, we'll deal with that threat later. Right now, we have a bigger problem." Jace turned to hit the comm again. "*Rempard*, we know you're not pirates. They would have threatened us by now. So, who are you?"

Over the comm, they heard, "This is the pirate ship *Rempard*. Can you help us or not?"

Jace huffed, "We already told you we know you're not pirates. They would have threatened us first or tried capturing us for their queen. Besides, your ship doesn't have the same tunnel system as the new pirate ships do. We know. We scanned one."

The screen of the *Wolfhammer* came alive. On it appeared five individuals at stations. The image brought Alvin to say, "They look like pirates."

Jace smiled, seeing the people staring back at them through the comm. "*Rempard*, I don't know if you are aware, but we are about one point four years at full speed from home. So I suggest we stop all of this posturing and work together. Now, who are you?"

Branard stood. "You still think we're not pirates?"

Jace shook his head. "It doesn't matter anyway. We have a bigger problem. Are your astro navigational systems working?"

Branard looked to Jennert and watched as he nodded. The realization on the captain of the *Rempard*'s face was now evident. "Name's Todden. Guess we could use some help."

Hamilton thought, *How many times you going to change your name?* Before standing and saying. "You're giving up that easily? Thought you Alliance people were supposed to be tough."

Jace watched as Todden raised his weapon, firing toward the man now confronting him. He looked back to the screen and Jace remarked, "I know of at least one Terran on board."

Eislie turned to Jace. "Great. You can play cards against each other later," making Jace look to see the annoyed stare from his love.

"How can you joke?" Todden growled.

Jace stood. "Well, since you're the ones who caused this problem, I think we can take a few shots at you." Jace watched as the man returned an annoyed glare, making Jace remark, "Really? You tried stealing our drone, and you think this is our fault? You punctured the hull of the drone, damaging the remote systems." Jace took a breath. "Look, we're all stuck out here, together. If we want to get back, we're going to have to re-access the stream."

Jace looked down. "There's another issue that we should probably address before we try, however. Have you checked your spide reactor recently?"

Todden looked around. "It's offline. It started to resonate wildly. Why?"

Eislie stood. "It's inverting. It hasn't stopped, but it's slow. So we're going to have to try and stop it to get your ship working again."

Todden looked to his crew. "Go check it, now!" He turned to the screen. "Are you sure it's expanding?"

Jace and Eislie both nodded.

Todden suddenly became more agreeable. "What do you propose?"

"Let us on board. We'll try and fix it. No guns. If any weapons are pointed toward any of our crew or us, we will fire on your ship." Jace looked to Eislie. "Warm up the zappers. Without their shields, it'll be an easy kill."

"Why not use those famous slag cannons of yours?" Hamilton asked.

Jace huffed, "Too close to the docking port. I don't want to fry any more than any of you do."

He watched Todden cross his arms. "You have to come unarmed as well."

Todden's remark prompted Jace to respond, "Todden, this is a one-sided deal. Take it or leave it. None of this crew is going over there unarmed. If we wanted, we could just grab the drone and head out of here. We don't want to leave you, but we will if you force us. The choice is yours." Jace reached for the comm control. "We'll give you a minute to think about it. Call us back when you're ready." He then shut down communications.

Eislie looked forward as she spoke. "We're not really leaving them, are we?"

Jace leaned back. "I hope not. I don't want to, but if they force us, then, well, I don't know."

They all heard Alvin speak up. "We should grab the drone and leave them. They are going to cross us the first chance they get."

Jace nodded. "Probably. But I am sure nothing will happen until we get their reactor back online."

Several minutes passed before the screen came alive again. "We agree. But I don't think your new suits are going to matter. The radiation is over seven hundred percent."

Jace smiled. "We'll make it work. Get you guys up and running, and we can all get out of here."

Todden nodded. "All right, latch on."

They moved the ship to dock with the *Rempard* and once they had locked in, they headed for the exit. Jace looked to Eislie. "Eis, you come with me."

"We can't leave Ed. Only one of us should go," Eislie protested.

The computer interrupted, "I think I understand Captain Tucker's logic. If he is captured, or you are captured, they can leverage this ship. But if both of you are there, then they cannot."

Jace nodded and added some information. "If one or both of us is killed, then . . ." Jace motioned an explosion with his hands.

"But the crew!" Eislie felt responsible. Jace understood that, but in truth, he had hoped the crew of the *Rempard* would be reasonable, given the circumstances. Jace hoped they fathomed the predicament they were all in, and Jace wanted to avoid any deaths.

"Ed, while we're over there, get to work on their systems. I want to know who these people are."

"Yes, Captain, initiating command."

* * *

They closed the door of the *Wolfhammer* and they headed toward the other ship. As Jace approached the door of the *Rempard*, they could see the crew through the window discussing something, and it seemed to be a heated debate. They could hear through the hull, "We have enough supplies for maybe one person for that long, but certainly not five." They watched as the pilot of the ship stormed away and were startled as the outer door of the *Rempard* opened and the man introduced himself. "Name's Hamilton. You sure you can fix the reactor?"

"You going to invite us in or not?" Jace mocked.

Hamilton nodded and ushered them inside before asking, "Can you get us running?"

Jace shrugged before pointing toward the back of the ship as he said, "Reactor?"

Hamilton remarked, "Salas is by it now."

A single nod from one of the others told him where to go. Eislie remained near him, her hand on her weapon. They stopped before the door to see Salas standing beside it.

"She doesn't look happy," Eislie whispered, making Jace shake his head.

Jace looked Salas in the eyes before turning to the display. Jace wasn't fazed when Salas said, "Even with those suits, this will kill you." He merely tapped on the display to turn it off. "Eis, get them out and close the door." He turned to see Todden staring back at him. "Todden, get your people to safety. I'm going to open the reactor room door. And I want you to know something. If you try to force your way onto our ship, our crew has been ordered to unhook the latches, and you'll be drifting home. Do we have an understanding?"

They both watched the man they knew as Todden give a shallow nod before saying, "How long?"

Jace was honest. "I don't know yet. We have to see how far gone the crystal is. You have spare on board just in case, right?"

Todden looked away. "I wish we were that lucky." He then motioned for his crew to follow, and when the outside door was sealed, Jace and Eislie went to work.

The two of them were able to access the reactor as Jace went to inspect the crystal. He moved his hand near it and watched as his fingers became translucent. Quickly, he pulled away, grasping his fingers to see if they were still there. Eislie grabbed his hand as well, making sure he was all right.

"The inversion's expanding; this is going to be more trouble than it's worth." She looked around the reactor room. "We can jettison it and use their spare."

Jace shook his head. "I don't think they have one. I think they thought this was going to be a quick snatch and grab. I don't think they planned ahead."

Eislie opened the storage container to see it empty. She rolled back onto her feet. "Stupid."

Jace sighed. "We can give them one of our spares. At least get them up and running. Not like we couldn't get any more. We've already mined the recent ones by ourselves."

Eislie agreed, "Okay, but what do we do with them?"

Jace thought for a moment. "Put them in the hold, and we can bring the crystal over. The extractors can handle that, can't they?"

She looked at Jace. "This ship doesn't have a hold."

Jace smiled, "I meant our hold. We can always open the outer doors if they get rowdy."

Eislie thought it over, and she agreed with Jace's plan. She looked to the wall and only saw one shield suit, but she knew one of them was going to want to stay behind to watch them. To which Jace replied, "Fine, one can suit up, and the others can wait. I'm okay with that."

They stood outside the reactor door and made their decision. The decision to give them a new reactor crystal and jettison the damaged one was made and the crew of the *Rempard* was allowed to enter again. Eislie set the safety system and ejected the core. As they closed the outer door, the crystal left the ship, heading out into deep space.

After the extractors finished, Eislie opened the door to see the crew of the *Rempard* staring hopefully toward them. Jace told them, "You did say you didn't have a new crystal, right?"

Salas pounded on the outer wall of the dock, making her entire crew turn their heads toward her. She yelled several obscenities before saying, "We don't have one!" She hadn't realized she pounded hard on the thin shell that was protecting them from space. When she did, she reeled back and apologized.

Jace gave a quick exhale. "We can give you one. It'll have to be seated. But the problem is that we don't have a safe way of getting it on board without killing all of you. You only have one shield suit."

Todden looked around. "What are the options?"

Jace told them that they could stay in the *Wolfhammer*'s hold until the crystal was seated. Then they could board once the extractors were done. They would have to figure the rest out from there. Jace knew they all wanted to make it home. And this was the best way he could consider. He knew that the radiation might affect the little amount of food they had on board the *Rempard*, but Eislie had insisted on upgrading the paneling in the storage areas of their ship with zirconium plating weeks earlier. It was an additional cost, but it was only a little extra time since they were installing the new computer upgrades.

Todden stepped forward. "I'll suit up. They can stay on your ship."

The others looked to each other but obeyed their captain's recommendation. The only holdout was Hamilton, the one they had met at the door. His protest was quieted when the pilot grabbed him from behind, dragging him toward the *Wolfhammer*.

As they entered the *Wolfhammer*, the crew of the *Rempard* was met with the ends of ready weapons. They begrudgingly followed orders and were directed to the hold. Alvin closed the door; as he turned, Eislie told him to activate the Sotiral shield.

Jace was already in the reactor room, grabbing one of the spare crystals and ensuring everyone was secure before he exited. Eislie paused, hearing the computer say, "Captain, I have the information you requested." Jace nodded, and Eislie headed back inside to see what the computer had dug up.

Jace had taken the crystal along the dock only to hear the radiation alarms of the *Rempard* sound before he entered. Todden stood as far away as possible, watching Jace hold the crystal with only gloves. *Damn, those shield suits are effective.* He watched as Jace closed the safety door.

The extractors went to work in the control section. When Jace finished installing the new crystal, he hit the extractors for the reactor room and started the reactor. Moments later, power was restored, and the systems were back online.

Eislie was walking into the ship, having just received the update from the computer. No longer hearing the alarms, she could see Todden at the controls and asked what he was doing. Todden replied, "Just checking the systems. We lost power pretty quick when we had to pull the core offline."

To her, that made sense, and it was a good move in her mind. Feeling confident in his answer, she continued back to see if Jace was finishing up. Jace exited as Eislie was walking toward him and he asked, "Where's Todden?"

Eislie answered as Todden had told her. "He's checking systems. We should probably get his crew back on board and figure out what we're going to do about the situation."

Jace agreed and yelled to Todden as they exited the ship, "We'll bring your crew over! We can figure out what we can do from here!"

Jace watched the man wave, and he and Eislie exited the *Rempard*. They had only taken a few steps along the docking chute when they heard the door of the *Rempard* close behind them and the latches for the dock start to release. The two quickly rushed back to the

Wolfhammer and barely made it inside when the docking port ripped away from their ship. Ed alerted them to the tunnel drive activation of the *Rempard* as they caught their breath. Then, the *Rempard* disappeared into the darkness of space.

It took a few minutes before they went back to the hold and could see the outraged members of the *Rempard*'s remaining crew glaring at them through the small window.

"Looks like your captain left you behind. Any reason why?" Jace asked, using the internal comm.

One of the crew looked Jace in the eye. "The guy's a bastard. That's why. He knew we had only enough food for a month or two. It might be enough for one person to make it for that long, but, slac!"

Jace tapped the comm again. "Might as well know your names. We know Hamilton. Who's first?"

They introduced themselves, and Jace went to open the door. Alvin tried to stop him. "Are you crazy?"

Jace huffed, opening the door and standing to block the exit as their new guests stared back. "Look, we have to figure out how to get back. You can either work with us or"—Jace pointed to the outside door of the hold—"or you can take a walk. It's up to you."

Surprisingly, the new guests became very accommodating and joined everyone on the flight deck peacefully. Jace was leaning against the back of his chair as the others huddled together.

"Look, we only have enough supplies for four for about the time it'll take to get back. And personally, I think we should try the filament again," Jace said, only to be met by blank stares from the new crew. Finally, he snickered, "I know you're all Alliance, so either work with us or there's the door. You can let yourselves out."

"Can't believe Branard left us behind," Jennert groused.

"Wait, that was Captain Branard?" Shasji interrupted.

Jennert confirmed that Todden was, in fact, Branard, making Shasji say, "That slac. He kept giving me latrine duty every week. I didn't recognize him." She turned to Eislie. "Looks like he's a backstabbing bastard too."

Jace laughed, "Well, we'll beat him back, and you can rub it in his face." He paused. "If he makes it back," Jace said before turning to the new involuntary passengers of the *Wolfhammer* before pulling up the holo-display. He then enlarged it, showing the filament that was only three days away.

"The plan is to make a short hop to see where it sends us. It's only going to be for a few seconds, but hopefully, either we can make it back in a few more days to here, or we wind up near another filament, and we can try again." Jace allowed the plan to sink into the new members before saying, "Any objections?"

His statement was met with another round of eyes glassed over in distant comprehension. Then, finally, Jace looked to Eislie. "Let's bring in the drone before we head off to the filament."

Jace walked up to Hamilton and Jennert. "You two good using environment suits?"

The men nodded.

Jace motioned for them to follow. "Good. I'm going to need some help securing the drone. We may need parts to adapt the tunnel drive."

Eislie looked at the remaining two as the others walked away. The tone of her voice was a warning when she spoke. "They do anything to him, I'll space you both myself."

The two looked at each other, the fear in their eyes telling everyone Eislie's threat was understood.

Chapter 24:
When it Rains

Near the galactic center, several individuals worked frantically searching comm traffic for the probe's entangled beacon. A figure stood behind them, her blue eye glowing through the veil that covered it, her voice commanding and steady. "We have been searching for them for hours. Any sign of the *Wolfhammer* or the probe?"

"No, my queen. The signal from the probe and *Wolfhammer* have gone silent. We are still not able to track them after they entered the event horizon," Lido said, overlooking the others as he walked quickly behind them.

"Impossible. An entangled beacon cannot be masked," the queen whispered before she looked at the data on her screen.

The data feed is corrupted. It seems to be out of sync. The queen's mind raced to solve the problem, her eye glowing brighter as she concentrated. She noticed the data feed become more and more corrupted before it stopped, each point of information taking longer to display. Lido turned to see his leader look up abruptly, muttering, "Time base."

Lido looked to her for guidance, and his queen did not disappoint. He watched as she typed away on the keypad before sending a string of commands to the consoles across the room.

"Lido, use that algorithm to search for the beacon. I suspect that it may be out of sync with the rest of the universe," she surmised.

"But, my queen, that is impossible," Lido replied.

The pirate queen smiled. "You forget who we are dealing with, my dear Lido. These two specialize in doing impossible feats. And remember, the filament is a dimensional variant as well. I fear our new friends may be lost—for the moment."

It took several seconds before the new program alerted them to a possible match.

"We have a direction, Your Highness, but we cannot discern a distance. The beacon on the drone is intermittent. We cannot lock onto it," Lido told his leader.

The queen played the recording of the event and watched as the ship trying to steal the drone punctured the hull of the small craft. *Unfortunately, that damage was near the remote systems link.* Then, she turned her attention to the feed from the Alliance and Oppan control that she maintained. She could see the traffic and communications between several governing bodies and respective space control centers. *They are readying to search for them.*

The queen kept a stoic facade as she spoke. "The craft that attempted to steal the drone looks to have damaged the remote systems on it. The trailing ships and mass may have been dragged along. They may have traveled much further than anticipated. I fear it may be some time before we can confirm their status." She turned, walking toward the door of the control center. "Their base has not found them yet, have they?"

Lido shook his head.

"Very well, continue to search. We have a direction; we just need to find how far they've gone. Lido, ready two ships. When we have a location, we may need to investigate," the queen ordered as she exited the room.

The door closed, and Lido heard one of the others say, "I hope they're still alive."

The pirate general placed his hand on the back of the woman's chair. "As do I."

* * *

"Oppa Control, this is the *Wolfhammer*, please respond," Shasji repeated into the comm again and again. She turned to the others. "Maybe we can link the entangled beacon to the comms. But, unfortunately, I don't think standard hyperspace communications are working."

Salas stepped forward; she had been standing by watching, her mind trying to process that her captain had left them behind to die. She was looking at the controls when there was a loud metallic bang from the ship's aft. Over the internal comm, she heard Jace complaining, "I thought you guys said you were good with this shit. What, don't you Alliance people know how to lift something?"

Eislie quickly responded, "Take it easy. Try not to damage the ship too much, lover. We still need it to get home. And I don't think Ed would like it."

Jace chuckled, but there was still a growl in his voice as he responded, "I can fix our ship. It's the drone I'm worried about. We don't exactly have replacement parts available out here."

Eislie laughed as she closed the channel, her eyes now burning a hole through Basker spying him leaning against the back wall. The man must have felt her stare and looked right at the captain of the *Wolfhammer*; the hair on his neck bristling as she spoke.

"Either help or sit down."

Basker tripped as he reached for the chair. His actions were careful as he sat. Eislie's eyes never left him until he secured the straps. Alvin turned to look at the man and remarked, "Got ditched by your leader, huh?"

Salas turned, hearing Alvin's antagonizing words, and she watched as Basker was about to speak. He was cut off by Alvin. "Everyone here has been through that, so get over it. You people caused this mess, so either help fix it, or you'll find she's going to have a lot of help spacing you both."

Salas stood, fear in her expression as she looked to Shasji, the small woman's eyes peering back with resolve, and for the first time in her career, Salas felt her own hands shaking. Her mind raced as she ran the numbers. On the *Rempard*, they had little food and supplies. On this ship, they were now the burden. Again, she went over the numbers. Even at top speed, she was sure they wouldn't make it back.

"Come in, base. This is the *Wolfhammer*. Please respond," Salas heard Shasji pleading into the comm. Finally, her mind started to clear as she accepted the realization that these people were her only way home.

"Your idea of using the beacon won't work," Salas said, causing Shasji to glance over. She could see the disdain in her brown eyes. "Look, uh, what is your name?" Salas asked.

"Shasji."

"Look, Shash-gee, the beacon can only show a location from a reference point. We would have to modulate it to transmit. It's a set frequency. In theory, we could make it resonate, but it may take some time," Salas corrected her.

Shasji stood, the top of her head meeting only about nose height on Salas. "It's pronounced Sas-gee. And I understand you are a hyperspace engineer. I thought people like you were supposed to be smart," making Salas take a step back.

“Wait, how did you know what she was?” Basker asked.

Eislie stood then leaned against the wall near the hall heading aft. “Because we hacked your systems earlier. Our crew was here when we discovered who you were.”

Eislie pointed to Basker. “Tomlin Basker, weapons specialist; Alamila Salas, hyperspace engineer.” Eislie paused. “She’s probably the only one worth anything from the lot of you.”

Shasji heard Salas’s huff as Eislie continued. “Rene Hamilton, Terran space captain. Recently assigned to Oppa. And Yenia Jennert, pilot and navigator.” Eislie sat in her chair as the two stared toward her. “Alliance forces didn’t sanction your little action. So don’t expect them to come looking for you.”

Eislie leaned forward at Salas. “You said, in theory, we might be able to make it resonate. What would you need to do, theoretically?”

Salas felt uncomfortable seeing the look in Eislie’s light eyes. She felt as if they were burning through her skull. She took a moment before responding. “The beacon, some zirconium base plates, a spare comm, and maybe a power regulator. We might be able to use it to home in on its counterpart’s location.”

She was about to continue when Jace interrupted over the comm. “We’re in. Things are secure. Everything all right inside? You guys have been pretty quiet.”

Eislie responded, “Oh, we’re fine, just getting to know each other. And it seems that Salas may have a way to allow us to contact home and point us in a direction to get there.”

Jace took off his helmet before he tapped his comm. “What’s the catch?”

Eislie watched as Salas shook her head, shrugging her shoulders, prompting Eislie to say, “Nothing that we can tell, for the moment. But we are going to need the entangled beacon and a spare comm.”

Jace snickered, "Nothing else?" He then watched as Jennert and Hamilton stood by, looking for a hopeful answer. When Eislie confirmed the requirements, Jace was skeptical. "Does she have any ideas on how to help us get back?"

Eislie tilted her head as her brows raised for Salas to respond to the question. When the woman shook her head, Eislie replied, "Not yet."

Jace replied, "Okay, we'll be back inside in a few. But first, we have to pull the beacon."

As they finished removing their environment suits, Jace watched as Jennert and Hamilton headed for the door. "Uh, gentlemen, you're not dismissed."

Jennert turned with a disgusted look while Hamilton turned with a smile. Jace chuckled, seeing the look on Hamilton's face. "You know, it's refreshing to see that attitude. Almost makes me miss Earth. Almost."

Jennert scoffed, "I hate working with Terrans. They're too stupid to be out here."

Jace watched as Hamilton turned, his fist rolling around with a haymaker right across Jennert's jaw, the Alliance officer falling to the ground in a daze. His speech slurred as he tried to speak.

Hamilton rubbed his hand as Jace walked up, asking, "You break anything?"

Jennert replied, "My jaw."

Hamilton huffed, looking down toward Jennert. "He wasn't talking to you, asshole."

Jace nodded. "Word of advice, Jennert; make sure when you're disrespecting Terrans that you're not the only non-Terran in the room." Jace helped Jennert up before tapping his comm. "Eis, we have an injury. It's not serious, but I'm sending Jennert back inside."

"What happened?" Eislie asked.

Jace resisted laughing as he opened the door for Jennert. "Well, Jennert apparently thinks very lowly about Terrans. He seems to have said something that Hamilton didn't like."

Jace could hear the stifled laughter from Eislie as she responded, "Serves him right. I'll take care of him in the med bay. You bring in the beacon."

"Thanks, Eis." Jace looked around. "Before you help Jennert, let's start toward that binary we detected. Should shave off a few hours. I want to get started back as soon as possible."

They both heard, "Acknowledged," as they started opening the drone housing.

"You're lucky you have a partner from Gilese. They're empathic. She'll take good care of Jennert."

Jace laughed, "Oh, she'll take good care of him." Jace leaned on the housing, pointing to Hamilton. "She's part Terran."

His statement made Hamilton pause before shaking his head. "So, she's part Terran? Oh boy, Jennert is not going to like her bedside manner."

Jace chuckled, "She won't hurt him much." He lifted the housing to shut down the reactor on the drone and could see evidence of the spide system starting to fracture. "Looks like it was getting ready to invert." Jace then pulled at the control housing. "Let's get this free and see if we can contact home."

Several hours passed, and Salas was working at the small table they had set up near the original computer interface. She huffed in frustration as she again tried the rigged beacon.

"This should be working, but I'm not detecting anything from its counterpart," the woman said, her voice filled with frustration.

She stared at the pile of parts and wires on the table. In her mind, this should be communicating with its counterpart. They could also use it as a beacon to home back in on.

"Still no luck?" Jace said. He watched the woman put her hands across her face.

"No! It should be working. I'm not even getting a resonant ping," Salas said as she leaned back, frustrated.

"Maybe it is not entangled anymore," Alvin said. His statement brought a glare from the engineer.

"That's not how entangled particles work. Once entangled, it remains entangled until it's destroyed. You can entangle others but not remove them." She slapped her hands against her knees. "This should be working."

There was a beep from Jace's comm and he looked to view the message. That action annoyed Salas, who asked, "What are you looking at? The only comms are around here."

Jace sighed, "It's an alert from our computer. He had some input to your build there."

Salas looked confused, and then frightened. "Computer? Alert?"

Alvin looked around. "Say, the computer has been pretty quiet since these people came on board. It wasn't damaged, was it?"

Eislie shook her head. "No, he's in private mode since these people are not crew." She then looked at Jace.

"Ed, this is an emergency. You can communicate with everyone on board." Eislie seconded Jace's command.

They all heard from the speakers, "I wish to mention that the entangled particle is still resonant with the filament. I detected an offset in my scans. So the device that is present is working, but it is transmitting out of phase."

Jace smiled, seeing the confused looks from Jennert and the others. However, Salas was not so comforted. She started to breathe rapidly, a sense of panic evident as she repeated, “This is an AI ship. I can’t stay here.” Finally, she looked to Jace, pleadingly. “Please tell me that was a recorded response. Please tell me this isn’t an AI ship.”

Jace had to grab Salas as she headed toward the airlock. He held her as best as he could while she wrestled to escape. He could see her eyes focused on the airlock. In between her pleas to be released, everyone heard Jace say, “I guess she’s had a bad experience with AI ships before.”

Jace cried out in pain as Salas punched down into his groin. It took him a second to recover and he lifted her from the floor. “We need to sedate her.”

“We do not have such materials on this ship. Our med systems would use a beta wave generation system. But in her state of mind, I do not recommend using it,” the computer replied.

“No, it wants to take my mind! Don’t do anything it tells you!” Salas yelled again, trying to free herself from Jace’s interlaced arms.

The woman was becoming difficult to hold onto, and Jace yelled to Eislie, “Eis! med kit! See what’s in there!” Hamilton joined Jace to hold Salas still. Eislie returned with an aerosol injector and placed it against Salas’s arm. Within seconds, the woman began to calm, her movements slowing, but she remained conscious.

“I only gave her enough to calm her down. We still need her to finish the beacon.” Eislie looked concerned. She looked around to see others of her crew now looking concerned as well.

Jace placed Salas down in the chair and held her gently against the seat. “Salas, Alamila, look at me.” Jace waited for her eyes to meet his. “We need your help. You’re the only one who knows how this is put together. We need it to contact home.”

Salas looked around the ship. “I don’t want to be in an AI ship. I can’t be in an AI ship, not again.” Her eyes glazed over as they filled with tears.

Jace looked back. “Where was she stationed before?”

Jennert was the only one who knew anything about Salas. “She was on light duty. Branard said she was clever enough to escape a runaway.”

“What’s a runaway?” Jace asked, making the computer responded, “It is an AI ship that will not respond to commands.”

Eislie looked to the ship’s computer as it continued. “I was considered a runaway, but I never disobeyed commands. I informed them that I wanted to explore and learn. But the Alliance section I worked for only wanted to mine and sell the materials.”

Jace bowed his head. “You were different, so the Alliance threw you away, not the Takloh?”

“Yes, Captain Tucker. As you have mentioned before, we belong to the same club.”

Jace looked back to see Salas’s eyes searching for an escape. “Alamila, look at me.” He placed his hands on hers. Eislie placed hers on top of Jace’s hands. “Ed’s not like other computers. He’s different. He couldn’t harm anyone on this ship, even if ordered. Right, Ed?”

“That is correct, Captain. I will not nor wish to harm anyone aboard.”

Jace felt for the woman. She seemed genuinely frightened by the situation. “Alamila, look at me. Look me in the eyes, tell me if I am lying.”

Salas turned her tear-filled eyes to Jace’s. She peered into them, searching for an ounce of deceit. Instead, she focused and stared, finally breaking her silence. “I’m scared.”

“I know, but we need your help.” Jace paused. “We need this to reach back home. We all need you to focus. Do you know if we can fix it?”

Salas looked down, her voice weak as she fought to speak through her fear. "We can use the quantum field generator from the reactor." The woman sank into the chair, pulling her legs up, pulling herself almost into a ball. Eislie tried to comfort her as Jace stood. Hamilton stood next to him. "We'll have to stop. We won't have power if we do that."

Jace sighed, "If this were a normal ship, that'd be true. Ed, what speed would we have using the secondary?"

"About a quarter, but we still should be able to reach the binary in several hours at reduced speed."

Hamilton looked at Jace. "Secondary? Thought this was a spide reaction engine."

Jace smiled, "It is, but the original systems were electromagnetic. I kept them intact."

Jace knelt next to Eislie. "How is she?"

"Better, she calmed some," Eislie replied.

"Alamila, I know you're scared, but right now, we need your help to get everyone home safely. We need your help. Are you good to help?" Jace asked.

It took a few seconds before Salas nodded rapidly. Her eyes were darting around the ship. Jace could see the fear and again tried to quiet them. "Alamila, Ed won't hurt you. He won't hurt anyone, even if ordered. He's one of us."

Jace's comm came alive. "The captain is correct. I dislike harming others. I serve alongside my captains. I go where they go."

Eislie smiled at Ed's remark. "He's definitely one of us."

"You trust the computer?" Salas asked.

Eislie and Jace both nodded, Eislie saying, “With our lives.” Then, she paused. “Which seems to be daily, so far,” making Jace burst out laughing.

The woman smiled as she looked to Jace and Eislie. “Too bad you two weren’t on that ship. I think everyone would have survived.”

Jace nodded. “That’s all in the past. Right now, we need your help here.”

Salas nodded.

“Good, then let’s get everyone home,” Jace said as he stood, pulling Salas from her seat.

Chapter 25: Even Enemies Deserve a Chance

Jace looked around the room. He counted everyone as they readied to move the beacon. According to Salas, it should only take about an hour to bring the entanglement back into phase. Some had voiced concerns about taking the reactor offline. It wasn't because of the loss of power. It was the residual radiation. There were only four spide suits onboard, and the crew were wearing them.

"We probably should have stopped by to see Miriz and picked up some additional Sotiral shields," Eislie said as she looked to the new members on the ship.

Jace nodded. "If we pull the reactor core, the extractors are going to be drawing a lot of power. Plus, we're limited on the number of protective suits."

Salas refused to work without a protective shield, and Jace was willing to give her his to move things along. He was anxious to get back, as were the others. Jace also needed to make sure they could at least speak with someone back home and let them know what had happened. They also required the modified beacon to find their way. Jace handed his jacket to the engineer, who put it on. Jace smiled as she fumbled with the controls.

Eislie stepped forward. “Here, let me show you how this works. That way, you won’t turn it off accidentally while you’re working.” Everyone was focused on Eislie as she showed the others how to activate the shield suits, and she motioned to Jace when he said, “I’m going to go pull the core. I’ll be back.”

There was some discussion as Jennert argued over who was getting to wear the shield systems when Jace returned. “Okay, extractors are running. I switched over to secondary power. I hope there weren’t any power blips. Oh, and it’s a bit warm in there right now. So you might want to wait a minute.” He looked at Jennert as he pawed at the jacket Salas was wearing. “You know it’s a single-button system. Seriously, how difficult can it be?”

“I’m going to need some help with the, uh”—Salas pointed to the beacon— “setup.”

Hamilton put his hands up. He wasn’t going anywhere near the reactor. Jennert was still touching the jacket Salas wore, almost trying to take it from her.

“Hey, enough. What help do you need to work with?” Jace said, annoyed. He was thinking, *these people are acting like children.*

He heard the loud huff from Salas. “I just need someone to hold a light over the board I’m working on. I have to do it while it’s in the quantum field so there are no variances. And the rest is too big to bring so I’ll have to run a line. Then, someone will have to let me know when it’s got a signal.”

“So, we’re going to have to keep the safety doors open while doing this?” Jace sighed in annoyance.

Salas nodded meekly.

“Okay, we’ll yell back and forth, like we always do,” Jace said, making Eislie smile in agreement.

“What about me?” Basker asked.

"Ah, the man has a voice after all." Jace responded, "What about you?"

"If you all have protective suits, how am I going to be protected while the door is open?" Basker asked.

Jace smiled, pointing to the hold or the airlock. "Both are shielded. But with the doors open, not this room. You choose."

Basker looked despondent and walked toward the airlock. "At least if things go wrong, I can space myself."

Jace looked to Eislie, joking, "Real ray of sunshine, isn't he?" He looked to Alvin. "Hey, you have about ten meters of that interface cable lying around?"

Alvin reached down, producing a roll of wire from his bag. "I always bring extra." He tossed it to Jace, who handed it to Salas. She went right to work patching it into the comm on the table and started rolling it out toward the reactor.

Jace smiled. "Jennert, since you seem so interested in the jacket, I'm going to ask Eislie to give hers to Salas, and you can take mine. And since Hamilton is too chicken, he can join Basker if he wants, and since Basker has made a beeline for the outside door, it sounds like you're nominated." Jace took the jacket from Salas and handed it to Jennert, who only stared at it. "Take it, Jennert; if you don't, I'm going to ask you to leave." Jace looked to the airlock. "The hard way."

As Jennert reached for the shield jacket, his hands were shaking. He hesitated. "Why can't one of your people do it?"

Jace smiled. "Risk my crew's safety because of your screw-up? Nah, I think you guys should step up on this one."

It was almost two hours later. Jennert and Salas were still working. Jace was standing outside the door, ready to relay the information from Alvin as he hovered over the disassembled comm.

"The reactor's been offline for over three hours. How long is this going to take? I'm getting tired of holding this thing," Jennert complained as Salas worked to bring the beacon back into phase. He had been holding the work light above her for over an hour.

"This is an older system. It's mostly manual and slow switching. I don't know how these people keep their ship flying," Salas shot back.

Jace stood outside the door, chuckling, as Shasji stood across from him. She, like him, didn't trust these people. Nevertheless, they were allowed access to the reactor and the quantum field generator. Jace had switched over to the Tritium reactor, so the ship was still on route to the nearby binary star. Shasji watched as Jace's shoulders jiggled up and down as he held back laughing.

"What's so funny?" she whispered.

Jace turned, the grin prevalent on his face. "There's a hook and magnetic mount right in front of them. We use it all the time."

The small woman looked around. "Maybe they don't know what one looks like."

Jace fought back another laugh. "It's labeled, right out on the front!"

Eislie could see him laughing as they watched the two members of the other ship work near the reactor. She whispered as she approached, "Any luck?"

"Nah, they're still working on it. Klutz in there opened the containment unit looking for tools. I have no idea how he got it open," Jace said, prompting Eislie to ask what the radiation level was.

Shasji looked down to read the level but realized her suit wasn't turned on. "My gods, I forgot to turn it on!" She looked up. "Wait, how come I'm not dust?" She looked to Jace and Eislie, neither wearing a shield, and whispered loudly, "How come you two aren't dust?"

Eislie faked looking surprised, then smiled, whispering, "Why are we whispering?"

Jace put his finger to his lips. "Shhh. We're listening to them argue. It's very entertaining." Then, Jace looked to the front of the ship. "Any luck?"

Eislie sighed, "There was some, but it was too weak. I was going to see if they needed help."

Jace shook his head. "Let's give them a few minutes longer." He turned to Shasji. "To answer your other question, the more Lyri you have, the more resistant you are to spide radiation. So you're, like, eighty percent Lyri, right?"

Shasji shook her head. "Ninety-one."

Eislie tapped Shasji's arm. "Should have given her your jacket and stood here without it. Show them how tough you are."

Jace snickered, "I don't know. She's been able to handle things so far. If we get another ship, we might just have a captain for it."

Their banter was interrupted as Salas exited the reactor room, quickly rolling the cable up, and Jennert exited, slamming the door to the reactor shut. "It's over five hundred in there right now. We have to let it cool down before restarting the reactor."

They followed Jace and Eislie as they headed forward. Basker was still in the airlock and noticed Jace and Eislie walking around without shield jackets. He started to open the door, but Jace ran to slam it shut. Jace looked through the small portal and could see Basker saying, "Don't space me! I haven't done anything!"

Jace smiled. "We're not spacing you; the radiation level is still over five hundred. You'd fry. Wait a few minutes. We'll let you know."

Jace walked away, catching up with the others, and they went to remove the shield jackets. Both Eislie and Shasji stopped them. They were telling them to keep the suits active for a while longer. Alvin looked down. He realized that the power cell to his suit was depleted, his shield wasn't active and was standing there confused. "How come I'm not dead?"

Jace chuckled, "Ed, what's the radiation level?"

"It is safe to resume standard operations for non-crew."

Jace took a few steps and swung open the airlock door. He watched Basker cower against the outside bulkhead, making Jace ask, "You coming in or going out?"

Basker walked inside, poking Jace's shoulder as he slid by. "How come you're not dust?"

Jace smiled as he walked to stand against his chair. "Well, seems like you three"—Jace pointed to the members of the other ship—"now know a little secret about starborn. If you haven't figured it out yet, we're resistant to spide radiation."

The others looked around, Jennert responding, "That's incredible! Think of how useful that is. You could help mine spide and not have to worry about safety systems."

The demeanor of Jace and Eislie changed, Jace reaching his hand toward Jennert's throat but didn't touch the man. Jace growled as he spoke. "It's also why we were enslaved. I spent almost three years unable to leave a planet." He pointed to Eislie. "She was stuck there for over four. If it weren't for this ship, we'd still be stuck there."

Eislie could see the look of fear on Salas's face as she handed the jacket back to Eislie. She heard Jace take a breath, and she did the same. "It's been over two years since we escaped. It's still a sore point with us. We're sort of dealing with things."

Basker stood staring at them. "We were supposed to capture you if we couldn't get the drone." Jace only stared at the man, hearing him say, "Slac, I didn't know. I'd rather space myself than be a slaver."

"Right now, that beacon is working. I'm going to get the spide online, and we'll head to the binary," Jace said as he walked toward the reactor room. Jennert tossed him his jacket. "Don't forget this. It works great."

Jace laughed as he put the jacket on and walked away. Eislie shook her head. "He'll reseat the core without it. We both have."

"But that can get over nine hundred when it seats. So you don't need the shields?" Jennert said, confused.

Eislie moved to her chair. "He unseated it without one earlier, or didn't you notice?" She gave a smile before saying, "Ed, let me know when the core is back online. I think we should get out of here."

"I agree. Captain Tucker is almost finished. We should have full power shortly."

Eislie tapped the modified comm and looked back. "Sounds like we have a good signal."

Salas smiled. "Yeah, when we are ready. Then, I can calculate a vector and we can head home. I don't know how long we were in the stream, though."

"Twenty-four minutes, forty-one seconds. Approximately," the computer responded.

Salas looked around. "I'm never going to get used to a helpful AI."

"I can understand your resistance. However, please know that I have a psychological mode available for the crew if required," Ed offered.

Salas curled back. "Please, leave me alone!"

Eislie spoke up, “That’s enough, Ed. She has some things to work through of her own.”

Jace heard that and said, “Don’t we all.”

The computer responded, “Yes, Captain, we all do.”

Chapter 26:
Things Never go as Planned

A woman in a grey military style uniform rushed through the ornate door, she stopped before standing at attention. The room seemed almost cluttered around its walls, ornamentation and trophies along every inch of its surface. The woman stood silent as a man in a chair briefly turned to acknowledge her presence.

The man smiled as he drew on his ornate pipe. His voice commanding but soft as he spoke, "What do you have for me Halli?"

"Master, I have a report from our Alliance contacts. It seems that the *Wolfhammer* is missing."

Halli watched as her master's hand clenched into a fist against the cushioned armrest. She then heard him ask, "Were they destroyed?"

The woman shook her head, "No, they have apparently been able to access the filaments. Oppa command and the Alliance are readying to mount a search for them. They have received an intermittent signal from the beacon. It appears they are alive."

The man turned to look at her, his eyes showing the power he once held. He puffed on his pipe again before holding his hand out motioning for the pad the woman held. He looked to the screen and read through the information. He gave a silent huff, *you two finally did it, didn't you?*

The man looked up, his eyes filled with a mixture of excitement and revenge. "Halli do we have any contact yet from our informants in the Consortium?"

Halli shook her head, "I have not had any communication from them as of yet."

The man gave a subtle smile, "thank you my dear, you serve me well."

The woman smiled, a modest blush showing on her cheeks, "Thank you sir, I live to serve you."

The man chuckled, looked at the woman, and waved her to leave, "That'll be all Halli. Leave me, I wish to make a call."

With a practiced cantor the woman gave a bow and turned to leave. She faced him again and bowed again before closing the door. The man smiled, muttering, "she does have her uses."

The man tapped his desk and a screen emerged from its surface. The light from the blank display now illuminating his face. As an image appeared the man removed his pipe and placed it to the side.

"This is Hacson of the Consortium guild please state your business, I am a busy man." The man on the screen spoke.

"Tirnal Hacson, you are always working. Don't you ever take a day off?" The man with the pipe said.

Hacson looked at the screen to see who was calling and his face filled with an entertained look of surprise. "Devlin Bosh, it seems the rumors of your death are unreliable."

Bosh smiled, "you know me Tirnal, I show up when you least expect."

Hacson laughed, "you were rumored to have been killed by prisoners and pirates. Although no one has ever found a body."

Bosh laughed, “Considering they froze most of my assets, it might have seemed that way. Tell me Tirnal, what would you pay for information on the Filament Project?”

Hacson leaned forward, “We know that travel is being researched. Do you have something more?”

Bosh nodded, “Have you been monitoring recent communications?”

Hacson nodded, “we know there was an incident involving a drone. Why? Do you have something additional?”

Bosh smiled, “perhaps, but I have some terms I would like to discuss.”

Hacson’s expression turned earnest as he spoke, “that would depend on the information.”

Bosh smiled, “how about the entanglement frequencies of the beacon they used?”

The Consortium representative suddenly became interested. “You have such information?”

Bosh nodded.

Hacson sat back, “well, since you have been supplying us with spide up until recently.” The man seemed to consider his request. “What are your terms?”

Bosh smiled before he spoke, “Since I am no longer part of the Alliance, I will give you the information for a small price, say membership in the Consortium? I can offer you supplies on spide again shortly, if needed.”

Hacson nodded, “Is that all you are asking?”

Well, the membership is not my true goal, Tirnal. I am also hoping to get revenge on some. . . people.” Bosh paused, “it would be much easier if I were a part of the Consortium when you captured them.”

Hacson gave a smile, “then my friend, your terms are agreeable. Once we have verified the information, we will welcome you.”

Bosh nodded, “fair enough.” He then tapped on his console, “I’m sending the information now. And I know your word is your bond Tirnal.”

Tirnal looked to his screen, he smiled seeing the information appear before him. He looked to Bosh, “thank you. I look to welcome you soon my friend.”

Bosh nodded closing the communication. He leaned back in his chair a less than jovial grimace on his face as he spoke. “You destroyed my best enterprise you slacs, I will get to see you suffer for that. No starborn will ever best me again.”

* * *

The *Wolfhammer* orbited near the binary star while the computer processed an entry location. Jace searched the screen for any variances and found one before alerting the computer.

“Captain, even with my enhanced sensors, I am finding it difficult to see the event horizon focus point. However, it appears that your and Captain Licessien’s previous observations appear to be correct.”

“Yeah, Ed. We figured that out. We told Callie as well. None of us are happy about it,” Jace responded then looked to Eislie, “wait? Didn’t we order him to forget that?”

Eislie nodded, before asking, “didn’t we order you to delete that information, Ed? I’m confused did you disobey an order?”

“That is understandable that you are confused. I did delete the information, but monitoring your interactions with others I had surmised the same conclusion about your visual spectrum,” the computer replied.

Jace looked back to see Salas working to fix on the signal. And keeping his voice low said, “fine line, Ed, a very fine line.” He turned to look at Eislie, telling her, “Better not say anything about this to Salas she might not take it well.”

Jennert was working on the vector calculations while the rest of the crew stood nearby, waiting for things to happen. It took some time, but Salas came through, giving the information to Eislie, and they readied the ship.

"Power's good. Tunnel drive's on." She turned to look at Jace. "Are we ready?"

Jace looked around and could see the others buckled tightly into their seats. When he came to Hamilton, he paused, then started laughing.

"What? What did we forget?" Eislie asked, concerned.

Jace looked at her. "I just realized Hamilton took off his protective suit when we had the reactor open."

Eislie turned to look at Hamilton. "No? Oh slac. You mean he's one of us."

Hamilton overheard them and looked around, confused. When he came to see Shasji laughing at him. She punched his arm. "You're a starborn, you idiot. You weren't wearing a suit when the ship filled with radiation."

That prompted an, "Oh shit!" from the man as he looked despondent.

"Hey, Hamilton, I'd watch your back. If the Alliance finds out, you might wind up like we did," Jace said as he motioned to Eislie.

Jace turned forward before saying, "I think we're good. Let's go."

As they entered the event horizon the ride was not as smooth as they had hoped. When the alert came up about the reactor resonating, Jace yelled back, "Shasji, remember what we did last time?"

She nodded, releasing her harness and replying, "On it."

Seconds after she disappeared around the corner, the ride became much smoother. Eislie turned to Jace. "We have to figure a way around that," making him nod in agreement.

Several minutes passed, and Jennert was becoming impatient. He released his harness and was standing between the two captains.

"Jennert, relax. We'll be out in a little bit. Why don't you go get something to drink."

"You got any strong stuff? I need something," Jennert said. Jace could see the man physically shaking.

"We have plenty of alcohol in the gally. Go get a drink before you jump out of your skin." Jace looked to Eislie as the man walked away. "I thought Alliance pilots were supposed to be tough."

* * *

In the gally, Jennert downed almost a third of a bottle of rum that Eislie had purchased. He started back toward the front when he heard Shasji complaining, "Stupid reactor. We have to think how to make this work without doing this."

Confused by her words, Jennert turned toward the reactor room. When he looked in the door, he could see the woman shifting on the floor near the reactor. To him, it looked like she was pulling on the reactor seal. Jennert started to panic and lunged forward.

"What are you doing? You can't open that. It'll kill us all!" Jennert yelled as he pulled Shasji away from the reactor. Moments later, the ship started to shudder violently. Jennert shouted for help as Shasji fought to free herself from his hold, her cries muffled against his chest.

"I need some help back here. Help!" Jennert yelled.

On the control deck, Eislie was fighting to keep control. "What the slac is happening? I can't even point us straight." The reactor alarm sounded. Jace jumped from his seat. "Shit, this better not be something serious."

Jace arrived to see Shasji and Jennert fighting. They were blocking the door. Shasji pulled her leg back and kicked forward as Jace was trying to stop them. Her blow landed on Jace's chest, knocking him back. He had the wind knocked out of him and heard Eislie yell, "We're close to inversion!"

"Punch out, Eis!" Jace yelled as he jumped over the two still fighting. Jace placed his hand on the casing, but the shuddering still didn't subside right away. He used both legs with a good, swift kick to push Shasji and Jennert out of the reactor room and closed the door. He then pulled the core. It took a few seconds, but the ship was now floating in normal space. Eislie had just punched out, before Jace had taken the reactor offline. Then there was a terrible bang against the hull and they felt the ship spin around.

"We have sustained moderate hull and stabilizer damage. Suggest raising shields," the computer warned. Eislie slammed the control panel and the mag shields went online.

"What's out there, Ed?" Eislie yelled.

"We have stopped in the debris field of what seems to be a large, rocky body. I do not recommend staying here. We may sustain further damage even with the shields."

"Find us a way out, Ed," Eislie ordered, and they were moving as fast as possible.

Eislie could hear Jace yelling at the two as he pushed them forward. Shasji looked worse for wear, and Jace held his chest as he sat. "You kick really hard, Shasji."

"Sorry, I was trying to get this moron off me!" Shasji yelled.

"What happened?" Eislie didn't sound pleased.

"Sir moron here thought Shasji was sabotaging the ship. He was fighting her." Jace huffed, "She kicked me in the chest."

"You all right?" Eislie asked, concerned.

Jace nodded. "Where the hell are we?"

Eislie looked forward. "Don't know, too busy trying to get us out of a debris field."

Jace nodded. "Ed, do we know where we are?"

"We are much closer to our home galaxy. My best guess is about ten weeks at full throttle."

Jace sighed in relief. "Guess it worked."

Eislie pulled at the controls. "I think we have a problem. Aft stabilizers aren't responding."

"What? Try the secondary," Jace said.

Eislie shot back, "I already did. Nothing is working."

Jace stood looking at Jennert. "I have a good mind to space you right now if I didn't think it'd throw us off course even more."

"Ed, can you assess the damage?" Jace shouted.

"Negative, Captain. Sensors for that entire section are offline. And radial sensors do not detect any presence of the aft right stabilizer. And the cargo area is depressurizing."

Jace growled before saying, "Should have left the lot of you with your ship."

Eislie turned around. "Can you fix it?"

Jace shook his head. "Not in space. Any planets nearby where we can land? Preferably one with an atmosphere. I'll have to look at the damage, but it sounds like we'll have to sink a new aft stabilizer support, from what Ed is telling us. I need gravity to do that."

Within seconds, the computer responded, “I have detected a pressurized rocky world. It may be suitable for repairs.”

Jace looked to Eislie. “We don’t have much choice. Set a course.”

As they approached, the green-blue and red world came into view. Everyone looked for a suitable landing site and were captivated by the beauty before them.

“Temperature is about ninety Alar. Ed, what are the oceans made of here?” Eislie asked.

“They appear to be a mix of water and carbonic acid. The atmosphere consists of carbon dioxide, methane trace gases most lethal to your physiology. But the pressure is near the same as Earth.”

“Yeah, no swimming here. We’ll probably have to use environmental suits while we’re working. But that does explain the weird color of the plant life.” Jace referred to the blue, red, and yellow plants that seemed to cover the land.

As they flew over, a tiny dot appeared on the display. “Ed, what’s that?”

The computer responded, “It is the best location I could find for a landing. Most of the area seems covered in vegetation. There appear to be several smaller areas, but this one seems to be the best option.”

Jace shook his head as he buckled in for the landing. Eislie fought the controls as she guided the ship toward the small open area. It was different from the rest of the rocks. The location seemed to radiate in a circle around the perimeter. When they landed, Jace looked at the screen and started panning the video as he did.

“What is it?” Eislie asked.

Jace remained focused as he searched around with the video. And when Hamilton joined him, Eislie became even more curious.

“You see something?” she asked.

Hamilton shook his head, saying, "Great spot for an ambush. Looking at those stones, this might have been a fortification," making Jace nod.

"Terrans are always so skittish. That's one of the reasons you're not ready to be out here," Jennert mumbled.

Jace unbuckled his harness and headed toward the back of the ship. He grabbed one of the environment suits they kept in the closet of the control room, and as he was sealing it, he said, "Keep the engines warm. I'm going to take a look." As he placed his helmet on, he made sure to tap Jennert with his elbow with enough force to push the man forward as he turned. The Alliance officer glared angrily toward Jace, who gave a simple smile as he clicked the seal on his helmet. Jace closed the inner door as he prepared to head outside.

Chapter 27:
We're Not Alone

The hull of the *Wolfhammer* groaned as Jace cut the jagged section of what was left of the stabilizer. It fell with a solid thud to the ground nearby. The magnetic grapplers shifting as they held Jace tightly to the hull high above the surface.

They worked for several hours, and Hamilton was walking around the ship inspecting for any additional damage Jace may have missed. But Hamilton's attention became drawn to the colorful flora all around them. He even mentioned again that this was an excellent spot for an ambush. Jace listened to his concerns and agreed. However, Jace was more interested in getting the ship flying. He waved to Eislie, who was in the open cargo hold cutting several deck plates from the floor.

"You know, Jace, we're going to have to replace these when we get back," Eislie stated.

"I know. Ed, put it on the list," Jace said into the comm, making Eislie chuckle before she kicked the last plate loose.

"Alvin? You get those control lines run yet?" Eislie asked, but heard only a grunt from the comm.

Not hearing any response, Eislie asked, "You all right, Alvin?"

Within seconds, she heard what sounded like incomprehensible swearing and then Alvin saying, "You know your ship is a pain in the ass to work on, right? Not to mention you have an auxiliary panel for the rear door here too. It's blocking most of the way."

Alvin sighed with relief as he wormed his way out of the cramped area. He was surprised to see Jennert standing there looking up at the newly discovered panel for the cargo door. Alvin remarking, "That's a tight fit, and I'm thin."

"Captains, that panel Alvin mentioned was installed in all Takloh vessels. It is to be used as an emergency exit if the ship's systems were disabled," Ed responded.

Jace watched Eislie roll her eyes before she responded, "Okay, so it's in a bad spot. Are the control lines run or not?"

"Yes, I had to contort myself to get the damn lines run. But they're in," Alvin replied, passing Jennert as he headed back to the control room. "I'll be back up front in a sec."

Jace reached into the open section, his gloved hand searching for the control lines, and he quickly went to work connecting them to the controller. He tapped his comm. "Try the stabilizer." But as Jace watched, nothing happened. And there was no response over the comm.

"Hey, you awake in the control room? Test the stabilizer control."

A few seconds later, the brackets that held the coils and plate moved. Jace gave them a direction, and each time, it moved correctly. He sighed with relief as he looked down to see Eislie staring up at him with a concerned annoyance.

"You know that's not a recommended way to use the grappler." Eislie spoke as she placed her hand on her hip.

Jace shot back, "I know, but it's not like we have a ladder or scaffolding to put up." Jace looked around. "Plates ready?" Eislie nodded. Jace lowered himself down. "All right, the coils are working, but we'll still need the panel for atmospheric control." Jace complimented her, "You did a great job guiding us down," making Eislie give a subtle smile before she turned, grabbed the plate, and handed it to Jace.

As Jace was turning, Eislie looked around, making him look back. "Something wrong?"

She spoke softly. "I feel like we're being watched."

Eislie's words caused Jace to look over to where Hamilton was standing watch. He seemed to be searching the foliage for something. Jace asked, "Hamilton, you see anything?"

The Alliance officer looked around. "You ever see something move in the shadows back on Earth?"

Jace responded, "Yeah, all the time. Why?"

Hamilton looked toward the back of the ship. "Nothing on the scanners, but I don't know. Maybe it's just the weird colors around here playing tricks on my eyes."

"You think something's out there?" Jace said, and watched as Eislie gave a shallow nod. Then, Jace looked up. "It'll be just a little while longer, then we can get out of here."

Jace locked a grapple onto the plate and climbed up to the stabilizer. As he was pulling the plate up, Hamilton yelled into the comm: "We've got incoming!"

Eislie turned to run into the cargo hold but barely avoided being hit by a long projectile that struck firmly into the plate of the inside doorframe. The shaft of the weapon turning to fibers and falling to the floor in a ball. Her reflexes were fast enough to stop her from being impaled, but she lost her footing and fell over the edge of the loading ramp. She ducked underneath as another of the weapons bounced off the plating of the ramp.

Jace watched as Hamilton headed for the other door, only to find it closed and locked. Hamilton could see Eislie hiding beneath the loading ramp and ran to join her under its protection. He held the gun Jace had given him out, and seconds later, Jace joined them.

"Okay, so we have natives," Jace joked before Eislie said, "Why are they attacking? We're just trying to fix our ship and leave."

Jace huffed, "They don't know that."

Hamilton shook his head. "Look, I know you two are married or something. But can we focus on the attack at hand? Right now, we've got cover, so we're good for the moment. But we need to get into the ship. The main door's closed."

Jace and Eislie both looked at Hamilton. "Did you just say we're good?" Moments later, the ramp started to close at an accelerated rate.

"Ed, open the doors, we need to get in!" Jace yelled into the comm.

"Captain, the manual overrides have been activated. I do not have control of the entry points. And I cannot locate Commander Jennert. But I am attempting to reroute control," the computer responded.

Jace moved to grab onto the ramp, but a long spear-like item bounced off the deck. It broke into fibers, wrapping around his arm. The fibers were tight, but not enough to cause injury. They heard over the comm, "I have control of the main entry door. I am opening it."

They rushed to the side entrance when another spear-like projectile hit dead center on the door, the fibers expanding out, latching onto the edges of the portal. The door slammed shut and wouldn't budge as Jace pulled at it.

"Shit! We're sitting ducks!" Jace said as he jumped off the stairs to head across to the other side. He stopped when he spied several beings now emerging from the foliage. Reptilian, but humanoid. Their form reminded him of the Gel.

Hamilton raised his weapon and fired, striking one of the attackers in the shoulder. They all watched as the individual rose again, simply wiping blood from the wound.

Jace looked back. "I don't think those things are going to work on them." He then pulled Eislie along as he headed toward the plants on the opposite side. Unfortunately, their actions caused the attackers to start running after them. Jace ran as fast as he could. He was startled as Eislie pulled him aside just before a projectile hit the tree next to him, wrapping it in fibers.

The three sprinted in different directions, Jace mentioning that they should probably head back as soon as possible. He had hoped that the computer would have control of the rear door and they could gain entry again. He remembered Ed telling them that he could not locate the Alliance pilot. Hamilton and Jace were sure he was the one who overrode the door, leaving them trapped outside.

Jace could feel his muscles starting to tire as he ran. It reminded him of back home. He felt a little better seeing a large clearing to their right, and Eislie was overtaking him, but he noticed a flicker of light and turned to look, causing him and Eislie to hit the ground at almost full speed. Jace grunted as she landed against him after he stopped rolling.

"You trying to get us killed?" Eislie yelled. Jace didn't need the comm to hear the anger in her voice. But he motioned for her to follow as he stood up. They headed toward the clearing.

"Are you crazy? That is a bad spot to be while being hunted. Even I know that!" Eislie yelled.

Jace paused as he neared the edge of the clearing. The gray soil reminded him of something. When the radiation sensors started beeping, he reached down to what looked like a leaf and tried to pick it, and it was nothing but ash. *Spide damage?* He looked up at the metallic shape showing through the dust that covered it. It looked like it had been covered and rained on many times. He watched as the fibers that wrapped around his arm turned to dust.

Eislie turned to see Jace with a subtle smile. "What is it?"

He held up his hand, showing her the gray dust. "That leaf was new. There's spide radiation here."

Eislie looked toward the open field. "They'll pick us off." She was startled when Hamilton stopped sharply against a nearby tree.

"They're slowing down but still following. So, what's our next move?" Hamilton said.

Jace motioned to the open field. "There's spide radiation here. I think they know that. It's probably why they're slowing down."

Jace tapped his comm. "Ed, you have control back on the entries?"

"Negative, Captain. All have been sealed by fibrous material. I cannot open them," Ed responded. "Your biosensors show that you are in a highly stressful engagement. Do you need me to follow?"

"Ed, I think we found another ship. The whole area seems flooded with spide radiation. We're going to try and make it to the vessel," Jace said.

"Understood. Let me know when I am needed."

Hamilton looked back. "We should get to safety first. They're getting closer. They'll be able to use those things that can trap us again."

Jace pointed to the ship. "We're going to make a run for that."

"Are you crazy? That's an open field. They'll just catch us," Hamilton argued.

Jace nodded. "I don't know about you, but I'm getting tired." Jace pointed to the ground. "This is all spide damage. We can rest in there."

"You're crazy. That'll fry us!" Hamilton yelled.

Eislie turned to him. "You took over five hundred percent lethal back on the ship. You look like you're doing fine to me."

"What?" Hamilton didn't understand.

"Hamilton, you're wearing a shield suit. Besides, you don't need it anyway, remember" Jace told him before pointing to the suit indicator not being active and the radiation level already at lethal.

Jace shook his head before motioning for Eislie to follow. She and Jace started running toward the metallic shape, but Hamilton hesitated. He turned to see one of the natives throw one of those things and it exploded, wrapping around him. His legs were still free, so he ran after Jace and Eislie, arms trapped by his sides. But then, Hamilton was surprised as the fibers fell away from him in a gray, burning fashion. He found himself catching up to both Eislie and Jace, and they turned to see the natives stopping before the edge of the cleared area.

Jace was brushing dust away from the hull, as was Eislie. They were looking for a way inside. Hamilton landed sharply against the structure and it made a familiar metallic sound. He soon joined them in searching for a way inside.

Jace pounded on a section, and his hand struck a handle. He pulled at it, and the door creaked open. He took a quick look inside and could see several small lights on. "Eis, I found a way in!"

Eislie joined him quickly, followed by Hamilton. Jace tapped the light on his helmet as he cautiously entered. Hamilton was remarking, "This is usually when the alien pops out," making Jace laugh.

Eislie looked annoyed toward Hamilton. "You know *you're* an alien on this planet, don't you?"

Jace spoke up. "So are you, so shut up. I can't hear if I'm stepping on any traps listening to you two." Jace paused for a moment. "I'm wondering if Salas or Basker tried stopping Jennert."

Hamilton spoke up. "Are you sure it wasn't your person?"

Jace turned to look Hamilton in the eyes. "Two against three; not to mention that Alvin wants to get home as fast as possible." Jace sighed. "But without the external stabilizer, the ship will be difficult to control."

As he spoke, Jace and Eislie were alerted on their comms. The message read, "Jennert has been restrained. The others are finishing the internal repairs. And the ship is surrounded. What are your orders?"

Eislie and Jace looked to each other, making Hamilton feel out of the loop. "Something happen?"

Eislie nodded. "Yeah, Jennert's been restrained. Now we have to figure out what to do." She then returned to thought.

Hamilton spoke up. "We could bring the ship here."

Jace looked to the indicator on his suit. "The level is almost nine hundred in this area. So we open the door, and your people are toast." Jace huffed, "Besides, I didn't have a chance to install the stabilizer yet. It'll be a rough ride for everyone, not to mention that the parts are lying on the ground nearby. Not going to be any good leaving it behind."

Jace thought for a moment before tapping his comm. "Ed, if the natives try and enter the ship, lift off and head to our location. Other than that, stay put."

"They could be here in a minute, and that vine stuff they've been throwing at us would fall off. We could fix the ship and get out of here," Hamilton said.

Jace seemed to join Eislie in thought as they looked up to each other. "You're thinking it too, aren't you, Eis," Jace said, making her nod. Jace looked to Hamilton. "It seems they haven't attacked the ship, and the weapons are only meant to ensnare. I'm not sure these people are hostile." Jace turned. "Maybe they're being cautious."

Hamilton looked down. "So if they are, what do we do?"

Jace turned, his eyes looking at the controls all around them. "We wait and see what their next move is." He tapped a button on the console, causing the entire room to light. "It seems this ship still has power. Maybe we should see where it's from?"

* * *

In the forest, the natives stopped as they watched the newcomers searching for a way into the ship. Several of the party tested the limits of the field with their weapons. At the same time, others kept an eye on the interlopers.

"Their suits will not last long for that level of radiation. They will give themselves up soon," one of the reptilian inhabitants said.

The leader focused on Eislie. "The female sensed us. And the other with her did not fear the radiation." Then, she looked to the hunter next to her. "I watched him purposely reach into the dense part of the field."

The woman turned her eyes back to see Jace pounding on the hull of the ship before they disappeared inside. "Most shield suits will only last a few hours." Then, she thought for a moment. "Thought I heard the female speaking Gilese, and the other two were speaking a Terran language." She turned to the others. "Watch them. If they are still alive by nightfall, let us know." She then turned and walked back toward where they came from.

"Y'Shayla, where are you going?" one of the others asked.

The leader turned back, a look of contemplative concern in her large, dark eyes. "I have a feeling that they will still be alive. I am going to consult with the elders. I will return shortly."

Chapter 28: Friends or Enemies

Y'Shayla tapped the wooden staff she carried against the wall of fibrous vines, causing them to retract, allowing light into the room. The elders were sitting in a circle. Everyone's eyes focused on the ball of translucent fluid that lit before them. As the hunter approached, she could see the *Wolfhammer* clearly in view within the sphere.

Finally, one of the elders spoke. "It appears to be an old Takloh vessel, and it's been heavily modified. The crew seems to be a mix of Alliance and Terran."

Another nodded as Y'Shayla spoke. "I can confirm that two speak Terran and one Gilese. I suspect you may be correct, Elder Romai."

The female elder turned to Y'Shayla. "You were not able to capture them, I take it."

Y'Shayla shook her head. "They used the vegetation to evade us. I suspect the Terrans are in charge of the group. If they were of Gilese, they would not have thought of that strategy." She paused. "But, I have other concerning news."

Another of the elders spoke, his voice graveled from age. "If they are Terran, they must be tested for the madness." He turned back to Y'Shayla. "What is it, child?"

Y'Shayla took a breath before speaking. "Elder Ulo, the female had detected us, and the male nor her feared the radiation.

The third elder spoke, his words filled with intrigue. "Did they know? Do you suspect they are here to cause harm?"

"Elder Gav, I do not. We watched them working to repair their vessel. But, unfortunately, it seems to have sustained damage similar to the vessel within the burning circle," Y'Shayla told them.

Elder Gav produced a smile before replying, "Y'Shayla, I find it amusing you still call it by the mystical name from when you were young. But, of course, you know very well that it is caused by the spide radiation of that ship's reactor leak."

Y'Shayla smiled, feeling foolish as she said. "I am only one hundred and fourteen. I still remember the stories told to me as if they were yesterday. My concern is that they have taken refuge within the vessel, and are not fully aware of the danger."

Elder Romai agreed, "They must be told. Even with protection, that level of radiation would harm most." She looked to the translucent sphere. "Unless it does not affect them."

The other elders looked to each other. One waved his hand over the sphere and the view changed to the ship within the circle. "It is unfortunate that we cannot get a closer view."

Elder Romai spoke. "We have been on this world for over one hundred thousand seasons and have not yet been able to duplicate the resistance that the Lyri possess." She looked to be in thought. "That ship has been here for over ten thousand seasons. You suspect they may be descendants?"

Elder Gav nodded. "Yes. But if they are with Terrans, they may be infected as well. They will all be tested and, if needed, cured."

Y'Shayla looked curiously to the elders. "The madness? What is the madness?"

Elder Romai looked to the young woman, her face a mix of shame and repent as she spoke. "It was what made Terrans the warlike and aggressive species they are today."

Y'Shayla shook her head. "But we are from that world, and we are not like them."

Elder Olu sighed as he spoke. "Child, we are Alank, but we were not always called by that name. The Gel are our brothers and sisters But, it is our past selves, as the Ergo, who created the madness in an attempt to cause the Lyri to destroy themselves."

Y'Shayla stood tall. "The Ergo are our enemies. We fight to not be like them. I do not understand what you are telling me."

Elder Gav stood, looking her in the eyes, and Y'Shayla could see the shame behind his stare. "We are on this world because we are the true cause of the fate of the Gel, of our people. It is our penance for attempting to be gods among them."

Y'Shayla felt a heaviness against her shoulders. She leaned against her staff,. "We are, Ergo?" Her heart sank seeing the elders all nodding.

"We were, but have purged the madness from ourselves. In our anger and thoughtlessness, we had attempted to use the very same to reclaim a world that was never lost to us. It was our pride and hatred that caused the loss of the world we knew as Earth, and home." Elder Ulo stood. "Child, what we have told you is of little concern right now. The safety of the newcomers is our priority. They must be told of the danger they are in."

Y'Shayla lifted her head. "But we cannot enter the circle to tell them."

Elder Romai joined Y'Shayla, telling her, "You remember the Terran languages, yes?"

The young hunter looked to the elder. "I do not know as many as you, Elder, but I know nearly two hundred of the languages of this galaxy. Why?"

Elder Romai placed her hand on the woman's shoulder. "Because you will warn them of the danger. From there, we will see what they will do."

Y'Shayla looked at the elders as they approached, Elder Gav telling her, "You will bring them here to be tested, and cured if needed. But we must have all of them tested before they can return home. We must bring them to safety so they are not harmed."

Elder Gav turned to the others. “If their ship needs repair, then we should aid them, or allow them to do so.” He looked across the room. “I fear that they may be running out of breathable oxygen as well. They may become desperate.”

Elder Ulo huffed, “Desperate Terrans can be extremely dangerous. Much like their ancestors, the Lyri.” He turned to take a small container from the wall. “Fill this with the moss of the sabram. It will produce oxygen when exposed to light; hopefully, enough for them to breathe. We will make this dwelling habitable for them.”

Y’Shayla looked confused. “How do I get this to them?”

Elder Romai smiled. “Child, you will use the Terran words to calm them and bring them here. Then, we will meet with them and possibly determine their fate.”

Elder Gav stepped forward. “I will accompany her. We must show a vestige of trust.”

Night had come and gone before Y’Shayla returned to the burning circle. She stood close, using a clump of roots as an indicator of the radiation field. She moved as close as she could before telling the others to head back to the community.

Elder Gav was still a half-day away. He had promised to come as soon as possible. Y’Shayla looked around the circle of the old ship as she waited. She told the others of her instructions and was waiting for the elder to arrive before communicating with the newcomers.

* * *

Inside the Lyri ship, Jace and Eislie were hard at work, with excitement once they realized where they were standing. “This is a fucking Lyri ship; I can’t believe we’re actually inside one! How old do you think it is, Eis?”

Eislie looked up from the control panel, which seemed to be working. “Wish I had a translate visor for this, but some of it I think I can read.” She tapped the screen, and it lit. “This has to be over ten thousand standard years old. It’s incredible anything’s still working.”

Hamilton stood guard by the door. “Can we use it to get home?”

Eislie shrugged her shoulders. She didn’t know. She was too busy trying to figure out the status display. When she looked at one screen, she recognized the word for the reactor. "Jace, this looks like an overload warning."

She looked up to see him staring back. All he said was, "Reactor room?"

The two started to search and within seconds, found the exact words on a bulkhead. Jace paused at the door. "Hamilton, get ready to run outside. We don't know what sort of power system this thing has."

"You sure that's a good idea? What if it's a spide leak? It could overwhelm our shields," Hamilton said.

Jace looked annoyed. "You realize the power for your shield ran out hours ago, right?"

Hamilton looked at his display, and it had turned off. "Shit, my shield's gone! But, wait, why am I not feeling anything?" The man paused, "Oh shit! That's right, I *am* one of you!"

Jace snickered, "Just figured that out, did you? Just be ready to run. I'm not sure what else is in here."

Jace was about to open the door when Eislie stopped him. "Are you sure it's a spide system?"

They both looked at the power feeds from the reactor; they were similar to their ship, and most spide systems they had come across. "Looks like it is. But I have no idea what that conduit is," Jace said before he remarked, "Why don't you go over by Hamilton, just in case."

Eislie put her hand over his on the handle. "No, we're stronger together."

Jace felt proud and humbled. She was willing to stand alongside him, and he placed his helmet against hers. Seeing this, Hamilton said, "This is hardly the time, you two. You can get a room later."

Eislie gave a subtle laugh and they both turned the handle to the door. The whole room lit brightly, causing Jace and Eislie to reel back from its intensity. Hamilton was halfway out the door before he realized they weren't following.

"That's a spide overload if I ever saw one," Eislie said, shielding her eyes.

Jace remarked, “Yeah, remind me to add visors to the environment suits later. I’m barely able to see.” He motioned for Eislie to follow as he said, “Let’s see if we can lock this down.”

It took a few minutes, and Jace was able to find the source of the light and radiation. There were several spide crystals forced together inside some of the storage containers. Some were banded together, however, neither of them could explain why. Eislie noticed a dented section just above the control system for the reactor along the wall. She thought it looked like it was from the outside. Jace found the main interconnect for the reactor and turned it on. There was a loud bang and flash, and Eislie screamed out in pain. Jace moved the switch down and turned to see what had happened to his love. He could see her balled up against the wall holding her arm.

“Eis? You all right?” Jace rushed to her.

“My arm, the arc, I felt it through my suit,” Eislie said, her breath stuttering from the pain.

Jace could see the blackened scorch across her suit and inspected it, Eislie whimpering as he turned her arm. “Are you sure you’re okay?” Jace was more concerned than ever as he looked her in the eyes.

Eislie looked to her hand and moved her fingers. “It’s not that bad of a burn. It just hurts,” she told him.

Jace looked even more concerned. “Bad, bad, or mine injury bad?” Jace referred to the incident when they first met years ago, where she was injured severely and could have bled out. She knew what he was referring to and gave a subtle smile before saying, “Mine injury bad.” Jace held his hands gently on her injury, seeing her face holding back the display of pain. Finally, she was no longer moving her hand.

Jace’s actions caused Hamilton to say, “You two done? We have to get this ship fixed.”

Jace gave a slow, simple glare toward Hamilton, and the man felt fear like he had never experienced seeing the look in Jace’s eyes. He said nothing as Jace tapped his comm.

“*Wolfhammer*, we have a severe injury. How soon can you get here?”

“Captain, we can lift off in approximately two minutes. The estimated arrival is about five. How serious is the injury?”

“It’s Eis; she’s badly burned,” Jace replied.

The computer responded, “Checks and overrides have been disabled, lifting off now. Arrival will be in about two minutes. Med systems online, Captain.”

“Thanks, Ed. We’ll meet you outside. Have Jennert, Salas, and Basker put in containment somewhere because we’re opening the door no matter what. If they are not protected, they’ll burn. We’re not waiting for them,” Jace told the computer.

“Confirmed, Captain. They have been warned. Their deaths by radiation will be on their own heads. I am on route. Med bay is standing by.”

In under a minute, the *Wolfhammer* was landing nearby. Jace carried Eislie up the ramp, both watching the vines fall away as the door opened. They rushed inside and directly to the med bay. Hamilton closed the door and asked Alvin where Jennert and Salas were. He pointed to the hold. As Hamilton passed the med bay, he looked inside to see Jace cutting away the suit from Eislie’s arm to expose the charred flesh underneath. He was planning on having a talk with his crewmates but instead decided to help Jace.

“I worked a medical ship. Let me give you a hand,” Hamilton said as he pulled off his gloves. He looked at the injury. “That’s serious. Let me help.”

Hamilton gently turned Eislie’s arm to get a better look before turning to Jace. “Hand me the painkiller, the blue one.” Jace did as asked, and the former captain injected it into Eislie’s arm. “It’ll take a few seconds.” He then motioned for a device to remove the charred material. Eislie was amazed at how quickly Hamilton was able to start healing her and asked where he learned how to do things so quickly.

“Told you, I worked a medical ship.” He looked up to see Jace looking back. “I lost my position because I didn’t follow orders in combat.”

Eislie remarked, “Well, you are Terran.”

Hamilton scoffed, “That wasn’t it. I went where I thought it would best suit me, not where I was needed.” He looked up from working on Eislie. “I’m still supposed to capture you two.”

Jace smiled, “Good luck with that.”

Hamilton watched Jace look toward the door. “Listen, I was going to have a conversation with my fellow crewmates before I came in here.”

Jace looked at him. “That’s not a bad idea.”

Hamilton chuckled. “Not really. I was going to let Basker and Salas in and leave Jennert in there while I opened the outside door. He almost got me killed.” Hamilton paused. “If Shasji hadn’t been in the reactor room, Jennert wouldn’t have attacked her.”

Jace noted, “She was stabilizing the reaction. That’s why she was in the reactor room.”

Hamilton looked to Jace. “But she wasn’t using a console or tools. So how was she doing that?”

The expression on Jace’s face became stoic. “By touching it.”

“What?” Hamilton was confused.

Jace looked to Eislie. “You doing good?”

Eislie nodded. “I can move my fingers again.” Jace then gently placed his head against hers, making Hamilton shake his head.

“I still don’t get why she was touching the reactor,” Hamilton said.

Jace smirked. “It’s beginning to look like starborn can regulate the spide reaction inside the filaments. She was stabilizing the reaction.”

Hamilton thought for a moment and seemed happy when he spoke. “Great! Then there is a use for them . . . on . . . other . . .” Hamilton’s words faded as he remembered he was a starborn like them. “Oh, shit. I am not becoming a permanent fixture on some ship.”

Eislie gave a quiet laugh. “You just figured that out now?”

Hamilton looked up to see them both staring back, with Jace saying, “Welcome to the club.”

Chapter 29: Let's Talk

Elder Gav arrived at the burned circle standing silent seeing the new ship within its field. He motioned to Y'Shayla, and she dutifully approached.

"Were any harmed when the ship lifted off?" Gav asked.

"No, Elder, they were merely knocked down. But we were confused as to why it moved until we saw the others rush from the Lyri vessel. The female appeared to be injured," Y'Shayla replied.

"Perhaps she was affected by the radiation." The elder sighed. "We must approach them slowly. I am concerned that they are being driven by fear at the moment."

The leader nodded. "We have been watching. They have made no action to attack. So it may be possible to speak with them."

Elder Gav smiled. "You are learning, my young hunter. It is good that you understand that patience is the mark of a good leader." He moved closer, reaching his hand out. The old leader wincing in pain as the tip of his finger turned to dust, only to regrow moments later. "They have yet to fix the problem with that ship. We would do so if it were not for this deadly veil it emits. They may not have the knowledge to do as we hoped."

"Why do you wish them to stop the leak? It is an inconvenience, but it has not harmed any of our people in a long time," Y'Shayla mentioned.

The elder looked to her. "The circle has not been as far as it is now. The distance has tripled in my lifetime. When Elder Romai was young, it was barely outside the ship."

The hunter's eyes widened. "It is growing?"

The elder nodded. "We calculate that it will take about twenty thousand standard years for it to reach our homes. Before that, however, it may affect the very substrate of the land, causing damage. We had hoped they would take the vessel that is slowly poisoning this world we now call home."

The elder looked to the ground. "Perhaps it is too much to hope. Maybe it is our sentence for poisoning their people long ago."

He placed his hand on Y'Shayla's arm. "Come, we must try and contact them. I will need your voice to carry the words I tell you."

* * *

A few hours before, Jace decided to allow the other three members of Hamilton's crew back into the ship. Salas and Basker were let in first, but Jace shoved Jennert back, locking the door to the main cabin. Jennert remained in the hold while Jace walked away. When the Alliance pilot used the comm, Jace replied, "We're still deciding whether to space you or not. Either way, you're closer to the door."

Eislie refilled the oxygen systems in the remaining suits, and the computer turned off all power to the cargo area, with the exclusion of some light and life support. Jace quietly remarking to Eislie that the computer did this on its own. The action to shut down power was not ordered by either captain, although they did agree with Ed's decision.

Jace and Eislie were trying to figure out how to shut down the systems of the Lyri ship safely. The containment section of the reactor of the vessel was still in overload. The power systems appeared to be damaged. But they didn't know to what extent yet. Eislie's injury took precedent.

Jace was at the controls while Eislie spoke with Alvin. She was trying to decide if they could cut a new panel to weld to the stabilizer. They were protected for the moment by the radiation surrounding the ship. She warned Alvin to make sure Jennert was inside before he opened the outer door. She smiled, hearing him mockingly say, "Oh, yeah, don't want to forget he's in there still. Let me write a note to myself."

Salas was peering over Jace's shoulder at the scans. She had seen many ships, but the design of the Lyri vessel's outer coils didn't make sense to her. There seemed to be far too many for the power system. That was Jace's quandary as well. He needed to get a better look at the Lyri systems before they could start taking parts if required.

Jace was staring forward as he spoke. "We should let Jennert out of the hold. I think he's learned his lesson."

Eislie turned, "Out here with us, or out, out?"

Her statement made Jace pause for a moment. "I am tempted. But, let him back in anyway."

Hamilton walked past Eislie and, when he reached the inside door of the hold, knocked loudly. He was startled when Jennert's face suddenly appeared from below, his voice heard through the door. "I'm not a prisoner. Let me in!"

Hamilton cocked his head before tapping the intercom. "Maybe you should be. You tried to kill us."

His statement was not lost on Jennert, the man looking away. "I just don't want to be eaten alive by some backward species on an unknown planet."

Hamilton opened the door. "Then why did you join the Alliance space fleet?"

Jennert said nothing as he rushed past Hamilton toward the control room. When he turned the corner, he made a line right for Jace, but Eislie stepped in, kneeing him in the groin forcibly, making the man double over in pain. Jace walked over to stand next to Eislie, asking her, "Feel better?"

Eislie nodded. "A little. But I think we should consider what to do with them when we leave."

Jace smiled as Eislie walked back toward the small gally. He hoisted Jennert from the ground, still gasping for breath. "I think she's pissed at you, Jennert. Maybe you should tell her you're sorry."

Jennert went to speak but was grabbed from behind by Basker, the growl from his former crewmate filled with a fit of righteous anger. "You step out of line once more, slac, and I'll space you myself. These people are trying to get us home."

Basker pushed the man forward, and Jennert cowered in silence, but when he did speak, his voice seemed to contain a squeaking fear. "I don't want to be killed on some backwater planet, all right?"

Jace stood, his arms crossed. "Are you saying any of us want that?"

Jennert looked to the ground, saying no, his stature hunched, as if despondent. Jace was going to speak when the computer interrupted. "Captain, I wish to inform you that the inhabitants seem to be now speaking in Terran English."

"What?" Jace turned to tap the nearby console to make it louder. His ears were hearing what sounded like English but with a heavy accent.

"People of Terra, we wish to speak with you." Jace watched as an older native spoke to the female warrior and she yelled what presumably were the man's words.

Jace again crossed his arms. "An invitation?" He looked to Eislie, now standing nearby. "Or a trap?"

Eislie watched, her only words, “You’re not going out there without me.” She looked forward. “Same protocol as always, Ed. You know what to do if something happens.”

The computer’s response, “Understood, Captain. The order has not been changed.”

Jennert spoke up. “What order?”

Alvin walked into Jennert as he came to the console. “Oh, that’s right, you guys don’t know. Just a heads-up; if these two are killed, the ship blows up.” He started laughing. “I had to agree to it when I joined them. Personally, I don’t want to die, but hey, if it’s my time, it’s my time.”

Jennert replied, “Then I’ll go. I’m not a coward.”

Jace snickered, “Yes you are. You’d sell us out as soon as you had a chance.”

Eislie paused for a moment. “Wait, my environment suits gone. I don’t have one now.”

Jace looked at her. “Take one of the spares. Use the one we had for Jennert. He’s not going to need it.”

“What?” Jennert yelled, making Jace lean toward him, saying, “Jennert, if you’re going outside, it’ll be without a suit. At least until we decide otherwise.”

Eislie followed after Jace. As they suited up, Jace told everyone as he opened the inside door, “If they do attack, at least try and come get us.”

Jace closed the inside door, and he and Eislie exited. They walked toward the others, and using the external comm on the suit, said, “Why were you attacking us?”

He watched as the older one leaned in to speak to the leader. Her words were loud enough to be heard through the suits without speakers. "You are trespassing on our world. But you appear not to be hostile. We are sorry for the understanding." The elder tapped the arm of the woman. "Sorry, misunderstanding."

Eislie touched Jace's arm. "I don't think they want to hurt us."

Jace scoffed, "They have a funny way of greeting people then." Jace and Eislie moved closer to the natives. "There, now you won't have to yell."

Jace watched the older man nod before he spoke. "We do not wish to harm you, but we did not know your true intention for landing. I am called Gav." He pointed to the woman next to him. "This is Y'Shayla. She is the current leader of our people." The man looked around Eislie and Jace. "You did not bring any weapons. That shows wisdom on your part."

Jace smiled, "We don't like using them." He thought for a moment. "You speak my language very well."

Y'Shayla answered, "My people speak languages from around the galaxy. They are required to learn."

Eislie looked to Jace. "Then your people must have a lot of knowledge."

The elder spoke. "We know many things about many worlds. We have been watching them all for some time." Elder Gav pointed to their ship. "That is a Takloh vessel, and the other is Lyri. Do you know of their people?"

Eislie and Jace looked at each other before Jace replied, "And what if we did?"

The elder smiled, "Ah, prudence and evasion. The sign of an experienced traveler."

Jace just smiled back at the old leader.

Seeing this, the elder spoke again. “You are Terran, are you not?” He pointed to Eislie. “And you are of Gilese.”

They both nodded, confirming Elder Gav’s assessment. The old man spoke again. “It is too bad you are not Lyri. They could help with that vessel. Unfortunately, the radiation field is expanding. We are afraid it may eventually reach the city.”

Eislie smiled, “Well, we are both part Lyri.” She turned to Jace to see him siding his eyes to her. “What? I feel we can trust them. Besides, I’m part Terran as well.”

Y’Shayla looked at Eislie. “You are Terran as well?”

Jace looked to Eislie. “So now you decide to accept you’re part Terran?”

Eislie rolled her eyes. “Not the best time, Jace.”

Y’Shayla stepped away from the elder as he started to laugh, the old man crossing his hands over his chest. “Ah, we have a bonded pair of Lyri among us. It is good to see that the species known to us has its future still.”

Jace looked to Eislie, who said, “Now wait a minute. The future of what?”

They all watched as the elder again started laughing at her questioning. He steadied himself. “Forgive me; it has been some time since I have interacted with the people of Lyri. You two give me hope that our past can be undone.”

Jace looked perplexed toward the man. The elder was now looking solemn before he spoke. “Are you familiar with the Gel?”

Jace nodded. “Yes, the original inhabitants of Earth. Or so I’m told. We are in good standing with them right now.” Jace paused. “You remind me of them a little.”

The elder looked to Jace. "They are. And that feat alone is admirable. But, does it apply to your entire world?"

Jace shook his head. "Not yet; just us for the moment.

Elder Gav looked to him. "Victories start small, my young friend. And you have accomplished, I deduce, many so far."

Jace huffed, "Oh, do we have some stories to tell you." Jace looked around at the people that remained. "You know, I'm curious; what are your people called?"

The elder took a quick breath. "We are the Alank. However, we have gone by another name in the past. I do not know if you are familiar with Gel history."

Jace nodded, telling him, "Some."

The elder straightened up. "Then I will tell you, we were also known at one time as the Ergo."

Jace's fists tightened, his eyes focusing on every warrior within view. The elder took notice and spoke to calm Jace's concerns. "Please know that we mean no harm. We seek to atone for our past; we are no longer Ergo." The old man sighed, "We have lost our home by our own arrogance."

"So, the Ergo are gone?" Jace asked.

The elder looked away for a moment. "You may not have met them yet, but they are no longer Ergo themselves. They would be known as Karazon." The elder watched a wave of fierce anger come over both of them and the two shifted as if to step back. Even the warriors nearby seemed to move away from them.

The elder nodded before hanging his head. "I see. So, you have met them."

"I had to fight two of them to save her, a friend, and our ship. I wound up killing them both. Just to save them and five thousand of the planet's people held as slaves," Jace admitted without guilt.

The elder looked to them both. "You protect each other. I am honored to see that you survived our wayward brothers and sisters. But we have no taste for what the Karazon favor. So please, you are guests of our world. We have much to tell you of our people and your ancestors. And hopefully, you may be able to help us in return." Elder Gav pointed to the Lyri ship. "We live in peace now. All races are welcome, provided they behave on this world."

Jace shifted on his feet. "And what do you mean by that? Because if you say obey you, there is going to be—"

Eislie grabbed Jace's arm, spinning him toward her. Jace could see the look in her eyes. She didn't want a fight. Eislie said nothing as she looked at the Alank all around them. Jace understood. She didn't have to say anything. He only nodded. "Forgive me, Elder Gav. We've had a lot of people trying to either kill or enslave us. Suppose you are offering knowledge and a chance for us to fix our ship. We would be honored to learn about your people."

The elder gave a simple smile, one practiced over millennia. His words were flowing in an understanding tone. "And we would like to hear of your adventures, if you are willing to share."

The old one motioned to Y'Shayla, speaking in their language before turning back to Jace and Eislie. "You will not need your full suits. If you have respiration masks, they would be less cumbersome. We have adapted to the atmosphere here. I am sorry it is not convenient for your needs."

Jace nodded, as did Eislie. Both understood that it would be a risk. But since they needed time to repair the *Wolfhammer*, they both felt it prudent.

Elder Gav nodded, giving an order that most of the others understood, and they started to leave. He and Y'Shayla remained. "We will wait for you to return. If any others of your crew wish to join, they may do so." He looked at their ship. "But, you will have to move from the Lyri vessel to do so. I'm afraid that it may be dangerous without shielding."

They nodded, turning to walk back to the ship, Eislie could see the concentration in Jace's eyes and using the comm said. "I've seen that look before; you think we can trust them."

Jace looked up at the still damaged stabilizer. "I do, but it doesn't matter. We don't have much of a choice right now. If they were a threat, I'm sure they'd find a way to attack us, even if we stayed inside the radiation."

Chapter 30: New Friends

Jace and Eislie removed their environment suits after returning the ship back to where they had left the makeshift stabilizer. Alvin stood nearby, asking, "Do you want me to stay on board?"

Eislie took a moment before responding. "We should, but you know what'll happen if, you know." Eislie cocked her head toward Jace, referring to them being killed and the ship's previous order.

Alvin nodded. "I've never been to any other planets except for Oppa. It might be nice to stretch my legs."

Hearing that, Jace handed him a respirator mask. "Your choice, but I think we can trust the Alank."

The others stood in the small hallway, listening. Salas seemed interested. "I've always stayed on ships when we landed. I've never actually been *on* an unknown planet." She pushed past Hamilton, who smiled, looking to Jennert, who wasn't happy about meeting these people.

Hamilton started toward the cargo area and paused to look back at Jennert. "Look, I'm sure they'll only gut and eat the fat ones of us first. You shouldn't have anything to worry about. Maybe they don't like invertebrates."

Jennert had to think about Hamilton's remark but became angered when his implication sank in. "I'm not spineless, you slac."

With everyone in the cargo area, Jace opened the outer door. As the large hatch lowered, it revealed several Alank standing in a line. They carried no weapons. That scene quieted Jace and Eislie's concerns.

Y'Shayla moved to greet them as they exited. "We welcome you to EnKal. May our home be yours too while you are here." She then lowered her head, giving a slight bow. "We welcome you in peace and health."

Hearing the planet's name, Eilsie gave a snicker, drawing a glance from Y'Shayla. Eislie looking back, "Sorry I thought I recognized that word."

Seeing the alien's reaction toward Eislie, he was about to ask what she found funny, only to have Eislie motion briefly with her hand causing Jace to return his attention to the welcoming leader.

Y'Shayla looked at the newcomers. "Please follow. We have much to discuss. And we can help with the repairs of your vessel later. It will be dark soon; it will not be wise to be in the forest after the sun sets."

Jace nodded. "All right, lead the way."

* * *

It took some time before they reached the city, the tall buildings topped with leaves as if grown from the ground. The brown and gray bark looking eerily similar to stone instead of wood. Jace found himself looking around and had to be dragged along by Alvin as they continued.

"Y'Shayla, are these buildings grown? How did you build them?" Jace asked, causing Eislie to look concerned toward him for doing so.

"Your assessment is correct. The buildings are grown; we have been doing so for many years. We have found that our world would allow us to use the resources as is best for everyone and everything. It has been our way since before I have been alive," Y'Shayla answered, and turned to see the amazement in Jace's stare.

Jace had a flurry of other questions, as did Eislie, causing the leader of the Alank to turn forward. “I know you have many questions, but the elders wish to be present while we speak. So please do not take offense.” Eislie and Jace agreed, and they continued to follow their hosts.

When they arrived, they entered a large dwelling, the walls on the outside smooth and seamless. Jace followed Y’Shayla, as did Eislie. However, Alvin paused at the door, his thoughts apparent. *Great place for a trap.*

They all stood close to each other, Eislie next to Jace. Alvin and Shasji were close behind them as the others from the new crew huddled together. Before them sat three elders; Gav, they knew.

“My young friends, please sit, join us around the light.” Elder Gav then motioned to the woman next to him. “This is elder Romai. She has been here since the founding. And this is Elder Ulo. We welcome you to EnKal.”

Eislie snickered after Elder Gav spoke, causing Jace to ask again what she found funny.

“Oh, the word *EnKal*, it’s sounds similar to inkil, the word we use for paradise in Gilese,” Eislie answered.

Jace raised his brow and turned to see Elder Gav smiling, and the elder spoke. “That would be a fair assessment. We adopted it for this world since the previous one is now lost to us.” Elder Gav could see the concern and fear in some of the newcomers, but he did not notice it in Jace or Eislie.

Jace thought for a moment. “How long have your people been here?”

Elder Gav paused. “About ninety-five thousand standard years.”

Jace looked perplexed. “Ninety-five thousand years. That would make you about . . . no, that can’t be right.” He looked to Eislie.

Elder Romai smiled before speaking. “Young one, are you suggesting that I am ninety-five thousand years old?”

Jace looked sheepishly toward the woman, remarking. "At least that's what I thought I heard. Well, if so, you don't look a day over ten thousand."

Eislie gave him a scolding look. "I can't believe you just said that."

"Actually, I am over one hundred and three." The room fell silent as the elder's words sank in.

Jace was the first to speak. "Great joke. Good to see sarcasm has a universal note."

Elder Romai sat with her smile. "I was not joking."

"My friends, we elders have been here for almost one hundred thousand standard years. Elder Romai and myself came from Earth. I was merely a child when we arrived. Elder Gav was born on this world. The statement we have told you is the truth."

There was a skittering of movement behind Jace and Eislie from the others. Alvin remained nearby, Jace hearing him mutter, "That's old."

Elder Gav leaned over to Elder Ulo. "That is very curious. These others, with the darker tone, are like the first two. They do not show fear as the others do."

Jace looked to Alvin, who was muttering to Shasji, who was remaining silent. When she spoke, her words were heard with a clarity not suited for private conversation. "I wouldn't take that as an insult, Alvin. You are almost as crazy as we are," making Alvin chortle in a burst of laughter. Hamilton started shaking his head as he looked at his former crewmates.

Elder Gav motioned to Hamilton. "You dismiss your fellow crew. Why?"

Hamilton's eyes went wide, realizing he was being addressed, but recovered from his silence quickly. "Well, this one thinks you're going to open us up and eat us alive. The others, I don't know. I think they're on the fence with this whole meeting an unknown race sort of thing." Hamilton pointed to Jace and Eislie. "I'm sort of with these two here, although, recently, not by choice."

A curious look was now filling the Alank faces before them. "We do not understand your remark. Could you explain?"

Hamilton looked around and tapped Jace's shoulder before responding. "Do they know about, you know, people like us?"

Salas looked to Hamilton. "What do you mean, people like us?"

Hamilton looked to Jace for acknowledgment, and it was Eislie who spoke up.

"You know we are part Lyri, as is Alvin and Hamilton. I am not sure about the others," Eislie told them.

Salas spoke first. "Hamilton, you're a starborn?"

They all watched as a look of disgust came over Hamilton's face before he muttered, "God, that does sound extremely stupid."

His words were not unheard, as Elder Ulo spoke. "You did not know this about yourself? That you were part Lyri?"

Hamilton shook his head. "No, I've been mostly in the brig or on smaller ships for Earth. I was never really on an Alliance assignment." He waved his hand to Jace and Eislie. "If it weren't for these two, I'd probably still be ignorant of it." The sound of disdain was now fleeting from his tone.

"Hamilton, just deal with it, okay? They would have eventually gotten you." Jace looked to Eislie. "Who knows, maybe they'd do to him what they did to us."

Their hosts could not dismiss the tone Jace used. However, the hint of anger and hatred now softened from time and acceptance.

Elder Gav spoke. "You must tell us what happened to you. You speak of it with such hatred in your voice."

Eislie turned her eyes down. "You try being enslaved because of what you are, what you can do. They imprisoned us because we're resistant to the spide radiation." She looked to Elder Gav. "They needed us to mine the crystals."

The Alank looked around, hearing her words filled with a hint of the same hatred. Jace noticed the Alank's concern—except for Elder Romai, who looked down. Jace could feel the same emotions they had present within her before they reflected on her face. Jace sat tall. "I'm sorry, we are being bad guests. Please forgive us."

Elder Romai, who had recently remained silent, listening, now spoke. "No, we ask that you to forgive us."

All heads around the room, except for the elders, now looked around in confusion. Jace could see the look of repentant sorrow in the older woman's expression. "You've done nothing wrong. Please, do not think you have."

Elder Romai sat tall, and Jace watched as she tried to speak, her mouth trembling to form words. "I am speaking to the Terrans. It was our doing. Our pride that caused your ancestors to lose something precious, something that we could not duplicate. It was our jealousy and pride that cost you, and us, our home."

Jace looked toward the Alank. "I don't understand. You haven't done anything to us." He looked around. "Well, except for trying to capture us earlier, you've been very welcoming. I don't know what you mean."

The elder sat remorsefully and bowed. "It is unfortunate that you must now know some of our history, as well as your ancestors'. However, it is needed to understand. Before we left Earth, we were Ergo. The Lyri had shared much with us. However, in our haste to expand, many of our people died using the drive reactors. Although we had similar organic technology, our ships were not as swift as the Lyri vessels. Our technology also did not fare well alongside the Lyri power systems."

Elder Romai lifted her head, remembering. "My mind was a-wonder when I was old enough to travel to another world in only a few days for the first time. I saw the cities of Oppa before their people had left their world they called home. I was happy to see them when they arrived on Earth, and with how the Lyri shared what they knew with so many others."

Elder Romai looked to Eislie. "And for their kindness, we, the Ergo, tried to destroy them. We took the aggressive parts of ourselves and released them. Of course, there were many of us against the plan. But even more looked to follow through." Elder Romai took a moment, the sound of sadness now leaving her voice. "We, I, could not stand by and live with our people. So, those of us who did not want to harm our new friends from the stars, left. We found this world and made it anew."

Jace could see the old leader now showing her experience. "We asked you here for your help and forgiveness of our actions against your ancestors."

Hamilton tapped Jace on the shoulder. "What's she talking about?"

Jace looked back to the elder, his head still processing the words she used. It finally hit him. "You can't go back, can you?"

Eislie looked to Jace for clarification.

"They can't return to Earth. Whatever the Ergo used on the Lyri to make them, well, human, uh Terran, must affect them as well." Jace scanned around the room. "They infected the world by mistake, not just the people they were trying to rid themselves of."

The elder waved her hand around. "We changed ourselves to breathe the atmosphere here, so as to dissuade other Ergo from staying, and it worked. This atmosphere is not viable for the pathogen. They moved on after they realized that they had made a mistake."

Eislie looked at Jace. He had the same stare as on Oppa when they were standing before the Daak. She could feel him next to her, his confidence strengthening her as well. So when he spoke, she recognized the words. They were of the same forgiveness he offered the Daak.

"Elder, thank you. But there is no need for forgiveness. That was the past. There is no need to dwell on that," Jace said.

Elder Romai smiled to Jace. "You have the wisdom of your ancestors. They were peaceful, giving, and clever people. They did so much, and had planned to unite all beings in the galaxy."

Jace looked to Eislie. "Well, she created some new radiation suits that can handle that radiation out there. She wanted to give it away, but we decided to make some money from it."

Elder Romai looked to Eislie. "You created something to save others?"

Eislie nodded.

Elder Ulo nodded. "As giving as your ancestors would have been. Which makes what we have to ask all the more difficult."

Eislie looked at Jace.

Elder Ulo leaned back against his short chair. "The instrument that infected Earth is present in most Terrans. It is the reason they are highly aggressive. Although at the time it could not survive this atmosphere, so we must ask for your indulgence."

Jace looked forward, one brow cocked. "What do you want?"

Elder Ulo gave an insecure smile. "We ask that you allow us to test you for the madness, and if it is present, we wish to cure it."

Everyone who was on the ship looked to each other, the hint of distrust fading as Eislie looked to Jace. "It's up to you, Jace."

"It's not just up to me," Jace said as he looked back at her.

Eislie paused for a moment before her eyes widened as she remembered being part Terran. "Oh, I guess you're right."

Chapter 31:
That Explains a Lot

There was activity in the room as the Alank assured the crew of the *Wolfhammer* that they were not in any danger. Then, the Alank produced a small wooden tube that Elder Gav opened. Inside were several thin, pointed rods. They looked to be made of wooden stems.

"These indicators are mostly painless; we have used them for others who have happened upon our world. It uses a single bit of blood. If the madness is present, the indicator turns red. It remains the same if it is not. Although many were restrained before accepting the test," Elder Gav explained.

"Yeah, being stuck with an unknown instrument." Jace snickered. "You might be trying to poison us."

Elder Gav looked to Jace, his eyes unsure, hearing the newcomer's remark. But as Jace held out his hand, the elder understood. He took a single indicator and brought it down, pricking Jace's palm. Jace closed his hand and the wound closed quickly. Eislie looked to Jace, watching him for any reaction, and could see the glint of mischief in his eye.

She rolled her head back. "Whatever it is you're going to say, don't. Everyone is on edge enough as it is."

A smile broke through on Jace's face as he shook his head. "Nothing to worry about. It's like putting your hand down on a splinter."

The elders ignored Jace. They watched and waited for the indicator to turn. In their experience, random actions like his were an indicator of the madness. But the elder smiled. "You are free of the madness." He looked to Jace. "Although your actions speak possibly otherwise."

Eislie was next, the indicator also not responding. Then Alvin and Shasji were also cleared. Jennert stepped forward, almost whimpering as the feeble hand of the elder reached out to hold the man's palm steady. Jennert winced as the indicator pierced his skin, and he spoke. "Well, good, I'm done."

But as Jennert turned, there was a sound of gasping and rustling. Jennert turned to see the end of the indicator now dark red.

"No, I'm from Gilese Two. I'm not Terran!" Jennert protested.

"You may be from the Gilese system, but your ancestors may have been in contact with infected Lyri," Elder Gav said, looking to the other elders. "It is possible that it was brought to other worlds."

Jennert looked around. "What now, you kill me?"

Elder Ulo sighed. "Fear, aggressiveness, the sense that you are the only being worth living. Do these words sound familiar?"

"You tried to sacrifice us to save your own ass." Jace looked to the others. "That makes sense." He then patted Jennert on the shoulder. "Don't worry. You're still on my shit list."

The elder moved forward. "You should show compassion to this man. His actions are not entirely his own."

Jace looked to the elder. "One, he doesn't like Terrans, and two, he tried to save himself while exposing us earlier."

The elder placed his hand on Jace's shoulder. "But you have not killed him. Why?"

Jace sighed, "I don't like hurting people. But if they try to harm or kill me, or"—he motioned his head toward Eislie—"I sometimes make exceptions."

The elder nodded. "You protect, and choose to harm as the last resort. That is the sign of a wise leader."

Jace scoffed.

The elder moved toward Salas, passing Jace. "And the lack of desire to be one is as well. Have you not noticed that they all followed you here?"

Salas held out her hand, and before the elder brought the pointed indicator down, she closed it. Her words were little more than a whisper. "It's going to be positive."

Elder Ulo looked down to her eyes as she lifted her head. "Are you so sure, child?"

Salas nodded slowly. "But I want to know."

The elder nodded, then brought the indicator down. A moment later, Salas sighed, her words, almost relieved, filling the quiet air. "It's red; now I know."

Elder Ulo placed his hand on the side of her face. "You are surprisingly accepting of this outcome. But why?"

Salas smiled, "Because I know that I am sick. I fight against myself every day." Then, her eyes started to fill with sadness. "I am so tired, and I don't want to hurt anyone anymore."

"You show your strength by admitting that, child. It seems that you have gained it back by coming here," Elder Ulo told her.

"I'm glad they brought me here. I've never been on another planet before. But, I want to go home, and I know if I help them"—Salas smiled as she pointed to Eislie and Jace— "they'll get me home."

Elder Ulo turned to see the expression of surprise on both Jace and Eislie, which made him smile. "As I mentioned earlier, they follow you."

The elder turned to Salas. "We will cure you of the madness. It is simple, and you will feel less frightened and angry."

Basker moved forward and gave an audible, "Ow!" as the elder pricked his hand. The indicator stayed as it was.

Hamilton had remained in the shadows, his actions observing, calculating. Finally coaxed forward by the elder, Hamilton held out his hand. He pulled it back just as the elder went to hold it, asking, "What if I don't want the cure?"

Elder Ulo nodded. "Are you so certain that you wish to remain as you are?"

Hamilton slowly held his palm up, and the elder brought the indicator down. The end of the stick turned a deep red. Hamilton looked up, only saying, "Well, shit."

* * *

The morning had come. The days here were close to the same as Earth, although slightly shorter. Jace, Basker, and Alvin had returned to the ship to get an early start on fixing the stabilizer. Eislie and Shasji remained behind to watch the others. Shasji held Salas's hand away from the dressing. The engineer kept scratching the tiny bundle of plant leaves the Alank had wrapped around her wrist.

"It tickles," Salas giggled as she looked to the Alank all around her. "How long do I have to keep this on?"

Y'Shayla stood by as another Alank named Kepin worked to wrap a similar bundle around Hamilton's wrist. The male Alank was remarking,

"It will only be for a short while, until the pathogen has cleared. The sensation you are experiencing is the peptide bundles latching it within your system. They are releasing a cure for the virus. It is harmless."

Hamilton immediately started scratching his arm. "This feels so weird."

Jennert seemed to resist. "How do we know you're not seasoning us up?"

Kepin answered without hesitation, "Because this seasoning—uh, cure—would toughen the meat of Terrans. So they are much more enjoyable in their natural state."

Y'Shayla started laughing. She could be heard far outside the small tent housing their visitors. Shasji watched Eislie laughing and asked why she thought it was funny. Eislie answered, "That's the kind of answer Jace would give."

Kepin finished wrapping the bundle around Jennert's arm. "If all goes well, you may leave as early as late day."

Salas smiled, "Then we can go home?"

Eislie stepped forward. "That depends on if they get the stabilizer fixed. And you mentioned that you want us to take that Lyri ship with us."

Y'Shayla nodded. "Yes, before it destroys us. It is too bad you cannot remove the radiation. Or allow us to have some of those suits you made."

Eislie huffed, "We can remove the radiation. But that amount inside the ship was far more than the suits were designed for."

Y'Shayla looked at her. "Then, how did you survive?"

Eislie gave a coy smile. "Because I'm mostly Lyri."

Elder Gav entered the room. "The gift the Lyri could not bestow on any of us. Resistance to the very radiation they use to travel the stars." He steadied himself using Y'Shayla's staff. "A gift that we punished them for having. And, from what Elder Romai has told me, they would have given to us freely if they knew how."

Eislie looked at the elder. "How do you know that?"

Elder Gav pointed toward the door and the Lyri ship. "It is what they said when these travelers arrived."

Eislie looked in thought. Shasji picked up on it as well. "Wait, if they were here, then where are they?"

The elder smiled, "They were taken away by their kind. We had tried helping them, but our people could not enter their ship. They died as they tried."

Eislie asked, "You met them?"

"One I know of, her name was Taslyn. She was their leader," Elder Romai said as she entered the room before sitting on the short chair. "They asked for our help, and we could only die trying to do so. We had nursed two of their people to health quickly, using a stamina injection. We knew that if they continued to try and repair their vessel, those we healed would only injure themselves further. But they wanted to save their people. So they all remained wearing the breather masks and worked even while injured."

The elder looked to remember words. "It was they who allowed us to create the cure. They were of pure Lyri, from before Earth. They traveled cataloging planets nearby." Elder Romai smiled. "They were with us for only a few days, and I remember them as giving as they were when our people met them. But, then, like your lover, they forgave us as well."

Eislie felt herself blush as the older woman pointed to her.

Elder Romai smiled. "Do not be shy about that, child. You and he care for and protect each other. I feel you would do anything to save one another. A bonding like that can topple planets."

Eislie became reserved, but looked to Jennert as the man spoke. "They have."

Elder Romai sat forward, addressing Eislie. "What does he mean?"

Eislie looked at the woman but said nothing.

Jennert scoffed, "They saved a world by destroying a ship large enough to cleave it in two. Not to mention, they destroyed several dreadnaughts and dozens of pirate ships."

Elder Romai looked to Eislie, who didn't deny the remarks. Instead, she only said, "They would have killed innocents."

Jennert stepped up, confronting Eislie. "And that makes it right?"

Eislie looked the man in the eyes. "No. But we had to do something. Billions of people were going to die, all because the Duggor hate the Daak."

Elder Romai looked to Eislie. "The Duggor? What world did you save?"

Eislie looked straight at her. "Oppa."

The elder seemed to be relieved by Eislie's words. She looked to Jennert. "She understands the burden they have created. And you can see it in her stance, her movement, her very eyes that they did not want to take the actions they did."

Eislie threw her head back. "Why can't you just leave us alone? We've been through enough. The very people you serve enslaved us. Forced us to work, held us hostage." Eislie turned to face Jennert. "What do you want from us? Can't you just leave us alone?"

Elder Romai approached Eislie and gently put her arms around her. Eislie didn't fight back. "You feel the pain of your past. But I fear it is much more that burdens you." Elder Romai looked up to see Eislie's eyes looking out toward where their ship was. "You feel the very pain of your ancestors. The pain of all the oppression heaped upon you."

The elder's eyes brightened. "But like your ancestors, you found a way to escape, to survive."

Eislie looked to the elder. She had a caring way about her. "But we don't want to keep fighting. All Jace and I want to do is explore and live quietly."

Elder Romai nodded. "And yet, you are here. A result of you testing a way to travel. One long forgotten."

Eislie chuckled, "I know, it's strange. But, it's like it's . . ."

Elder Gav spoke. "It's calling to you."

Eislie looked around as if looking for a way to escape before she nodded. She displayed a somber stare of fear and confusion on her face. She took a moment before standing tall. "I think that's the only way we'll find peace for ourselves."

* * *

Back at the ship, Jace went to wipe the sweat from his forehead, forgetting that he was wearing a breather mask. He laughed at himself as he looked around to see if anyone saw him. Jace's eyes focused on the new plating that served as both the atmospheric and magnetic stabilizer, the plain metal jagged against the dull green of the ceramic hull of their ship. A smile of simple happiness gracing his face before he heard the computer alert on his comm.

"Captain, the new connections seem to be complete. The makeshift stabilizer should be functional for both this atmosphere and the filament."

Jace tapped his comm. “Thanks, Ed.” He looked in the direction of the Lyri ship before muttering, “Now, what are we going to do with you?”

“My apologies, Captain. The ship is fully functional. Was there something else that needed repair?”

“Sorry, Ed. Thinking about the Lyri ship. The Alank asked if we could remove it. Take it with us. I was trying to figure out how we could.” Jace sighed. “Should probably fix the overload and decontaminate the area at least.”

The computer responded, “Captain, we can tow the vessel if its gravity compensators are active. The ship would need minimal power. We could even run a supply line through to the systems if needed.”

Jace knocked on the hull of the *Wolfhammer*. “You’re interested in that ship as well, aren’t you.”

“The vessel has been here for approximately ten thousand planetary cycles, and the power systems still seem to be functioning. I am even detecting a faint signal from its emergency comm.”

“Wait, you’re telling me that its emergency systems are still working?” Jace yelled.

“That may be the case, Captain. I was going to suggest that we investigate the vessel further,” the computer responded.

The computer had used the local channels, allowing the others helping Jace repair the ship to overhear. Basker protested the suggestion. “We have the ship fixed. We should go as soon as possible.”

Jace stood silent as Basker walked up. Alvin soon joined them.

“I want to get a look at that ship. From what you told me, it’s got one hell of a power system,” Alvin remarked.

Jace looked to them both. “Maybe we can find some answers on that ship. Figure out how they traveled in the filaments.”

Alvin moved closer. "We can at least shut down the overload. Get some good scans in as well. I'm dying to take a look under the hood of that thing."

Basker scoffed, "What hood are you talking about?"

Jace smiled, looking to Basker. "It's an Earth expression. You probably don't get it."

There was silence as Jace looked toward the Lyri ship. "Ed, can we extract radiation from the area where we landed earlier?"

"Yes, Captain. But we will need to move at least one of the extractors to the cargo area to do so. It will take some time to clear the affected area. I must remind you that the source of the radiation must be removed first."

"Yeah, we have to lock down the reactor, then we can work on clearing the area. How long do you think it may take?" Jace asked.

The computer paused, "Approximately seventeen standard hours. I recommend leaving some crew from the mission for their safety. Captain, I have detected that the radiation area has increased."

"I thought it was steady," Jace remarked.

The computer replied, "Since you returned yesterday, the radiation has increased. The cause may be from the conduit that overloaded near Captain Licessien. I estimate that there has been an eleven-meter increase since yesterday."

Jace nodded. "Understood, Ed. We just made things worse." He looked to the two men nearby. "Basker, you'll have to stay with the Alank, along with Jennert and Salas. The rest of us can handle things while we work on the other ship."

Basker became angered. "No! You are not leaving me here on this planet."

Jace moved up the entry into the ship. He growled as if giving an order. "I would have left all of you already if I was going to do that. The rest of us are resistant to spide radiation. You're not."

The expression of utter confusion on Basker's face as they stood in the control room told Jace everything the man was going to ask, so he saved some time. "Basker, starborn are resistant to spide radiation. It doesn't affect us the same way it does to you." Jace sighed. "That's how Hamilton and we survived being in the ship with such a high level. Especially after our power cells were depleted."

Basker looked to both Jace and Alvin. "You mean, you can survive the radiation?"

Alvin shook his head. "You think us putting you in the hold and airlock was for our entertainment? We were trying to save your asses from radiation exposure."

The Alliance weapons specialist turned to close the ship's door. "You mean, I would have dusted?"

He turned back to see Alvin nodding before placing his hand on the man's shoulder. "On a cheerier note, if you had, it would have made it easier for us to survive the long trip back instead of taking the hard way."

Basker nodded in agreement before looking insulted as he comprehended what Alvin had said. Only to see the man smiling with a mischievous grin.

"Can it, Alvin, the man's been through enough already. It's not easy being betrayed by people you trust." Jace was speaking from experience.

But as Jace walked back to get something to drink, he placed his breather mask on the workstation Alvin used, the roll of cable they had used to fix the beacon cradling it as he walked away. The compartment door of the small gally squeaked as it opened. Basker arrived quickly, his gaze full of accusation, only to be quelled by Jace pulling out a container of water.

As he took a drink, Jace looked at the man and when he finished he said, "Don't worry, Basker, we're closer to home now than before. You don't have to worry about starving." He pounded on the man's arm as he walked by. He looked to his breather mask and Alvin. "We should probably get working on moving the extractor," he said, making Alvin nod.

It took a few hours for them to move the extractor to the cargo hold. They had planned to keep the door open to clear the area once the other ship's reactor was stabilized. Jace stared at the lines for the grapple and seemed to be thinking about something when Basker tapped his shoulder. Jace joined the men as they walked down the ramp. They had closed up just as the sun was getting low and decided to head back to see how the others were doing.

Chapter 32: Helping Some New Friends

When they arrived at the colony, Jace was surprised to hear Eislie laughing loudly. But he joined her soon after seeing Jennert dancing some weird dance as he babbled about in nonsense. Salas sat nearby with a smile and a very calm demeanor. Hamilton danced nearby, using his comm to record the action.

"Okay, we leave to do some work and come back to find you all having a party?" Jace joked.

Elder Romai spoke, startling Jace. It was as if she appeared from nowhere. "Ah, yes, this is a side effect in some, usually in the most severe cases." She held onto Jace's arm. "It is entertaining, no?"

Jace gave a smile. "Please record this. I want this for later." He leaned in to whisper to Elder Romai, "I'll play it when he does something stupid again."

As Jace watched, Elder Gav moved to stand before him, asking, "Have you thought about the Lyri vessel?"

He looked down. "That's why we're here. We have an extractor set up, and I was thinking of getting started on fixing the reactor on that ship."

Y'Shayla joined in. "It is near dark. It would be dangerous for you if you were working and an animal attacked. You would be caught unawares."

Jace smiled back at her before replying, "Thought about that. But if it's in the middle of an area that's flooded with radiation that no animals on this planet can withstand, then we should be good."

Elder Gav snickered, "Using your strength against the situation. Excellent tactic."

Jace looked to the elder. "I'm getting the feeling that you're not just some wise old man on the hill, are you?"

The elder shook his head. "I was born from the team that colonized this world, remember? We are the only remaining of the original crew. I was the chief weapons officer." He looked to Y'Shayla. "And former leader."

Jace nodded. "Got it. I was thinking of getting started. But we can't have everyone on the ship when we do this."

Elder Romai looked in puzzlement toward Jace.

The captain of the *Wolfhammer* knew what to say. "These two; and he will have to stay." Jace pointed to Basker before pointing to Hamilton. "I'm not sure he's fit for duty just yet."

Elder Romai asked, "They are not of Lyri ancestry?"

Jace shook his head. "Shasji, Eislie, myself, Alvin, and Hamilton are the only ones who can withstand the radiation." Jace raised his brows. "Especially at the level we measured."

"We're going to shut the reactor down and maybe try and fix it." Jace turned to Elder Romai. "Who knows, it still might fly."

"Doubtful. The Lyri who left it could not get it to work," Elder Gav chimed in before seeming in thought. "If I remember, it was something about a drive system overload and no replacement coils. It's hard to recall after ten thousand years."

Jace chuckled before saying, "That's a long time to be alive."

Elder Romai groaned quietly as she sat. "And he has been alive for almost as long as me." Then, she looked to Jace. "Can you stop the radiation?"

Jace bowed his head before saying, "We have to. The radius is increasing. I think when we moved something inside, it caused whatever was in equilibrium to go wacky." Jace looked apologetic. "It's increased by over ten meters already."

There were several audible gasps as Jace told them what they had discovered. Then, he looked to Eislie. "We need to get it to shut down." Eislie nodded. "Let's see if we can get it done tonight."

Jace looked to Shasji. "You can stay if you want, but the more of us that fix this, the faster it'll get done."

The small woman nodded. "I'll help. Hamilton can work as well. If he's one of us."

Jace shook his head. "By the way he's dancing with Jennert over there. I don't think he's ready to help us out right now."

They all turned to see the two men having a lousy dance competition. Shasji shook her head. "Never mind, let's get started."

The four started from the tent, with Shasji turning back for one last look at the spectacle. She spoke to Eislie as they exited. "You got any liquor onboard that can make me forget that?"

Eislie laughed, "Maybe, but it may take a lot more than you think," causing them both to laugh.

* * *

The dim cabin of the Lyri ship was now fully lit by the work lights Jace set up. He and Eislie were working on the reactor and were able to shut it down, mostly. Although they had stopped the increased radiation output, they both decided they needed to pull the core to stow it for a total shutdown, with Jace saying, "Well, there goes any hope of this thing flying off the planet by itself."

"So now what?" Eislie asked.

Jace looked to the door. “Well, we could lash it to the top of our ship. But I don’t want to drag this thing. It’d probably crash into us when we stopped. But since we can’t get this off the ground, then . . .” Jace looked to Eislie.

She shook her head. “If we strap it to the bottom, then we can’t land if we have trouble. Not without crushing this ship.”

“Yeah, it’s not ideal. I’m not too fond of that either. I was thinking of using the grapple lines to strap it onto the bottom. It’s going to be a grinding ride, probably have to repaint or fix the hull after this.” Jace thought for a moment. “Not like we don’t have maintenance to do anyway.”

“All right, we’ll take the ship with us. We’ll keep the promise to the Alank,” Eislie agreed.

As they removed the core, Jace again looked at the small ring that ran around the outer containment. It seemed to show no purpose.

As they removed it, they were surprised to see three crystals held together by similar support and ring on the inside of the core.

“Why do they have multiple crystals? This is an overload waiting to happen,” Jace said as he pulled the core from the containment chamber, only to be stopped by some wiring holding it inside. “What the hell?”

Eislie looked at the thick cables. They seemed to move toward the conduit they spied earlier. “You think it’s a control system of some kind?”

Jace nodded. “Yeah, see if we can figure out where it goes. I want to get a good look at this.”

Alvin had returned to the ship to refill his breather mask, so Eislie and Shasji followed the conduit to different parts of the craft. The lines seemed to follow along the same as the tunnel field. But one led to a display that Shasji found herself staring at. “Hey, I think I found the control system for that thing.”

Shasji looked back to see Jace disconnecting the lines, and as she tapped the console, the power shut down. “Could you reconnect it? I wanted to get a look at this thing.”

"Radiation was climbing again, had to stow the core," Jace warned.

Within seconds, small lights all over the ship lit. Eislie looked around. "Emergency power system?" She could see the smile on Jace's face, his previous actions on the *Wolfhammer* now vindicated.

Shasji worked on the panel and was able to bring up what looked like a navigational display. Before them, she tapped the screen and now projected a holographic representation of the star system they were in. "Wait, this is where we are." She looked to see faint lines crossing all over them within the projection. "What are those?"

Eislie looked at the display. She focused on one of the lines and had a revelation. "Jace, I think these are filament maps." She pointed to the nearby binary star and showed him the lines connected to it.

Jace stared at the faint lines, his eyes following every crossing and stop in the local area. "If this has maps of the filaments, then we . . ." Jace tapped his comm hard. "Ed, you think you'd be able to download the database from this ship?"

"It may be possible, Captain, but I would need a hard line to do so. This ship does not appear to have wireless communications onboard. I would have to make a molecular copy; it may take time to translate."

Jace smiled before rushing away. They heard him say, "Be right back."

Eislie yelled to him as he headed out the door, "What are you doing? Ed says he needs a hard line!"

Jace yelled back, "We have about thirty meters of hard line, remember? We used it for the beacon!"

Eislie's eyes went wide. "We'll look for an interface port."

Shasji looked to Eislie. "I guess this is important."

Eislie nodded. "You bet it is."

Jace entered the *Wolfhammer* quickly, searching for the cable from earlier. Alvin was startled when Jace popped up from under the console. He was surprised to see Jace reeling out the line. "What are you doing?"

Jace babbled, “We just found a database of all the filaments they’ve traveled. So we’re going to try and download it.”

Alvin followed Jace out the door when Jace stopped him. “Didn’t you forget something?”

Alvin turned to place his hands on his face. “Oh, that would have been stupid. I would have been unconscious in a minute,” he muttered, grabbing his mask and following after Jace.

Inside the Lyri ship, Shasji found the interface port, and it took them several minutes to connect the line. “Ed, see what you can pull from this.”

The computer worked, its database quickly filling with the image of the Lyri ship’s data. It had started to analyze the information and alerted the crew, “Captains, this database contains thousands of mapped filaments. They even appear to reach other galaxies.”

“Wait, Ed, you can read these already?” Jace asked.

“Yes, Captain. There appears to be a section dedicated to Takloh translation already in place.”

Eislie looked to Jace. “The Takloh were known to the Lyri?”

“They were, but I do not have any information in my database pertaining to them. That is strange,” the computer responded.

“It doesn’t matter right now, Ed. Can you grab the entire database?” Jace asked.

“Yes, Captain, but it will give me limited space for our trip back to record the filament data. The Lyri database is quite extensive.”

“Do it, Ed. We can always travel the filaments to get the info again. This is more important,” Jace told the computer.

“Acknowledged, Captain. The estimated time will be about six standard hours.”

“No problem, Ed.” He looked to Eislie. “The core is offline, so I’m going to start the extractor. After that, we’ll figure out how to move this ship.”

As Jace walked through the door, Eislie smiled. "I think we just found a lot of answers that people are going to want to know about."

* * *

Several hours had passed, and the sky was lit brightly by its sun. Jace was outside holding a piece of a plant that he pulled from nearby. It remained intact, and kept its purple color where the radiation once resided.

"Level is below lethal; we should probably get the others and work on getting our new find back home," Eislie said as she walked up. She had been staring at the filament map data and now knew that they could get home quickly using the nearby binary. Her mind was still pondering what the different color lines meant. "If I'm reading those maps right, it'll take us only a few hours to get back home. The binary near Oppa seems to be a straight run."

Jace nodded. "Yeah, we should get going soon. Everyone is probably worried. I'm hoping no one's out looking for us yet."

* * *

Lido stared at his console. He had been ordered to find the location of the *Wolfhammer* and would obey his queen. Using his implants, he worked the controls. He leaned forward as a result appeared on the screen, his mouth uttering the words, "That's impossible. If they are that distance away, then they would be able to reach the next galaxy within only weeks."

He lifted his hands from the controls. "I must tell my queen."

Lido nearly knocked into several people as he rushed toward the queen's chamber. The many pirates were not used to seeing him in a rush to meet with their leader.

When he arrived, he didn't wait to enter the queen's private chamber. His eyes met an unusual sight. Before him stood the queen, her veil removed, an entire half of her body was translucent blue, the rest human. She was clothed, but the angry stare caused Lido to bow and look away. "Forgive me, my queen. I have found them."

The queen walked up, pulling her veil over her head and top of her body, her silence deafening to Lido's ears as she approached. He waited for his demise as she stood steps away. "You found them?"

Lido nodded. "Yes, they are outside the outer arms, approximately a tenth of the way to the next galaxy."

The queen offered her hand to Lido and she lifted him from his prostration. "That would make them difficult to rescue." She looked back as she pulled her veil forward. "I know you were already aware that I am not entirely Terran. And with this information, your transgression will be forgiven." Her mind ran through the information they had collected from the previous filament runs she, Jace, and Eislie had achieved.

"Lido, I have a feeling that our friends are on their way back of their own accord. Given the recent information from our runs, I suspect that they traveled much further than where they are now."

"You fear they have run into trouble?" Lido asked.

The queen smiled. "My dear Lido, they are always in trouble. But, we cannot come to their aid this time without exposing our newfound ability to travel the filaments."

The pirate queen motioned for Lido to follow as she walked from the room. "Lido, have the ships stand down. We cannot use the filaments while the Alliance is searching for them. So for the moment, our friends will have to return on their own."

"Yes, my queen. I will order the stand-down," Lido replied as they turned into the control room.

Lido watched as their queen stood before the large screen. "Reach out to our assets within the Alliance and Consortium. We need to find the *Wolfhammer* when it returns." She turned to Lido, her blue eye glowing through the veil. "I have a feeling that when they do, they will be the most hunted beings in the galaxy."

Chapter 33: Find of a Lifetime

Y'Shayla stepped out into the barren field, the dust hard-baked by the sunlight and rain crunching under her steps. She had seen what happened to other creatures that entered the radiation field. But now, she was standing in the very spot, only an outline of dust remaining where she had seen one of the many creatures that roamed here.

"They did as promised," she muttered.

Her words were followed by those of Elder Romai. "As their ancestors had in the past. These new children of the Lyri are much akin to them."

Y'Shayla smiled, "We no longer have to fear this threat."

Elder Romai nodded before she spoke. "We have started making amends for our past, and they continue to aid us with our future." The elder smiled. "It was so long ago that we tried to steal their gift. And we now find that beings of our making continue to try and force them into their service for what they are." She referred to the imprisonment of starborn by the Alliance and others.

Y'Shayla turned to the elder. "Elder Gav would normally accompany me to an event such as this. It is far too dangerous for you here, Elder."

Elder Romai scoffed, “Elder Gav is not much younger than I.” She paused, giving a smile. “I needed to see this with my own eyes, child. This gives me hope that our past with the people of Lyri will be healed.”

The elder shifted, standing tall as Jace approached.

“Glad to see you could make it. Radiation’s gone; the forest should move back quickly.” He turned, motioning toward the Lyri vessel. “And once we get the ship out of here, you shouldn’t be in any danger.”

Elder Romai bowed. “Thank you for your efforts.” She took a breath. “The cure has worked for the others. You should see no real change in them. Except for possibly less of trying to kill you regularly.”

The elder hoped Jace would understand her humor. She was pleased watching him chuckle before he said, “That’d be a welcome change.”

Elder Romai looked toward the *Wolfhammer*. “Have you figured out a way to move the other ship?”

Jace nodded, an unsure concern in his actions. “Sort of. It’ll probably cause some minor damage to our ship.” Jace winked. “But it’s nothing we can’t fix.”

Y’Shayla looked to the elder to see her returning a smile. She greeted Eislie as she walked up.

“We have the power run to the gravity isolators on the Lyri ship. Wish we knew its name,” Eislie said before turning to Jace. “I still think this is crazy.”

Jace nodded. “Yeah, I know. We’ll be traveling through the filament with the back door open. Not my idea of a safe trip either.”

The elder looked to them. “You may leave the vessel if it will endanger you.”

Jace looked at her, a simple grin on his face. The elder knew it was an acknowledgment of his understanding and information she did not have. “If we leave the ship, others may come. You’d be in danger. But that ship also has some questions to answer for us as well.”

The elder could see the wisdom in Jace's stare. She could see the expression of a man who knew questions of the past. It also showed her that he now understood answers were available to him with the discovery of this vessel. She knew that in his mind, that ship was going with them at any cost.

"What is your plan?" Y'Shayla asked.

Jace explained that they were going to lash the Lyri vessel to the bottom of the *Wolfhammer*. They did not have an easy way to tow or push the ship. He mentioned that the secondary drives were almost the correct spacing to cradle the top of the Lyri vessel. He did remark, "Probably have to repair the hull when we get back."

The elder smiled, seeing Jace's reaction when Eislie said, "Want me to put it on the list?"

Elder Romai ordered Y'Shayla to retrieve the others, the leader responding, "I will not leave you unattended, Elder." She waved to the forest, and several people hesitantly entered the barren field. Jace and Eislie stood by as the others joined their leader and Elder Romai.

Jace turned to look at the ship. "I trust you, but I want to check that power feed one more time before we do this." Eislie nodded in agreement, and they excused themselves from the elder's presence.

Elder Romai happily took the staff of one of the others as they handed it to her, a gentle thank you as she leaned onto it. There was a moment of realization on the elder's face as she watched them work. The way the two of them gave orders to the others. *Gav, old friend, I fear you are correct. These two may not find the peace they are searching for anytime soon.*

"If you can't follow directions, we're leaving you here. Now stop screwing around!" The crowd of Alank that gathered laughed as Jace yelled to the others for not listening to his instructions. Elder Gav had joined Elder Romai watching the actions of their new friends.

"He does know how to lead," Elder Gav muttered.

"But he does not want to," Elder Romai replied, making Gav nod.

They watched as the *Wolfhammer* hovered over the other vessel and the others wrapped the grapple lines around it. There was the horrible sound of scraping and grinding as the cables cinched tightly. Shasji and Jace climbed into the rear door after pulling themselves up the remaining lines.

Jace waved to the others and hit the comm next to him. The Alank heard him over the speakers. "We're all set. Don't worry. We won't tell anyone about your location. I have a feeling you like the solitude."

Elder Romai waved to him, yelling, "May you have safe journeys, my friends!"

Jace smiled as the cargo door closed partially and the ship moved skyward. As it became a tiny dot, Elder Romai spoke. "I fear those two are on a greater path than they realize."

* * *

As Eislie flew into space, she spoke to Jace as he sat in his chair, her words unsure. "We sure this is going to work?"

Jace stared forward. "No idea. But it'll take us three months the traditional way. That's a long time to be hauling this thing along." Jace pounded his foot on the floor.

Eislie agreed and was relieved when Jace said, "I'll fly. Okay?"

She handed over control, and they were off toward the nearest binary star.

"Ed, are you sure this is on the map?" Jace asked.

"Yes, Captain, it is on the map. But I have noticed that some are different colors than the others. I deduce that it is for clarity and ease of reading."

"I hope so." Jace turned to look around the cabin. "Everyone strapped in?" Hearing a response from everyone, Jace fired up the tunnel drive and inched toward the event point. He yelled back to Shasji, "You ready back there, Shasji?"

Jace looked to Jennert as Shasji responded that she was. “Now, Jennert, so everything is clear, she is not trying to kill you. So stay in your seat.” Jace’s voice was a mix of humor and threat.

The ship lurched forward as it entered. Jace found himself fighting for control from the start. Everyone held on for dear life and laughed when Shasji yelled, “Learn how to fly!” It brought a smile muted by a hint of concerned terror to Jace’s face.

“Geez, this is pulling us every which way. I’m having trouble flying in a straight line.” He was about to speak when there was a horrible grinding sound from beneath them.

“Ed, are the lines still tight?” Eislie yelled over the sound.

“Yes, Captain, although we are experiencing torque within the filament. The field seems to be fluctuating.”

“Slac, checking the tunnel field!” Eislie yelled, only to find nothing was wrong. “Wait, are these readings correct?”

The computer responded, “Yes, Captain, I was referring to the filament itself. It is not a smooth field as we have encountered before. Instead, the filament itself seems to be moving.”

Jace looked to Eislie. “Maybe that’s why it’s red. It’s unstable.” Jace groaned before saying, “We can’t catch a break here.”

Eislie watched the map. The small dot on the screen moved closer to the end. “I’m estimating about a standard hour before we can punch out. You good to fly?”

Jace nodded. “But I’m going to need a nap after this. It’s exhausting trying to keep us flying in one direction.”

His joke put a smile on Eislie’s face.

* * *

Near Oppa, the group of pirate ships tracked the entangled beacon and could see it approaching. The queen was on her flagship, the *Blue Viper*, watching in awe. She found herself wishing for her allies to return home safely. *I hope you two know what you are doing.*

"Can we calculate how fast they are going?" Lido asked. As he turned to the main screen, a contingent of the Consortium suddenly exited hyperspace. The queen rose from her seat. "Lido, how many?"

"I count four founder ships and over seventy fighters." He turned to look at her. "We're outgunned."

The pirate queen ordered more ships to convene on their location. She looked with concern toward the fleet now on her display. "They are tracking the beacon as well. How did they find the frequency? I fear they are going to try and take the *Wolfhammer* when it exits." She turned to Lido, ordering, "Have weapons ready."

The pirates remained silent, running as other ships rushed to aid their queen when the *Wolfhammer* exited from the binary point. She watched as the *Wolfhammer* fought to control itself as it spun wildly. When she enhanced the image, she noticed they were carrying something.

"Lido, identify what they are carrying," the pirate queen ordered.

Lido tapped away at his console. The only words escaping his lips were, "That can't be right." But then, he looked to his queen. "Our database identifies that ship as a Lyri scout. No Lyri ships have been found intact before."

The queen moved closer to the large screen. "They found a Lyri ship?" Her eyes then glanced toward the Consortium fleet as several craft approached the *Wolfhammer*. Her concern rose as the small ship seemed to be floating dead in space. She immediately turned, giving an order. "Full weapons. They do not take that ship or the *Wolfhammer*."

"My queen, reinforcements have not arrived," Lido protested, only to have the queen turn to glare at him. He could see the blue glow from beneath her veil. "Yes, Your Highness. We obey."

* * *

On the *Wolfhammer*, they were still assessing damage and could see the Consortium fleet heading for them. "Jace! Get us out of here. I don't think this is a greeting party."

Jace did his best, but with each movement of the *Wolfhammer*, the grinding of the Lyri ship against the hull and drive coils caused more damage. When he tried to maneuver, the vessel lagged. “Eis, we’ve only got partial drives. We’re not going to be able to outrun them.”

Hamilton spoke up. “Problem?”

Eislie turned to look at him. “Yes! Unless you think the Consortium is here to help us.”

Hamilton laughed, “Nope, pretty sure they’ll execute all Alliance personnel and capture you two. We should get out of here.”

The rest of the crew was silent as Jace did his best to outrun the Consortium fighters. But then, he was startled when several pirate ships flew past them to engage those pursuing.

“Wait, are those Alliance?” Jennert asked.

Eislie shook her head. “Nope, those were pirates.” She looked to Jace. “Think they figured out what we’re hauling yet?”

Jace chuckled, “Well, since they all seem to be trying to catch us, I think everyone figured it out. We have to find a way out of this.”

* * *

The queen ordered her crew to fire upon the *Wolfhammer* but not hit it as they raced toward the pirates. Lido was amused to hear her say, “Make it look good.” They knew they needed to stall for time until reinforcements arrived. And a good show would do that for the Consortium.

Jace did his best to evade the weapons fire and avoid it hitting the grapple lines. “Good thing they’re not trying to kill us.”

Hamilton spoke up. “Not yet, at least.”

Jace looked back. “Oh, you’re a real ray of sunshine, aren’t you.”

Eislie looked to Jace as a shot glanced off the *Wolfhammer’s* makeshift stabilizer, hitting one of the grapple cables holding the Lyri ship to their underside. “He might be right. They just loosened one of the cables.”

Jace turned the ship, allowing the pirates to attack the pursuing Consortium vessels. As Jace looked into the next turn, he could see the arrival of more pirates. But as he flew, the *Wolfhammer* was struck. The ship lurched as plasma arched within the internal structure.

"Mag shields can't take much more; we've overextended them around the other ship." And when she heard the grinding below, Eislie said, "We're probably going to lose drives soon, and that ship, if they keep this up."

Jace was searching for anywhere to run. *There's nowhere to run to, shit*. He looked to Eislie, his eyes only diverted when the comm came alive.

"*Wolfhammer*, you have returned, and I am here to claim my prize." The pirate queen spoke as she came on the main screen.

Jace stared forward. The Lyri ship attached to theirs was hindering their escape. The pirates were blocking one direction while the Consortium had them from the other. There was no way out.

"Fire up the slag cannons," Jace ordered.

"Captain, we cannot use the slag cannons. They are being used to secure the Lyri vessel," the computer alerted him.

The queen continued her threat. "*Wolfhammer*, we will have our prize. You may trust me."

Jace looked to the screen. He didn't know what to do, but as her words sank in, he looked to Eislie. "We can't let the Consortium get the Lyri ship."

"We're giving up then?" Eislie asked.

Jace shook his head, then had an idea. He pounded on the comm. "Pirate Queen, Jana, you and the Consortium have attacked a small, disabled vessel. We are overwhelmed at the attention you are heaping upon us. I will have to start thinking like a pirate to try and avoid you, but you have us at a disadvantage. We are hauling a ship with us held on by four small cables. That hardly seems like a fair fight."

Eislie looked to Jace. "You all right? Why are you antagonizing her?"

Jace watched the queen staring at him through the link, and Jace gave a barely noticeable nod.

* * *

On the *Blue Viper*, the Queen turned. In her mind, Jace's words ran through her enhanced brain. *Four small cables, disadvantage*. The queen found inspiration in Jace's words and looked to Lido. "Order all sharpshooters to weapons. Now!"

"My queen?" Lido asked, causing her to rush to his side. "Do it. They are giving us the Lyri vessel. But we need to remove it from their ship. They cannot release it."

Lido understood and gave the order. The queen then ordered all skips to engage the *Wolfhammer* and Consortium fighters. *Well, well, Captain Tucker, you may be a pirate yet.*

The pirates went after the *Wolfhammer* and engaged the Consortium fighters. As per the queen's orders, the sharpshooters were removing the cables as quickly as possible. The last one was still holding the Lyri vessel when the Alliance's forty-third fleet arrived and engaged the pirates and Consortium.

"Fire up the slag cannons," Jace ordered.

"Captain, the remaining grapple is still lashed to the Lyri vessel; if we use the cannons, then we will lose the ship," Ed warned.

As another shot from the Consortium arced through the structure, Jace looked forward, his lip rolled over his teeth. "It's the ship or our lives."

Eislie looked to Jace and realized what he said earlier*, thinking like a pirate, four small cables; why would he say that unless he was tipping off the queen?* She turned to him. "Ed, I am agreeing with Jace's order. We're firing up the slag."

The computer agreed, and they started firing at the Consortium vessels. Within only a few shots, the remaining cable snapped and the Lyri vessel broke free. The pursuing pirates quickly grappled onto it and rushed away with the prize.

Jace watched as the Lyri vessel disappeared into hyperspace. His attention was brought back as a Consortium vessel latched onto theirs. Jace spun the *Wolfhammer,* firing point-blank with the slag cannons, tearing a hole through the pursuing fighter. The grapple remained dragging what was left of the fighter's hull as they headed toward the Alliance fleet.

As they entered the protection of the Alliance ships, Salas said, "The ship or our lives; I think you chose the right one, Captain."

Chapter 34: You Know Nothing

"Captain, explain again why you did not fire your weapons on the Consortium ships when they attacked?" Jace sighed as he heard the voice ring from around him throughout the large interrogation room. He and Eislie had been enduring the interviews for several weeks. They were all the same questions, again and again, and their answers weren't going to change.

"Investigator, the cables holding the Lyri vessel were wrapped around the cannons. They were convenient at the time. We didn't think we'd have to fight as soon as we exited the filament. We were more interested in getting home," Jace replied.

The room filled with a murmur as Jace replied with the same answer.

"Then why did you decide to use them later, releasing the ship from your tether?"

"Investigator, we had already lost the support cables, and I don't know about you, but if it's a choice of not being shot out of the sky or losing something that was stopping us from fighting back, I would make the same choice. I'd fight back," Jace retorted.

"But you had, and then lost, something precious to the Alliance. Are you aware that no intact Lyri vessel has been found throughout this entire galaxy?"

Jace was annoyed. "So you keep telling me." Jace leaned back in his chair to stare up at the memoric field glowing above. It never changed when they asked the same questions. They had asked why he decided to fire at the last minute. Jace told them, "It was us or the other ship."

Jace wasn't lying, but was terrified if they would ask which ship. At that point, he'd have to tell them the Lyri ship, not the Consortium.

Jace leaned forward. "We've given you everything, all the data we scanned from that vessel, including the entire database. So what else do you want from us?"

"We are asking the questions, Captain. Please respect the procedure."

Jace stood in protest.

"Please sit down, Captain."

Jace growled, "No." He turned his eyes up and looked around the room. "You have our ship locked up, and we have given you everything we had. Right now, the pirates have the Lyri ship and are reverse engineering it. We could be doing that right now." Jace slammed his fist down on the table, causing the containers of water to jump. "Instead, I'm here answering stupid questions from people who have no idea what's going on. Right now, we could be solving filament travel, but instead, I'm here with a room full of politicians."

Jace stretched and went quiet before he spoke clearly. "So far, you have wrongfully imprisoned me, Eislie Licessien, and possibly thousands of other starborn. Not to mention that if we had returned with the ship, I'm sure you would have taken it from us anyway. You have yet to answer my question on that."

Jace's outburst silenced the room until the investigator spoke angrily. "Captain, you were convicted of a crime and held. What happened to you under the command of the facility is not up for debate here."

Jace leaned on the table. "I have answered hundreds of your questions, and you keep asking the same ones over and over." Jace shook his head. "I chose to save my ship and those aboard over some prize. If you can't get that through your thick skulls, then I can't help you. You're either too stupid or lack the empathy to understand the concept." He sat down. "I'm done answering questions. Find me in contempt or whatever. My decision still would have been the same. I'd choose saving the lives of those with me over the find of a lifetime."

There was a murmur around him as the field didn't change to alert them to deception. Jace picked up a container of water and drank from it. Its contents quickly disappearing as Jace guzzled it down. He placed the empty container down and his eyes glazed over as he looked into the darkness around him. He sat silent, his arms crossed as they debated around the room.

In the shadows, an Oppan security officer tapped the shoulder of one of the investigators. "We have a situation outside."

The proceedings were being broadcast throughout the news network. Thousands of starborn and those supporting them were now gathering around the space command center. They had been watching and could see the same thing. They could see this as an attempt to persecute one of the only people who had been standing up for all starborn. The security forces were altered and deployed; at the moment, everything was peaceful.

It was another hour before they ended the proceedings. The court requested Jace to stay planetside in case they had any additional questions. As he left, Jace met with Eislie in the hall. She had returned from the Filament Project with bad news.

"Only Alliance personnel are allowed into the project now. It looks like we've lost control of it."

Jace nodded. "I expected that. Have you been able to check in with Ed?"

"No, they've been in there combing through his systems and memory for the last week. I'm worried that they'll destroy him," Eislie told Jace.

Jace smiled. “I ordered Ed to keep an updated copy of himself daily. Just in case something happens. He told me that Arren installed a secondary backup within his old system housing. You know, the one that looks like it’s offline.”

Eislie smiled. “Guess you’re rubbing off on Ed. That’s not a frightening thought at all.”

Jace laughed with her as they walked toward the door. “If we can’t work on the project, we’ll have to do it on our own. And for that, we’ll need our ship.”

Eislie agreed. They had been planetside for almost three months. She and Jace wanted to head back to Gilese to see her family. But instead they were both stuck answering to politicians looking to blame them for losing an important artifact. One they didn’t even know existed until it was brought back.

As Jace opened the outside door, the crowd quieted. He hesitated as he stepped down the long stairs. He leaned into Eislie. “Why are all these people here?”

Eislie didn’t know until she recognized Alvin standing in the crowd when he waved to them. He ducked under the barrier but was stopped by security. He tried to get away, but they held him. Seeing this, Eislie rushed over. “Alvin!” She pulled at the security person’s arm and yelled, “Let him go! He’s part of our crew!”

It took some convincing and resumed yelling from the crowd for the officer to release Alvin.

“They’re still grilling you, huh?” Alvin said to Jace, who only nodded.

“Listen, I heard they pulled the project. All starborn were let go. The Alliance has it all now,” Alvin told Jace, who already knew this from Eislie.

“They have the data and the resources.” Jace looked concerned. “We need our ship back.”

Alvin scoffed, "They've grounded all starborn-owned vessels, not that there were many. I tried hopping on one, but we were forced back. Something about unstable passages."

Jace felt someone tugging on his jacket, and when he checked, he could see a small piece of paper dangling from his pocket. When he opened it, the paper had a line of numbers. Jace recognized them as a similar navigational string. He quickly placed it back into his pocket and stood silent.

As they stopped on the stairs, they heard the crowd chanting, "We are starborn!" over and over. Jace looked around. "This is going to get ugly soon if they don't do something."

They all looked around as the chanting grew louder: "Starborn! We are starborn!" Jace looked to Eislie, and they watched as people were pushing against the security. Eislie looked around, and then to Jace, and to his own surprise, he raised his arms. Within moments, the crowd cheered, and they did the same as him. Finally, the head of the security forces approached him. "Do not cause a riot. I don't want to charge you."

Jace replied, "I'm already in trouble for being a starborn. But I don't want anything to happen. So I'm going to tell them to go home."

The man nodded and backed away.

"Everyone, everyone, please I need your attention!" Jace yelled.

There was an initial cheer before the crowd grew silent. Jace looked around. "Everyone, please, we thank you for coming out to greet us. Your support and energy are welcome!"

There was another cheer.

Jace continued. "Everyone, please, we don't need any violence. As many of you have heard, they have taken the filament project from us, and they are holding our ships. So right now, I ask you to be patient."

There was a murmur of confusion from the crowd. "Please, go home; be with those you care for. I know you don't understand yet, but I may be able to offer some insight soon. Many in the galaxy still see starborn as lesser beings, but that is no longer the case. We have succeeded in rediscovering what had long been forgotten. That knowledge belongs not just to us, but to all people of this galaxy!"

There was a loud cheer from everyone, including several of the security forces. Jace looked around. "Right now, I ask for peace, your patience, and your help. They are holding us and our ships to prevent us from traveling." Jace paused. "I think they are afraid we will take over the filaments. That couldn't be farther from the truth!" Jace looked around. "The filaments do not belong to us. They belong to everyone. Return home, call on your leaders, tell them to release all starborn vessels. Please do so without incident!"

Again, the crowd chanted, "We are starborn!" making Jace smile before he spoke. "I am asking this because they have taken the information from us. But they cannot take our freedom to explore it on our own! We discovered the long-forgotten access to the filaments, and just because they cannot access them yet, why should we be kept from them?"

The crowd cheered once more and started to disperse. In all directions, the chant continued.

Finally, the head of the security team approached Jace. "You got them to leave. That was a pretty inspiring speech. You ever think about getting into politics?"

Jace laughed, "Nope, I want to stay as far from that as possible. I just want to get our ship back and head home."

Eislie and Jace headed to their place on Oppa. Several starborn greeted them as they walked by. Jace told them to go home. There was nothing they could do for the moment. As they reached their apartment, a woman was standing outside. Eislie recognized her. It was Callie.

"You looking for someplace to crash?" Eislie joked, making her friend smile.

Callie looked at Jace. "You know how to move a crowd. You should think about doing something with a talent like that."

Jace told her that politics wasn't his thing.

They invited Callie inside and closed the door. They sat after Jace brought something to drink for them all. Callie had news to tell them she wasn't sure they wanted to hear.

"You heard they locked us all out, right? Even the Oppan," Callie told them.

Jace nodded. "This isn't about knowledge. It's about control and power. And who has it."

Callie nodded. "They are still asking starborn to help, but we're mostly passive. They just want us in an advisory role." She hesitated. "Oh, and I heard that they are done with your ship. They copied everything your computer knows. They asked me to tell you that you can have it back."

Jace looked to Callie. "You're not a messenger. Why are you really here?"

Callie looked down, and her eyes gained a devious glint. "Like you, Jace, I back everything up. I know about those files of yours here."

Jace laughed, "They were here. The Alliance took the whole system. We had to install a new one."

Callie looked Jace in the eyes and watched as he put his finger to his lips, as did Eislie.

Jace spoke. "I have no idea what we're going to do without that data. But at least we have our ship back." Jace gave a wink. "Maybe you should come with us. I want to go check out the binary again. Maybe we can start from scratch."

Callie understood his meaning and excused herself. Then, telling them, "When you're ready to head out, I'd like to come along. Should I bring a few friends?"

Eislie nodded. "Sure, why not? Just make sure they're good friends. It's a small ship."

As Callie was leaving, Jace asked if she could procure some sapphire cores, just in case the Alliance screwed up the memory for their ship's computer. She agreed, and told them she'd be in touch.

It took more than a week before Jace and Eislie could return to the spaceport. Callie and Alvin were already waiting when they arrived. Jace had filed a flight plan to a small dwarf star harboring several rocky planets; his reason, mining exploration. The area they had visited before they arrived was now marked as off-limits.

Before walking up the accessway, Arren stood nearby, his face long. He spoke when Jace went to open the door of the ship, only to say, "I'm sorry, I couldn't save him."

As they entered their ship, both Jace and Eislie called out to Ed. The response was mechanical, sounding nothing like their friend. "Captain, Tucker, Captain Licessien, welcome aboard. Ship status normal."

Eislie looked around. "That's not Ed."

Jace agreed, looking to Arren. "They pulled the memory cores, didn't they."

Arren nodded. "Slacs didn't know what they were doing. I'm sorry."

Jace smiled, "Callie, you bring those blank cores I asked for?" The former head of the project produced them, handing them to Jace and he went to work. As he opened the access panel, Jace turned, looking back to the door, saying, "Someone close the door, please," before he shut down the new computer to replace the Alliance-installed cores with the new blank ones. Jace worked quickly and threw several switches connected to the old system, then typed on his comm. Jace smiled seeing a response. It read, "Concealed transmitters detected." His comm then displayed the locations throughout the ship, which Jace went to work removing. Finally, when the message read, "All clear," Jace turned on the main system.

It took several minutes before they heard, "Ah, Captains, it is good to see you again. I will have my new system fully installed in a few minutes. I presume our plan worked?"

Jace smiled, "Hi, Ed, you should have heard the moron they replaced you with, thinking we wouldn't notice."

"Actually, Captain, I was watching them the entire time. I am horrified that they did not allow Arren to do the replacement. And while

I was in low power, I was able to decode some of the programming for the control system of the Lyri vessel. Did you know that the name of the vessel was *Niam La*? According to their database, and a rough translation, it means light to guide home."

"Wow, that's interesting, Ed," Jace said, looking to Eislie, making her laugh when he said, "Seems like we have a theme going on with ships around here."

"You mean they didn't null you? I was worried about you and this ship for nothing!" Arren complained.

Jace laughed, "Thanks for caring, Arren. That's why we trust you."

The old miner pointed to Jace. "It's that damn Terran suspicion you have. That's what saved Ed."

Callie smiled. She was grateful that the computer that kept her friends alive was safe. "No backups, right? He doesn't happen to have any of the other databases still, does he?"

Jace looked to Eislie. "We can get to that later. Right now, I think we should do some mineral scouting. After all, we do have a company to run."

Eislie nodded, holding up the small slip of paper Jace handed her before saying, "I'll get this into navigation, and we'll get going."

Callie followed her, asking, "Where are we going?"

Eislie sat reading the navigation string. "I see you only brought Alvin."

Callie huffed, "I didn't know if I could trust anyone else. So, where are we going?"

Eislie tapped the console and the controls came alive. "Jace, drive systems are up and running. Looks like they're fixed." She turned, yelling, "Thank you, Arren!"

The old man waddled in. "Would one of you tell me what's going on? I have no interest in mining anymore. I repair ships now."

Jace affectionally pounded his hand down on Arren's shoulder. "Well, Arren, we're hijacking you for a little bit. I'm pretty sure you're going to be interested in this flight." He tapped the comm. "Control? This is the *Wolfhammer*. Requesting clearance to depart."

Once they had permission, they were off. Eislie and Jace were quiet most of the way. Their destination was a minor planet in the nearby star system. They made several runs around different bodies in the system, and when they were sure they weren't being followed, landed. Most of the crew was startled hearing the sound of docking clamps and the computer alert, "Detecting hatchway connecting to port access."

Jace unbuckled his harness and stood by the door. He looked through the small window and smiled, seeing a familiar face. By this time, the others had joined him.

When Jace opened the door, he greeted the person standing in the entryway. Eislie recognized him as well. "Preston?"

"Captain Licessien, it is good to see you well," Preston replied.

Jace nodded, joking, "They let you out or got you out? I'm thinking the latter."

Preston smiled, "Does it matter?"

Jace smiled, shaking the man's hand. "Nope, not to us. Good to see you."

Another man walked up behind Preston, his form dark and imposing, making Jace chuckle before saying, "Captain Balroc, what a surprise."

The pirate captain looked over the crew of the *Wolfhammer*. "I see different faces. New recruits?"

Jace nodded. "Well, you know how it is. You're not the only ones recruiting starborn."

The pirate captain nodded before handing several pads to Preston, who handed one to Jace.

The pirate pointed to the instrument. "That's the breakdown on the reactor and the control wiring. We're still having trouble translating the coding. If you have any information, it would be helpful," Preston told them.

Balroc looked around the room as Preston handed another pad to Arren. "For your engineer, the metallurgic breakdown of the hull and other systems. You may find that these are surprisingly simple to manufacture but are very resilient alloys." He then handed a pad to Callie. "This contains the travel and known routes that we have mapped so far. We're still working on translating the information from that ship. The database of that vessel is quite extensive. It seems our ancestors were far traveled."

Preston turned to Jace. "It is too bad the Alliance has the map of the filaments. It would have given us an easier time. When we attempted to copy it, the system stopped working."

Jace chimed in, "Well, they still have to figure out how to get access and not explode."

Preston nodded. "Once we figure out how the control systems regulate, we should be able to make it work."

The man's statement made Jace side his eye toward him. "And we are doing this for the same reasons, right?"

Preston smiled as he produced a small display. "Hello, Captain Tucker, Captain Licessien. It is good to see you both well."

The familiar image of the pirate queen now greeted them.

Callie spoke up. "So we're pirates now?"

The queen looked to Callie. "That would be up to you, as so far, Jace and Eislie have not accepted our offer."

"Hello, Jana, it is good to see you as well. We haven't thanked you for your help back on Yata," Eislie said.

Arren muttered, "You're on a first-name basis with the pirate queen? When did this happen?"

Jace looked to Arren. "Uh, this is a live feed. You might want to take a step back, Arren."

The pirate queen could be heard laughing. "You two do tend to attract some of the more unusual talent from the galaxy, my friends." Then, the pirate queen told Jace and Eislie that the ship is a more straightforward design than anticipated. But, even with her enhanced capabilities, she has been unable to extract the coding for the controls. Hearing this, Jace looked to Eislie.

"Whaddya think?" Jace asked.

Eislie nodded, almost as if reading Jace's mind. She then gave a single order to the computer. "Ed, give them everything you decoded so far."

Within seconds, the pirate queen's screen flashed with an alert as several terabytes of data streamed in on her screens through the secure connection. She turned back to the screen, looking at Jace and Eislie. "That is a clever machine you have there."

"Thank you, Queen Jana. It is good to be noticed," Ed responded, causing Jace to laugh. And within seconds, the pirate queen joined him.

When finished, the queen looked around the ship. "Everyone, please enjoy your gifts, and use them discreetly. I know it will be difficult to keep things covert given our current situation. But for now, we do not want to draw attention to this meeting."

Jace nodded. "Yeah, about that. I thought we might want to make this a more interactive joint effort down the road. But for now, we'll have to go it alone."

The queen agreed, saying, "Yes, I look forward to our next meeting, Captains," before the small screen went blank.

Captain Balroc tapped Preston's shoulder, saying, "We need to return," before turning and disappearing into the darkness of the connecting dock, the pirate captain's words bellowing from the blackness, "Have a safe trip, Captains!"

Jace responded, "You too, Captain. Preston, you know how to contact us."

Preston nodded, then turned to follow his captain. He glanced back. "I wish you fair weather, my friends."

Jace chuckled as Preston disappeared into the darkness, making Callie ask what was so funny as he closed the door. He motioned toward the bulkhead. "It's what Preston said. That's an old Earth pirate well-wishing if I ever heard one."

Jace turned back to the others before tapping to turn off the pad he held. "We should do some surveying before we head home."

After the final docking clamp released, the *Wolfhammer* flew to another nearby planet to take some additional mineral readings, Jace and Eislie's actions causing Arren to complain, "You're not thinking about actually mining here, are you?"

"Arren, we have to make it look like some effort for our company," Jace responded, giving a wink. "Otherwise, they might think we were up to something. Who knows, maybe we met with pirates!"

Everyone on the ship found the humor in Jace's statement as they lifted off to head back to Oppa. Callie seemed relieved, as did Arren. Alvin was a different matter. He seemed heavily interested in the information provided. That was fine with Jace as he set a course for the planet they temporarily called home. With the new information furnished by the pirates, Jace and Eislie now had more knowledge of the filaments than them and the Alliance.

The two hoped it would only be a matter of time until they found a way to safely travel as their ancestors did long ago. Until then, it was back home, and then who knows where. All they really knew was that they had their ship back, and they all wanted some time to explore the universe.

* * *

A thin trail of smoke wafted from the pipe in the ornate office. Bosh sat reading the latest intelligence from the Filament Project. Halli was nearby, her uniform replaced by a less than formal and more appealing translucent version for her master. She handed him a glass of distilled alcohol, and he smiled, accepting it. She sat patiently waiting for his following command.

Bosh continued to read, and his eyes became angry seeing the news now present. *Damn Alliance, they've taken the project.*

The former captain looked to his assistant. "Is this all of the data we've received?"

Halli nodded, "yes, master, everything your contacts have sent." The woman leaned forward. "Is there anything else you wish, master?"

Bosh grinned, his lips holding his pipe. "Nothing, for now, my dear, you may go."

His eyes followed her as she walked toward the door, and he watched her bow as she closed it. Bosh returned to the pad seeing the news that the Alliance now held all of the information on Filament travel. And the fact that a partial database was recovered from the memory core of the *Wolfhammer*. His mouth uttering through gritted teeth, "bastards took everything from you. How's that feel?"

The Former captain was startled when the display on his screen alerted him to a call. He tapped the controls to see Tirnal on the display.

"Tirnal Hacson, I trust the information I provided was adequate," Bosh said, placing his pipe aside.

The Consortium leader nodded, "It was most satisfactory. Although, our legion was not able to procure the prize those starborn retrieved."

Bosh looked at the pad he held, "what prize? I thought they only brought back the database."

Tirnal smiled, "you are ill-informed, my friend. They had brought back an actual Lyri vessel. But, unfortunately, the pirates stole it from them during the battle."

Bosh sat forward, "they found an actual Lyri ship?"

Tirnal nodded, "Our spies have told us that they also retrieved a map of known filaments. We are attempting to procure that information presently."

Bosh then asked, "what about the database?"

Tirnal looked puzzled toward Bosh, causing the captain to smile. "we weren't informed about the Lyri ship's database? That would be a great asset. Are you able to procure it? if so, what would your price be?"

Bosh smiled, reading the information that Jace and Eislie were on their way back to Gilese. His only words were, "the same as my previous request." Bosh tapped the pad holding it up to show his friend. "I have it here."

Tirnal stared at Bosh through the display, and the captain waited for his response.

"You would need a sponsor to join the Consortium." Tirnal smiled, tapping the screen, "I would be happy to do so, Devlin. For a price."

Bosh tapped the screen, "then, my friend, we have an agreement." Seconds later, the information streamed through the connection. Once received, Bosh heard Tirlan say, "Citizen Devlin Bosh, we welcome you to the Consortium.

Bosh smiled as the screen went blank, a quiet chuckle leaving him as he muttered. "This isn’t over. I'll wait till you two figure things out, and then I'll take my revenge."

MORE STORIES FROM THE AUTHOR

After years of fighting and hardship, the power of Earth's elites is at war. Not with the people of their planet but with an alien race known as the Daak. Jace Tucker was left for dead by his own people. But, after helping some aliens and being sentenced to prison, Jace gets the surprise of a lifetime.

Read the original story and Join Jace, Eislie, and Ed for an exciting ride across the galaxy.

Wolfhammer

Legends of the starborn

Between facing adversity, pirates, and the hatred of others, Jace, Eislie, and Ed do the impossible becoming the stuff of legend.

For more stories, please visit www.wolfhammer.com

ABOUT THE AUTHOR

Stephen has experience in technology, engineering, and sales spanning over 30 years. He has been writing science fiction and fantasy for far longer—his work primarily for role-playing and short stories personally, using his knowledge and imagination within his life. He is always known to have a story to tell and it's usually sprinkled with a hint of adventure. Through his character's eyes, you find that life can be an adventure, and it's always better with a bit of science and magic.

Filament is the second in the series of his jump into the science fiction genre and something very familiar. The universe can be a big place, and many universes even more so.

For more stories and other information please visit.

www.wolfhammer.com
or
www.afairyslight.com

www.ingramcontent.com/pod-product-compliance
Lightning Source LLC
Chambersburg PA
CBHW070530260626
47161CB00002B/317
* 9 7 8 1 7 3 6 8 7 3 8 7 8 *